Chapter - 1 - The Times, They Are A Chang...

Ariadne sat with her back to the captain, her disdain could be heard a league away as she sighed at their current predicament. She knew that it was a risk, taking up the lieutenant's role with Seamus Hawthorne at the helm, but with being the first woman to take on the title, she felt it necessary to take the first position thrown her way. She knew that never backing down from a challenge would get her into trouble one day – today was that day. Ariadne should have realised the implications of sailing with a man like Hawthorne and abandoned ship before she had even set foot on the HMS *Daedalus*, abandoning any dreams she had of ever making a name for herself with the Admiralty in the process.

Of course it had been a shit posting, why had she not seen that? She should have listened to the rumours on the dock. Seamus Hawthorne's reputation as a captain was tarnished with many tales of his infamous exploits, and that was putting it kindly. She'd taken it as a tall tale. How could any captain worth his salt lose a ship to mutiny? Well, now she knew. She was silently fuming; Seamus could hear it loud and clear. Here she was, stranded on an island in the middle of the Caribbean, bound to an idiot.

"They even took my best fucking cutlass! It was my grandma's! She would be turning over in her grave if she knew it was in the hands of some *scurvy mutineer*. I have had that cutlass since the first day I was put to sea with Captain Smith on the *Greenwich*, and that was damn near fifteen years ago!" Ariadne's tirade was incessant, and she had subjugated Seamus to it for a good while.

They had not even spent so much as a single night in that beautiful new ship, and she knew he was ashamed of it. Ariadne felt her anger was valid though – he deserved the verbal abuse, even in the face of propriety.

On the other hand, Seamus did have some winning qualities which, when she wasn't angry, endeared him to her. For one, he was very vocal about his love of strong-willed women. The first story Seamus told was about his upbringing and how his mother would boss the men of the family around. She liked to muse that this was why he had accepted her as his lieutenant so easily. Having her around reminded him of home. And when you're over a thousand leagues away from familiar lands, having things around that reminded you of them kept you grounded.

The second was the give-me-adventure-over-anything attitude that he seemed to carry so well. Not a suitable quality for a captain of His Majesty's Navy, though. He acted more like a privateer, which probably was what had gotten them into this mess.

Ariadne thought that it was a mix of things, really. Trying to endear himself to a new crew by being overly familiar — wrong choice, especially this close to Tortuga. The recent loss of his old ship to mutiny. Stories get around quickly, which is surprising with how long it takes to send letters. The time-honoured tradition that, or as she put it "silly superstition", women bring bad luck at sea. She felt this was boys being boys, afraid of change, trying to ward off the inevitable. So she let that one slide. Let them see what luck can be had at sea with Ariadne Smith at the helm.

That was before she ended up at the business end of a mutiny herself.

The last feather to break the horse's back was this damnable mission that the admiralty had sent them on. It clearly spooked the crew, because, as soon as the sailors found out where the *Daedalus* was headed, the crew's displeasure was apparent with protesting moans that would put the bustiest of wenches to shame. The closer she brought the ship to its destination, the louder their protestations sounded, and as soon as they were far enough out, away from prying eyes, the call for mutiny was raised.

So here she was, stranded on an island in the middle of the Caribbean, with her captain.

Ariadne was done with being angry. It was time for action; time to get off this isolated paradise and seek retribution. They may have taken *Señor Stabby*, but those scallywags had forgotten to check her boots. Happily concealed in the side of one lay the key to their salvation, and she had spent the best part of the last hour working it out of there. But once the metaphorical ship had sailed on her anger, Ariadne kept getting side-tracked, and the dagger kept sliding back down. Now it was out, and she needed to manoeuvre over to where it had plopped in the sand.

Seamus had been unusually quiet. She could sense he was feeling bad for their predicament. She knew it was not all his fault; it was those damnable superstitious fools. Times were changing, though. They had to get their heads out of their arses and look to the future. No good berating the snakes now, they were long gone. Ariadne leaned into Seamus.

"Push this way. I managed to get my dagger out."

"Good show, Lieutenant!"

She managed to shuffle over to the blade, with the captain's help, like some sort of horrific crab monster. Finally, with much labouring, Ariadne cut the bindings that bound them. The two were now free, thanks to her. She stood up and dusted herself off while stretching her stiff muscles. She watched the captain do the same, assuming he was brushing off the embarrassment as well as the sand. She was now free to roam their island and new permanent home.

Ariadne knew where she was; she had plotted the damn course. She and Seamus had set sail from Tortola, which had been captured from the Dutch some eight years ago. They were there to '*colonize the newest acquisition of the British Empire, Anegada*', or so the captain said. It seemed that it wasn't everyone's cup of tea. The moment they arrived at their destination, she was bound to Seamus and left on the beach to die. Maybe if they were lucky, a pirate like the infamous Blackbeard would happen by, or perhaps the ever-more encroaching Danish would make a surprise appearance since they had been impinging ever more on Tortola's doorstep these past few years.

Either way would probably mean death, or worse, pressed into service. She knew she couldn't stomach working on a Danish Vessel, and she knew for sure that Seamus would rather die – they were so unadventurous.

"I know little of this island, captain, save what you told me. Anything you left out that may make this awful situation more bearable?"

"Ah yes, well, it was part of some project started by Samuel Pepys once he started to reform the navy. The admiralty tasked us with protecting the fledgeling forest here and to ensure that no enemies of his Majesty got close enough to lay a spyglass on it. It's a bit of a weird order, and you know how I like to hear adventure ringing in my ears, but I'm duty and honour bound to protect His Majesty's interests."

Ariadne thought about their current predicament. It would be weeks before anyone could get to them from Tortola, maybe even months if the tropical storms arrived early. They had been sent with a few weeks worth of supplies to get the ball rolling and were to use the stockpile of chopped down trees to build shelters and form a colony. Now, the tools and food they were sent with were sailing away to some godforsaken piratical haven.

"We are going to have to go native, captain, and cobble something together to survive. We need shelter and tools to hunt, especially if the approaching storms hit us. If there's one thing you can count on in this part of the world, it's those incessant storms and howling winds."

"Of course, Ari, you have the right of it. You don't mind if I call you Ari, do you? I grow tired of propriety quite quickly, and if we are to be here a long time, let it be as friends. I've been considering this myself. If we find this stockpile of logs that the admiralty mentioned, we can fashion a shelter in no time at all."

Ariadne had mixed feelings about that. She supposed that if they were going to be stuck here for a while, she would rapidly get sick of being called lieutenant. "What's the point in keeping up propriety if there's no one around to observe it?" she posed to the captain.

"Seamus." The captain held out his hand towards her.

"Well met, Seamus." Ariadne grabbed hold of his hand and greeted him, as if for the first time.

"Now we are better acquainted, let us speak plainly. I must apologise for stranding us here; I blame myself. I should have been less familiar with the crew, more authoritative. I didn't learn from the last affair, it seems."

Ariadne was no longer angry at their situation. It was all in the past. She smirked and decided to test the boundaries of their new friendship. "I blame you too, ya idiot! Who loses a ship? Twice!" She could see the embarrassment creeping back in over his face and she backpedaled. "I'm just messing with you Cap'n." Feeling that she should not broach that subject with such coarseness next time, she decided to change the subject.

"Why do you suppose they were so adamant that we protect these trees? They look just like the oak trees from home."

She watched Seamus mull over his thoughts.

"According to the admiralty, the trees were brought here as saplings and planted on Pepys' orders. Some sort of scientific experiment to help win the war against the Dutch. I'm surprised they survived the salty climate; though they seemed to have adapted to it quite well."

"I suppose it's as wet here as it is back in England, ey cap'n?" She needed to lighten the mood. She had spent far too long being angry, and Seamus had that ponderous look on his face that suggested he was contemplating his failure. "We can do this, captain. We'll make some sort of shelter. If we build it within the forest, it will offer us some protection. I could craft us a bow; we would be able to hunt food for the next few weeks. The mainland should be sending another ship out here to check on us, perhaps the *Neptune* or the *Vanguard*."

Ariadne watched as Seamus' rugged features filled with determination; she seemed to have been able to pull the forlorn captain out of his dour mood with her words. For now.

"You're right of course. Ari, we should make a start. It will almost be nightfall."

She followed the captain up the beach towards the stockpile of felled trees, spying crates as she did. "Oh-ho, look what we have here. Looks like they left some supplies as well. Let's check out what's in these." She motioned to the boxes. Cracking open the first large one, she discovered tools: hammers, saws, and other gear that she was sure would help their predicament.

"Tools, my friend! We find ourselves better equipped, more so than an hour ago. What else do we have here?"

Ariadne explored a crate set under some palm fronds, while Seamus started marking out the best logs to use for their shelter. "Well, well, well, what do we have here?" She swept off the top of the crate and examined its hidden treasures. "Sails! Seamus, look at what the gods have deemed to leave us in their infinite wisdom."

Seamus appeared at her side, looking confused. "Why would they leave these? Especially in the Caribbean. You never want to be caught with your sails down, pirates could be waiting just over the horizon."

"Speaking from experience, cap'n?" She smirked. Ariadne quickly changed the subject again. "Well, it's their loss. I have a better idea than a log cabin, much quicker, too. We can use these to form some sort of tent and brace them to the trees. If we work together, we can get these up and have a fire going before the sun sets. Those fronds will make for excellent kindling."

Hours later, Ariadne watched the sun setting on Anegada. The two pioneers had successfully erected the tents, and Seamus was off collecting more kindling for the fire. She was scouting for the right branch to whittle down and craft into the perfect hunting implement. It turned out that the dead palm tree leaves *did* make for great fire starters. The look of excitement on Seamus' face as he got the fire going, rekindled a bit of hope for the future in her mind. She was doubly hopeful that it had had the same effect on Seamus.

She was also feeling the buzz of adventure, even in the face of such dismal treachery. Granted, she didn't know whether they would be able to gather enough food to survive, and she had no idea what would happen if the storms came while they were still here. Hopefully, someone would turn up soon. Yet, here she was, on an island, fighting for survival, and there was something primal about that—woman versus nature, the ultimate adventure.

She was alive though, and so was Seamus, and that was what mattered most. *We just need to survive on this tropical island until help arrives. Maybe we don't have to stay? Perhaps we can craft a boat over the week and use it to sail to the mainland?* She mused at the thought of charting a course back, and that it relied heavily on the direction of the winds. If she wasn't careful, they could both end up in the middle of the North Atlantic, and that would be a bit of a predicament indeed.

"Ah, that will do."

She had found the perfect branch to carve and mould into shape. There was only one thing to do, and that was to climb up and cut it off. Thankfully, she had brought one of the saws she had found in the crate; it would have been a horrible task with the knife they had freed themselves with. Ariadne patted her old friend.

Given her past experience climbing trees, scaling this one proved a breeze. Her brothers would have been proud. She smiled at the memory. Ariadne secured herself between two of the failed candidates and proceeded to saw at the branch, making sure to keep her balance. She was almost through. She perspired lightly under the tropical heat as her final stroke severed the last inch of bark on the branch. Then, the most curious thing occurred.

The branch floated away.

Ariadne jumped down from the tree, confused. She decided to try again, this time with another branch. *I must be losing my grip on reality, maybe it's the heat or my exhaustion.* She shook her head to try and knock out the crazy. She moved to cut off another branch, one lower down this time, nly to be met with the same result.

"Huh." She slapped her cheeks to check that she wasn't dreaming. She was definitely already awake. "One last attempt." She cut another branch, similar to the last, but this time caught it as it tried to escape. "Not this time, my friend!" She tapped the branch against the tree, testing its existence. It felt the same as any normal branch. She broke it in half. The true test of reality she felt. Nothing seemed to be different. Except... she released her hold of the two halves.

Away they went. Skyward.

Ariadne felt dumbstruck, staring at the sky and lost in her own thoughts, wondering if she had finally lost her sanity.. She had no idea how long she was like this, but was brought around by a light touch on her shoulder, making her jump almost completely out of her skin.

"Ari? Is everything ok?"

"Oh! It's just you, Seamus. You scared me half to death." Ariadne stood there, her hand on her chest. "I did not hear you coming. I was just trying to get a branch to make a bow, while we warmed ourselves by the fire, and I swear, the strangest thing just happened." She was bewildered and her friend looked overly concerned for her.

"What happened?"

She sighed a little, she did not look forward to cutting off another branch. As if she needed *more* confirmation that she was losing her mind. "It's better if I show you, it's hard to find the words to express my consternation." She found the nearest subject of her distress and started to saw, grabbing the branch before making the final cut. She spied the look of bemusement on Seamus' face as he waited in anticipation for the revelations she might reveal. All she had in her hands were more questions.

She turned to Seamus and showed him the branch in her hand. Ariadne tapped it against the tree trunk as before, making a dull thud to show that it was, in fact, a branch. Then she held the limb out to Seamus with a hesitant grimace.

"Try and take it," she motioned to him.

As soon as Seamus placed his hand out for the branch, she let go, and, in a slowly ascending instant, she shared her befuddlement with Seamus. She looked questioningly at Seamus as he stood there, aghast, staring into the sky as the branch left her hand and floated into the heavens.

For what seemed like an eternity, she stood there, watching the branch reach its zenith and, finally, disappearing, before Seamus broke the tension.

"Did we fall asleep? Because I feel as though I am dreaming. Or did we really just witness that branch fly away? I presume the same thing happened to the other branches you cut."

She nodded to the confused captain. "Aye, I mean, I guess we could try again, but I fear the same outcome would only occur again."

"Am I asleep, Ari, this is beyond rational belief. How do you explain such an occurrence?" She watched as Seamus slapped his cheeks.

"Tried that, Captain, we aren't slumbering in our tents. It's a mystery to me. One would presume, logically, that these are not normal oak trees from England." Her brain was ticking away, trying to fathom the mysteries of the island. She could see Seamus was also cogitating on the matter at hand.

"Agreed. If one were to continue in a logical manner, then the Admiralty knew about these specific trees, and that's why we were sent here to protect them. But they must have known about these peculiar properties? Why didn't they keep us apprised of such absurdities?" Ariadne could see that Seamus was increasingly pulling himself out of the shell he had created and becoming more like his normal self.

"Maybe they had no idea. Maybe they sent us out here to protect Pepys' project, but didn't know what they had created?"

"And what is that, Ari? Floating trees? What on Earth could they use them for?" She watched as Seamus sat on the ground, hands cupping his head, massaging his temples. She could tell he was growing wearier by the minute. "This is making my head hurt."

Ariadne couldn't help but agree with him. "I feel like I've been in the rum for a night or two. Maybe we should sleep on the matter at hand, and, hopefully, answers should be readily available to us in the light of day."

"Yes, I think we should. Lead on."

She made it back to camp with Seamus, and the two made themselves as comfortable as possible under the newly made tents. The fire warmed her face relentlessly. It was nice. Comfort wrapped around her, lulling her into a dream-filled state.

* * *

The warm Caribbean wind whistled through the trees and blew the scent of Old England through the island, caressing the cheeks of the intrepid adventurers and billowing the sails of their makeshift tents. While the waves of the North Atlantic crashed on one side, the Caribbean on the other, the trees grew silently as they had done since they were first created in a dusty laboratory back in London. Little did anyone know the true consequences of what that meddling would breathe life into, especially not two unsuspecting members of His Majesty's Navy.

It started with a deep tearing coming from far underground, followed by a low rumble. Not enough to wake anybody, but just enough to cause some concerned frowns to appear on the nocturnal denizens milling about the island, looking for their next meal. The tearing became more evident, as veins of earth opened around the edges of the forest, allowing the sound to escape more loudly. Yet, they still slept.

The earth let out one last groan as it released its grasp on the forest and allowed it to find its way into the world. For a moment, the forest didn't know what to do with its newfound freedom, and, if it could feel, it might have felt a little scared at its new grasp on reality. But as soon as it found its footing, its first few steps into this new world were bold as it ascended into the sky.

The new floating forest grew as tired as its occupants. If it could think, it might have mused, *That's enough for today, I might try moving again sometime tomorrow.* Promptly hanging in the air, as giant, slumbering forests are often wont to do. There it slept, a half a mile above the rest of the island, as peacefully as Seamus and Ariadne in their tents.

* * *

Ariadne awoke feeling groggy. "Well, that was a weird dream," she muttered to herself. Looking over to Seamus, she saw him still slumbering. She always awoke at the crack of dawn, this was her forte. She loved to get a head start on the day.

The embers of last night's fire were almost out, and this made her sad, it was quite a chilly morning, considering. So she made it her first task to look for more kindling. She was sure Seamus would approve of a warm welcome to the day. Off she went, wiping the sleep from her eyes and allowing the world to focus. It wasn't long before she reached the edge of the forest, where the good stuff was, near the stockpile.

Except the stockpile was not there. Nothing was, just a big blue never-ending sky.

She turned around, slightly concerned that she was still asleep, and started to walk back to camp, pinching herself along the way. The realisation of the moment revealed itself to Ariadne exponentially as she got closer to camp, and it quickly dawned on her what she had seen.

Ariadne broke into a quick-paced march, as she was still unsure whether or not she might violate some sort of equilibrium. The moment she arrived at the camp, Seamus was just coming out of his tent, yawning. He was stretching off the last vestiges of sleep, preparing his body for the day, and, hopefully, answers. She had to break it to him gently, having no idea how he would react.

"Seamus, I require your assistance over by the stockpile, for a moment."

Seamus broke out of an extremely long yawn, seeming not to hear her. "Good morning. I don't know about you, but I slept like a log. This mystery and intrigue must have taken more out of me than I realised!"

Ariadne felt a little nervous at what lay in store for him, "Aye, me too. I could use a hand with the kindling."

"Of course, my friend, lead the way."

She played with the idea of just telling him then and there, giving him time to acclimate to the whole notion. Yet, she felt that letting him experience it for himself would be the better of the two options as they walked through the forest. Seamus looked like he had something on his mind.

"I spent my waking moments thinking about how best to craft a vessel so that we can sail to Tortola and inform the mainland of our situation, and our findings. We would have to be very careful not to fall victim to the storms. But I feel that if we can get a vessel crafted and in the water in the next few days, we could be back before the wind direction even changes."

She could sense that they were getting closer to the edge of the forest.

"I thought of something similar myself. At least, I did up until this morning, when I saw this." Ariadne motioned to the edge of the forest.

She watched as Seamus glanced over to where she had pointed, hoping that he could cope with the worsening of their current predicament.

"Where has the world gone?" Seamus seemed a little scared. Ariadne watched as he scrambled away from the edge. She had had some time to come to terms with their new existence. This was not their world anymore, not the one she had grown up in. This was one she had no concept of, at least not at this moment in time, so early in the morning.

"Look down." She joined him at the edge of their new world, and the two of them glanced down, being cautiously joyful at the sight of their old world below them, half a mile away.

"Well, I see, that's how things are now. I don't mind saying, Ari, I don't quite care for this surprise, but I shall grow accustomed to it, in time."

Chapter - 2 - We Did Start The Fire

The fire had been burning for several minutes.

From beneath the deck, a roar could be heard as the powder kegs exploded, bringing with it an excellent morale boost for the hoard of fearsome pirates and adding nicely to an altogether satisfying blaze. There was something about the flames licking up the sails that pleased Captain Rackham.

'Captain' was merely a stolen title, much as the many things he and his crew took. To them, he was Jack. To the lucky few who managed to survive his onslaughts, one name was whisked windward – Calico Jack, the terror of the Caribbean.

"Survivors, Captain!" the new recruit shouted to the heavens.

Jack peered portside into the briny deep. "So there are, Bill." He took a bite out of the apple he had procured from the French vessel. "Ten doubloons on Red-shirt. Any takers?"

Bill looked inquisitive. "What are your terms?"

Jack cast his eyes over the water and took another bite out of his apple. "Red-shirt gets eaten by the sharks first." He peered towards the island in the distance. "Before he gets to that island over there." Jack grinned at the sharks' fins, making a beeline for the hopeful swimmers.

He watched Bill weigh the coin purse attached to his belt.

"Aye, you're on!" Bill flung the captain his share of the recently acquired booty. "I'll take the white shirt. Looks like he has weaker legs!"

The crew let loose an almighty cheer. There wasn't much chance for entertainment at sea, and this is what passed for it. It had been a while since this congregation of piratical bastards had had an opportunity to raid and pillage a fellow navigator of the sea. So the moment that the *Trident* appeared over the horizon, the *Kingston* crew pounced into action and chased the French frigate with all the zeal and enthusiasm of a hungry shark.

The Captain stirred from his thoughts.

Jack noticed that the sharks were not alone. Some friends had also arrived for a quick feast from the east. It wasn't long before the sea was churned into a bubbling red soup. One of the sharks took a bite out of the white shirt. He cried for his *maman*. This roused a hearty cackle from the gaggle of pirates. Second to go was red-shirt with an assault from the rear. Both bodies bobbed up and down in the waters, ripe for the picking. Both wore shirts stained with blood. Jack grinned.

"Well, well, well. It looks like Calico Jack wins again!" The pirate captain threw the core of his apple to a watery grave and proceeded down the steps to his cabin.

"But my man died first! The white-shirted Frenchy had his leg bit off." Jack could see that Bill was angry. He played a dangerous game arguing with this captain, but it had been a bit of a quiet few months, and the coffers were looking depressing. Bill had just bet his entire share.

Jack placed an arm around the dishevelled new recruit to ease any fleeting notions of mutiny. "Now, Bill, look over there." He pointed with his already-drawn cutlass. "Tell me what you see."

The two eyed the mess of body parts and unsatiated sharks.

"I see that both Frenchies are, in fact, wearing red shirts," grinned the pirate captain. The blood had seeped through White-shirts' ribboned garments and stained. Logically, he was the winner, but a lot of pirates weren't as logical as him.

Jack could see that Bill saw red. Not only in the water, but it was also now colouring his vision too. He had to strike before Bill got the better of him preemptively.

"Cheater!" Bill screamed.

Enraged, he had gone for his dagger and made ready to stab Jack. Yet before he could, he had three inches of steel and a handle protruding out his chest.

Jack let Bill settle with the notion of dying.

"Oh." That was all the punctured pirate could utter.

Jack tightened his grip on the handle and kicked Bill off his blade, onto the deck of the *Kingston*. "Looks like the sharks will be having dessert today. Throw him overboard, lads!" With that, the crew picked Bill up and flung him over portside. His body made a commotion as it hit the water, which signalled to some of the less fortunate sharks that there was still food to be had. "Poor Bill, he wasn't long for this world, what with his poor eyesight," Jack lamented, watching the water froth red.

The pirates laughed with maniacal ferocity.

The *Trident* was almost under; Jack's latest offering to Davy Jones. All that remained were the masts and blazing sails. He pulled himself away from the dancing flames to return to his cabin. Yet, before he had even reached the door, another call came from the deck.

"Another survivor, Captain!"

Jack could feel his eyes rolling into the back of his skull. "Leave him for the sharks; we don't need any more entertainment. I have much more pressing matters to attend to." He eyed his cabin door anxiously.

"This one's laying on a chest, Captain."

The pirate captain's hand rested on the doorknob. His eyebrows raised inquisitively. "Why didn't you say that before? Is your heart even in it anymore, Sebastian? A treasure for me means treasure for all. You would think a man of learning, such as yourself, would be more concise with the pertinent facts."

Sebastian gulped. "Yes, Captain. I'll try to be more succinct with the truth in the future." Jack had stolen him aboard many months ago. *Stolen* was putting it nicely. Calico Jack attempted to be whimsical with his benevolence once in a blue moon and Sebastian had seen that firsthand. His was a scholarly vessel heading to research some of the flora in the Americas. That was before his pirate bastards got their hands on the man's equipment. The crew told Jack that they liked him around because of his endearing qualities, *the cut of his jib*. He knew Sebastian had no idea what that meant. The men found him funny-looking, but the captain, well, he kept him around for some intelligent conversation.

Jack sauntered over to starboard and placed both hands on the taffrail. He gazed avariciously at the garishly dressed Frenchman draped over the sizeable chest. "If this were a tavern, Sebastian, I'd have shot the bugger and claimed the wench for myself. What is she still doing in the water?" He questioned the scholar with an accusing look and a slight caress of his cutlass.

Sebastian looked at the captain with a hesitant grimace. Jack liked to give off the impression that he was one of two things, angry or aroused.

"Sorry, Captain, I'll get the men to retrieve her straight away. What about the survivor, Captain?"

"Ugh! Must I do everything around here?" Jack's utter disgust trailed off as he stormed into his cabin. With the door finally closed, Jack was able to continue with his unfinished business. "I hope I didn't miss anything, Anney? You know how much raiding gives me the horn."

"Aye, ya sick bastard, that's why I love ya."

Anne Bonny lay in the bed, the words flowing from her lips. Jack removed his belt buckle, dropping his lengthy cutlass to the deck.

She lay there playfully twirling her fiery red locks, enticing him back to the bed she had kept warm.

It had been several delicious minutes as the two pirates entwined, partaking in each other's vices, both of one mind. Each lover moaning and asking for more, but, before they could complete, there signalled a hurried knock on the other side of the door.

"Captain, you should come look at this."

"Good gods, man. What is it? Can a pirate captain get no peace aboard his own, stolen, vessel?"

Jack marched angrily over to the cabin door, not even bothering to dress. He swung it open with a great, sexually-frustrated, ferocity.

"Sebastian. Really? If this is something that could have waited, you will find yourself at the end of a very short plank."

Sebastian glanced down at Jack, immediately overcome with embarrassment.

"Errr, it's just that, well. . ."

"Spit it out, man! You're acting as if you've never seen a penis before." Jack stood in the doorway fuming, hands on his hips, foot tapping away.

"Well, it's just that the chest is a bit devoid of treasure *per se*. It's just filled with documents, papers, formulas. That sort of thing. Nothing valuable to a pirate."

Jack had stopped tapping and raised his eyebrow. His face was a nice shade of vermillion. "I really hope there's an *and* after that sentence, Sebastian, because my patience is waning. You haven't told me why I shouldn't be telling the lads to get the extremely short plank ready." Jack could tell that Sebastian was very reluctant to share the next bit of information with him. The man was due for a beating.

"Well, sir, you see, the prisoner is jabbering on in French."

There it was.

"Sebastian, Sebastian, Sebastian." Jack shook his head. "You know the rule with prisoners, don't you?"

Sebastian gulped. He had made an error.

"No prisoners?"

"No prisoners," the captain confirmed.

"It's just that he seems to be making a lot of articulated gestures towards the chest and its contents. Like they are important." Sebastian stood there expectantly like he was waiting for something, yet all that was happening was that Jack was getting angrier.

Jack stood staring. Still naked.

23

"Important, as in profitable, captain." Jack felt Sebastian push him along the thought process.

A lamp flickered on in the back.

"What is all this commotion over a chest, Sebastian?" Anney had risen from Jack's bed, a look of pure disdain on her face.

"Go back to bed, Anney. Don't bless Sebastian with your presence. He's taken a prisoner." Jack could hear the groan from behind him, followed by the patter of feet back to the bedroom. "Let me put some clothes on, and I'll grace this prisoner with my presence. You have dodged the plank once again, my friend." Jack saw the look of relief brighten Sebastian's gaunt face as the captain closed the door and returned to his lover.

Now, fully satisfied, fully dressed, and donning all his pirate accoutrements, Calico Jack looked like he could frighten the barnacles off a hull. *Beat that, Blackbeard.* He stood there admiring himself in the mirror until he was satisfied. He was going to give this French prisoner a piece of his mind. If Sebastian weren't going to get the beating he so rightly deserved, this man would be the recipient of some harsh words, maybe even more brutal actions. Jack sauntered down to the brig and was presented with the very entertaining image of Sebastian trying his very best to communicate in French.

"Well, well, Sebastian, am I led to believe that you have more use than a pirate with two eye patches? Have you got anything useful out of the poor bugger?" Jack growled at the prisoner. He tried to sound more menacing and less like an angry badger. He hadn't had much chance to growl at prisoners, partly because he didn't like keeping them around longer than a heartbeat, and partly because he usually just flashed his cutlass at them to make them talk. This was different, though. He was trying something new.

The prisoner looked frightened and seemed very adamant about relaying some sort of information about the chest. Jack was in a better mood now than when Sebastian had ruined his earlier rendezvous with Anney. He decided to give the man the benefit of his benevolence. Just as long as he came up with something worth his time. He was a very busy pirate.

Jack leered at the prisoner. "Can you make any sense of what he's saying?"

"Well, Captain, he keeps mentioning *revues*, which are journals, and something about *des arbres,* which I think is a tree?"

"You're asking me, Sebastian? Gods, man, don't fail me now." Jack felt as though his eyes would never stop rolling whenever Sebastian was concerned. He moved over to the scholar and started to massage his shoulders. Jack felt Sebastian tense up as if, for some reason, he felt as though his life was on the line again. "Relax, Sebastian. Calm yourself. Make yourself useful to me, and everything will be fine. Tell me, my friend, what's the French for gold?" He felt Sebastian relax under his hands.

"*L'or,* captain."

"Very well, Sebastian. Ask the man if this is worth anything." Jack motioned to the bare chest. He grew more impatient with every breath the prisoner took. Jack watched as Sebastian tried his very best to ask if the chest was worth any gold, but his French was either useless, or this Frenchmen was a bit dull in the head. Jack chose to accept the former.

"I'm guessing you can't understand me. *Parlez-vous anglais*?" Jack's last-ditch effort to commune with the Frenchmen. The Frenchman just shook his head, and Jack sighed. He pointed to the chests. "*Revues,* how much *gold*?" Like any foreigner who wanted the listener to understand what he was going on about, Jack emphasized gold. He flicked a doubloon at the prisoner. The piece of gold bounced off the man's chest and fell to the floor. Something must have clicked for the Frenchmen because a look of understanding washed over the man's face.

"*Beaucoup d'or. Sans prix.*"

Jack looked at Sebastian expectantly. "Pray, tell me that meant what I hope it meant, Sebastian? So help me God, if he didn't allude to untold riches, I shall be very upset. Mainly with you." Sebastian gave him a look of pure relief and, some might say, quite a smug smile. That was all the affirmation Jack needed.

"Yes, Captain. Lots of gold."

"Well done, Sebastian. See, that wasn't so hard, was it?" Jack patted the man on his shoulder. That was the only bit of praise he felt the scholar deserved after interrupting his liaison. Jack went to leave the brig but then turned to Sebastian. "Find out everything you can about these journals. If I'm going to barter a good price for them, I need to know what I'm dealing with, savvy? I know it's going to be hard, Sebastian, but try not to annoy me with small details again, I'm looking for big details." Jack turned back to leave but stopped mid-step.

"Oh, and Sebastian."

"Yes, Captain?"

"I need this man to think he's going to live. So relax. Milk him for all the information he's worth. Then have the boys take care of him. You have 'til we get to Tortuga." Jack left this time. He could feel Sebastian's disappointment oozing from the brig. As he marched up onto the main deck, he spied Anney draped across the wheel. She was fully clothed this time, much to his dismay.

"My, my, don't you look the part." Anney smirked at him. If he had a heart, it might have melted. Jack had lost his train of thought and was beginning to wish that she was back in his bed. "I was going to come to find you and divulge the particulars of the chest."

"Aye, I think you did enough divulging earlier." Jack flashed her a devilish grin as he joined her on the poop deck.

"I thought it best to set sail for Tortuga. The lads will want to be spending their coin, and I feel you have some business to attend to, what with that chest of yours."

"Excellent. I feel we might be swimming in doubloons shortly. Enough to quit this place entirely and let the other pirate captains pick the carcass clean. We can head to a place where there is less chance of being hanged. Let me know when we get there."

"Aye, Jack."

He vaulted over the rail and onto the main deck and entered his cabin for some well-earned rest. *It's hard work being a pirate.*

Chapter - 3 - To Boldly Go

Ariadne was growing accustomed to the sight already. She felt disconnected from the old world, with the treetops now brushing the clouds, but she also felt something else. There was a place inside her that thought it always needed to be part of something new and push the boundaries of what was acceptable - her grandmother had been the same. It must have skipped a generation because her mother was the height of propriety. She had begged Ariadne not to join the navy, saying that only bad things would come of it. *Well, look at me now, mother.*

Planting both feet somewhat tentatively within this new world, Ariadne wondered how far Samuel Pepys' chaotic experiment had stretched. *Had he planted these magnificent oaks anywhere else? Were there more floating forests out there?* She surveyed the newly airborne island's perimeter, taking extra care to pay homage to every step she took, never knowing if the ground would suddenly fall away into the sea below.

The wind was much stronger up here, Ariadne had a horrid feeling that it might blow the island apart. Yet, she stood true and firm.

Much like a new ship, she had decided to give the island a name. She had mulled it over for a while before deciding on *Selene*, after her grandmother, who had inspired her so much. Ariadne felt she would have been proud to bestow her name to this beautiful marvel.

While she explored the extremities of their new reality, she had sent Seamus off to inspect the forest itself, to see if anything could aid them in their dilemma. That and Seamus' air legs were not as attuned as hers yet. She smirked. He seemed much better in the centre away from the edge. She didn't want to concern him further, especially after he had finally managed to maintain his constitution. Ariadne took to the situation a whole lot better than he. She was glad for it; if they were ever to survive this unfortunate turn of events, she would need a hardier constitution than his. She knew he would get there eventually, *he just needed time.*

* * *

She had been walking for what seemed like miles before Ariadne decided that nothing new could be gleaned from the perimeter and made her way back to camp. Something caught her eye in the distance, near one of the bigger trees in what she presumed was roughly the forest's centre, a blemish in the soil. Ariadne Smith was never one to back away from adventure, even the whiff of one. So, she made her way over to investigate.

As Ariadne got closer to the tall oak, she made out what looked like steps cut into the soil, circling the tree's perimeter, leading down into the ground. "Curiouser and curiouser." She cautiously approached the large oak and proceeded to move down the stairs. It looked as though someone had dug them out with tools, but for what purpose she could not fathom. The soil staircase spiralled down into darkness as it delved deeper into the ground. She followed it until the last of the light died away, and all she could see was black. *What good is exploring this strangeness without light?*

"I should return with a torch."

She spoke into the darkness to ward off any would-be assailants, but there was no one there, just the darkness.

* * *

"Ah! You have returned; I was beginning to worry."

"Sorry cap'n, I was waylaid by a mystery."

"More mysterious than a floating island? I will trouble you for an explanation in a moment, for I have urgent news regarding our return to the mainland!"

"I see! Pray tell me this joyous news so you may rejoice alone no more."

Seamus looked excited. "Well, while I was scouting the interior, I thought more about our situation and possible solutions. I had designs for a raft swimming around my head for the longest time. Yet, now we find ourselves a lot closer to the clouds than I would like. I feared that it was no longer a viable option. So, I made my way back to camp." She watched him pace around the fire, the same one they had lit that morning.

"Did you find anything of value in the forest?" *Maybe he came across another staircase*, she mused.

"No, I'm afraid not. Yet, upon my return, lost in my thoughts, a great billowing sail greeted me. Flapping up in the air and let loose from some of its bindings. I feared some ghost had come to haunt me!"

Ariadne sat by the fire on the edge of a log, captivated by Seamus' performance. She hadn't seen him this animated since she first came aboard the *Daedalus*. It was good to see her friend finally revived.

"Then, like a ship coming over the horizon, it dawned on me. Why not remove the raft entirely?" She watched as Seamus grabbed hold of a nearby axe and cut some of the tent's reattached bindings. The sail flowed freely up into the air billowing in the updraft.

"We are going to sail the forest, Ari!"

Ariadne shrugged. "Sure, why not. I mean its absolute madness, but no less mad than being stuck on top of a flying forest. How are we even to craft such an endeavour?"

"Ah, well, you see, I had envisioned something akin to a frigate, but we would have to make modifications to take into account we are flying a forest and not sailing a ship." She watched Seamus pace back and forth, his vexations apparent, sighing.
She could sense he was having difficulty with the particulars of the operation.

"I was hoping you might have some input as I seem to be falling short on the logistics of the entire matter."

Ariadne laughed into the air. "Ever the visionary Seamus. Don't worry. I'm sure it will all work itself out. In the meantime, I fear we should explore our other mystery."

* * *

Ariadne led Seamus through the sea of oaks while carrying torches, cloth, and flint. All would be needed to better illuminate the passage that carved into the floating island's depths.

"Steps, you say? Leading to darkness? Well, that is intriguing. I dare say this only adds more to the mystery we find ourselves in. You did right to wait to investigate. Who knows what lurks in the shadows?"

Ariadne was not taking any chances this time. She had Seamus bring an axe from the supply crate and she had her trusty dagger close by. "Well, it was more the light, really. Where is the sense in exploring a pitch-black staircase when you cannot see? But I suppose you are right; I wouldn't want you to miss out on all the fun."

"Ha! Right you are. You say this particular oak was near the centre of the island?"

Ariadne scanned ahead, fervently looking for the discolouration in the soil. "Yes, we should be getting close. I mean, it didn't take me long to get back to you, so we should be there so---" She trailed off as she fell head over heels through the earth.

"Ari!"

Her face may have been full of dirt but she could hear Seamus' panic-stricken cries. She was one with the earth. There was dirt everywhere, but at least she had found the staircase. She needed a moment to adjust and come back to the land of the conscious.

The earth groaned or was it her. It was hard to tell. Ariadne sat herself up, dusted herself off, and looked up to see Seamus peering over the edge of the pit, relief, at seeing her unhurt, in his eyes. "Told you it was close by." She stated with a pained emphasis. Ariadne rose to her feet, brushing the sun-bleached mess of hair out of her face, and nursed the bump on her forehead.

"Thank goodness you're okay, I feared you were gone for good!"

"Just a bump on the old mind-box cap'n, nothing to worry about. At least we found the stairs." She bashfully replied. Ariadne held out her hand for Seamus to help her out of the hole she had momentarily disappeared down.

"Right you are. Let's get you out of there."

Ariadne pulled herself out of the hole, using Seamus' hand as leverage. "Aye Cap'n. Let us light those torches and investigate further." She watched as Seamus wrapped the cloth around the makeshift torches. He was taking great care not to let go of them. Carefully, he passed one to her, then proceeded to light the one he held with the flint. It sparked to life with relative ease, and he was then free to light hers as well. "These torches won't last long, the wood doesn't seem to burn as well, so we will only have a limited amount of time.

"Aye, aye, cap'n. Shall we see what the forest has in store for us?" she posed to Seamus with a wild glint in her eye.

"Lead the way."

Ariadne crouched as she probed the darkness, the last of the sun's rays no longer visible. Now she was relying on the torchlight to explore the depths of this earthen staircase.

She continued down cautiously, using the torch to light her path. *Praise the light.* "Careful here." She relayed to Seamus. The walls dripped with the captured rainfall that had soaked into the earth, and some of the larger stones had come loose from their place and demolished some of the steps. It was a tricky descent, but she eventually came to a wide opening, cautiously entering, torch first.

Ariadne had uncovered a humble cavern with Seamus joining her shortly after. She raised her torch into the darkness to see how far it actually went, which wasn't very far. The oak roots had run deep, bursting through the cavern's crest and spreading out over the roof of the cavern like a spider's web. She waved her torch around, exploring its depths, hoping to uncover some clue as to the purpose it served.

"It'll be better if we split up. You go that way and I'll carry on this way."

"Good idea Ari."

She watched as Seamus inched away, gripping the cavern's walls for stability until all she could see was his torchlight traversing around the cavern. *Hopefully, he doesn't run into any monsters in the dark.* She pressed on further along the opposite wall. Eventually, the light from her torch exposed more roots, which seemed to be concealing another passage, one which led away from this chamber.

"I think perhaps the mystery runs even deeper," she called in the direction of the light of Seamus' torch. "There appears to be some sort of passageway leading away from here. I'll follow it, see where it takes me."

"Do be careful Ari." The reply echoed around the room, eventually reaching her ears.

She delved into the roots, hoping over the main branch and squeezing between several smaller ones. "What madness is this, pray tell?" She whispered to the darkness as she explored the new depths, travelling down the tunnel. It was a good job she didn't get claustrophobic, the walls closed in, some of the soil had come down and caused the path to become tight and the air became thinner. Roots dragged at her mess of hair as she ducked down to clamber through the dark. Eventually, she felt like the space had opened up and she was finally free from the confines of the tunnel. Ariadne cautiously tested the limits of this new opening with her torch, hoping to uncover answers, but only illuminating more questions in the form of a lone skeleton.

"Seamus!" She cried into the darkness. *Hopefully, he heard that.* She brought the torch closer to the skeleton hoping to uncover some clue as to who this was, and, more importantly, why they were here. After the initial shock of discovery, she was beginning to feel exhausted from the constant adrenaline rush, the excitement of having another mystery to solve. The skeleton in question was lying prone on a makeshift bed, the floor below it stained red with old, dried blood. *He's been here a while then.* She explored the room further. Scanning the space with the torchlight uncovered tables with odd equipment on them, shelves filled with labelled books, and bottles, with cuttings in, next to some dusty-looking microscopes. *Curiouser and curiouser indeed.*

"Ari, are you well?", came a call from the darkness.

"Unless the dead are about to rise up, I think I'll be okay. But you really must see this, it's remarkable." She swung the torch towards the passage in an attempt to light the way for Seamus. Eventually, additional light blossomed in the darkness, heralding Seamus' arrival. "Ah, good, you found me! Feast your eyes on this," and, with that, Ariadne lowered her torch to reveal the skeleton lying on the makeshift bed.

Seamus almost jumped out of his skin. Ariadne began to chuckle at his fright. "It's just a skeleton. No monster in the dark." She shook the skeleton's hand at him, making ghostly noises as she did. Seamus shuddered and straightened his jacket.

"Yes, well, it was just a bit of a surprise that's all. You could have warned me." Ariadne was still laughing.

"Is this a living space? Or at least, was it?" She watched as Seamus kneeled to inspect the inhabitant closer. "Dried blood. It seems that whoever this was bled out. This dank cave was to be his final resting place."

"It seems it was much more cap'n. See here; tables with bottles, scientific equipment, books." Her light shone over the table, enough to allow Seamus to gaze in wonderment. "And here are tree cuttings and microscopes." She manoeuvred her torch's light to illuminate the cavern further. "It seems to be some form of laboratory."

She watched as Seamus moved over to the bookcase. "Look at all these books on botany and alchemy."

Ariadne joined him by the bookcase, her torch exposing the titles as she moved down the shelves. "And these here, journals! These could reveal what this person was doing here. We best head topside before our torches run out. We'll never be able to find our way out otherwise."

"Good idea, Ari. Let's grab as many books as we can and take them back to camp. Hopefully, they bring forth light where there once was darkness, and help us uncover this mystery."

Ariadne grabbed as much as she could safely hold and passed her burden to Seamus. She then picked up a similar number, ensuring that she would be able to return topside without spilling any. "There must be a better way of taking these with us?" *Hang on; a plan is formulating.* She pulled the scrunched up sheet off the bed, placed the books in the centre of the sheet, then fetched the rest, adding them to the growing pile. Picking up the corners, she turned the bed sheet into a carry-all. *Much better.* "Leave no book behind." She mused to a very bemused looking Seamus.

37

She retraced their steps with great difficulty, passing the roots with the carry-all proved quite difficult but she managed to squeeze it through some of the larger cracks. Then up the spiral staircase. Their vision blurred when sunlight greeted them as they exited, slowly normalizing as their eyes focussed on the natural light of day.
"We'll leave the torches just inside the mouth of the tunnel, so they don't take a trip to the clouds."

"Good thinking Ari. Now let us get these back to camp. Hopefully, they hold the key to some much-needed answers."

"Lead the way cap'n!"

* * *

Ariadne had taken to reading a journal on the short hike back to camp, eager to expose the secrets beneath its cover. She followed Seamus who was carrying the rest of the books, her head buried in the book, occasionally glancing up to check the path ahead for hazards.

"April 3rd, 1673, we finally arrived in the Caribbean with our consignment intact. No contact that raised any suspicions of note upon the journey. It seems we were not deserving of further investigation. For this, I am glad. Can you imagine the look on their faces if they came aboard and all they could plunder were saplings?"

"Seems like he was here a long time. This journal is from April."

"April 15th, 1673, I have finally ascertained the best spot to be cultivated in order to ensure the success of this batch of saplings. The crew has been busy planting them and digging out a living space and laboratory. Somewhere away from the tropical elements

of this island and somewhere I can inspect the roots through the years of growth. I have enough work to be getting on with and enough supplies to last me for months. Pepys assures me that he will have fresh supplies for us shipped from the mainland so that my experiments may continue." Ariadne was growing more intrigued with each turn of the page.

"I'm assuming the skeleton down in the cavern was the owner of this journal. Seems he was sent here to carry out further experiments."

"I think you might be right, Ari. This journal here talks about possible applications for the mature trees. It seems this botanist was very aware of the tree's abnormal properties. Here."

She took hold of the journal and flicked the pages to where he had indicated.

"*June 5th, 1678, the oak has grown healthy, as expected. It was a good choice to splice. The fact that it can grow in any climate helped with the process. In some cases, the experiment seems to have accelerated growth. For example, the giant oak above the main cavern, its roots have broken through the ceiling and begun to sweep across it slowly.*

"*June 7th, 1678 Experimentation continues on the branches of some of the more mature trees. I feel that the most peculiar attribute I have uncovered from these experiments is the material's persistence at floating into the clouds. Remarkable. Who would have thought the combination of Botany and Alchemy could produce such things. The material offers countless applications; housing, inaccessible fortresses, weapons, trade, not to mention the implications this will have for the Navy.*"

"There are some sketches and diagrams. Look, here is something that resembles a bird. Reminds me of Da Vinci's notebook. In any case, it sounds like this is the true intent of being sent here. Yet why would the Navy not confide this intelligence with us? And where is this scholar's crew?" Seamus was turning a new shade of red. She liked to think it was a mix of concern and anguish.

"I'm sure the answers lay somewhere in these journals." She placed a hand on Seamus' shoulder in reassurance, "Don't worry, we'll get to the bottom of this and get back to the mainland."

"Right you are." He seemed to be a bit more accepting of the whole situation. "Let us get back to camp."

* * *

Ariadne Smith had spent many moons under the stars as a child. The sky tonight was providing a particularly clear view of the constellations. She sat by the crackling fire looking up, the peace and tranquillity whisking her back to those days when she had not one care in the world. Well, unfortunately, she had one now, and it was what was keeping the fire burning. She threw another palm leaf on the blaze and returned to her seat, her back to the oak nearest the heat.

Learning the constellations was, of course, her first foray into navigation. She would have been no use at charting courses at sea if she had not. Seamus sat close by, reading various journals, scouring each page as if he were looking for clues to El Dorado.

"What was the first constellation you had the pleasure of discovering, cap'n?"

He pulled himself out of his current journal as if breaking from a spell. "If memory serves me right, it was Orion."

Ariadne was impressed. "The Heavenly Shepard? He doesn't seem to be out tonight."

"No, I haven't seen him for many months."

She was reminded of the normality of only a few months ago, in stark contrast to how different things were now. She knew that normalcy would never return. She breathed a heavy, nostalgic sigh for the loss of what was once, and would never be again. She could sense Seamus' heartache creeping back in, so she quickly changed the subject. "I remember mine well," the memory brought a smile to her face. "My grandmother used to take me camping when I was but a young thing, all hair and boundless energy. We would practice sword fighting and hunting by day; then she would teach me the constellations and the history behind them. She was a very knowledgeable woman."

Seamus looked impressed. "She sounds like a formidable woman indeed."

Ariadne crept closer to the fire to breathe in that wonderful campfire scent. "Aye, you would have liked her; she would have kept you on your toes, no doubt."

Seamus laughed heartily; it was a welcome sound to hear, something different from the wind howling around them. "I bet she would. But what about your first constellation?"

"Ah, well, let me see if I can find it." She gazed through the opening in the forest and scanned the heavens looking for the stars she knew so well.

"There she is! Andromeda. Beautiful, isn't she?"

"Indeed, a picture of beauty. Tell me, Ari, did your grandmother tell you the tale of Andromeda, how she became placed in the heavens for all to gaze upon?"

"Of course. Although I did not like that she was so reliant on Perseus saving her. I thought she should have got out of Ethiopia the moment sacrifice was even mentioned. Who sticks around to get tied to a rock at sea to wait for death? An idiot that's who. A beautiful idiot."

She sighed, remembering only mere days ago being tied to a rock herself. She glanced at Seamus.

"Yes, well, I fear you have the right of it." Seamus returned to the journal he was reading.

"Tell me, have the journals been fruitful? You've barely spoken a word all evening, your nose has been glued to a book."

His nose poked back over the book. "Well, take a look here. From what I can gather, the Admiralty had no idea what this botanist was doing out here. He writes here of being sworn to secrecy by King Charles II himself, that Pepys was merely funding it. Apparently, the war with the Dutch was not going so well. Charles needed to secure money for it but was having no luck at home, so he had to rely on French subsidies. He knew the Dutch fleet was strong, but he vowed to Louis XIV that he would make a stronger fleet. French and English botanists and alchemists allied across the channel to make a lighter, more durable material to make the combined fleet fast and devastatingly brutal. So, they discovered a new technique called..."

She watched as he flicked through the pages.

"Splicing. Where the alchemists could combine elements with the oak saplings during the germination process, they were hoping to find a way to mix the properties of some elements with the main source material. The trials also highlighted that heat seemed to generate faster growth rates in some of the testing batches, hence why they were out in the Caribbean, I suppose. You don't get much sun in old England."

"Too true, cap'n! Is there any mention of what happened to the crew, or how the man died?"

Seamus picked up another journal and flicked through the pages in a flurry.

"There is no mention of the crew's fate, only that there are several entries across all the journals of the ship making trips to the mainland for supplies. He marks when they returned later in the week. Yet in the last entry, there is no mention of a return. Could be anything, Ari; pirates, the Dutch, bad weather, mutiny." Seamus let that one linger in the air.

"I see. What about the botanist?"

"Well, I was just getting towards the end of the last journal. He makes mention of spotting a vessel on the horizon."

"September 29th, 1680 It has been over a week since my crew set off for supplies. They should have returned by now. The ship that has been haunting the eastern horizon is not flying our colours. I fear

for the safety of the experiment if they start to advance closer. Hopefully, my crew has just been temporarily detained."

"September 30th, 1680 My crew still has not returned come the midday sun. The vessel on the eastern horizon is advancing towards the island, but my fears have subsided, for I have identified the vessel as a French frigate flying the ensign of King Louis XIV. Hopefully, the vessel bears my fellow scientists with news of their own experiments, or at least the notion of some fresh fruit."

"October 1st, 1680 The French frigate has anchored offshore, and three smaller vessels now make their way to the island. I shall head down to the beach and greet them."

Seamus' eyes scanned ahead, frantically searching through the remaining pages.

"This doesn't bode well, Ari. We need to get back to the mainland as soon as possible."

"What does it say? What happened to the botanist?"

He passed her the journal. Ariadne solemnly read from the top of the last page.

"They betrayed us, those damnable French. I managed to make it back to my laboratory, but I am losing a lot of blood. I do not think I will see the next sunrise. They have taken them, all my notes on how

44

to splice the seeds. Please, if my crew returns or you happen upon these journals by chance. Take them to the King, and you will be greatly rewarded."

Fear and anguish crept over Ariadne's face as she stared into the burning embers of the fire.

Chapter - 4 - Pieces Of Eight.

The *Kingston* glided through the water, like a bird slicing through the clouds, her enemies now left in her wake. As bold as day, Jack stood, admiring the progress she made from the bow of the ship. This was his thinking space. All he could hear were the waves bowing to his ship's will, and the sea parting just for him. He felt well-rested, but Sebastian had given him some vexatious news. News that required more than a modicum of concentration.

"Tell me again, Sebastian, in terms that a layman may understand, and please do try and remember that my generosity is all but spent on your last endeavour."

Sebastian looked sheepish. "It might be a little difficult to sell the chest's documents."

The veins on the side of Jack's head were throbbing with a renewed vigour. "What, exactly, is the problem, my friend?" He placed an arm around the cowering scholar, thoughts of pushing Sebastian from the figurehead suggestively flouncing in his groggy head. Or, at least, dangling him from it. He mused long and hard about that, but she was a lovely figurehead, all delicate oak curls and seductively supple tits. It would be a shame to mar such a delectable creature, and he had already spent enough effort pulling himself away from Anney.

"Well, Captain, they would be of no use to a pirate. Present company excluded. The cost of these documents is well beyond the aspirations of some common pirate from Tortuga. Think bigger, Captain."

"Mainland bigger?"

"Royally bigger."

Jack's eyes grew large, thoughts of his rise in status dancing in front of them. "Admiral Rackham?"

"Try Lord Rackham, sir."

The urge to subjugate Sebastian to ease his stress was leaving him and being replaced with a warm feeling of euphoria. "I knew it was a good idea to keep you alive. You will live another day, my friend!" He squeezed his pet with a renewed vigour. Sebastian looked terrified, *good that should keep him on his toes*. "Follow me to my cabin, away from prying minds. You can divulge the particulars to me before we dock in Tortuga."

* * *

Jack sat in the ostentatious captain's chair in his cabin, legs splayed, one leg hitched on the armrest, his bulge centre stage. Sebastian's gaze couldn't escape it, and it amused Jack to think that the scholar was sitting there uncomfortably, searching the room for something else to look at.

"So, you're saying that they invented something? What invention could be worth all this bloodshed and chicanery?"

"Er… as far as I can translate what I'm getting from the prisoner, the Sun King himself, Louis XIV, sent them on a mission to sever ties with King Charles. They were collaborating with something, together, in the Caribbean, but you know how volatile kings can be.

They go to war over the slightest besmirching."

"Are they at war?"

"I don't think so; not yet anyway. I think Charles has more to worry about at home, going by the reports. Maybe the Sun King is licking his lips at the thought of lapping up the leftovers once the dust has settled."

"Interesting. Now, continue telling me how I become a lord, Sebastian."

"Well, captain, it looks like the Sun King wished to acquire these documents." Sebastian waved the journal at him. "At any cost."

"What's so valuable that a king would send a covert force, to the other side of the world no less, to collect a few documents?"

Sebastian looked mentally exhausted. "This is where the translation got a little...er...fuzzy."

"Now, now, let us take this slowly, my friend. You wouldn't want me to look like a fool in front of a King. Especially if you did me the dishonour of mistranslating the prisoner." Jack fidgeted with the cutlass resting at the side of his bejewelled throne, growing impatient. "What exactly did you tease out of the Frenchman?"

"I think, maybe, I should just show you. Frenchie was spouting all sorts of nonsense that I either mistranslated or is just complete insanity. That is until we found this on his person. Then things became clearer."

Jack's curiosity had peaked. He stopped placing his bulge on parade and playing with his cutlass suggestively. The pirate captain sat forward, ready to absorb anything Sebastian had to share with him. He watched intently as Sebastian pulled out a single vial from his person. The inside housed a single splinter of wood.

"It just so happens that you have expertly stumbled on to a king's ransom, Captain."

Jack eyed the vial with the same desire he observed his wenches, with arousal coursing through his veins and suffusing his gaze.

* * *

The sun and the moon had passed from horizon to horizon, and the crew had finally made it back to Tortuga. Jack's mind was racing, trying to process all this information. He sat there, musing, weighing up his choices. His mind had initially been intrigued by the mention of gold, and what he could buy, but another path weighed heavy on his mind.

"The decision facing you in his moment, Captain, is which monarch you wish to hold accountable for the punitive interest in transferring such valuable tomes."

"Keep it down, Sebastian. We don't want this information getting back to any of the other captains, like Hornigold or Vane. God forbid this should get to Blackbeard; that pompous toad. All curls and smoke, like some cheap parlour trick." He was thankful that, upon inspection, most of the bar's patrons were too inebriated to care. One couldn't be too careful though.

Jack sat in the most disreputable bar-- if you could call it a bar --in Tortuga. It was a mere shack with chairs, and alcohol happened to be in the vicinity, but it felt like a home away from home. Jack had been in port two days now, and, after the initial whirlwind of activity that comes with being in Tortuga, he now had time to mull over his choices. Who better to mull it over with than his pet, Sebastian, and Anney.

"This seems like a lot of trouble for some books, Jack." Anney wasn't sure about the whole venture, not one bit.

The vial's existence had been sworn to secrecy even from Anney. If Sebastian were to ever tell her about its existence he had been threatened with the pain of a most excruciating death. He learned a long time ago not to keep all his eggs in one basket, and Anney was a basket that found it very hard to retain eggs. Jack could hear the rowdy cheers of randy pirates, and he revelled in them. This was his world; comfortable, adventurous, and libatious, but Jack feared that he would need to venture far from it in order to take that step towards what he had decided. If he could use these secrets, he and Anney would have something better than all the riches a pirate could ever wish for. They could have their home back and be free from the fear of hanging.

"These journals hold secrets, Anney, secrets a king would betray another for at a moment's notice. Secrets of all kinds, love. Ones to win wars, that describe machines that could turn the tide of battle, and even a few that hint at the mysteries nature still keeps hidden. The Sun King went to a lot of effort to obtain these secrets, being even so bold as to sail to my waters, and steal my treasures!"

"*Our* treasures, Jack, and don't you ever forget it." Anney glared at him.

"Okay, okay, *our* treasures. I want to do what's best for us. Do you want to keep pirating till your final days, Anney? A life being chased by privateers, by the King's navy? A life where one day we wake up with a noose around both our necks? A life where Sebastian has no one to teach him the ways of the world? Or do you want what we dreamed of?" He watched as Anney's eyes turned inward and glassy, the dream she knew all too well playing behind them. He knew he had won her over, and she couldn't resist.

"I, for one, would appreciate seeing home again. The land of civilisation; free from coconuts and palm trees, and a little less rape, murder, and pillaging." The words sprouted from Sebastian's mouth like a siren that couldn't sing.

"No one asked you, Sebastian. Do I not keep you in the civility you are accustomed to?" Jack was faux shocked at his protestations. He turned to his lover to renew his efforts, but he didn't need to push very hard. She had that look in her eye, and she was licking those juicy lips like she had a thirst. Jack steered himself back on course. "Anney, I need your help with this if we are going to do it. The men will not like sailing into unfriendly waters. So I need your help to work your charms on the lads, make them pliable to *our* plans."

Jack watched as the gears ticked over in Anney's mind. "Take your time, lass, this is a tough decision." He suggestively stroked her arm with only the slightest touch, watching the hairs stand on end as he passed over them.

She smiled at Jack, the spark of wild adventure in her eyes. "What of these news reports, Sebastian? How tempestuous are England's waters?"

"Mostly political, with a dash of assassination thrown in there. The papers are calling it the *Rye House Plot*. A failed attempt at assassinating Charles and his brother. The rumours are that the masterminds were Protestant politicians, but going by recent developments, it could be an effort to destabilise the region by the Sun King."

"I think that might work in our favour." Jack stared into space his machinations spreading out before him in his mind.

Sebastian looked confused. "How so?" he looked deep in thought, "too many people are looking for a step up. Suppose we head in there with our -sorry- *your*, little chest of mysteries. We won't even get close to the king. There is also the fact that every member of the crew is wanted, dead or alive, by King Charles' jailors."

"What are you thinking, Jack?" Anney looked at Jack with concern, "What are you planning?"

Jack felt that this wasn't the right place or audience for a lengthy discussion of his tactics, these things were best discussed in secret - especially a plan of this calibre. He had no idea how Sebastian would react to his real plan, he felt it best if he got the measure of the man first and just went along with Sebastian's get rich quick scheme. He gave Anney a little shake of the head, signalling that he would discuss it later with her and returned his attention to them all. "Ugh! Yes, as much as it pains me to agree that Sebastian is right, I fear that French waters should be our destination." Jack threw the scholar a sinister glance, heavily laced with the threat of a beating. Sebastian raised his hands in defence.

"Captain, as much as it pains me to lower myself to piracy, I think the Sun King would be your best bet to fleece. He has the most to gain from these secrets, therefore, the information is more valuable to him. Things back home are not good. Politics and assassinations aside, the king is in ill health and fighting against parliament. The Sun King seems like your best bet."

Jack placed his hand on Sebastian's thigh, dangerously close to his crotch; he could feel him squirm over the awkward silence. "My friend, I didn't think you had it in you. You constantly surprise me. Can you imagine, Anney? Sebastian is turning into a pirate under our tutelage!" He laughed heartily, along with Anney, while Sebastian sat there silently in a sea of discomfort under Jack's touch. Once Jack's laughter had died down, he raised his flagon and, with a little coaxing, the three finally sealed the deal with a clink of their three drinks.

***

While the crew slept off the night's rum on board the *Kingston*, Jack was creeping about, trying not to disturb them. He had slipped out of his sheets, leaving Anney to recover from their vigorous love-making, while he went to find Sebastian to carry out their own *unique activities*. It wasn't long before he found him, sleeping in a barrel, as he was often wont to do. "Sebastian, wake up." Jack shook the scholar awake like a ragdoll, covering his mouth to stop any screams escaping. It had the desired effect; Sebastian woke with a muffled shriek. Sudden realisation blossomed in his eyes, as he saw Jack looming over him.

"Captain? Where am I?"

"You fell asleep in a barrel again. I swear you're a devil when you're drunk, my friend."

Jack watched as Sebastian struggled to remove himself from the barrel, before relenting to his better half, well, quarter, and giving the man a hand. "Now, now, Sebastian, as quiet as a mouse, if you please. I need your help with something. Mum's the word. Just like with the vial." Sebastian nodded in agreement, staying silent, awaiting further instructions.

"That's a good chap. We need to take a short trip, you and I. But first, we need to make a little visit to the brig."

Sebastian followed the captain down into the dark depths of the *Kingston*'s brig. As Jack approached the cell, he spied the dim features of a man in solitude. "Sebastian...what is this prisoner still doing here?" Jack was disappointed. "I told you to kill him once you had squeezed out his secrets." All Sebastian could do was look on in failure. "Just when I thought you were learning..." Jack strolled over to the guard, who was passed out from his night's activities and lifted the key off him. Jack unlocked the cell to the sleeping prisoner. "Let this be a lesson to you, Sebastian." Jack removed his cutlass and ran the prisoner through in one fell swoop; the prisoner didn't even have a chance to let out any blood-curdling groans. "Never. Leave. Unfinished. Business. Now clean off my blade." He handed his reluctant student the cutlass.

"Yes, sir."

"We can't have any witnesses to our activities tonight. Thankfully, this drunken fool is well out of it."

"What exactly are we doing down here, captain?" Jack moved out of the cell, towards the chest that was nearby.

"You and I are going to take a little trip with the contents of this chest. So get to packing them into this crate," Jack patted the crate to the chest's side, as Sebastian handed him back the cleaned weapon. Jack grumbled in his direction as he examined the blade.

"It'll do, I suppose." Jack returned the cutlass to its rightful place on his belt before moving on.

* * *

Jack and Sebastian had loaded the contents into a rowboat and were making their way from Tortuga to Haiti, a short row but tiresome nonetheless. "Why exactly are we burying the very thing we intend to sell, Captain?"

Jack was busy tending to his nails as Sebastian propelled the rowboat along with pure mental fortitude. That, and Jack had informed him he had noticed some hungry sharks a few meters back, and neither of them fancied being a late dinner. Jack chuckled to himself. *That will teach him to soil my clothes with French blood.* He watched as Sebastian rowed away from the non-existent sharks.

"Well, Sebastian. I lay naked in bed, after satisfying Anney several times, wondering about our little conundrum, and how best to deal with it." He watched Sebastian squirm on hearing the graphic details. "I thought to myself-- we don't actually need to take the contents of the chest with us. It just wouldn't be the smart thing to do. Say we made it all the way to France, unmolested. Furthermore, say we arrived safely in the court of the Sun King. What's stopping him from just taking what he wants from us?"

"Mayhap some of my intelligence is rubbing off on you, captain?"

Jack was impressed. It wasn't often Sebastian had the balls to throw a taunt his way. Jack let the question linger in the air just long enough to let the scholar think he had made a mistake...*There it is.* Before Sebastian could get out his apology, Jack splashed him with salty seawater. "Ha! I'll soon have ye talkin' like a pirate. Arrrgh!" Jack mocked him with a heavily laced accent.

55

"So, we are going to bury the contents on the island we are heading to?"

"Aye, matey!" Jack continued talking like the quintessential pirate. Sebastian sighed at his antics. "Yes, that is correct, my friend. We will take these secrets and bury them where no man will find them, save us, *and only us*. Savvy?"

"Aye, cap'n." Sebastian grinned at him.

"Oho! Very good." Jack felt something he hadn't in a long time, apart from the few moments he was alone with Anney. But this was different. He couldn't pinpoint what exactly it was. Maybe comradeship. *I mean, my crew I can count on, mostly. Yet I wouldn't trust any of them as friends.*

"I think we are here, Captain."

"Excellent. Now, we must be quiet and observant, my friend. I don't know who is in charge of this island, but we don't want to alert them to our activities." Jack stood at the bow as the boat glided on to the sand, carefully checking their surroundings. "Come, the coast is clear." He led Sebastian up the coastal path leading away from the beach, and into the forest. The terrain suddenly changed to bare soil with roots sticking out of the ground, no trees were in sight. Just a great hollow. They stumbled down into the large clearing.

"Huh...I could have sworn there was more trees here. Nevermind, ay? Here is as good a spot as any." Jack sat himself down on a boulder and watched as the scholar rolled up his sleeves and started digging.

"Captain, what are you going to ask for if we get to the Sun King?"

"*When* we get to the Sun King." Sebastian stood corrected and continued digging. Jack wondered for a moment, "I suppose I'll ask for a lordship and all my sins absolved, and, let me assure you, I have done some sinful things, my friend. Money is always nice. A place where I can hang my boots. Big enough for me and Anney, maybe space for a servant…" He eyed Sebastian with a testing look. "…or a friend."

"I'm sure he will give you all you desire, Captain. Especially when he sees the gravity of the situation he finds himself in. You have all the pieces; he has the board. He can't play at war until he gives in to your demands."

Suddenly Jack felt a gaze upon him, and it wasn't just Sebastian's adoring eyes.

"Shh, Sebastian, what was that? I hear rustling."

Jack turned his back to the scholar and scanned the tree line. *Hmm, no one there. It's just paranoia.* He turned back to Sebastian and gave him a questioning look. "Must be my imagination. As you were…" A loud thud was heard behind him again, causing his body to chill.

"I heard it that time, Captain."

"You finish digging and get that crate buried. I'm going to check those noises out." With that, he drew his cutlass and advanced upon the loud section of forest. Jack edged ever closer to where he thought the sound had come from, feeling both alive and aroused at the thought of imminent action. It had been a while since he'd had a good sword fight. *It's about time I brush off these cobwebs!* The bushes ahead of Jack started to rustle as he inched closer, adrenaline pumping through his veins. Pausing when he reached them, he carefully thrust the blade into the bush, parting them as silently as he could.

A screeching, furry mass darted out of the bush, nearly making Jack lose the contents of his bowels in his breeches. Jack blew out a sigh of relief. "False alarm, my friend, it was just a damn monkey."

"Thank God. Well, we are all done here, captain. The crate is six feet under, where it shall remain until we return."

"Let's get back to the *Kingston*." Jack collected Sebastian and led the way through the tree line, a chorus of rustling following their wake.

"Captain?"

"Probably just more monkeys," Jack whispered, concern evident in his voice. "Nothing to worry about, I'm sure."

Chapter - 5 - Teamwork Makes The Dream Work.

"You know this is the definition of insanity?" Ariadne shouted down from midway up a large tree. Seamus had had the mad idea of turning the island into a flying forest, and ever since he had caught up to speed on the journals, he had been working more fervently to accomplish that goal. Nothing like the threat of war upon your homeland to speed up the process of converting a floating forest into an airship.

Seamus had reduced the tree to just it's trunk, by removing all its branches, and he was making the final cuts through the base of his tree. "Just a few more swings of the axe, I think, Ari. Are you sure that rope is secure?"

"It's no Palomar, but it's the tightest bowline you've ever seen!" Ariadne had secured a rope around the middle of the tree she had wrapped herself around and the same rope to the base of the tree Seamus was felling. They had planned to let his float up until only the last quarter was below the treeline. Then Ariadne would secure it to hers, creating a massive makeshift mast from which they could hang a sail. It was tentative at best, but they didn't have any better ideas. She watched from her lofty perch, cringing, as Seamus swung the axe, finally breaking through to the other side.

Seamus dived away. She was pretty confident the tree would just drift up, but she guessed he hadn't reconciled with the whole idea of floating trees yet. The tree was free now, and, for a second, it just hung there, deciding what to do, before slowly starting to ascend. Ariadne smiled as it did, while Seamus picked himself up off the ground.

"Well, I'm glad that tree decided not to flatten me."

As he stood there laughing at the tree, she watched it make its way to her. She had no idea what would happen when the two collided. Ariadne was hoping that it would be a gentle affair and that the bindings would hold. Yet, she and Seamus were pioneers on this frontier. There was no telling, with absolute certainty, what might happen. So, she would just have to brace herself and hope for the best.

Ariadne watched through slitted eyes as the makeshift mast sauntered nonchalantly towards her.

"Brace for impact!" Seamus shouted to her as he ran for cover behind the nearest oak.

She grabbed hold of two branches for stability, but she need not have bothered. For the moment the trunk collided with hers, it ricocheted off with an oaken thud, continuing its path past the treetops. It didn't get much further before the bindings pulled tight, and the log came to rest in place. She felt a cheer was necessary.

"Huzzah!" Seamus had preempted her thoughts.

Ariadne grinned down at him. "Looks like we've taken the first steps towards building the HMS *Selene*."

"*Selene?*"

"My grandmother. She was very much my inspiration when I was growing up. She inspired me to join the navy, to be on the frontier, where the adventure was. She'd be smiling down on me now if she could see me." She sat there reminiscing on days gone by, of the days when Selene was still with her. It didn't take much for her age-roughened words to come back to her.

Advance. Advance. Deflect.

Riposte!

Well done, Ari. Let's go again.

Advance. Pivot. Retreat! That's right, Ari. Don't let anyone get an edge on you. Someone spins you around; you give them ground. Examine what they are going to do next. Be calm. Be methodical.

She shook herself out of the memory, her last good memory. It was from the period just before she had set sail on her first voyage, the one captained by her uncle on his ship the *Greenwich*. She was still only a child and her grandmother a force to aspire to. Now she felt old, disconnected from that part of her life. So much had happened since then, and she felt there was still much more to come.

"Ari?"

"I'm okay, cap'n, just lost myself in a memory for a moment." She moved up the tree; heading for the log that had pulled its bindings taut and came to rest high above her.

"A good memory, I hope?"

"Oh yes, swordsmanship with my grandmother. She was determined to drill me in all I needed to know before I left for the *Greenwich*. She knocked me on my arse so many times. It was infuriating. But I got up every time, and I persevered."

"Determination to succeed!"

"More like bloody-minded stubbornness. Got that from my mother." She continued ever upwards, finally reaching the base of the mast. "We need to bind at least the lower quarter to this tree, for the strength. Once the wind strikes the sail, there will be a lot of force exerted on this joint. I'm going to need to bind it as tightly as possible. How much rope did you find?"

"I think we should have enough. We could use the cord from the tents since we won't be needing those for much longer."

"It should hold, we only really need one good trip, right?" Ariadne began to bind the trimmed oak to the tall support tree with the lengths of the rope she had brought up with her. "The fun part is going to be fixing the yard, for our sail, to the peak of our new mast." She grinned. "Have you found a decent substitute yet?"

"I do believe so. I had to weigh it down after trimming it. I believe I can let it float up, attached to a rope, and you should be able to secure it from there. What do you think?"

"I think I've been climbing masts since I was eight years old. This should be no different. No riggin' this time, though, I should be a little less cocky about my abilities until after the deed is done!"

Seamus laughed heartily. "Right you are, my friend!"

Ariadne gauged the top of the mast and steeled herself for the climb. *Exude confidence. Find handholds. Secure footing. Climb. Check the route. Climb.*

She heard the limb snap beneath her feet.

"ARI!"

Legs meeting air. Falling. Need something to grab onto. Falling. I'm going to die. Falling. "Oof!" *Winded. Alive. I'm okay.* She opened her eyes. Two branches had broken her fall, knocking the breath out of her. She laid there dazed for a moment before checking how far she had fallen. She turned, gingerly, to peer past herself. *Oh good, not too far.* It felt like she had been dropping for an eternity.

"Ari! Are you ok? Are you alive?" She could hear the panic in Seamus' voice.

"I'm good, I'm alive, I think." Life slowly returned to her as she tested her extremities. "I've still got some wind in my sails." She could hear a huge sigh of relief below her, followed by rustling. Seamus was climbing the tree, his broad frame eventually blocking out the sunlight as he stood over her on some branches, checking her for injuries.

"You frightened the life out of me; I thought you were as good as dead. What would I do here without you? Who will I reminisce with about the time I was the subject of a second mutiny? Or, the time we found ourselves on a floating island?" Seamus grabbed hold of her hand so that he could pull her up.

"What about the time we turned it into a flying ship!" She exclaimed as she allowed him to do so.

"You are truly ok?"

She gave her concerned friend a fervent nod. *My friend.*

"I wonder if you would do me the honour of being less stubborn, and allow me to do this. I can't have you doing everything. We need to share the load." She sighed, resigning herself to allow Seamus to have his way. She wouldn't admit it to him, but the fall had taken more than the breath out of her lungs, and she didn't mind showing a little reliance on Seamus while she recuperated.

"Sure, where did you leave the yard?" She slid back down the tree, her muscles aching, reeling from the shock of the fall.

"It's tied up there, next to the stump, probably hiding in the treetops somewhere. Just follow the line."

She left him there, to ascend the mast, while she went over to the stump. Spying the rope tied to the tree nearest to it, Ariadne followed the cord with her eyes all the way up. *There she is.* The trimmed log lay nestled, in between the leaves and branches of the surrounding trees, the line keeping it anchored. She returned to concern herself over Seamus' ascent above the treetops, as she untied the yard and dragged it across the sky like she had a cloud on a lead. Seamus was almost there. She watched as he carefully climbed the looming oak.

"Alright, alright, no need to show off," she shouted up. "Shall I start unreeling the yard towards you, Seamus?"

She watched as he secured himself to some branch stubs, checking his surroundings before mentally preparing himself. *Don't fall.*

"Yes. I think this is good. Let it up!"

Ariadne slowly released the rope, allowing the yard to ascend towards Seamus, perched high above in his lofty roost. She watched as the log floated into his waiting arms.

"Gently does it. Just hold it there, while I secure it."

She tied the rope to the base of the support tree and stood back to watch him work. Worry washed over her as Seamus manoeuvred himself over to the floating log. Grabbing it with one hand, he slung a rope over with the other, wrapping it around in a cross pattern several times, before tying it off.

"There, all secure!" he bellowed down. "She's ready for the mainsail, once we have the steering masts set up and braced!"

Ariadne racked her brain to try and picture what he had in mind. "I don't think I quite follow."

She looked on as Seamus made his way down the mast, swinging between branches and sliding down the trunk until he finally made it to the ground. "I've had the idea swimming about in my head for a while. We can do a number of things on a ship to steer it, as you well know. But what about in the air? We don't have a rudder, and there would be no way to use a rudder to steer the island anyway. We don't have an anchor either, but I fear we shall need one before we get to where we are going."

"I have some thoughts on that, Seamus, but carry on."

"So, there is only one possible solution that I can see." She watched on as Seamus grabbed hold of a sharp rock, crouched down, and started drawing in the dirt. "This is the island, and here is the mast we have just erected, with a sail for illustrative purposes, of course."

She tried to stifle her laughter at the child's drawing before her. "Very informative."

"I'm no Rembrandt, but it will have to do."

She stood there, giggling. Seamus jostled her with a smile. "I'm glad you approve of my artistry. It will surely be the thing that saves the day!"

Ariadne finally managed to get her laughter under control with some effort. "So how do we steer her, cap'n?"

"Well, I was thinking. A gaff and a boom on each side of the island. Here and here. Attached to a tree we shall call, the steering mast, for that is what we shall use it for."

She examined his drawing closer as he drew two parallel lines pointing outwards of the island on either side of the *Selene*. "Seamus, I apologise, I must have not slept very well last night." She pinched between her brows. "Do you mind going through that again, more slowly this time?"

A hearty chuckle left Seamus' lips, "I know you've not been long a lieutenant, but you do know that the gaff is the spar that helps bend the sail, right?"

Ariadne rolled her eyes, "And the boom is the lower spar, yes, of course, I know that, Seamus. What do you take me for? An unseasoned landsman? I was having difficulty following along with your childish drawings after I've barely slept a wink."

"Next time we get stuck on a floating island, I'll make sure to practice my art skills beforehand, just give me a warning if we are to ever be in a similar situation." He replied, shooting her a cheeky grin. "We can fashion a pulley system and have a sail furl out in the middle of the gaff and boom, on each side. We can pull out the sail on the opposite side, depending on which way we need to steer. Or we have them fold in and when we need them fold them out, like a schooner. What do you think?"

She stood there, musing over the question. "We would need to have them fixed. I don't think there is enough rope to have them pull in and out, because we need a lot of rope for the anchor to be effective. I can't see any way of reliably hinging them either. There's going to be a lot of force on them when the wind hits, and when the island manoeuvres, they'll break apart with the stress."

"That's what I was afraid of." Seamus breathed a heavy sigh.

"Yes, one of us is going to have to shimmy over the side of the island to attach the pulley system for the sails." Ariadne let the thought hang in the air for a moment, while she pictured herself carrying out the task. She shuddered.

"It should be me."

She laughed haughtily. "Oh, should it? Pray tell me why that is."

"Well, I'm a man, I should be doing this…"

"Oh, please! Spare me the chivalry. If we are to be friends, Seamus Hawthorne, let it be known that I don't take kindly to chivalrous acts. It paints the female of the species to be something that is weak, something that needs to be looked after and nurtured like a sickly pup. Am I a sickly pup?" She stood there with her hands on her hips, challenging him.

"No, of course not, I would never..." Seamus cheeks as red as a sailor's tan. He paced around as if searching for the words. "I think you are the most courageous woman I have ever met. Daring to venture into a man's world with only your stubbornness and a sense of adventure."

"Only?"

Seamus stood there, stammering, "Y-y-your incredible knowledge of the stars, and I'm sure your expert sword skills."

"The best damn sword slinger in the Caribbean!" Ariadne's scrunched up brow relaxed, to be replaced with a grin.

Seamus breathed a sigh of relief. "Gods, Ari, you are a force of nature."

She picked something from her nails and polished them on her lapel. "Aye, that I am. Just remember those words when I'm dangling from the mast over the side of the island."

Seamus looked deflated.

* * *

"So, we have both the gaffs and the booms for the project?" Ariadne sat by the fire, warming her hands. They had spent the rest of the day cutting down and trimming logs for the sides of the island. She was now spent from the day's activities, so they had both decided it would be better to do it when there was light again. She jested that it was so she could see what lay below, but, in reality, she was tired.

"Aye. All four present and accounted for. If we get an early start, we could have it done within the day; I would wager."

"I believe we will." Ariadne yawned. One of those over the top yawns that stretched her whole body. "Do you have any idea about our destination?"

"As it happens, I do. I've been mulling it over. The original plan we had was to make it to the mainland, inform the Governor, and hopefully obtain a new ship back to England to report the news. Unfortunately, I fear the winds are picking up in the wrong direction. So we are going to have to go with our backup plan."

"Which is?" She didn't like the sound of where this was going. It was crazy enough to fly the island across to the mainland; anything other than that would surely be folly.

Seamus pulled a branch out of the fire and started drawing in the dirt by the fire.

"Oh, are we drawing again?" She grinned.

Seamus snorted. He continued to sketch lines on the ground. "Here we are." He pointed to a sausage shape in the dirt beneath him. "This is the fun part." He drew a sad-looking boot in the dirt far away from the sausage shape. "This here is Merry Ol' England. The wind is blowing towards her, Ari."

"Surely you jest, Seamus, we are taking a massive risk even attempting to take this to the mainland, and that is assuming it even works. You want to take her across the North Atlantic, all the way to English waters? What if the island breaks up on the journey, which very well could happen due to the wind. We'd be adrift in the middle of the ocean, with no hope of rescue."

"Where is your sense of adventure, girl? What would Selene say?"

He had pushed the right button. *Goddammit, Seamus.* "You want us to hitch a ride with the trade winds? On this?" She waved her hands around.

"Yes! Exactly that, my friend. If we can capture the breath of the wind god Zephyrus that will push us across the tropic of cancer, it should get us all the way to Africa." He drew a crude elephant's head under the sad old boot that represented England. "Mustn't forget Spain!" He fiddled some more in the dirt. "So once we hit the Saharan coast we will hopefully be able to manoeuvre the island northwards up the coast of Spain." He drew a line signifying the course of the *Selene*. "Then, it's just across the top of the Bay of Biscay, and we are a stone's throw from the Channel!"

"What you ask for is all reliant on *Selene* staying in one piece. You know that."

"She will, Ari, I have faith. I have to. It is the quickest course of action from what I can fathom. If we sail the island to the mainland, by the time we get a ship to transport us to England, it will be too late to avert any disasters occurring as a result of these wonderfully powerful secrets. You've seen what this experiment can accomplish. If the French had these secrets, *when* the French have these secrets, England would no longer be the greatest power in all the seven seas. She would be reduced to ashes by a mighty fleet of flying ships under the power of that damnable Sun King."

She knew he was right. If whoever stole those secrets was on their way back to French waters, they must delay no longer. No matter how dangerous it would be. She was becoming more resigned to the idea, but she still felt she needed to voice her concerns, regardless. "We don't even have a compass."

"We will use the stars." Seamus smiled at her, his dimples melting her fears away.

"What if we break apart?" She was still mildly concerned about that. Rocks had been dropping off the bottom of the island since it had first risen. They would wake her up in the night with a loud crash. At first, she had no idea what it was until she saw one drop from the edges, resulting in the same solid thud.

"We'll cross that bridge if we come to it. We could build a raft from the surplus if it comes to it. It won't though. Ari, we can do this.

Think about what they will write in the history books about this moment. A floating island, the HMS *Selene*, first of her kind, dominating the London skyline."

Now she was defeated. "If this is what we must do, then so be it. Let us do it in a blaze of wondrous glory!

* * *

Ariadne hadn't been able to sleep. Her mind was filled with worries regarding the days ahead of them. She wasn't a great fan of heights, yet she had been adamant about threading the pulleys on the steering masts. *Hoisted by my own petard.* She was also serious about her concerns regarding whether they would break up over the North Atlantic. At least, in that case, they would just drop into the ocean. Alternatively, the thought of breaking up over land filled her with dread. The journey was necessary though if they were to avert subjugation by a French king. So she had preoccupied her mind with her anchor project. She hoped it would work, but there were a lot of unknown factors that she just couldn't confirm.

Seamus roused from his slumber by the side of the dying fire. "Good morning." He looked questioningly at what she was working on. "Have you had any sleep?"

"Not really, no. Maybe a few hours. I needed something to occupy my mind for a moment or two."

"Pray tell me what this monstrous thing is?"

"It's the anchor, obviously." Seamus looked at her like she was mad. "My grandma and I used to weave wicker baskets when I was little. It used to help me work through my frustrations and any problems I had. Thinking about her yesterday, and the time we spent, gave me the idea for this." She rolled the giant wicker ball that she had been working on around.

"Explain how this is going to keep us anchored." Seamus seemed intrigued.

"Easy. I've created a hatch in the wicker here. We roll this over towards the back of the island, or at least relative to whichever way we are flying at the time. Fill the wicker ball with large rocks and then close it. Bind the last of the rope to the ball and tie the other end to a tree. Hmmm, We are going to need some kind of winch system to lower it; God knows that just dropping it won't work. Nevertheless, when we need to stop, we just push it over the edge. Hopefully, that does the job and slows us down." Ariadne was hopeful. She had to be.

"That might just work, my friend!"

"Aye, if it doesn't slow us down, at least we will have a way to get down."

"Oh, you wish to slide down the rope?" he laughed sleepily.
"There's the adventurer I took on as my Lieutenant."

She smiled at him, her eyes wary. "I even had time to catch us some rabbit," she said, nodding over to the fire to emphasize her words.

"I thought something smelt good; I have been starving for days. Where did you find them?" Seamus stood and crouched over by the roasting morsels, his mouth watering at the thought of gnawing on the meat. Ariadne could hear his stomach growl as if it were purring at the food on display in appreciation.

"They actually woke me up during the night. Inquisitive little things must have decided to warm up by the fire. Little did they know they were offering themselves up to the island's only two predators." She sat there, grinning.

"You are a true huntress." Seamus tucked into the nearest rabbit, a look of divine euphoria spreading over his face as he devoured it. "So, after breakfast, should we continue with our plan?" He spoke with a full mouth.

"Sure, why not? I was just thinking it was time for some more death-defying jaunts."

It wasn't long before she had finished her rabbit and satiated the groaning in the pit of her stomach. She felt slightly more alive. Seamus had finished his and was busying himself collecting the gaff and boom; he had left them where he had trimmed them down, with rocks to stop them from flying away. She was using the time while she waited for him to finish the anchor off.

Ariadne heard low thuds in the distance, seemingly getting closer. She wasn't worried that the island was falling apart because she could simultaneously hear Seamus grumbling. She scanned the area to see if she could spot the noisy captain.

She spied him carrying both the gaff and the boom like it was nothing. "Oh, you brought both," she shouted to him.

Seamus was finally back at camp with one of each under his arms. "These trees are light, even for such unwieldy things, it's going to make transporting them to the island's extremities easy. We just have to remember not to let them go before we have bound them properly. Oh, and they like to bump into everything, as I have obviously found." He sounded frustrated, but things were about to get a lot more fun.

"Yes, hence the difficulty in manoeuvring through the forest. But look, I discovered something." He checked his surroundings and proceeded to jump into the air. The scene that played out was strange, but no stranger than what they had already lived through. As Seamus jumped into the air, it was as if he was a leaf dropping from a tree. As he descended from the apex of his leap, he carefully floated back down to the ground. She stood there amazed, the effect was minimal, but the logs did slow his fall.

"That's amazing, at least we have a second option off the island once we reach England."

"What do you mean?"

"The journal, the possible applications, didn't you say there was a picture of a bird-type structure? Mayhap this is what that was referring to. All it needs is some structure to it and some cloth for steering. Like wings?"

"Oh, excellent, I think I'll stick to climbing down the rope, for now, thank you." Seamus did not seem like he was sold on the idea of leaping off and floating down to the Thames.

"Maybe as a backup plan, then?" Seamus eyed her with a wary cock of the eyebrow. "Okay, maybe a backup backup plan." She grinned at him.

"We shall see. Let's put the idea in the insanity pile, for now, where it belongs." He rolled his eyes at her idea. She could tell he wanted to distance himself from that idea as much as humanly possible.

Ariadne seemed interested in the rope adorning the logs. "What's that wrapped around the logs for?"

"I see you have spied my pulley system, I crafted it to easily unfurl the sails. You see here at the tip, I just wrapped the rope around the log for strength, then left a loop of it tied off here to thread the sail line through. I did the same further down near the other end of the log." Seamus looked proud of himself.

"Mighty fine work. Hopefully, it works in practice."

"Shall we affix these to the 'steering masts', my friend?" He seemed eager to get to work.

"Seamus, I would love nothing more than to be dangling over the edge, looking into the abyss." She relieved him of one of the logs and followed him to the first site at the edges of the *Selene*.

* * *

She and Seamus had toiled hard to get the gaff and boom fixed securely. The two lengths of wood loomed far out over the edge of the floating island; the sail needed to be large enough to gather enough force to turn the *Selene*, as she was now known. They had bound them to the closest trees on the edge; the boom attached near the ground, and the gaff installed just shy of the treetops. Thanks to the weightlessness of them, the logs were pretty easy to manoeuvre and bind into place. All that was left was to pass some rope through the crude pulley system and attach the sails later. All she had to do was shuffle out along each log.

"At the fear of sounding like an archaic beast, you don't have to do this." It was like Seamus could sense the dread in her. She was ok with most heights, one had to be while working on a ship, but this was different. Her back was still tender from the fall the previous day as well.

"Watch a force of nature at work." She put on a brave face and gave him a slight smile, hopefully fooling him into thinking that she was fine.

The climb to the top of the 'steering mast' seemed to take forever, but eventually, she came to the gaff at the top and straddled it. Ariadne peered back down the tree and gave Seamus a nod. She had tied the rope to her waist for ease of access, so she removed it now and passed it through the first loop of the pulley system. She felt safe here; she was still over the *Selene* at this point.

Now for the far loop.

She sent her mind to somewhere else as she made the first few shuffles along the gaff, away from safety. Her legs dangling down over the edge. "Are you sure the bindings are secure, Seamus?"

"Yes, I'm sure; I double-checked them myself. You have nothing to fear, my friend. Just remember; keep moving."

He's right. Keep moving. Advance. Advance. Deflect.

She took it one shuffling movement at a time, deflecting the fear away as she inched along the gaff. Taking her mind to happier memories and trying desperately not to look down. She was doing so well at avoiding doing that until she reached the end where the last loop was. Ariadne untied the rope from her waist once more and laid down on the log to pass it through, her heart beating in her chest, thumping against the oak. This was when she made the fatal mistake of peering down to the lands beneath her.

Shit! I am so high up. I can barely see the world below us. What if I fall? They won't be able to find the pieces of me to send me back home.

Panic started to set in.

"Are you ok, Ari? It's just; you don't seem to be moving." Seamus shouted to her, clearly sensing she was in trouble.

Get it together, Ari! You don't want to embarrass yourself again. You fought for this.

Advance. Advance. Deflect.

She pushed the negative emotions away with sheer will power and came to her senses. "I'm good!" Her voice quivered from the adrenaline that she so sorely needed. She passed the rope through the loop and tied the rope back to her waist for the return journey.

Advance. Advance. Deflect.

The trip back was less eventful, and she managed to keep her eyes on the log for the majority of the journey. Only allowing herself to look when she had reached the safety of the tree she had climbed originally. "One down!" Affirming her success to her worried friend. She affixed the rope to the 'steering mast' and descended to the boom.

"Good show, Ari!" Seamus was beaming. He patted her on the back in a show of camaraderie. "I don't think I could have done that myself. You are something else." He was trying to cheer her up, and she knew it. It was working.

"Well...I am a force of nature, you know." She grinned as the two shared a hearty laugh.

"One more to go on this side. Are you ready?"

She nodded, and Seamus tied the second rope to her midriff after passing it through the first loop.

"You are good to go," he exclaimed as he patted her shoulder.

She straddled the boom and advanced. It was easier this time; she even chanced a little peep over the side as she went. It was going smoothly, the adrenaline was powering her past the halfway point, and she imagined herself back on solid ground. She was there, finally, at the last loop of the pulley system. She untied the rope and passed it through, just as before. After tying it back to her waist, she returned to the starting point, inching ever closer to the *Selene*.

Suddenly, out of nowhere, the wind picked up speed and ripped her off the boom.

All she could feel was the absolute inevitability that came with falling to her final doom. *This is it. I'm done for.* The wind rushed past her as she fell from the log, and all she could hear was Seamus screaming her name. She closed her eyes and waited for it to be over. But even before her life had begun to flash before her eyes, she felt a great jolt at her waist. *The rope!* The world came back into focus as she hung there, dangling off the boom, nothing but empty sky beneath her.

"Ari! My heart can't take any more of this! Thank God you were tied on. Are you ok?"

"I take it back." She mumbled.

"What was that?"

"I said, I take it back, you can do the next one." All she could hear was Seamus' joyous laughter.

She felt tugging at her midriff as Seamus pulled her up to the boom using the pulley system.

"At least we know that works!"

She grabbed onto the log and pulled herself up, embracing the boom as if it were some long lost family member. Slowly, Ariadne made her way back across to safety without any further complications. Seamus was there to greet her, grabbing hold of her arms and pulling her back to the ground, embracing her as if she had almost died. She felt safer.

"It'll take more than a gust of wind to kill Ariadne Smith, my friend." she squeezed him tight.

"Now, let's get to the other side of the *Selene* and take care of that other gaff and boom." She grinned as Seamus released her. Ariadne followed Seamus back into the forest as they both went to battle the elements once more and finish this project they had started.

Chapter - 6 - Hidden in Plain Sight.

Jack had managed to slide back into bed without arousing his sleeping beauty. He and Sebastian made it back before the sun started to peek over the horizon, a mix of ambers seeping into the purple canvas of the night, extinguishing the stars as it did. Last night was a duplicitous affair, but he assured himself and his partner in the act that it was a necessary evil. *Never play all your cards at once, Sebastian.* He had tried his best to explain it to him in a manner better befitting the scholar, but all that came out were card analogies.

The treasure was now hidden. All Jack needed was the vial to win over the Sun King. Proof of his word. *We will need supplies, it will be a long journey, and the North Atlantic is a treacherous beast, especially this close to the Caribbean. We would have to go under the guise of a merchant flag so as not to arouse any suspicion. We will have to keep a keen eye out for other pirates.* In any case, they needed to visit the mainland first to get what they needed.

"Morning, my love." Anney stretched like a cat in the warm sun, her body glistening in the dawn light. He admired every undulation, rubbing his hands up the fiery pirate's curves.

"What happened to you last night?"

Shit!

"I needed to clear my head. I was out on the main deck, with Sebastian, going over the plan."

"Sebastian was not with the fairies? I'm surprised he was even coherent after all you plied him with last night."

Jack chuckled. "Aye, I had to pull the pickled scholar out of his barrel. He was like a fish with no fins."

Anney looked confused. "It's too early for your bilge. What did you fella's decide?"

Jack was dreading this part; he knew how she felt about the mainland. "Anney, we need supplies, so you know what that means. We need to go to Monte Cristi." Anney sat up in bed, the sheets rolling off her naked body, and she cradled her head as if she were nursing a numb skull.

"Fuck, Jack, why do we need to go there? It'll just dredge up the past, and you know what she's like. She will sniff something out. She's a beastly devil that one."

"You don't have to go, you know." He knew she needed to though. As soon as he set foot on that sand, she wouldn't do business with him unless Anney were there. Yet, he had to say it.

"You're full of shit, Jack. You know I have to be there. Otherwise, she won't trade...Fuck!"

Jack put an arm around her in an attempt to console Anney. She shrugged it off -- He was well aware of the history there. Anney was his ace-in-the-hole, though. He knew he'd get a decent deal if he placed her in the firing line. She'd be fine. He just needed to convince her that she would be.

"It was a long time ago, Anney. She'll have forgotten all about you."

"Oh please! With these tits?" She offered the aforementioned pair up, underlining them with her hands. "Besides, you don't know the woman, she never forgets. She's like a damn elephant."

"We need this stuff now, love. Time is of the essence. We can't have any other pirate sauntering over to the Sun King's court and taking our prize. If there's anyone who can get us the things we need in quick time, it's Mary Read.

She looked like she had given up hope, like a sail with no wind behind her. She was defeated. "Oh, God, Jack, fine. You'll be responsible for the consequences, though."

"You won't regret it, love."

She might.

* * *

Jack, Anney and Sebastian had all been suitably welcomed into the morning and had been dropped near the docks of Monte Christi, to make their own way there in a sailboat. "I'll tell you why she hates the place, my friend. Monte Cristi is a fine example of why pirates are a true breed of hardy bastards."

"I don't hate the place, Jack, it's the people there I hate."

"Shush now, Anney, I'm telling a story."

She let her rage out on the seawater with a swift slap.

"Back in the early sixteen hundreds, around eighty years ago, Monte Cristi was a thriving hub of pirate commerce. When pirates were real pirates, Sebastian, not these flouncy, swashbuckling codpieces, they'd come here to barter their filthy ill-gotten gains, and trade was thriving. The governor was revelling in riches, and the king was none the wiser. Until some privateers became savvy and decided to trade in secrets that weren't theirs to sell."

"What happened next, and why are we rowing if this is a merchant dock?"

"If you wait, Sebastian, I'll tell you." The scholar went back to focusing on rowing.

"Now, where was I? Ah, yes, trade capital. Well, once the king got wind that his fancy new colony was trading in pirate booty, the very nature of the beast he had been fighting against, he razed the place to the ground. People and all. No colony of his was going to trade with filthy pirates."

"Let me guess, Jack, they didn't stop trading?"

"Right you are, my young pirate. Even though the king's privateers burned the town to the ground and killed most of its inhabitants, a small minority survived and bloomed. Monte Cristi wasn't the same, but it grew, with the same pirates' help, which gave it its reputation. Things didn't seem quite right, though."

Anney sighed. "Until a pirate came along that saw what the place needed and decided to use her skills to revive what was lost. That pirate was a young Mary Read. My lover."

"Ex-lover," Jack interjected. "And way to spoil a story, stealing the final lines. Anyone would think I had offended you in some way."

Jack was the recipient of the nastiest look he had ever received from her. "If looks could kill, Anney."

"And why are we rowing instead of just sailing into port?"

"Good question, Sebastian. I couldn't know how Mary would act. So I told the men to sail back to Tortuga if we weren't back by nightfall."

"Makes perfect sense." Sebastian rolled his eyes. "I look forward to planning our escape from inevitable doom, cap'n"

"Anyway, there you have it. Mary has been running this little trading emporium out of Monte Christi for the past five years. Never letting it grow too big, hiding her operations away from anyone who isn't of a pirate-y persuasion. It's the best-kept secret on this side of Tortuga."

"This should be fun!" Sebastian grinned as he continued rowing towards Monte Christi's dock. Anney groaned with appreciation, while he just laughed at their predicament. Jack was already growing fonder of the new Sebastian. He was more relaxed than the scholar of before, not a snivelling, worrying mess anymore. Jack would need to make sure he didn't relax too much. He wouldn't want the man utterly unafraid of a beating. His next goal was to hear the scurvy seadog swear. That would amuse him.

Jack and the gang drifted towards the harbour. "Woah, Woah, Woah, slow down, my friend."

The scholar looked inquisitively at Jack for answers. "What's wrong, Captain?" his gaze swinging to Anney for a clue as to the pirate's consternation.

"Jack?"

"It's too quiet. You can always hear the hustle and bustle of market life before you even see the dock. Take her in steady, Sebastian."

"Aye, Captain."

The rowboat cruised around the coastline, making its way to the harbour. Jack scanned the cliff tops, coves, and beaches for any sign

84

of life. *None.* "Around this rockface, we should be able to see the dock." He moved to lay at the bow of the boat, his spyglass to hand. Sebastian had stopped rowing and was letting the vessel drift around the corner, allowing the dock to reveal itself.

"A ship. No strangeness there in a dock. Let's take a closer look." Jack spied through the device.

"What do you see?" The scholar waited with bated breath.

"Nothing good, my friend, take the boat back to that cove there. We shall sneak into town."

"What did you see, Jack?" Anney seemed mildly perturbed.

"I fear we have come at a most inopportune moment, love, we seem to be interrupting a business transaction between your ex-lover and Edward bloody Teach."

"Truly?" Anney seemed a tad worried.

"I spied, with my pirate's eye, the *Queen Anne's Revenge.*"

Anney cursed violently.

"Mary can take care of herself. I'm more worried about our particulars if he catches us. Especially after the shenanigans, we've put him through."

"Who is Edward bloody Teach?"

"Oh, Sebastian, my uninformed friend. Only the most notoriously named pirate in the Caribbean, apart from myself. Edward Teach is a pirate that strikes fear into many. Though not me, of course."

"Is that why we are sneaking into Monte Christi?" Sebastian asked with a smug grin on his lips.

"Mine is a calculated retreat, thank you, Sebastian. It would do us no good at all, especially before our little expedition, if we were to invoke the ire of the pirate king himself."

"Blackbeard won't be happy if he finds us here, Jack."

"I do wish you wouldn't call him that, Anney. It only adds to his bravado."

"Well deserved bravado, I fear, captain. I haven't heard of Edward Teach, but I have heard of his alias, and it's not all swashbuckling adventure."

"Oh, Sebastian, it's all puffed up pageantry to frighten the privateers." It suddenly dawned on Jack why Monte Christi was doing so well. "That's why they won't touch this place. If they think they are going to feel the wrath of Edward bloody Teach, they'll leave this place well alone." He spat in the sea, trying to remove the bad taste from his mouth. "The last time we were here together, we left on some pretty bad terms, Anney. I don't know how we will get what we need and deal with both a pissed off Mary Read and an angry Edward Teach. Maybe we should just head back to the *Kingston* and find another port town further along the coast. One that doesn't have a bloody hornet's nest to poke."

"No, Jack, I need to make sure she ain't strung up. Doing business with Blackbeard is a fickle thing. She might be in trouble. Even after what I did to her, I owe her that much."

He sighed heavily. "Okay, love, we'll sneak in, keep to the shadows."

She placed her hand on his, giving him a look he had not seen for many moons, a gaze that imparted a thousand words yet uttered none.

Jack sat weighing up the options, while Sebastian manoeuvred the vessel into the cove. "There's an ominous-looking grotto in this cove, Captain."

"Have not a worry, my friend, we used this grotto to escape damn near five years ago now. The passages within should take us right where we need to be, under the governor's house. When they burnt the place down, they uncovered the tunnels. A secret escape route for the governor. It's how a lot of the old merchants survived the razing."

They passed under the grotto entrance, the waves licking up the edges of the mouth. All Jack could see was darkness, but he knew what awaited once his eyes adjusted to the inner sanctum. It was a place he and Anney often visited alone, away from the eyes of her lover. The sea had eroded its way deep inside the place, leaving a stone shelf to dock the rowboat to, with several paths leading from the main chamber.

"Oh my, this is nature at her finest. Carving such a wondrous cavern for us to enjoy." Sebastian seemed elated.

"Aye, Jack and I would often frequent this place when we were secret lovers. We made it somewhat cosy." She grinned at Jack.

"Oh look, Anney, our old makeshift bed is still here, do you want to give it a good thrashing for old times sake."

"Not in front of the kids, Jack."

Jack could feel Sebastian glowing with embarrassment from the other side of the rowboat.

"You two are insufferable sometimes."

Sebastian had brought the boat to the edge of the rock shelf and thrown the mooring rope over the side. Jack watched as he jumped out and secured the boat to a thick stalagmite. The boat now secure; he was free to stretch his legs while Sebastian helped Anney out in his wake. *The place hasn't lost any of its old charms*, he thought as he stood there admiring his old lover's retreat.

"Beautiful, isn't it?" He placed an arm around Sebastian. "It makes a difference to be fully clothed. The number of times Anney and I have lost ourselves down here, and I mean in every sense of the word, literally and figuratively." Anney gave him a cheeky grin.

The scholar groaned.

Sebastian attempted to sway the conversation in a less erotically charged direction. "What's the plan, Captain? Once we get to the town, what are we to do?"

"Well, my friend, we shall discuss the plan on the way. Time is of the essence!" He directed his friend to the tunnel, which would lead them to their goal. "Just take care while you're on the rocks; they can get quite slippery when wet." Jack looked hungrily at his lover, while Sebastian groaned like an old weathered ship.

* * *

"And that's why we don't let monkeys on deck anymore." Jack led the two through the pitch-black tunnel, straining his eyes and ears for any sign that the passage was about to end.

"What did you expect with letting that little bastard on board, Jack?" Anney shuddered.

"I don't know why you thought you could train it, Captain." Sebastian seemed like he was about to launch into a lecture on the latest scientific knowledge on the topic.

"Pause that thought, my friend," Jack whispered. "I see the light. We must be under the house." Jack edged closer to the source. His body was breaking the shafts of light as he moved silently under the exposed floorboards. "See? They rebuilt the new governor's house right on top of the old foundations. Hopefully, she didn't secure the hatch. Otherwise, we'll have to find another way in. Are you two savvy with the plan?"

Anney gave a curt nod.

"Aye, Captain. Sneak in, listen, and learn. Help Ms Read if we can. Don't needlessly endanger ourselves."

"...and get our supplies." Jack jogged the scholar's memory.

"Yes, of course."

It had been a while since he had seen Mary. The last time he was here, in this passage, he had been with Anney, and they were running away together. The two of them had helped her set up this place. It was a different time then. Jack was a newly minted pirate, and Anney was young and in love with Mary. She had big ideas, and Jack was eager to prove himself. He couldn't have foreseen falling for Anney and stealing her away in the dead of night. Now here he was back in the place where it all started, ready to bring the saga of Mary Read full circle.

Jack pushed his ear to the floorboards. He couldn't hear anything but the beating of his own heart. "I think the coast is clear." *Now to try this hatch,* he thought to himself, giving a gentle push against the boards. *Nothing.* He pushed a little harder, and this time, with a little increase in pressure, the hatch popped up a little. He looked over to Sebastian. "It just needed my special touch." He could hear Sebastian's exasperation filling the air.

He popped his head above the floorboards, checking the room for inhabitants, but to no avail.

"The coast is clear."

One by one, the three sneaky pirates filed out the secret hatch and into a room that looked very much like a cellar. Because it was. Wine now lined the walls in this dusty old memory of a place. "Looks like she's been busy." Jack picked up a bottle of something that looked, French. He pulled the stopper out and took a swig. Spewing out the contents, he passed it to Sebastian. "Tastes like piss."

The scholar-turned pirate took a good long sniff of the bottle. "Hmm, yes, a very floral bouquet." The refined gentlemen took a sip, swilled it around in his mouth, and daintily spat it out. "Hints of strawberry and melon. Yes, very nice. The lady has good taste."

Jack looked at him, disgustedly. "You like it?" He whispered in an incredulous tone.

"I think the problem here is that you are so used to that pig swill you drink. You've killed your taste buds with rum."

"And whiskey! Also, how dare you. Rum is the lifeblood of a pirate," Jack argued with the gentleman.

"Shh! Someone is coming." Jack looked over to Anney, who had been busying herself by the cellar stairs. A look of panic creased her face.

"Quick, behind here," he motioned over to the thick casks near the back of the room, providing natural cover for two pirates and a sommelier. The three hid as best they could, peeping through the cracks that the casks formed so that they might spy the unwanted guest.

The door opened with a thunderous crack. The wooden boards of the stairs creaked ominously as heavy footsteps descended. Jack tried to angle his sight to see the producer of this melodious entrance but to no avail. They were still not in view.

"God damn pirate bastard, coming in here, bossing me about. I didn't spend all that time as Mary's first mate to be ordered around like some common scullery maid by Edward bloody Teach."

It was music to Jack's ears, but before he could even formulate a sentence, Anney sprung out from hiding to confront the disgruntled sailor.

"Hector!" Anney clearly startled the man. The poor wine collector nearly jumped out of his skin. However, his fear melted away and turned to joy as he realised who had cost him his dignity. She ran over to hug the surprised old seadog.

"What are you doing here Ms Anney?"

Jack and Sebastian both came out of hiding to join the two. Jack eyed the sailor up. His blonde curls had now been mostly replaced by a mass of grey, but his piercing blue eyes and strong jawline still made the man unmistakable. "Hello, you old barnacle, still as gorgeous as ever." Jack grinned at his old friend.

"Master Jack, and who is this?" Hector motioned towards Sebastian.

"This is our confidant, and pirate in the making, Sebastian Bellamy." The scholar bowed.

"Pleasure, sir, I'm sure." Anney released her grip on Hector and allowed him to regain his composure.

"It's been five years, what are you doing back here? Now is not the best time to be in the court of Mary Read."

"Is she ok, Hector?" Anney looked searchingly into the old sailor's eyes for answers that might not be as forthcoming as his words.

"Oh, she's fine, miss. Don't you worry a jot about her."

Anney seemed relieved. "So she isn't in trouble? We thought with the dock being deathly quiet, and the *Queen Anne's Revenge* docked, that she had gotten herself into some heavy debt with that bilge rat that passes as a pirate."

"Miss Read is fine, Anney. It's just business. Honestly, you don't need to go barging in there saving her. You'd only be causing yourself more unnecessary trouble. She seems to be quite comfortable now with that lecherous turd." Hector scowled as even the thought caused him to vomit internally.

Jack perked up. "What's this business with Teach? What's he doing here?" He asked inquisitively.

"That scallywag." Hector spat on the floor while Jack grinned. "He turned up shortly after I helped you two escape. The two have been whispering in each other's ears ever since, turning Ms Read more bent than usual." The grumpy sailor kicked the dirt.

Jack was beginning to see the bigger picture that Mary's first mate had found himself in. "Cutting ol' Hector out of the loop, I reckon?"

"You have the right of it, Master Jack." Hector looked sullen, constantly eyeing the cellar door. "I can't tarry much longer over tales of the past; the pirate king will be wanting his wine."

Anney grabbed hold of his hands, staring into his soul. "Come find us, Hector, tell us what's happening here."

The old sailor looked hesitant. "His *lordship* is keeping me quite busy, fetching this, cleaning that." He looked bashfully at Anney, who was engaging her best charm offensive.

Just like I taught her, clever girl.

"But, I'm sure I can find some time during the night to come and catch up with old friends."

Jack patted Hector on the shoulder in quiet celebration, causing the weathered first mate to grin at the reunion. "You remember where the passage under this cellar leads?"

"Aye, Master Jack."

"Meet us in the grotto at the end. We will keep the embers burning."

Each friend, old and new, clasped forearms and parted ways. Jack and his friends slunk back into the shadows, and Hector returned with the wine.

What are those two bilge rats up to?

* * *

"Anney, come lay with me, don't worry about Sebastian. He can lose himself in one of the tunnels for a few moments." He eyed his lover suggestively, patting the makeshift bed beside him.

"Good lord, can't you two keep the filth to a minimum while we are hiding underneath the pirate king and his mistress?"

"I wish I could, my friend, but the lady has needs and desires. What kind of captain would I be if I didn't take care of them?" He questioned the scholar solicitously, with an added raised eyebrow.

"Give me strength." Sebastian sighed as he walked off down one of the other tunnels looking for peace and driftwood for the fire.

"He's right you know, Jack, we should keep our wits about us. We don't know what's going to come down that tunnel tonight." Anney looked slightly worried.

Jack sat on their old bed reminiscing about all the sunsets they had watched together from this view. The grotto entrance gave the most amazing vantage point for it, a view they had spent many nights celebrating with the most passionate sex he'd ever cared to commit to memory. "How many more do you think we will get to appreciate, love?" Nodding to the sun floating on the horizon. He kicked off his boots and started taking off his shirt.

Anney looked over to where Jack had pointed and bit her lip. She turned to him lying there in a state of undress, the heart in his burly chest beating at the sight of her. Slowly, she moved over to him, making no effort to rush things. Her look had turned from one of nervousness to desire as she stood there, her features glistening in the last of the dying light.

She moved over to him, he knew his cheeky grin and dimples would be setting her desires afire. They had seen a hundred sunsets together, but this one would be marked by something memorable if Calico Jack had anything to say about it. She stood over him, taking him all in.

Anney knelt down, taking his head in her hands, working her calloused fingers through the rivulets of dark salty hair. She tugged his hair back allowing her to fall into his lips, caressing them with her tongue. She pushed his head playfully away and walked off.

"Keep it in your pants, sailor. At least till we are back on board the *Kingston*."

Jack let out a sexually frustrated groan, as Anney sat near the grotto opening to watch the sun disappear with him.

"Do you remember that day, Anney?"

"The day you and I ran away from this place?"

"Aye," Jack came to sit by her side. "Do you remember what I promised you?"

Anney laughed, "which time? A man will promise the world to a woman if he can get his prick wet." They both grinned.

"I mean the promises that counted."

"Aye, Jack, you promised me you'd take me away from this place, that we would see the world, that we would get a place together and fill it with children."

"How am I doing on those, love?" Jack felt desolate.

"Well, we are currently back where we started. We haven't left the Caribbean since we departed from this place and the only child we have is currently looking for firewood." She let out a sigh.

"Once we figure out what's going on here, we'll carry on with the plan. The secrets we have will truly set the cat amongst the pigeons, enough so that we can win back our homelands I wager. I will not break the promises I made. You have my word."

Anney lent on his shoulder. "Let's just enjoy the sunset for now."

It had been five years since they had left this place, under the cover of darkness. In those five years, he had stolen a ship from some Jamaicans and used it to plunder and pillage across the Caribbean. Taking some large ships in the process, to add to the fleet. They had grown to be rich-comfortable pirates. But the lifestyle had tied them down to this place. Now he had the key to open the door out of the Caribbean and get everything that he had promised. All he had to do was sail across the world under a merchant flag, make his way to the court of the Sun King and bargain with him. *Easy.*

"Not interrupting anything am I?"

96

"Hector! I'm glad you came." Anney jumped up to greet her old friend.

"We were just admiring the sunset, reminiscing." Jack stood up to grab hold of the sailor's arm.

"I come bearing gifts, ya scurvy hounds." Hector handed him a sack filled with food and wine. "Let it be known that Hector of House Lothar is a good host."

"Now there's a name I haven't heard in a long time." Jack went straight for the wine, uncorking it and taking a huge mouthful. "How is the old guard?"

"Scattered and rudderless, there were rumours of a reunion a few years back, but that isn't why you are here this day."

Jack was here for that very reason, but he didn't want to get his old friends' hopes up just yet. He needed to at least have his plan in motion before he attempted that. "No, I'm afraid not, my friend. That time will come, one day, but it is not this one. We came for supplies. I am taking the crew to seek an audience with His Majesty Louis XIV."

"Why on earth would you go there?" Hector seemed intrigued.

"Let's just say the winds have become favourable. There's a chance we might be able to reposition ourselves in a more agreeable location."

"And the price?"

"Knowledge, my friend."

There came a clattering from down one of the tunnels. Then a voice.

"It's just me, I dropped the driftwood. Have you guys finished your vigorous lovemaking?" Sebastian's disembodied question lingered in the air.

Jack grinned at Anney. "We are all fully clothed, Sebastian, for now."

Sebastian appeared from the tunnel he had disappeared down, his arms full with driftwood for the fire. "This should keep the fire going till morning."

"Good man, come take a seat so we can continue our discussion." "Welcome, Hector. You made it. Hopefully without arousing any suspicions?" The scholar waltzed over to the fire, throwing a few logs on and sat down to warm his hands.

"I have my ways." He gave Jack a knowing look.

"So what did I miss while I was in the tunnels?"

Jack gave Hector a little shake of the head. "Nothing much, my friend, we were just discussing what the situation is topside."

"Well, I can tell you now, and with certainty that you won't get any supplies here. Edward and Mary are loading up the ships for their own quest it seems. They are having the men take everything we have to sell and are heading off to do something I am no longer privy to."

Hector seemed upset. The Hector of five years ago was Mary's closest confidant, her first mate. He had a lot of say in the way things were run, he set up the merchant connections and ran the day to day stuff for her. Now it seemed he had lost a lot of that power and was running around for Edward Teach.

"How did things get this way, my friend? You two were as thick as thieves and now what? You're the maid?" Jack was struggling to comprehend the situation Hector was in.

"It started small. Edward arrived in Haiti some four years ago, the business was okay. You two had been gone a year and Mary had finally gotten over you Ms Anney. She was focussing on trade, building up this place to its former glory. When he arrived, he came with ideas and whispered them in her ear. Business started to grow and we had become the hub for pirate trade. She became more invested in listening to him when his ideas paid off."

"Rumours of his alias started spreading about that time also."

"That's right, miss. He started to build up his reputation as Blackbeard." Hector spat in the dirt. "His reputation even overshadowed Miss Read's. Then he became the self-proclaimed pirate king. Taking twenty percent of earnings in the process."

"The price of his protection I presume?"

"Aye, Mr Bellamy, very astute. His visits have been less frequent of late. But a couple of days ago he arrived and hasn't left since. He's been whispering in her ear again, and this time she won't tell me a thing. The only intelligence I can gather is from lurking in the dark. However, even that doesn't tell me much. They are being very secretive."

Jack's interest was piqued. "What did you learn from the shadows, my sneaky shark?"

"Only that they are planning to sail east. Everything else is whispered behind closed doors." The old sailor seemed upset that he couldn't offer more information.

"What could they be doing taking all these supplies East?" Anney questioned the group.

"I don't know, but we shouldn't worry about them, or Mary." He looked into her eyes with reassurance. "She seems to be doing just fine. We need to think about where we are going to get our supplies and a merchant flag."

Hector perked up a little with a grin reaching from ear to ear. "If it's a subterfuge you are looking for, I think I know where you can find what you need."

"Truly? You may have won the day for us yet, Hector of House Lothar. Tell us what you know, friend!"

The four friends huddled around the fire conspiring by twilight, as the sea crashed against the walls of the grotto drowning any plotting in a crescendo of white noise.

* * *

Chapter - 7 - Flight of the HMS *Selene*

Seamus sat across from Ariadne, grinning like the cat that got the cream. "What?" They sat by the fire warming their bones. It had been a thoroughly long day finishing off the construction. They had finished erecting the 'steering mast' on the opposite side of the island and attached the sails to the ropes they had painstakingly threaded. So they were almost ready to depart. Just one more night of much-needed rest, and by the dawn of a new day, they would be ready to set sail.

"I'm just saying, it's as easy as that."

He had spent a good part of the night reiterating his thrilling adventures on the gaff and boom spars. Seamus was even going as far as to embellish a few facts, like the fact that he walked the boom. *Definitely didn't happen.* Ariadne had also spent a good portion watching him reenact a few of the more precarious parts of his adventure. He unmistakably seemed more alive than in recent days.

Seamus had no trouble with his spars, no near misses, or tumbles, and he was lording it over her. It was nice to see this side of him, but also equally frustrating. She had only had a chance to know him as her Captain, before arriving on Anegada, and since their time on the island, he had only shown one side of himself. After getting us both stranded here, recovering from his embarrassment, and finding himself in this situation. He was finally coming into himself. Gone was the captain she was loath to be stuck with, now he was more like Seamus Hawthorne, one of the crew. He was becoming more like a dear friend.

"Once I had conquered the gaff, the boom was a breeze. I mean, okay, I might not have walked across, but it felt like a breeze. I don't know why I'm telling you. You were there! It was just so thrilling, Ari."

After her near misses that morning, they had decided to recover a little from the nerve-wracking escapade she had put them through. After a short rest back at camp, they left to carry out the necessary work, grabbing everything they would need. Seamus was eager to get the task over with, there was so much to do, and they needed to catch the trade winds as soon as possible. He had his spars up in quick time, while Ariadne made extra care to strengthen the bindings.

Once that was done, Seamus was free to thread the rope through the loops. Just as before, he took the top spar first. Seamus couldn't help but show her up, pretending to fall off, *bloody fool*, general scoundrel behaviour. But he did get the job done. *Well, blow me down, that's a swashbuckler if ever I laid eyes on one.*

"...and the view, you didn't tell me how breathtaking the view was. At first, yes, I could feel the weight of my position, so high above the ground. My head did spin. But once I got used to it, it was rather quite impressive."

Once that was complete, their next task was to take down the tents and prepare for hoisting the sails in the morning. They had even found some extra lengths of sail in a rogue crate they had not opened yet, which came in handy for the 'steering masts'. It had been a long day, but they managed to rig up the sails with no significant hiccups. She had even found a little time to finish off the anchor project she had been working on in her spare time. She could have finished it during the flight across the North Atlantic, but she always had to be the efficient one.

"Yes, well, my fall earlier on the main mast got me all disorientated of a sort. I blame that for showing me up, like some useless landlubber. If I hadn't felt so groggy afterwards, I would never have fallen. You are just lucky I didn't embarrass you by doing all the work. Imagine having an enfeebled woman saving your arse. What would the boys back at the Admiralty say?"

Seamus laughed. "I'm sure they would have something to say, some harsh ribbing, no doubt. That doesn't matter to me, though. What matters is that we get back in one piece to warn the king, even if...even if I don't make it." He had turned sombre. "Ari...if something were to happen to me on the way. Would you do me the honour of telling my family that I love them? And, that my thoughts were of them, till the end? That I was brave?"

Ariadne looked concerned. "Where is this coming from? You're going to be fine. You can tell them yourself. Hells, we both will."

"It's a dangerous business we find ourselves in, Ari, I nearly lost you twice, in two days! You remind me how treacherous this place can be. Here's me larking about with my own mortality. I forgot how panicked I was at your misfortune. I apologize for playing the fool."

"Think nothing of it. I'm just glad the task is done. I'm glad you managed it better than I. It puts things in perspective if you think about it, we just need to be more respectful to *Selene*. Otherwise, lord knows what we might forfeit." She patted the ground as if to soothe the beast.

"You are quite right, my dear friend. The trip we are about to make is treacherous. As you say, the island could fall apart, and we could drop to our doom. I want you to know that as your captain, I promise I will do everything in my power to make sure that you at least get back in one piece."

"Seamus; We will both make it back. I promise *you* that. We will *both* warn the king *and* tell your family what a brave little captain you've been."

A grin spread across Seamus' face.

"There we go much better. Now, you are sure of our direction?"

"My lady, I have been wandering these seas since I was a boy. I could chart our course blindfolded. I've been charting the stars nightly, taking care to note the stars which appear in the eastern sky. For the past few days, Perseus has been chasing Andromeda across the night sky, with Cassiopeia trailing behind. So if we head for her during the night, we will end up west eventually over the course of the next few nights. We just have to follow the sun eastwards by day and chart our course through Perseus, then Cassiopeia. They are both very prominent in the night sky this time of year." Seamus stated matter of factly.

"I concur, I too have noticed the same constellations haunting the horizon. Do you know the tale of Perseus? I know we discussed Andromeda before."

Seamus had returned to his zesty form; his interest peaked by myths. "Aye, that I have. Legendary Greek hero, slayer of the gorgon, *Medusa*, destroyer of the sea monster, Cetus. Thrown into the stars as a testimony for challenging the gods."

"Can you imagine how Perseus must have felt, with the gods throwing everything at him just to stop him from saving Andromeda?"

Seamus pondered the question for a moment. "I imagine he might have felt a little like us in our predicament. Except we have no monsters to slay. Yet." He grinned.

"Wait till we catch up to those double-crossing French scallywags. I, for one, will hunt them to the edges of the world, if that's what it takes to get our secrets back."

"Huzzah!" Seamus seemed to be mulling something over. "Tell me, Ari, have you ever done much hunting?"

"I presume you mean animals? Aye, I've done my fair share of hunting back home."

"Your Grandmother?" He asked her with a look of impressed bemusement.

"Indeed. She would take me on trips into the wilderness and teach me how to hunt and track. Lessons I have not forgotten, obviously." She flashed the bow at her side. "I still remember the mantra she used to repeat over and over."

Focus. Take aim. Breathe. Release.

Seamus broke her out of her reminiscence. "So when we get home and inform the proper authorities, of course, you will have to take me hunting sometime."

"I would like that." She smiled warmly at him. "Do you think it will end there, Seamus?"

"What do you mean?" He asked inquisitively.

"Do you think once we've spoken to the Admiralty, or the king, that everything will go back to normal? Once we've warned them about what has transpired on this island. The experiments, and what they have created and how the French came to this place and stole the findings of our poor scientist."

Seamus looked slightly melancholy. "No, I don't suppose it will, will it."

"We shall see, only time will tell. We at least have to make the crossing first! Promise me we will take out time to go hunting when we return. I just want something normal in all this madness." Ariadne pleaded with him.

"I promise; as your friend, once we are back home, you and I will do this. Before the Admiralty decides to send us back out into the world again on some godforsaken errand."

* * *

Ariadne awoke at the crack of dawn, eager to start the day, the day they would set sail for merry old England. The two friends had fallen asleep by the side of the campfire talking of times gone by. Old memories resurfacing like a whale coming up for air. Once one comes up, the whole pod does, getting the conversation flowing. With each passing story, she felt like she was getting to know the real person beneath the facade of the station, the true nature of her captain.

Seamus was still asleep. He must have tired himself out with the rush of adrenaline yesterday. She didn't want to wake him just yet. The man looked a shade of how he first looked onboard the *Daedalus*. Most of his uniform had come to some disrepair. The jacket was lost, and his waistcoat tattered. The buttons were gone, his shirt dirty and dishevelled. His hat was long gone. He had lost that the first night they spent there, possibly animal-related, there had been many dastardly monkeys back in Anegada, not so many now. His face had the same chiselled good looks; the only difference was that his clean-shaven face had been replaced with scruffy brown stubble. He almost looked handsome.

Focus. I should try to hunt for some food before we go. Who knows what the animals will do once this place starts moving.

Ariadne had spotted a good place to hunt the day before, while they were fixing up the last of the sails. She was sure that she had spotted a deer, but only a fleeting glance from the periphery of her sight. If she could track it and kill it, well, that *would* be a feast fit for two hungry officers.

She stalked through the forest, taking care not to make too much noise, just like her grandmother had taught her. She had to come from downwind, so that the deer if it was there, wouldn't catch her scent. *Quiet steps. Be wary of your surroundings, Ari.* This proved to be a bit of an inconvenience because she had to trek a long way and trackback. *No matter.* She clenched her bow and made her way back to where she thought she had last seen the creature.

She bent down to examine the ground; her bow slung over one shoulder and the quiver on the other. Ariadne brushed away some of the leaves to no avail. She advanced to the next section, quietly creeping along with the dead leaves and soil, carefully avoiding broken branches, brushing away more leaves as she did.

Tracks. I knew it, I was right!

The deer was here somewhere. The tracks were fresh, visible, not covered in leaves. The mud was still moist, not old and dry as if they were from hours ago. All Ariadne had to do was take her time following them, being as quiet as possible. She crept silently through the trees, stalking her prey.

"I want you to be ready for anything, Ari. I know you are only a child now, but there will come a time, and it will come when you need to be more than you are—when you have to fight to survive. Our family's past, present, and future is in your hands. And I will

see that you are fit to protect it. You are the key to our salvation— my sweet Ari."

"Grandma, what are you talking about?"

"Quiet child, your prey awaits you. Breathe. Pull back the string. Release."

Ariadne brought herself back to the present. Her bow now in hand, arrow notched. She was going to show Seamus what she was made of, not the clumsy fool she had been the past few days; he would be impressed when she came back with a deer on her shoulders.

She crouched down, minimising how much of herself was visible. Her bow was on point sweeping from left to right, scanning the direction in which the tracks pointed, looking for the next clue which would tell her which direction she should go.

There, a broken branch.

She followed the path of destruction. The deer had left signs everywhere; the tracks and broken branches led to a clearing a few feet away. Ariadne made her way silently to the clearing, hoping to catch a glimpse of the deer before it caught wind of her. She tread carefully through the opening, taking care to lessen the noise from her feet and control her breathing.

There it is!

She had spied the deer in the clearing, not too far from her current spot. It hadn't spotted her yet, and that's the way she wanted to keep it. She notched the arrow and aimed at the unsuspecting deer, already tasting the roasted meat on her tongue. She began to salivate. She slowly and decisively pulled back on the bowstring to its full extent. She meant business.

Focus.

Take Aim.

Breathe.

Release.

The arrow let loose, flying through the air in an arc towards the target. Ariadne watched as it swept across the forest in slow motion towards its mark. The deer heard the twang of the string, picking up its head to better locate the sound, but it was too late—the arrow headed for its mark directly into the deer's heart with a wet thud.

"It takes more than skill to end a life, child. You've got to have the guts to go through with it. The knowledge that you are ending a life, but for the greater good. For the benefit of the many. This deer's life might have ended, but it will feed your family tonight. Do you understand, Ari?"

"Yes, Grandma."

"One day you might have to end a life to save your family, how do you feel about that?"

"I don't know, Grandma."

"That's ok, Ari, you don't always have to have the answers. We can always be happy with small victories."

"Huzzah!" She allowed herself to bask in this small victory before attending to her downed prey. The deer's laboured breathing was rhythmic. It was still alive, but not for long. The creature lay there, its breath slowly dying away, the panicked look in its eyes as it finally spotted its predator. It was in pain; she had to put it out of its misery. Ariadne took out her blade and did the deer a favour, before thanking the goddess of the hunt, Artemis, for this bounty.

"Repeat after me, child."

"Thank you, Artemis, for teaching me the skill and the knowledge to take this animal's life and with it feed my family. Just as my ancestors taught me."

She placed the deer on her shoulders. It wasn't too heavy, nothing she couldn't handle. Then she carried it back to camp.

I'll show him hunting.

Ariadne sauntered back to camp with a smug grin on her face.

* * *

"Good morning, my friend! I see you've been busy. Is that a deer?" Seamus seemed jovial.

"Aye, I spotted her yesterday. Decided we would need a good few days worth of food for the journey." She was still smug.

"Good show! I knew you could hunt but look at the size of that creature. I can't wait for you to show me a thing or two with the bow. Whatever happens, when we arrive, we are going hunting, mark my words."

"It was nothing really, anyone with a bow can take down a deer if they learn the skill." She was beaming with pride.

Seamus stretched the morning cobwebs off, with a yawn that might have swallowed her whole if she had dared to get too close. "I think perhaps that it is time for us to make ready, Ari? If we can get hold of the morning trade winds, we should make great headway towards the coast of Africa."

"Of course, let me just hang this somewhere safe. I'll take care of it later once we are away." She straddled the deer on a couple of high up branches so that no curious critters could take a nibble of the fresh kill.

"To the mainsail!" Seamus was in high spirits, and she had to admit that she was too. They were finally going to see if this plan even had a chance of working by taking the first step. If all went well, they would be home within a week. If a bird could make it across in several days during migration, she was pretty sure the *Selene* could do it in the same. Although, she was a giant bird sailing across the clouds. *Perhaps she could beat that.* She patted the tree as if to commune with *Selene. Don't fall apart on me, dear.*

She picked up the spare rope, just in case, and followed Seamus. She felt a little tight in her chest from the anxiety. Everything was relying on the mainsail working, and the hope powering her through this was just enough to keep her moving. Seamus seemed in good spirits, more accepting of where he was. "You seem different."

"How do you mean?" Seamus looked puzzled.

"Well, may I speak freely?"

"Always, my friend."

"From the moment we were marooned on this island, you seemed to take everything with a grain of salt. You acted like it was nothing, that we were marooned here, and that if we waited long enough, things would get better, or someone would come along. Then whenever some new mystery befuddled me with its complexities, you seemed to take those in your stride like it was a normal day at sea."

Seamus seemed to be thinking over his response.

"I'm sorry, I didn't mean to offend."

"No, don't worry, I can see how that would be frustrating for you. I just needed to reflect on my actions since we were marooned here. The first few days we were here, I expected someone to come along and save us. As a captain, I felt totally out of my element. I'm used to having people around me to take care of my every whim on board. Imagine a captain with no crew if you will. I just expected us to batten down the hatches for a few days, and we would be off that island." He mused further.

"Understandable, but you are more capable than you know. You've proved that over the past few nights." She tried to diminish some of the feelings of a personal attack that Seamus might have.

"That is kind of you to say. I think it just took me a bit of time to break out of the uselessness. Then the forest happened. I mean, you took to all of this so well, and I just couldn't believe my eyes, going even so far as to *take it with a grain of salt*. I think it took nearly losing you to snap me out of it. I needed to be more active in our salvation. I know you are a very capable woman, Ari, but you can't do everything. As your captain, I won't let you."

"Is that an order?" Ariadne grinned.

"Yes, I do believe it is." He grinned with smug satisfaction.

"I didn't take to this as well as you think, Seamus, I was terrified and puzzled at our predicament."

"Well, you didn't show it. You were quite admirable."

"I knew that if you were as worried as I was, it wouldn't help to have two people at their wit's end. I needed to ease you into the world in which we find ourselves."

"You should have slapped me out of it. Ya scallywag. We both need to be on the same page, from now on." He smiled at Ariadne.

"Deal." She shook his hand to solidify their partnership.

"Ah. We are finally at the mainsail. Would you care to say a few words? We are about to set sail on the maiden voyage of the HMS *Selene*, after all." He waited for her response.

"To the *Selene* and all who fly in her. May her voyages be smooth and short. May she never fall apart and let her inhabitants fall to their doom." She laughed.

"Huzzah! Let us be on our way. If you would help me with the honours."

She grabbed hold of one of the ropes, while Seamus went over to the other one.

"Together now!" He ordered, with a much more authoritative command.

They both pulled their ropes down while the sail snaked its way up the mast using the pulley system in place. It worked magnificently, and the sails raised up the makeshift mast picking up the wind as it did. Billowing eastwards. The sail was now fully erect and gathering wind. Now all they had to do was wait and see.

"At least it didn't snap off." Ariadne chanced a jest.

She looked over to Seamus with a questioning expression.

"I don't know, my friend, maybe give it some time?" Seemingly understanding her apprehension.

As soon as the words had left his mouth, there sounded a deep rumble underneath them, and the wind howled like a ferocious wolf. The ground shook, knocking Seamus off his feet. *She's falling apart!* Ariadne thought as she withstood the initial movement. She had been expecting at least some motion, but this was much more than what she was anticipating. The sails were taught, and the trees were creaking, but the mast held. The sound the *Selene* made as she flew over the North Atlantic was that of the wind whistling through the trees, just more prominent. *Typical Grandmother, always having to make herself heard.* The rhythmic sound of the wind rushing the oaks was accompanied by the crashing of stones dropping from the bottom of the island.

"We need to make sure she's not losing too much earth." She rushed to give Seamus a helping hand.

"Of course! It would be best to check from the back. We would be able to see it there, I'm sure. Let us head to the west of the *Selene*."

114

Ariadne raced through the trees with Seamus at her tail. Eventually breaching the edge of the forest and arriving at their destination.

"Careful now, Ari. Let's take care not to end up over the edge. I won't be jumping in after you." He scrunched his face up in a grin, his dimples more prominent.

Ariadne crouched to the ground and crawled to the edge to peak down. The loud rumbling and popping had been replaced with a low hum. The sounds could only mean good things, she hoped.

"The stones seemed to have stopped falling, and we feel a bit more stable. I can't see anything else dropping off. We are moving away from Anegada, though. So that's good news!" She was excited now that the prospect of breaking up upon starting the journey had passed.

Seamus pulled her back to safe ground and embraced her in celebration. "We did it, my friend! Pioneers in the field of airships!"

"We will be home before you can say *Shiver me timbers*, cap'n."
The two grinned at each other as the *Selene* made its way across the North Atlantic like a lost cloud.

Chapter - 8 - Stealing Fire from the Gods.

Jack had been sitting listening to Hector for a good while. He couldn't believe the balls on this sailor. Hector wanted them to steal one of Edward Teach's ships. He wasn't so brazen as to suggest they steal the *Queen Anne's Revenge*, but still. Ballsy move. Teach must have royally pissed the old barnacle off.

"I think if subterfuge is your game, then you need to look no further than the eastern harbour."

"Let me get this straight, old friend. You want us to march across Monte Christi, walk up the dock, and onto one of his recent acquisitions, the HMS *Neptune*. Steal it. Then be on our merry way?" Jack asked Hector incredulously.

"Oh, she's grand, Jack, Teach stole her off some pompous Captain breaking her in. She's a newly built, ninety-gun, ship of the line. It doesn't look anything like a merchant's vessel, but at least she'll be well-armed. It's fully stocked with everything you need for a long trip, I know because I loaded it myself. The flag has already been replaced with one stolen from a French merchant vessel. Most importantly, you'd be sticking it to that scurvy, syphilis-infested, black-bearded weasel." Hector sat there, revelling in the warmth of his own plan.

"Also, it's dark out now, it would be the only real way of getting anywhere since the *Kingston* has probably gone back to Tortuga," Anney interjected.

Jack mused for a moment. "*We'd* be sticking it to him because I want you to come with us, old man. I won't leave you here alone with Teach cracking the cat-o-nine." Hector had put his life on the line for them when he helped them escape. Jack was sure as hell not going to leave him here to be some puffed up pirate's maid. Even if he would have to insult the man to get him to leave.

"I couldn't leave Miss Read on her own. I promised to look after her. Even if she has abandoned me to that tar." Hector looked downtrodden.

"Mary will be fine. She's a big girl now. Playing at pirates with Teach. I seem to recall a similar promise was made to us." He nodded at Anney.

Anney perked up. "Maybe this isn't the time to talk about that." She glanced over at Sebastian.

Jack wasn't taking no for an answer. "Before we sailed so far from home to this godforsaken rock, you made an oath to Anney and me. You made an oath to *our* King. That you would protect us from harm, and aid us should we ever need it."

"These are different times, John. Our home is all but gone. There's nothing to fight for anymore. Like I said before, the Brass Roses are spread far and wide. There is no leadership, no direction. Which wind would you have us take to get home?"

Jack stared into the flames licking at the logs.

Sebastian perked up at the mention of the Brass Roses. "Um...What are we talking about? And who is John?"

"Never you mind that."

He turned his attention back to Hector. He knew exactly what to say to get the old bastard to change his mind. "Then it's true, these really must be the end days of Lotharingia. Because that would be the only time that a Knight of House Lothar would become an oath-breaker…" Jack let that hang in the air, while Hector registered his abuse.

Hector turned bright red. "How dare you, boy! You know not what you speak of. An oath-breaker? Hector of House Lothar does not break oaths. I was there at the battle of Nancy, fighting alongside my fellow knights, where were you, boy? Still suckling at your mother's teat, no doubt. I was there when the Dukes of Burgundy were burnt alive by Greek fire. Where were you? I was there when our homes were trampled on by French soldiers, scrambling to stake their claim."

Jack watched as Hector stood up from the fire and stormed about the cavern. "Your mothers, they came to *me*, I swore to them that I would protect you, that when the time was right, I would help you reclaim our lands. Is the time nigh, John, or do you wish for another helping hand with some labour of love? You promised to lead your people, John, and now look at you, some fancy puffed up pirate, and you dare to call me an oath-breaker."

He stood up and knelt by his old protector, pacing back and forth. "Hector, I'm sorry, dear friend, let me explain. I need that fire if we are ever going to reclaim our homelands. All I ask is that you forgive my terrible attempt at swaying your decision and listen to what I have to say."

Hector paused for a moment, taking in the sight of his ward kneeling to him. "Fine! Have it your bloody way, ya knave!"

Jack was grinning from ear to ear. "So you'll come?"

"I didn't say that. I'll listen to what you have to say." Hector kicked dust into the fire, flaring it up into the grotto ceiling.

"Good because I have a plan." Jack looked devilish as he leaned into the fire to get closer to his companions.

118

"Oh, you do, do you? Tell me, what does this boy think he can do?" The bite had mostly been taken out of Hector's voice, replaced with a more inquisitive tone.

Jack turned serious, placing his hand on his cutlass. "For a start, you can stop calling me, boy. You know who you are speaking to."

"Very well. What can John of House Rackham do?" Hector stated matter-of-factly.

"It's Jack, and if you calm down, I'll tell you."

Hector breathed in, then exhaled his anger. "Go on."

Jack turned to Sebastian. "Sebastian. What is about to transpire here you must tell to no one. Upon pain of a most stabby death." He patted his cutlass. "If you are in, just say aye, and we can continue. If not, take a walk."

Sebastian looked around the fire at the others, all looking at him expectantly. "Well, I've nothing better to do. Aye. I'm in." Sebastian leaned in.

"Very well, then listen closely."

* * *

The moon was out in full this evening; Jack loved her as much as he loved the stars. If there was one thing he enjoyed about being a pirate, it was that he always had the chance to appreciate a clear night, with the stars out showing themselves off like twinkling jewels. He hadn't had much of a chance to appreciate them on this night, which made him agitated and eager to get this jaunt over and done with.

"How much can these boys drink?" Jack asked to no one in particular.

They had been hiding in the shadows for at least ten pints, and Sebastian was getting fidgety.

"Sebastian, what are you doing back there? Are you coming on to me, lad?"

Sebastian huffed. "You couldn't handle this, cap'n, I assure you."

Jack turned to his partner in crime with a look of complete and utter disbelief. "Sebastian Bellamy, was that sass emerging from your lips?"

"Aye, cap'n, I believe it was." Jack could feel him smirking in the dark.

Everyone, it seemed, was either now too drunk to be alert or asleep. Jack prefered the latter, but he could work with the former. He had lost patience watching the ebb and flow of the dock from hiding. Sebastian was behind him, watching his back, or at least pretending to. The conversation in the grotto had been extensive, but he had put a lot on the scholar. "I hope I can count on your discretion, friend?"

Sebastian had been lost in thought for a while; he had hardly spoken since his remarks on whether he could keep up with him. "Yes, of course. No one will learn of this from me. I, for one, find your history remarkably intriguing."

The dock had grown eerily silent. Perhaps it had been quiet for so long that the alternative was disconcerting. In any case, he knew it was time to move.

"Shh, now is not the time." Jack had noticed that the dock had been clear for some time now. *They must have finally drunk enough.* It was almost time to make a move for the *Neptune*. Anney and Hector were out there somewhere. They had split up to better cover all angles. It was a tricky business stealing a docked ship. He felt that they would rather not be found out until it was too late, but accidents happen. He searched for her red locks in every dark foreboding corner of the town. *Where are you, love?*

"Can you see her?" Sebastian was peering over his shoulder, whispering in his ear, like a lover in heat. Jack shivered.

Finally, after moments of searching, he saw her. The moonlight reflecting off her perfect features, her red curls effortlessly cascading down her face. Those pouting lips he had been longing to kiss since the grotto.

"There she is," Sebastian whispered.

"Aye, I can see that, friend." Jack shrugged Sebastian off his back.

He gave the signal, to show that the coast was clear, and waited. Jack watched as his lover scanned the town looked for stragglers. Hector was behind her, crouching behind a crate, checking the area they had come from. Jack saw Hector suddenly turn when Anney mouthed something to him. He watched as the old sailor moved to her side. She must have spotted something because she was holding up her hand for them to hold fast.

Jack looked to where she and Hector were gawking. He could scarcely believe his eyes. Exiting out of the tavern was none other than Edward Bloody Teach, all curls and beady eyes, and Mary Reed by his side. Looking like a couple of loved up drunks, flouncing about, holding each other up for leverage. "Look what we have here."

Sebastian peeked around the corner. "If I was a betting man, I'd hazard a guess that that was Blackbeard, which, using my powers of deduction, would make that Mary Reed?"

Jack sighed gently and turned to stare at Sebastian. "I told you not to call him that. You are just pandering to his ego. It's like some damn bad luck. You call him that, and he gains more gravitas." He spat on the floor.

Sebastian had offended him, he returned to watch the scene unfold.

"Well, if you ask me, he doesn't look that foreboding. Just like a normal pirate with a curly beard." Sebastian retorted with remarks loaded with reparations for his transgressions.

Jack grinned. "That's the spirit, friend." He enjoyed the fact that Sebastian was pandering to him, trying to cheer him up. *Is this what it feels like to have a friend?* He mused.

"She is stunning, though. I can see why Miss Bonney and Mr Teach would bed the woman. But going by his looks, how did he attain such a lofty goal?"

Jack tried to stifle his laughter. "Oh, Sebastian, you know how to cheer your captain up."

"I try, sir." The scholar had a smug grin on his face. "It looks like they are bedfellows, though, in both business and love."

Jack looked impressed. "Aye, very perceptive, it looks like the two are in cahoots, bonking every chance they get. Look at them, they are all over each other."

"Just like you and Miss Anney." Sebastian sniped.

"Look who's getting bold." Jack laughed quietly as he grabbed hold of his friend in a headlock.

Once he had finished horsing around with Sebastian, he looked over to Anney. He didn't know what to think of her mood. Maybe seeing Mary happy with someone else would give her closure, seeing her drunk and loved up. Or perhaps she felt relief that Mary was okay and not under some sort of duress. Only time would tell. That was a conversation for when they were safely reunited with the *Kingston*. For now, she seemed to be watching them like a hawk.

"Well, at least that ties up that loose end. If Mary is truly in no danger, then we should be free to carry on towards French waters." Jack was relieved. He bore no ill will towards Mary, but he needed Anney focussed. Jack didn't need her to go on a fool's errand to save someone who didn't need saving. Even if Hector had attempted to put her mind at ease, he knew Anney she would always be worried, but she couldn't deny her own eyes.

"Quite. Miss Read seems to be fine, Hector need not worry about her, nor Miss Anney."

"I do wish you wouldn't call them Miss, Sebastian. There's nothing ladylike in their manners. Anney, especially." He cocked an eyebrow at the scholar.

"You may be trying to turn me into a pirate, cap'n, but I'll never lose my manners. I will always stay true to myself. It would belittle my father's teachings. God rest his soul." Sebastian made the sign of the cross.

Jack watched the two lovers wobble off to the governor's house, that they had so sneakily graced with their presence only recently--at least the cellar. He watched as the two giggled their way through opening the door. Edward's cackle sending chills down his spine. He shuddered. They finally made it through the threshold and disappeared inside. Jack looked over to Anney, mouthing the words, *are you ok?* She nodded in reply—a *conversation for another time, perhaps.* Jack motioned the signal to advance forward. They stepped lightly to the next building while making sure that Anney and Hector were following suit.

Jack continually scanned the area looking for Edward's black-hearted crew or Mary's buccaneer-turned-merchants.

They could see the dock now from the corner of some shacks on the outskirts of the town square. He signalled over to Anney to look. As he did, the door from around the corner of the shed they were hiding behind opened up with a surprising creak. He and Sebastian jumped back around the corner into the dark. The torchlight overhead illuminated a shadow creeping slowly from the door, which preceded a great lurching figure stumbling drunkenly from the shack. *This is one of Edward's.* He was donned in pirate's regalia, but it was the ripe smell emanating from the man that really sold it to Jack. The scurvy seadog stretched his weary muscles right next to them as they hid, bathed in the night.

Jack held his breath while holding his hand over Sebastian's mouth.

The substantial oaf eventually lumbered off towards the tavern.

Jack looked disgustedly at Sebastian as he removed his appendage from the scholar's mouth. "Did you just lick my hand?" He whispered in outrage.

Sebastian panicked. "No! It's the moisture in the air, I swear."

Jack eyed him with some suspicion but decided to let it slide, wiping his hand on his breeches.

When the oaf was decidedly far enough from earshot. Jack and his three companions slunk down the dock's path, covertly moving from shadow to shadow.

Jack turned to Sebastian at the final stretch of their sneaky adventure. "I need you to go and take care of that dastardly deed I asked you to do."

"Aye, cap'n." Sebastian nodded in affirmation.

"Remember, you must be as quiet as a mouse." Jack watched as Sebastian went around the back of the building they were currently stationed at and made his way towards the dock. Jack continued making progress towards the pier, while Anny and Hector were one step ahead of him.

They were all finally there. Jack crept down the wooden dock to regroup with Anney and Hector, the planks straining under the weight of every footstep. "Which one is it, old friend?" He questioned Hector.

"This one right here, Jack." He motioned to the ship on the left.

Jack seemed taken aback as he laid eyes on the vessel as it was now right in front of him. "Of course she is, how foolish of me." He chanced a hearty laugh. "You were right. She looks like a damn fine ship, ninety guns, you say? She looks undamaged, how did Teach manage to take her without damaging her?"

"The way that prick bragged about it, he made out like he just walked on board and the captain shit his breeches, then jumped overboard to escape his wrath. I reckon it was some landlubber captain though, freshly seasoned, no leagues under his boots."

"She is a beauty, she definitely needs someone to show her the ropes." Jack grinned at Hector.

Anney huffed. "Let's get on deck before you get your horn on Jack, you can admire her curves once we are safely away."

Jack grinned, "How right you are, Anney."

He made his way up the gangplank of the *Neptune*, stroking her taffrail as he passed. "Yes, she will do nicely." The two swashbucklers trailed shortly behind him. *My ragtag group of sneaky thieves*. Jack scanned the main deck; thankfully, there was no one in sight. He just hoped there was no one below. *That would be unfortunate. Sebastian would loathe having to clean the blood off my new ship*.

Jack looked around as he heard wooden squeaks emanating from the other ship. Sebastian was making his way down the gangplank as lightly as possible and rejoining them on the main deck of the *Neptune*.

"All done?" He quizzed the saboteur.

"Aye, cap'n. She won't be making sail anytime soon." Sebastian was grinning at him, awash with adrenaline.

Jack was amused at his friend's new demeanour. He was making great headway to becoming a true brethren of the coast. "Good job, my friend, make sure I reward you once we are in safer waters." He gave the scholar a hearty pat on the back.

"Make ready to set sail," Jack whispered to the group. He watched as Hector went off to slip off the mooring ropes and double-check the anchor wasn't down. *Now that would be embarrassing. The old barnacle hasn't lost his skill, that's for sure.* Anney positioned herself by the wheel, ready to steer the *Neptune* out of the dock. *Typical Anney always needs to be in control.* He sighed. *I guess I could help Sebastian, maybe that could be his reward. The pleasure of my help.* He mused, watching Sebastian struggling with the mainsail trying to make ready. After the amusement had passed Jack went over to help his friend with the sails.

"Together."

He pulled the rope alongside Sebastian, the struggle finally over, as the sail rose up the mast smoothly.

"Hopefully, there's enough wind to push us out, my friend."

"You are just this moment, considering that?" Sebastian asked with wild eyes.

Jack stood there, admiring his new surroundings. "Yes, well, if we planned every little detail, that would be no fun now, would it?"

Sebastian laughed nervously. "I suppose not, cap'n."

The mainsail was now raised to its full extent, Jack was grinning, *she is a pretty ship fully erect*, he thought. The wind had finally caught, he could see the sails being pulled taught, filling up with warm tropical winds. The mast began to creak as the mainsail pulled the ship forward. The easterly winds blew the *Neptune* smoothly away from the dock. *Excellent, she's moving.* "Good job, Sebastian." *Praise well deserved.*

All they had to do now was make sure that no one noticed a ninety gun ship-of-the-line, with a full cargo, sailing away in the dead of night. Once they were out of the dock, they could unfurl the other sails and put some real distance between them and any potential problem.

"Hey! Who goes there?" A voice shouted.

I spoke too soon.

They had been spotted. Jack stayed cool, calm, and collected as he often wanted to do when panic was called for. Some scallywag on the dock had heard the sails billowing and ship creaking and had come out to inspect. The unwanted guest appeared from one of the buildings lining the port, and Jack thought that he looked a lot like a potato with features. It was dark though, he gave the spud a little leeway. He was more worried about the noise coming from the potato's mouth.

Jack stood by the taffrail, full of cocky swagger, his hand upon his cutlass, watching as the vegetable tried to chase the *Neptune* as she drifted alongside the dock.

"Nothing to see here, my good fellow, go back to sleep," Jack shouted at the troublesome tater.

"Captain! Someone's stealing the ship!" The voice filled with panic, causing Jack to perk his head up in alarm.

That's all I need. Jack held his head as if a headache was starting. He looked around, checking for any more alerted denizens of the dock, and then in the distance, a commotion was stirring.

"What's going on here? You lily-livered bastards! Who do you think you are, stealing from me? The Pirate King!" shouted the object of Jack's hatred. Blackbeard emerged from out of the governor's house, running towards the dock in a state of undress. Jack had well and truly stirred the hornet's nest now.

Shit. "Well, it could have been worse."

"How so, Jack?" Hector retorted.

"The man could have had no pants on." Jack quipped.

Hector wholeheartedly agreed with him on that point.

Jack focussed his attention on the ship's wheel. "Anney set sail for Tortuga."

"Aye, aye, cap'n."

"Let's just hope he doesn't start chasing us," Jack exclaimed to the heavens. He strolled up onto the poop deck with Hector behind him. They came to rest behind Anney, watching the scene unfold.

"You think he won't?" Hector asked him incredulously.

"Oh, I think he will, I just thought maybe if I said it, some god watching over us would be listening." Jack grinned.

Sebastian had joined them at the taffrail on the poop deck. "I think he's running for the other ship, cap'n." The scholar had a smug grin on his face.

"Well, he's going to be pleasantly surprised when he tries to set sail to catch us isn't he."

"Oh?" Questioned Hector.

Jack strained his eyes to focus on the trouble brewing as the *Neptune* moved closer to open waters. "I had Sebastian leave him a little surprise, just in case he ever dared to chase us after we repurposed his vessel."

Jack stood at the aft with Hector and Sebastian, watching all the rats scurry out of the tavern, and surrounding buildings, making a drunken run for the other docked ship. He grinned as Edward ordered his men around, shouting at them to make sail.

Only for the mainsail to be completely cut away from the mast. Leaving Blackbeard and his crew scuppered and unable to sail. Unsurprisingly, Blackbeard was fuming.

Jack was happy, and not to mention, slightly aroused. He stroked his cutlass.

Hector laughed heartily at Edward's misfortune, slapping Jack on the back.
"Good show, Jack, I should learn to trust your judgement."

"I'm going to need your support in the coming days, my friend, now more than ever. I have big plans for us." Jack mused.

Hector seemed slightly concerned. "You've proven yourself capable with this little escapade, that's for sure. But it's going to take a lot more than some pirate chicanery to do what you are planning."

"Oh, trust me, I've had five years to plan this: every eventuality, every hiccup, every turn, and twist. I just needed the right key to get through the door. Now we have it." Jack patted his jacket pocket.

"We shall see, Master Jack. We shall see."

Chapter - 9 - Starry, Starry Night.

Ariadne was peering over the edge with Seamus at her side. They were both admiring the immense mass of blue ocean underneath the *Selene*. She had been on her current course for a day and a night now, and the dawn of this new day was clear enough for them to check for any loss of mass. The edge was mostly soil, but some parts were exposed roots where she could clearly see through to the ocean. Luckily no more had dropped off in the past day that they had heard, which meant that the *Selene* was happy enough with her current motion and had decided to stay in one piece. For now.

"There they hoist us, to cry to the sea that roared to us, to sigh to the winds whose pity, sighing back again, did us but loving wrong." It was early, but she had enough energy for a witty remark.

"I didn't know you were a fan of the comedies?" Seamus grinned at her.

"It's been known for me to stray down the South Bank from time to time. Who knows, maybe Prospero is to thank for all this sorcery." She waved her hands about indicating the flying island.

Seamus laughed. "The Tempest! Excellent, my friend."

"Well, as far as I can tell, without the aid of a compass, of course, we are still making headway to the east. We followed the sun's course yesterday, and it set over the horizon in which we are moving. So I'd say that was pretty successful. Then, during the twilight hours, we've been pursuing Perseus." Ariadne asserted.

She and Seamus had taken shifts through the night to make sure they were still keeping course. Seamus had taken the first shift but had neglected to wake her upon the agreed-upon time.

"I said when the moon was at its zenith, not during its descent." She chastised Seamus.

"Ah, sorry, my friend. Forgive me, I know the past two days have been a challenge, and I need you in top shape, just in case anything untoward were to happen. You are up now, anyway. How do you feel?"

"Well rested." She smirked. "Are you going to get some rest?"

"No, I think I'll stay up a little, keep you company. The stars have been captivating me tonight. I would admire them a little longer."

"Tell me about your childhood, Seamus, entertain me of your past conquests. Dazzle me with your witty anecdotes."

Seamus laughed. "My childhood is nothing to write home about. Definitely nothing noteworthy."

"Oh come on, there must be something that happened to young Seamus. Where did you grow up? What were your friends like? Did you ever get into any shenanigans? What was your first kiss like? What were your parents like?" She quizzed him voraciously.

He sighed while stoking the fire with a branch.

"Ari."

"Hmm? Sorry, what was that?" She shook the memory from the forefront of her mind.

"That's ok, my friend, I was just saying that we should be on course if we follow the sun this day. If not, we might have to test out the steering masts." She winced. The memory of her near-death

133

experiences had not left the periphery of her memory yet. Every time she thought about it, she felt a little bit nauseous.

"Don't worry. I've been mulling this over. If we need to make minor adjustments to our course, we can twist the sail slightly. It should give us enough momentum to correct our course."

Ariadne was slightly relieved. She could handle that. "Some minor adjustments in our course should be no issue. When we reach the coast of the Sahara, we need to worry about the stability of the steering masts. Otherwise, we could end up somewhere over Africa."

"I agree, we shall consider our options when the time comes. You need not worry, though. I have faith in our ingenuity and the strength of our will to survive this." The man oozed charisma. She had no idea how he kept up his positive outlook.

"Oh, I know we will, do you know why?"

"Because my charisma is rubbing off on you?"

"Seamus, if you ever rub off on me, I will make it my goal to make sure you walk away from that encounter with your manhood detached." She stared at him with a demeanour that meant business.

Seamus was silent. He looked slightly worried. She decided that she had let the threat linger long enough and let out the laughter that was welling up inside.

"Oh! Very good, Ari. Haha." He had been defeated.

"What I meant was. The reason we are going to survive this is because I need to teach you how to hunt." She jostled him with her shoulder. "Can't hunt if we don't survive," Ariadne said matter-of-factly.

Seamus beamed at her. "When this day is over, my friend, we should know if we are on course."

She pulled herself away from the edge; it was almost mesmerizing watching the water far below, with the low hum of the *Selene* in the background. Ariadne had grown to love the sound of the wind blowing through the trees, the leaves rustling as the forest raced over the ocean. She pulled Seamus back from the edge and helped him back up on his feet.

"Thank you. Shall we try some of that delicious deer you hunted for us?"

"Oh, for us, is it?" She cocked an eyebrow at the captain.

He was growing wise to her sassiness. She could tell because he didn't miss a beat. "But of course! I shall help skin it and prepare it, I can at least do that since you went to all the trouble of catching it." She grinned

"That's mighty kind of you, Seamus."

"Err, just one thing?" Seamus looked a little embarrassed.

"Oh?"

"I'm not quite sure how to do those things," he said sheepishly.

Ariadne laughed heartily to any god that was listening. "Don't you worry, my friend, I shall teach you."

* * *

Ariadne sat back at camp, the deer roasting on the makeshift spit. Seamus sat watching it intently. He had done a good job, he was a bit squeamish at first, which was hilarious, but he really got into it. Maybe he wouldn't be so bad at hunting after all. It was midday, and she was going over the journals again, checking out the diagrams.

"Some of these sketches are quite entertaining. There are some diagrams here of using the new oak to build ships of the line. Can you imagine? A fleet of flying ships, under the command of King Charles. No enemy would be able to defend against that. Especially not the French."

"Powerful ideas. Let me have a look."

Ariadne showed him the images from the journal. "Oh my, she is beautiful. Who knows, one day we may all be commanding a flying ship of our own." The *Selene* rumbled. "Not one as good as you, old girl." Seamus patted the ground. Ariadne was staring into the fire that was roasting the deer, her mind wandering.

"I actually grew up in Deptford. Naval family, you see. Had to be close to where the ships were being built. You never know when there's a war on. After that, it was Chatham. We moved around a lot. I lose track in my head sometimes."

"I can sympathise with that; we moved around a lot too. Didn't get much chance to make friends. My grandmother helped with that, though; she kept me entertained with various things to learn, things a child would think boring."

Seamus looked melancholy. "Aye, well, I had my time filled up with learning too, but it wasn't the kind that you had the freedom to explore. My time was spent preparing me for a place in His Majesty's navy. I didn't have the luxury of keeping friends. Not that there was any time to make them between moving." Seamus seemed resentful of that fact.

"What about your mother and father?" She asked Seamus.

"Mother, oh, I do have fond memories of her. She was always there, if ever I had a scrape, she would pick me up. If ever I had a question, she would do her best to answer it." He seemed lost in a sea of memories.

"What about your father?"

"Father was hardly there; he was off defending the country from whichever enemy the country was at war with. He'd return from time to time, though. Always to make sure I was learning my constellations or learning regulations. Then as quick as he would appear, he would be gone just as fast."

"At least you had a father, even if he was there for some of the time. I don't remember mine much. Mother always talked about him as if he was there for the first years of my childhood, but I don't recall."

The ground rumbled again, snapping her out of it. Ariadne was a smidge concerned.

"I take it, you felt that too?" Seamus was on his feet. "We should check the crow's nest."

"Since when did we have a crow's nest?" Ariadne was puzzled.

"While you were off galavanting with your giant wicker ball, I thought it best to make myself useful."

"So, you crafted us a crow's nest?"

"Aye, that I did." Seamus was one sentence away from earning a usefulness point.

"Is it safe?" She braced for the answer.

"Of course, I jumped up and down on it myself." He seemed rather proud of that fact.

Point earned. "Fair enough, lead the way." She followed the inventor to his invention.

"So, you're telling me you had no friends growing up?"

"Oh no, don't get me wrong, Ari, I did have friends, briefly. But by the time I had made them, it was time to move on. It was like a cycle of renewal. I would make friends, then I would move. We had just moved to Deptford, and my mother shooed me out to go play with the children on the street. I must have been about five. I had made friends with one child, Adam. We got on really well; some might have even called us good friends. But once his real friends showed up, he became mean and threw rocks at me."

Ariadne held his hand. "I'm sorry that happened to you. Children can be real pricks."

Seamus smiled at her. "I ran into my mother crying, she was busy entertaining. I can't remember much after that. My memory is foggy when it comes to my childhood. I do apologise."

"No, it's ok, my friend. I'm glad you shared this with me."

Ariadne had followed Seamus all the way to the mainmast. They both stood at the base, staring up.

"Magnificent isn't she!" Seamus was exuberant. He had done a thing on his own that he was proud of, and she could tell. He was the same when he had fitted the gaff and boom to the steering mast—full of life.

"You did good, I have to admit. May I climb into your nest?" She asked with a raised eyebrow and a slight cock of the head. Seamus looked slightly deflated. "Unless you want to mount her again?" Ariadne decided to err on the side of basic politeness.

"No, no, I shouldn't have all the fun." Seamus raised his hands, offering the climb up to her.

"As long as you're sure?" She made advances on the mast, double-checking with Seamus with each step.

"I mean, I'm sure it's safe up there." He paused like he didn't believe what he was saying.

"You're sure?" She checked a final time. "I'm just going to go ahead and climb up." She inched up the mainmast, checking Seamus' reaction every other branch.

It was a very uneventful climb. That didn't stop Seamus shouting up every foot, making sure she was good. She had learned from the last ascent she had made to secure each footing on the mainmast. Ariadne was almost past the sail; she could almost grasp the rim of the crow's nest. She took a moment to affirm her safety to the worried captain below before pulling herself up into the makeshift viewing platform.

Ariadne didn't know why, but she felt the need to double-check Seamus' safety test. She braced herself and gave a little jump. Everything was still attached. *Huh, he was right.*

The view was amazing; she could see for leagues. The vastness of the ocean surrounded her on all sides. She felt exhilarated. The wind whipped her locks into her face like a tumultuous tempest, and she was reminded of the first time she ventured into a crow's nest.

"Can you see, girl?"

Captain Smith had done Ariadne's mother the honour, or so he put it, taking her under his wing. She was only nine, but it had been decided that her unruliness could only be rectified at sea. After her Grandmother's passing, there was no one but her mother to contend with a wild child- so she was sent to her Uncle -Captain of the Greenwich.

It went as expected at first. She ran circles around him on the main deck while trying to chastise her for unruly behaviour. So it was no surprise that when her uncle asked her not to climb the mainmast, whilst they were fleeing from a Dutch fleet, that she did anyway. They had been at sea for what had seemed forever to a little girl, but more like three weeks. Their vessel had been in the process of being stalked. Although, it seemed that they had been blessed with the will of Poseidon because they had caught a wind that had allowed them to outrun their stalkers. Or so they hoped.

She had climbed into the crow's nest to double-check they weren't hiding over the horizon. It was very windy, and the climb was exhaustive, but she made it. During the climb, she realised why no one else had attempted it, while the wind tried it's very best to pull her off.

"Well?" Her uncle shouted up to her?

"I see them, Captain, just on the horizon. They must have caught the same wind." She heard a lot of cursing from below. "Language, Uncle. What would your sister say?" She might have been a headstrong nine-year-old, but she was a sassy one at that.

"All is not lost, Captain, I see a reef to the east. Perhaps we can scupper them on that, or at least slow them down."

"Excellent idea, Ari."

"Ari? What do you see?" Seamus shouted up at her.

She strained her eyes to check the horizon in the direction the *Selene* was headed. *Is that?* She could hardly believe what her eyes were seeing. *No, it couldn't be.* Ariadne wiped the tiredness from her eyes. *It is.* "Land ho!"

"What? You can't be serious, my friend, we've been at sea for what? A day and a half, going by the sun." Seamus hadn't believed her because she could hear the sound of disbelief shimmying up the mast to join her.

Ariadne scooted over carefully, still unsure of Seamus' engineering, allowing him to join her in the crow's nest. They both stood in silence as the two friends watched the mass on the horizon growing bigger.

"I can scarcely believe it. How can this be?" Seamus still couldn't believe his own eyes.

Ariadne mused over the questions hanging in the sea air. "I can only fathom that perhaps the mass of the forest and the speed with which we have covered the leagues are *not* comparative to a migrating bird."

"That must be some kind of record," Seamus exclaimed excitedly.

"Should we perhaps start turning?" She hadn't had time to process the dreaded 'steering masts'. It was inevitable though, that they would have to use them. Sooner rather than later.

Seamus sensed her hesitation. "We should wait. We could be off course. It may be an uncharted island. When we get closer, we should be able to tell if we have hit the West Coast of Africa from the Saharan dust."

"Let's head down and make our way over to the forecastle. We'll be able to see the land without the fear of falling to our doom from your construction." She chanced a quip at Seamus' expense.

"I would stake my life on the sturdiness of my crow's nest." He stated adamantly. She watched as he rattled the rail of the platform, only for it to wobble beneath their feet.

They both froze in place.

"Yes, well, maybe we should get down. Lead the way, my friend." Seamus hurried her down as the crow's nest creaked in a nerve-racking chorus.

Whether it was the excitement of land being sighted, or the need to get to safe ground urgently, Ariadne reached the floor quicker than she ever had. She practically slid down the tree, with Seamus following shortly. She and the captain made their way to the forecastle in double time, racing through the sea of oaks, jumping over exposed roots.

Ariadne raced from the main deck as fast as her little legs could carry her. The crew was bracing for impact. The scuppering hadn't worked, and the Dutch fleet had gained on them. Her uncle in his boldness decided that if he was going down it would be with a fight. So he had turned to face them.

It had been quite a heroic last stand so far. The Greenwich had snapped the mast of the Olifant, which had been left in the distance. Smith had then rammed the Dolphijn and pushed the damn ship into the reef. It was beautiful. The real struggle came when the Hollandia appeared from nowhere, blasting her eighty-two dutch cannons into the broadside of the Greenwich.

The Greenwich was no match for the Hollandia. As she fired upon their vessel, the crack of the cannons would always stick in her memory as the most frightening thing she had ever heard. Her uncle decided to do the only thing left in his repertoire. Board her. It seemed a bold move, especially to young Ariadne.

"Brace for impact," the captain shouted as he steered the Greenwich into the enemy's broadside.

She remembered it like it was yesterday. The ship rattled like it had just been hit with a considerable squall as the two collided. Splinters and debris flying everywhere. Men shouting, the crack of pistols and the sharp ringing of steel on steel. The smell of smoke and blood tainting the air. It felt like it was never going to end, but then it did. As she opened her eyes, her uncle stood over her.

"Get up, Ari. You need to see this." He seemed exhausted, the adrenaline was wearing off.

"I said, you need to see this, Ari." Seamus was excitable. He had reached the forecastle first.

Ariadne broke through the treeline to be greeted with a lovely view of the ever-increasing landmass on the horizon. The air had a slight tinge of redness to it which she had not seen before. She held her hand up to try and feel the hazy air, but then it dawned on her what she was looking at. She had noticed flecks of yellow sand in the dirt. They were on course. They had hit Africa. She beamed at Seamus.

"We made it my friend!" The two friends embraced as they jumped up and down in celebration.

"We need to steer the *Selene*, Seamus, so that the coastline is on our starboard."

"Good catch, I almost forgot, in all the excitement. To starboard!"

She followed Seamus along the perimeter of the island, the Sahara coastline looming in the distance behind them. Ariadne's mind wandered back to Seamus' late night revelations.

"What about mischief? You must have put your mother through some nightmares?"

Seamus smiled. "Aye, I got myself in some scrapes. I was chased by the neighbour's children once, I'd grown tired of their bullying, so I'd decided to stick up for myself. Can you imagine, Ari, a scrappy young rake of a man standing there bold as day telling ten other children to go bother someone else."

"Oh, aye," she giggled. "What happened?"

"Well, they didn't back down, that's for sure. They chased me through Chatham docks, hurling abuse, and stones to boot. They were fast, but I was faster. I managed to crawl through the gates of some old dock while they busied themselves searching for me."

"I'm glad." She smiled at Seamus. She had started to feel a little sorry for young Seamus, but it had also allowed her a window into why Seamus was like he was now. He'd never really had friends growing up, and his eagerness to make up for that now was reflected in how he ran his ship.

"It wasn't all bad. I had stumbled upon a place where I could be at peace, somewhere I could study alone and not be chased by gangs of youths. Watching the masts travel over the horizon day after day was soothing. It was a place lost to time, that no one needed anymore, no one except me anyway."

The boom spar of the steering mast peeked around the corner, looming over the edge of the island, as they raced along the edge of the forest. It was finally time to test whether they had it in them to turn the *Selene*.

Seamus could see the apprehension in her eyes. "Don't you worry, I have faith. They will work, my friend."

"And if not?"

"Then, we will get through this together, you and I." He placed a hand on her shoulder in reassurance.

The Seamus of old had gone. He had been replaced with this new creature that was trying its very best to look after her. To be worried when she was hurt. To make sure she made it home in one piece. She felt as though she didn't have to deal with everything herself anymore. She had a friend in this world that would be by her side no matter what. Whether they found themselves marooned on an island together, or flying a floating forest towards the African coast. He would be there.

"Let's get this sail unfurled." She went to grab the ropes they had attached to the sail to extend it out. Seamus grabbed the other.

"Together." She smiled.

Ariadne watched as the sail made its way between the two spars to its full extent, the wind pushing at the cloth as it did. The gaff and the boom were staying put. They were working.

Seamus was grinning, "See? I told you they would work."

"Now we just need to see that they turn the *Selene.* Then we can celebrate."

The two of them stood in front of the sail, watching the coastline in the distance.

"There!" Seamus was the first to spot it. "She's moving, slowly but surely. Can you see it, Ari?" He jumped up, punching the air. "Huzzah!" He was so happy, it was good to see. She felt that they had been through so much that a turn of good luck was in order.

She could see it, the *Selene* was slowly moving as they flew closer to land. The coastline was drifting to the right of them, to their starboard. She was so relieved.

As soon as she could see the ocean in front of them, she knew it was time to reel the sail back in. "I think that should be enough, shall we pull it in?"

"I think that would be wise. We don't want to turn back on ourselves." He grinned.

They both started to pull the sail in. "You love it up here, it's really brought out the swashbuckler in you. I think you'd enjoy another trip back and forth."

He laughed heartily. "That I would. But we have business to attend to first. That and a particular someone promised to take them hunting." He raised his eyebrows in her general direction.

The *Selene* started to rumble again like it had hit another squall. The oak creaked and cracked with the change in pressure, and suddenly, the boom ripped away from the tree with a terrible crunch, the sail in tow behind it. The wind flung the spar directly towards Ariadne. She had no idea what to do. She had done what she promised to never do and let the panic seep in. Ariadne was now frozen on the spot as she braced for impact.

As if from nowhere, Seamus barged her out of the way. The log continued on its path and whacked him straight across the chest, knocking him unconscious, before hurtling into the sky.

She picked herself up and rushed to his side. He wasn't breathing. She panicked; she had no idea what to do. She started beating on his chest. "Wake up, damn you, this isn't over, you don't get to die." Ariadne searched her mind; she needed to find the answers. She needed to save him.

"You see this, Ari. This is what happens when you back a Smith into a corner."

Young Ariadne stared wide-eyed at the death and destruction around her. Men were milling around the main deck, picking up the enemy fallen, throwing them overboard. Cannons were being pushed back into place, and mooring hooks were being removed.

"My first thoughts were for the crew, Ari. When I knew we were being stalked, I put them first. I fled so that they might survive. Always remember that life is worth preserving. Never go into battle against an overwhelming number. Unless you have to. If you are backed into a corner, go hard or go home. Never panic in the face of adversity, stay calm, keep your thoughts collected. That's how a Smith has survived for many generations, and that's why the Smiths will live on for years to come. Now help make ready for sail. You did good today, Ari, your father would have been proud." He patted her on the shoulder.

Ariadne breathed, she could feel the anxiety welling up in her, but she needed to store it away for later. She had things she needed to do right now.

Breath in and out. Focus.

She checked his heartbeat. It was weak, but still there. She tried to recall her training, her mind raced, a piece of literature she was given once she passed her Lieutenant's exam wandered into her mind. A french manual directing one in the art of an experimental technique called resuscitation, but that was for drowning victims. She figured that this was the same principle. Seamus had stopped breathing.

Ariadne tilted his head back to make sure his airway was open. She pinched his nose, took a deep breath, and placed her lips on his, exhaling into his lungs. *Nothing.* She tried again. *Still nothing.* "Breathe damn you, Seamus!" Again, she filled his lungs, and she was beginning to lose hope. The moments of breathlessness dragged, she thought that it was over, her efforts were in vain. Seamus was gone.

Seamus stirred, his eyes flickered, and a small groan left his lips. The emotion that had been welling up inside Ariadne's chest finally came crashing out. She was so relieved. "Are you ok?" He mumbled at her.

"What?" She wiped her tears away.

Seamus coughed, clearing his throat. "I said, are you ok, Ari?"

She laughed. Here he was nearly lost to the world, and all he was bothered about was her. She sighed. "Aye, I'm okay, Captain. You?"

"Maybe just a little bit sore, nothing too major. Just need to walk it off." He winced in pain as he laughed. Ariadne moved to comfort him.

"You just stay still for a little while, there's no rush to get up." She sat by his side, stroking his hair.

"Did we make it, Ari?"

"Aye, we did. *Selene* is on course for England."

Seamus relaxed a little. "You did good…proud of you."

"Shh, get some rest." A tear rolled down Ariadne's cheek. *Stop, he's ok.* She sighed with relief.

"Ok, just going to have a little rest. Just a few moments." He dozed off while the African coastline passed them by as they made their way North.

Chapter - 10 - Forming the Fellowship.

"Sebastian, that was so good, I do believe my breeches got a little tight." Jack was in such a good mood. He despised Edward bloody Teach, and he had just stolen a ship from under the bastard's nose, leaving him with a red face to go with his lady-like curls. *Thanks to this magnificent rapscallion!* He pounced on Sebastian, rubbing his head for any luck that might care to fall his way.

Sebastian laughed. "Get off ya...lily-livered strumpet."

Bless him, he tried. Seamus grinned. "Is that colourful language spouting from those lips? I do declare, my good sir." He bowed to the scholar.

Sebastian bowed back, "I thank you, my good sir."

He revelled in his mischievous deviants, enjoying their high spirits, while they horsed around on deck, even Hector was smiling. They had unfurled the full complement of sails and were making good headway back to the *Kingston*. He was surprised Teach hadn't made any extra attempt to follow them. At least not yet. The man was such a scallywag, he wouldn't put anything past him - with good reason.

Jack watched as Anney and Sebastian danced around the mainmast.

He had no intention of souring his mood with thoughts so wretched. The rest of the night was for revelling because as soon as they had reunited with the *Kingston*, they would be on their way towards the English Channel. Plenty of time to be wary of slippery eels like Teach worming their way into his plans.

Hector had returned from his rummaging. "I found some rum in the captain's quarters, some la-de-da officer of His Majesty's navy liked the good stuff."

"Oho! Excellent find, my friend, and some glasses? Fancy." Jack was pleased that there was something to take his mind off that turd.

The old sailor was a very resourceful man that was one of the things Jack liked about him. That and being a piece of his past that he wanted to keep secret--as did they both. Hector poured some of the sweet liquor into one of the fancy glasses and passed it along to him. He then poured a glass for both Anney and Sebastian. They had both sniffed the rum in the air and had decided that dancing was an activity best enjoyed with said rum in their bellies.

"A toast to the new ship, Captain," he asked Jack.

Jack raised his full glass in the air, spilling some of the contents all over the poop deck. The rest of the skeleton crew remained silent. Waiting.

"To dastardly deeds and daring escapes!" The four friends all cheered with much vim and vigour

"Huzzah!" The rum had gone straight to Sebastian's head.

"I would bless our new ship on the voyages, and the battles, in which she is about to partake...under my loving touch, of course." He stroked the ship's wheel.

Sebastian groaned. "Get a room, that man!"

Jack and the others laughed heartily.

* * *

Hector had taken the wheel of the *Neptune,* while Jack and Anney were at the aft. They were sharing the port bottle Sebesatian had pilfered from the other ship. He was currently questioning the old sailor about his lineage, leaving him and Anney to have that heart to heart he had meant to have with her.

"They grow up so fast, don't they? I remember when he couldn't even hold his liquor. Now, look at him. Talking Hector's ear off, no comfy barrel in sight."

Anney laughed as she took another swig of the port and past the bottle to Jack.

He turned to face her, brushing those fiery locks out of her face so he could get a better read on her, and as an added bonus, the moonlight reflecting off her features was giving him the horn. Which he positively intended to deal with once they had arrived back at his old ship.

"So, I wanted to talk to you truly, before we start slurring words." He was trying to be sincere, but he was finding it hard. All he could think about were several naughty positions he wanted to tire Anney out with later that morning.

Anney placed her hand on his. "I'm fine, Jack, don't you worry about me. You've promised some pretty big things, and it's going to need a lot of planning, and let's be honest, some dumb luck."

Jack offered himself up. "Funny you should mention that because big things and dumb luck is my speciality." He grinned as he cocked his eyebrow.

Jack continued, "but seriously, love, I'm not just here to be your sex slave. I can lend an ear if you need to talk things through."

Anney smirked at him, but it was just out of courtesy. He knew that because as she took another swig out of the bottle, it slowly faded away. "I hurt that woman, Jack. We both did five years ago. Now, look at her, shacking up with that prick, doing God knows what in the east. I don't know what I expected to find when we got here, I just wanted her to be ok, happy."

"She did seem like she was having a good time." He knew it was a mistake the moment it left his lips.

She gave him her best incredulous scowl.

He raised his hands in defence. "I know, love. What could we have done, though? Stolen her away? We'd have had Teach on our aft for sure. Then what?"

She sighed. "I don't know. Jack, if it were anyone else. It's bloody Edward Teach. He's as rascally as they come and a black heart to boot. She did seem loved up though, don't you think?"

"If it were anyone else, we wouldn't be having this conversation," he affirmed. "Mary's a big girl, Anney, she can look after herself. She has done so since we've known her. She never took shit from anyone while we were around, she certainly won't now."

"Aye, you're right. Mary will be fine, God help Teach if he ever rubs her up the wrong way." She seemed satiated by the conversation.

Jack looked mischievous. "Speaking of rubbing up," he shouted. "Did I tell you that Sebastian came on to me while we were sneaking through Monte Christi?" He jumped on the scholar. "I don't think he could handle this, though, do you, Anney?"

Anney giggled alongside Hector as he rode Sebastian around the poop deck like a horse. When he charged his trusty steed at Anney, he noticed something from the aft in the distance. Something faint. Something on the horizon.

"Hold fast, Sebastian." He jumped down and tried to shake the fog from his mind.

"What's going on, Jack?" Anney was searching where he was staring.

"Hopefully nothing, love. I thought I saw something in the distance. A light maybe." He was sure he saw something; it wasn't there now.

Anney sniffed the bottle. "Maybe it was just the port, it's quite strong stuff."

"Yeah, maybe." Jack wasn't convinced. He decided to stand vigil at the aft of the *Neptune* until they had reached the *Kingston*. He didn't want to leave anything to chance, especially after their escapades in Monte Christi.

* * *

It was almost time for Helios to ride his horse-drawn chariot over the Caribbean sky. The sun's rays had already begun to poke forth from the briny deep, as Jack kept watch over the horizon to the aft of the *Neptune*. Anney was making herself comfortable in his new bed, while Hector had scuttled away to his own little corner of the ship. Apparently, he had already moved his things to this ship for the journey he would have been making with Mary. Sebastian had taken the wheel and was manoeuvring her around the isle of Tortuga to their destination.

"Spot any more lights, cap'n?" Sebastian was yawning. It had been a long night.

"Nothing yet, my friend." He was tired too. The concentration had drained him.

"Could have been a passing ship, perhaps?" the scholar mused.

"Perhaps. Tell me, Sebastian, I've had a chance to mull over a few thoughts during our journey. What we are about to do is going to be very difficult, but the outcome will be very rewarding. I need to make sure that everyone is invested in the plan and that our motives are aligned. Hector, his vow binds him to us. His order can be trusted. I know his kind, they do not sway easily, and they are loyal to their house. Anney and I grew up in the same lands, from different Houses, yes. But we share the same passion, the same goals. I know this to be true because I know the woman. But you, Sebastian, you are the wild card. I would know your true intentions."

"That's a reasonable desire, cap'n." Sebastian continued to steer the ship.

Jack watched as he thought about his words carefully.

"Tell me, we stole you off some vessel heading to the Americas. Why haven't you tried to escape?" Jack questioned him.

Sebastian laughed. "While it is true, I have thought about it, and had many opportunities to run away, yet still I remain."

Jack tried to dig a little deeper. "But why? This is what I need to know. If we are to align on this venture together, I must know that you aren't going to run off when I need you the most."

"Have you forgotten that I was a scholar when you dragged me off the *Artemis*? You and I have found this thing; it defies all logic, all the things I have read in my books. I must follow this thread, I must be there when the curtain is pulled back."

Jack laughed. "So, it's knowledge you seek?" This is why you have not run away?"

"Not entirely. I considered running the first chance I got in Monte Christi, but Edward put a scupper in that plan. I must admit, I did have designs on returning for the contents of that chest we buried. Then, following my own path home and demanding answers from the King."

He couldn't believe what he was hearing. "It's very bold of you to reveal this to me, Sebastian. Why didn't you?"

The scholar thought long and hard. "It was you, Jack, you inspired me that night in the caves under Monte Christi with your tales of land once lost that could still be reclaimed. Your home, your family, your heritage. These are all things that I take for granted, and to hear you speak passionately about taking them back from the French, well, your zeal swayed me."

"I always was good at rousing the men." He smugly polished his lapel.

Sebastian hadn't finished. "It wasn't just that which stopped me from running."

"Oh?" Jack was intrigued.

He watched as Sebastian fought with the words. "As good as you are at speeches, you make a better friend than a jailor. You stopped berating me and threatening me with a beating and started treating me like a companion, as a confidant. I will always appreciate that, even if you did kidnap me from my own vessel."

Jack was impressed, never had he heard so much honesty from one man. *Nay a friend.* He was satisfied with Sebastian's answers.

"You know, you're still not too big for a smacked bottom?"

Sebastian smiled. "Of course, cap'n."

"I would be very upset with you if you double-crossed me, my friend, so don't." He grasped Sebastian's forearm to seal the bond.

Sebastian gripped his forearm tight. "Deal, just promise me one thing, Jack."

"What's that?"

"That you will teach me the most important knowledge of all." Jack's eyes grew wide as he drew in closer.

"Which is?" Jack was concerned he could not promise something he did not know.

"I've always wanted to know the secrets to charm the female of the species."

Jack laughed. "You need not bother with that, my friend, they are a troublesome lot."

He and Sebastian laughed as Anney emerged from below them onto the main deck.

"What are you lads conspiring about?" She spoke with a half yawn, half stretch.

"Oh, nothing really. Sebastian wishes to know how to talk dirty to women."

Sebastian was flabbergasted.

Without missing a beat, Anney replied. "Then he shouldn't come to talk to you. Sebastian, you come to me if you need to learn that particular art." She said with a straight face.

Sebastian laughed heartily while Jack had been mortally wounded. Sebastian's eyes lit up.

"Ship ahoy, cap'n! It's the *Kingston*."

Jack stopped pretending to be mortally wounded and raced to the forecastle. "Aye, there she is, Anney, in all her glory. Right where we told her to wait."

"You best signal her, Sebastian. Otherwise, she'll take us for an actual merchant vessel, the crew will try to mount us." He could never fail to keep Sebastian on his toes.

The scholar was panicking. "What are you going to do?"

"Anney and I are going to do some catching up." Jack grabbed hold of Anney's hand.

"But what if they don't see me, and they just start firing?" Sebastian's tone reached a greater level of panic.

"Pray they see you, I suppose. I have faith in you, my friend."

Jack waltzed off to his new quarters dragging along a more than pliable Anney.

* * *

"We nearly fired on ya, Jack! Had it not been for ya man waving his arms about like a flailing squid, we wouldn't have recognised ye." The crew was more than happy to see their Captain back.

"Aye, lads, we had a spot of trouble back in Monte Christi. On account of their being a scurvy bilge rat there, going by the name of Edward Teach." The crew all spat on deck. He smiled.

"It's good to have ya back, cap'n, the crew was worried about ya." Jack loved his crew, they were such bastards when it came to pirating, but they really were the most loving that Jack had the pleasure of sailing with.

"It's good to be back, my friends. I have missed you all dearly." Jack bowed to his audience. "How do you like her?" He motioned to the *Neptune*.

"She's a fine ship captain. To whom do we owe the honour of bestowing this beauty upon us."

"Stole her from right underneath Teach's nose!" He revelled in the piratical bastards' whooping and yelling in happiness.

"Came running after me with his breeches around his ankles, he did!" He embraced another round of raucous laughter.

"Thank you, thank you." He bowed profusely.

"What now, captain?" The crew was all waiting with bated breath for their next order.

Jack thought for a moment. "Now we have some business to attend to, and I'm going to need you to listen to me till the end. For we are about to take a long journey, but it will make us all wealthy men. That I can promise you."

"Of course, cap'n, whatever it is you want us to do, we got your back." That made him smile internally.

"I'm glad to hear that, my friends. Truly." Jack stepped back on board the *Kingston*. He brushed his way through the men placing his hands on each of their shoulders as he passed. Affirming their worth with a look he had perfected over the past five years. "Each one of you here has proven to me time and again your skills as a sailor, a pirate," he turned to one of the sailors in the crowd, "a lover." They let out a burst of hearty laughter while ribbing the singled out sailor.

Once the laughter had died down, he continued, "I hope that I too have proven that you can count on me as your leader, your captain, your counsel." He walked over to the ship's mainmast and mounted a crate so he could take them all in. "I feel we share a bond, you and I, that nothing would dare break. We have protected each other through war!" The crew cheered. "Through politics," they roared with all the breath they could muster. "I have fought, and I have bled, till there are no more enemies at our gates," he bellowed into the crowd, "and I have done this by every one of your sides," the crew were in the palm of his hands, he could feel it with every cheer. "As God as my witness, I would bring you all back from the very brink of Davy Jones' locker, *my friends!*"

Jack attempted to quiet the men with his hands. He allowed the huzzahs to die down to a low rumble.

"Now I call upon you, *my friends*, for it is I who is at the brink, it is I who has enemies to fight at the gates. My home lies in tatters! Ripped to pieces by hungry kings. They say we are nothing! These kings flick us off their boots like we are dirt, and they send privateers to seek us out and blast us to hell." The rumble of the crowd was intensifying. "Do you know what I say? I say we show them what us pirate bastards are made of!" The crew was riling each other up. "I say we take the fight to them!"

The cheer was deafening - he had won them over. Anney, Hector, and Sebastian revelled in the emotion.

It was good to be back.

* * *

Jack stood with Anney, on the poop deck, watching the crew cheering and drinking till their heart's content. "It's good to be back in friendly waters."

"Aye, right you are love, you can't beat a nice bit of sneaking about in the dark, though, that's where you and I have all our fun." He grinned at her.

"To *sneaking about in the dark*!" Their cups collided in unison.

Jack sighed; he was searching for the right words.

"You good?" Anney took a swig from her cup.

"I don't know how to put this, Anney, but I'm in love with another woman." Anger flashed across her face.

"She has curves in all the right places, the way she feels under my touch, she's just so smooth and tender." Her face was almost as bright as her hair.

"Who is she, Jack? I'll kill her!" Jack tried to defend himself from the blows.

"But the thing I love most about her is the way she glides through the water, it's just so... rhythmic." He burst out laughing.

Anney walloped him. "Ya bastard, Jack, You're talkin' about the damn ship, aren't ya?" She scowled at him as he continued keeling over in hysterics.

As soon as he had overcome that, he returned to his first love. "Now, Anney, you know you're the only one for me. You will always have a place here." He took hold of her hand and placed it on his chest. "You feel that, love. It beats for you." There was no anger in her face anymore, just pure wanton desire. "That's why I want you to have the *Kingston*." He loved how the look of surprise took over her face so quickly. "You sail her better than I, anyway."

She chanced a grin "Aye that I do. It's about time you gave me the ship. He and I have been getting better acquainted over the years."

"Oh, it's him, is it? Last I checked *she* still had tits on the figurehead." He loved the back and forth they had.

"Aye, well, that's the first thing I'll be buying when we get paid - a lovely carved merman to adorn my ship." She playfully retorted.

"Well, I hope you two are happy together!" He let the silence hang in the air until he could leave it no longer. They burst out in laughter together.

"Seriously, though, we've got a long journey ahead of us. Perilous, some might say. I have faith, though, we will win our home back, Anney. Together."

* * *

Jack stood on the aft of the Kingston, taking in *her* curves one last time before Anney added a penis to her. His piratical bastards had drunk themselves to sleep. One last huzzah before the journey began, he had no idea when they would get another chance. His inner circle was solid. He knew where their allegiances lay. He knew they would see this through to the end. Whenever that may be. His crew were behind him no matter what, he would need them in the coming days. All that remained was to keep an eye on that worrying light on the horizon. His watch continued.

Chapter - 11 - Welcome to Merry Ol' England.

Ariadne had spent a good portion of the morning tinkering with Seamus' crow nest while he rested at camp. She wasn't getting up in that deathtrap without her own reassurances. Ariadne had climbed up in the early hours before Seamus had awoken and fitted some extra spars and bindings to secure the platform. Now completely satisfied, even passing the fabled jump test, she chanced an attempt to complete her goal. The good thing about being this high up was that one could see for miles - more so than from an ordinary ship's nest. So she was up there from the crack of dawn looking for landmarks, making sure their path stayed true.

Come on, I know you're out there, I can practically smell the worship.

She had moved a lot when she was young, as she had told Seamus. She didn't go into the breadth of her travels, though. Ariadne only vaguely remembered the place, but before she left with her uncle, she and her grandmother would make a pilgrimage to the west coast of Portugal every year. There, high up on the Sintra Mountains was a lone monastery. She enjoyed the trip, but the only real details she could remember were her grandmother telling her that the Order of St Jerome took them in. Her grandmother would never tell her why, only that she was too young to understand.

Now she was searching for the place to make sure they hadn't strayed too far off course. *Shouldn't be too hard.* She had spotted the Canary Islands. From this high up, the paradise islands looked rather romantic. *Let someone else get trapped on them. I've had my fair share of paradise islands.* There was also the constant threat presented by the Barbary Corsairs. A set of pirates that were more twisted than Blackbeard. They had plagued those isles for damn near a hundred years. *Imagine if I commanded an airship, there would be nowhere those scurvy pirates could hide.*

The *Selene* ploughed through the clouds, wisps curled up the billowing sails. Suddenly, the sky came into view as the floating island burst out of the other side. Ariadne could see the sea now, and the coastline. She scanned it closely, looking for those distinctive features. A grin spread across her face. There it was. Amidst a sea of green, those whitewash walls and spires, that place of pilgrimage. The memory of the building, and her visits, clearer now that she had chanced a better look at it.

"Not that I don't appreciate the adventure, Grandmother, but why do we come here every year? We walk up the mountain, through the forest, and into the monastery. I play with the nuns while you talk to Monks."

"Oh child, there's so much you don't know. So much, you don't understand. One day, when you are older, I will tell you of your family's origins. Until then, we will make this pilgrimage together, because I want you to remember this."

"Remember what, Grandma?"

She mused for a moment while choosing her words carefully. "That some legacies are worth saving. The Order of St Jerome is dying; every year, there are fewer monks, who will remember them, who will remember us, Ari? We travel here every year so that we may keep each other's legacies alive. So that one day, when you are old enough, you can continue both."

The wind whipped the sail, rousing Ariadne from her thoughts. They were almost home. She had calculated that it had taken them a day and a half to reach the coast of Africa. The sun had been just past its zenith. The distance they needed to travel to England was roughly two-thirds of that -- *As the crow flies, of course*. If the *Selene* had made it to the coast of Portugal overnight, that had to mean that they were at least half a day from the Channel. Meaning that she should be back in her own bed by nightfall. *I need to tell Seamus.*

She clambered out of the crow's nest and carefully moved down the mast past the sail. The morning light grew dim as she breached the canopy and made the descent of the support tree with great caution. After Seamus' accident yesterday, they didn't need two people out of action -- especially this close to home.

Ariadne needed to collect something first. She had set up a little experiment of her own towards the forecastle, and it had proved quite effective. She was only disappointed that she hadn't thought of it in those first days of parched throats and cracked lips. She made her way to the front of the *Selene*, where a plethora of palm leaves were arranged near the edge of the island. She hoped to be able to collect moisture since they had been travelling through clouds daily.

Sure enough, much to her jubilation, the leaves were a veritable source of water droplets. All Ariadne had to do was curve them, then gently pour them into the cups she had found. She had seen them when she went to check on the botanist's earthy home for more intelligence. She carefully curved the palm leaf to her mouth and watched as the raindrops collected in the centre of the frond then raced down to her waiting lips. Elation spread across her face as her thirst was finally quenched. She hadn't realised how thirsty she had become until the first gulps touched the back of her throat.

She quickly collected some more water in one of the cups, repositioned her leaves, and made her way back through the forest to Seamus, a smile spread across her face.

"Why are you smiling, child?"

"A knight gave me a flower, Grandmother."

"A knight? What would a knight be doing all the way up here?"

"He said that he was here on a pilgrimage. His eyes were so blue! His hair, golden curls. He said that he was in the Order of the Brass Roses."

Her grandmother seemed reluctant to believe her own ears. "What did you say?"

"Oh, Grandmother, his eyes were as blue as the ocean, and his hair golden…"

Selene held out her hand to silence Ariadne. "Focus, child. Did the knight mention the Brass Roses?"

Ariadne shook the stars from her eyes and focussed. "Yes, he said he was from the Order of the Brass Roses. Why?"

Selene looked at the monk she had been talking to with a look she had never seen in her grandmother's eyes. If she had been a bit older, she might have recognised it. Hope.

As she got up to see the knight for herself, Selene stood still in her tracks. The Brass Rose was standing in the doorway, all smiles and valour, with their arms stretched open. "Lady Francis, as I live and breathe, it is good to see a familiar face, and one as beautiful as yours."

Ariadne had never seen her grandmother blush, but her cheeks seemed to beam as red as the rose crest on the knight's chest. She embraced him as Ariadne stood there, jealously, wishing she was embracing him too. Then a thought crossed her mind.

"Grandmother, why does the knight call you Lady Francis? Your name is Selene Smith."

The knight looked over to Ariadne, a calculating look in his eyes. "You must be little Ari." He stroked her hair. Now she was blushing. "The last time I saw you, child, you were still crawling on the floor. It is good to see you took your grandmother's looks."

"I do not remember your face, but it is good to see you again, Sir Knight. Will you sit and eat with us? You must tell us what you are doing here. Where are you headed?" Ariadne was eager to learn more about the man.

"She has your manners, Selene. Looks like you are teaching the girl well." Selene smiled at the man.

"Of course, it would be an honour, my lady." The knight bowed in acceptance. "I'm here for the same reasons you and Lady," he looked to Selene for the correct name.

"Smith."

"Lady Smith and I come here to remember. To preserve." The knight turned solemn as he became introspective.

Ariadne remembered the words her grandmother had used. "To keep our legacies alive."

The knight looked up from the ground and smiled at her; she swooned at his dimples. "You have the right of it, Ari. As for where

I'm headed. I'm heading to the new world, to return when the time is right. This land holds no place for people of my creed."

Selene seemed sad as she placed a hand on the knight's pauldron. "Won't you keep two ladies company for a few days? Tell us of your travels?"

The knight smirked. "It would be my pleasure."

"Would you like some water? The climb up must have been tiresome."

Seamus roused from his slumber. The cup Ariadne had carried from the forecastle, nestled on his parched lips. She watched as he took a sip, then a gulp, as he came around.

"How are you feeling, old man?"

Seamus spluttered as he drank the water. "I might be old, but I was still spry enough to leap to your defence, again, my lady."

"At least the log didn't knock the sense of humour out of you." She grinned at him.

Ariadne emptied the mug into his mouth, then went to sit over by the fire. "I have been back up the crow's nest to check on our surrounding landmarks."

Seamus lifted himself up on his elbows with a pained expression, his chest still feeling the knock he had taken. He cocked his eyebrow, "my tottering crow's nest?"

"Don't worry, I secured it."

"What did you see? Are we on course?" Seamus moved himself over to the fire to warm his bones.

"I was looking for a specific place near the coast of Portugal, a monastery on the Sintra Mountains. Thankfully, I found it poking out of its home in the forest. Which means we are at least flying alongside Portugal." Ariadne became lost in thought. Seeing the old place had resurfaced some old memories. Memories she hadn't realised were there, and they were uncovering questions she had never found the answers to.

"Excellent news, my friend. How long till we reach England?"

Ariadne roused herself from her thoughts. "By my estimations, *if* we stay on course, we should be able to see the white cliffs of England by nightfall."

"You jest?" Seamus didn't believe her.

"No, my friend, the *Selene* is making good headway. It took us the night to reach Portugal. We should be passing over her now."

"Over her? Are we over land now?" He seemed excited.

"Aye, the *Selene* was heading slightly into land during my last observations. The tidal winds will be brushing the coastline, pushing us along with the tide. That brings us halfway to home, at least from the Saharan Coast. Don't worry, everything will be fine. If we need to make a course correction, we can always twist the mainsail."

"Yes, I think that might be our only option. I don't think we will be able to repair the Starboard 'steering mast' in time." Seamus seemed satisfied by the progress the *Selene* was making.

Ariadne continued to be distracted by her own thoughts.

"Is aught amiss? You seem lost in your own mind this morning." Seamus seemed concerned.

She stared into the flames, warming her hands, deciding how to explain the questions she had. To her, they were long-standing questions she had from childhood. To Seamus, they would seem like gibberish with no actual context. It was a conundrum. She decided to just start with the basics.

"Seeing the monastery again brought forth some old memories, memories I thought lost to time."

"Happy memories?"

"Confusing memories. Memories that provide ponderous notions about my life, my past, my future."

Seamus reflected on her words. "You know, I am here for you. If you need help fathoming the depths of your consciousness."

"I appreciate that my friend, I'm just finding it hard to order my thoughts. I feel that there are memories below the surface tugging away at the curtain, waiting to be exposed." Ariadne's mind mulled over the memory that had recently been brought to light. "My memories of the monastery seem far more extensive than I had previously thought. The many years at sea must have pushed the information deeper, to make room for relevant memories. Tell me, have you ever heard of the Order of the Brass Roses?"

Seamus thought long and hard. "Tell me more about what you know of this order. Were they a religious order? From where do they hail?"

"Where to begin." Ariadne couldn't help but be flustered by the struggle to pull forth pertinent facts from her own mind.

"Take your time, Ari, I am not going anywhere."

Ariadne slowed her breathing and pushed her mind back to the memory. "I was but a girl of nine. My Grandmother and I would take a pilgrimage to the Sintra Mountains, yearly. To preserve our legacies, she would say. I would go because I knew a long trip at sea would get me away from chores. It was more than that for my grandmother. When I pushed her on it, she deemed me too young to understand. Only leaving me with the very vague notion that they had helped our family in the past and that we needed to remember and preserve each other's order."

"The Order of the Brass Roses?" Seamus enquired.

"No, the Order of Saint Jerome, a religious sect of monks and nuns. They ran the monastery," she clarified.

"I can see why it would be confusing, all these orders. So they helped your family in a time of great need? It seems your grandmother owed them a lot to make such a journey every year."

Ariadne continued recounting her memory. "I would talk to the nuns and play in the courtyards. We would only be there a few days a week at most. Then we would sail back to England."

"Have you ever spoken to your mother about it?" Seamus interjected.

"Mother and I have barely spoken. She has become ever more reclusive to me since my grandmother passed."

"Well, we shall figure it out together. What about this other order?"

She inhaled while she ordered the memory, then slowly exhaled. "One day, a person calling himself a knight turned up. I had thought such things a legend, but there he was, all blonde curls and blue eyes, a breastplate with a rose crest on the chest. I stood there with my bloody mouth on the floor like a lovesick pup."

"What did he say to you?"

She pushed hard, searching the memory. "The knight asked me to go tell the monks that he had arrived."

A look of understanding washed over Seamus' face. "So, he was expected." The understanding was replaced with frustration at the problems she was facing. "If we could stop the *Selene* easily, we would halt our journey to take a trip down memory lane."

Ariadne smiled, as she placed a hand on his shoulder. "A trip for later, perhaps."

"What else happened with the knight?" Seamus enquired further.

"He met with Selene, the two seemed to know each other, they acted like old friends. He was very charming. Called my grandmother Lady Francis. Which is another question my brain can't fathom." Ariadne felt a little puzzled.

"Because you are a Smith? Perhaps it is a maiden name?"

"Hmmm, maybe. Perhaps that was it. The knight told us he was there on a pilgrimage too, and that he planned to travel to the new world. That he was to return when the world was ready for people like him again." Ariadne poked the fire with a stick, causing new life to be born in the fire.

Seamus was scratching his head, his face filled with thought. "How curious. I can definitely see why this would cause you some consternation. Perhaps you should talk to your mother when we return, maybe she can help illuminate the recesses of your mind."

"If only it were that easy, my friend. She can be quite the mute on subjects when she wants to be."

Seamus seemed almost as frustrated as her. "I'm sorry I could not be as much help as I hoped. I know nothing of either order. Let it be known that I will help you uncover these mysteries, once we land on solid ground."

Ariadne smiled. "Thank you, Seamus." She placed a hand on his shoulder. "Tell me, how are you truly feeling?"

He winced as he moved his joints, testing his limits. "I can move a little better, my chest is causing me a little aggravation, but I should be ok when nightfall comes."

"That's at least some good news." She wasn't sold on his assessment. "Talk to me, Seamus. Tell me about your family. I need to hear something normal to take my mind off all this ponderous thought."

"There's not much to tell, really." Seamus stared into the fire with a blank expression.

"Is there a Mrs Hawthorne? What about a little Seamus running his mother ragged?" She chuckled at the thought.

Seamus managed a little laugh. He placed his hand to his chest, felt through the fabric to something beneath. He pulled out a locket attached to a chain around his neck and unclipped it to release the secrets inside. He gazed upon the pictures inside before removing the chain from his neck and passing the locket to Ariadne.

Seamus' face was pained and apprehensive. She hadn't seen him like this before. "My wife and child."

Ariadne looked at the portraits in the locket. "She is beautiful, Seamus, how did you get such a fair maiden?"

He chuckled lightly. "I used to be quite the catch, you know, back before the sun and wind had their way with my skin."

"And your boy, I'm glad he got his looks from his mother. I can tell he's going to be a real charmer when he grows up. What's the little heartbreaker's name?" She passed the locket back to Seamus.

"Noah," his voice cracking slightly.

"I can't believe you haven't spoken about them the entire time we have been on this island jaunt."

Seamus sighed a little, his eyes glazed over. "They are not a topic I broach lightly. I may seem a hearty individual most of the time, but there are things in my past that pain me to relive."

Ariadne felt like a fool. How had she handled that so horribly? *Ugh. The jibes.* "Seamus, I am sorry. If I had realised, I would not have poked fun. I should have picked up on your reluctance to share."
You've been with the man day and night. Why didn't you pick up on this? Curses, Ari.

176

Seamus smiled solemnly. "Do not beat yourself up, my friend. You couldn't have known. Truth be told, there is little to tell. It is just a sad chapter in my life, one that I must sometimes read again. It is good, it keeps their memory alive."

She felt awful. "Please, do not feel as though you need to share; I would not cause you pain," She paused for a moment. "If you wanted to talk about it, though, I will always be here." She shuffled up to him and rested her head on his shoulder. They both sat there, watching the flames dance. Letting the time pass.

"We were childhood sweethearts, you know. My wife and I. Remember the pier I told you that I had found? To escape my tormentors. She found me there, my place," he thought for a second, "Our place."

Ariadne raised her head from his shoulder and turned to listen. To learn. She took his hand as he continued his story.

"We would meet there frequently. You see, she too was tormented by the same bullies. *'Can I share your sanctuary?'* Those were her first words to me. Of course, I obliged. Father didn't raise a scallywag. She was beautiful, and I was silenced by her beauty. You should have seen me, I was a stuttering wreck." Seamus laughed. "Y-y-yes, of course."

Ariadne smiled at him.

"Weeks went by before I finally plucked up the courage to ask her name. *'Elsabeth.'* The floodgates of conversation now open; we would find any excuse to meet up in our place. Our past, present, and future discourse all took place here. Over the next few months, we knew everything about each other. We were quite inseparable. Talking turned to courtship, courtship to marriage, then, when the time was right, Noah came into our lives. What a bundle of joy he was."

She noticed a tear roll down his cheek. "You don't have to carry on if the pain is too much to bear."

"It's okay, Ari." He gave her hand a little squeeze.

"He was such a lively boy. The moment he was on his feet, he was off exploring. He would run circles around Elsabeth. Always asking questions, such an inquisitive mind."

"Well, at least he got something from you," Ariadne chanced.

A little smile spread across his face. "My brave boy." Seamus grew reflective.

"What happened?" She pushed.

"It was while I was away at sea, the letters came too late. Noah had been taken ill - the plague. By the time I had sailed back to be with him, they were both gone. Noah, from the black death," Seamus paused, collecting his thoughts, his voice beginning to break further. "After that, she couldn't live with herself, knowing that every time she looked at me, she would be reminded of our son. She ultimately took her own life, and I never saw them again. Just one day—one letter—and I had lost everything."

Ariadne felt the tears warm her cheeks, then patter onto her knees. "I'm so sorry, Seamus. I feel devastated for you, that you had to go through that."

Seamus leant over to console his friend. "It's fine, my dear. These things happen. It is part of life. I know that somewhere they are watching over me. Who knows, maybe some god placed them in the stars."

Ariadne had so many questions. She didn't want to berate him with them, though. They could wait; they weren't necessary. What was important was that Seamus understood the importance of keeping the memory of his legacy alive. It meant the world to him. If she ever made it back to that monastery, she would say a prayer for him and make sure to keep his legacy alive.

Ariadne felt some silence was needed to remember the dead. So they both sat there in silence, reminiscing about the fallen.

* * *

The sun had reached its zenith. The morning had been both frustrating and saddening. Yet, Ariadne felt as though her relationship with Seamus was strengthened. She had always been the strong one, the adventurous one. However, after Seamus' revelations, they had left her distraught, broken. She had looked at the pieces of his life, and for the first time in her life, felt like she wanted to just hold him -- to make everything better. At the beginning of their odyssey, she had very little respect for the man, stuck on that beach, but now she looked up to him. The man had been through hell and made it out of the other side with his sanity intact.

There were things that didn't need to be said. Things that were communicated with a knowing look or a reassuring touch. They both saw something in each other that was lacking in their own life. The need to protect, to help, to honour. These were the ideals that had been forged in this place. This was the bond that would never be broken. She would make sure of that.

Ariadne needed to check on their position. They had been talking for hours, and time was ticking away. It wouldn't be long until they would reach the channel. Ariadne stood up and rested a hand on Seamus' shoulder.

"Nearly home, my friend."

"Do you need help?" Seamus got up with a pained expression on his face.

"Not with this. I just need to check our position from the nest. You can help me with the anchor." She smiled at him as she walked off towards the mainmast.

The walk was short, she didn't really want to think. The morning had provided a mild pain in her head to form. She just needed to stay focused on their immediate goal of getting home. Once she had reached the mast she made her ascent, hopefully for the last time.

Ariadne scanned the horizon for familiar landmarks or at least some indication of their position. The *Selene* was back over water, the view from the aft was more land. They were approaching a coastline. *Going by our last position, I'd say we were over the Bay of Biscay.*

The sea was disappearing fast. She could only presume they were coming up on France if only she could spot some distinguishing feature. *There it is! The Loire river.* At least she hoped it was. She scrutinised the river further until finally, she spotted the isle of Nantes, which solidified the *Selene's* position. The only trouble was they were on the wrong side of the Loire. *A little course correction should help with that.* Ariadne took in the scenery, nothing like being on top of the world to put things in perspective. She traced the

Loire as it swept across France. Just as she was about to make her way down, she spotted a Chateau in the distance.

Dozens of Chateaux littered the river, but there was something about this one that polluted her mind with a vague recollection. It stood taller than the others around it. The architecture was similar to the rest. As the chateau grew closer, pockmarks became visible on the turrets. She tried to figure out what they were but couldn't get a good look at them. Then, as if struck by lightning. A memory. She tried to pull on it to recall it clearer, but the image seemed to be veiled with mist.

The rain dripped from Ariadne's hood as she stood holding her mother's hand. She could hear shouting in the distance. Horses galloping. She turned to her mother, who was searching, through the storm, a look of panic on her face. Her mother squeezed her hand. A horse-drawn carriage breaks through the night, the horses snorting hot breath into the cold air. Relief spreads across her mother's face.

They were warm now, the rain was not falling on their heads. The carriage bobbed along as the coachman yelled at the horses to make them gallop faster. Shots are heard in the distance. Ariadne buried her face in her mother's lap. Darkness.

Frustration spread across Ariadne's face. The more she pushed, the more the memory edged away from her mental grasp. It seemed that the recent brush with the monastery on top of the Sintra Mountains had opened the gate to more memories. Ones that had stayed locked away inside her mind. She was definitely going to have to speak with her mother about this. The other memory she could have just swept to the side, but this newly resurfaced one she needed answers for. *Why were we running? Who was hunting us? Where were we running from?*

Ariadne shook the questions from the forefront, leaving only the background in focus. Her main goal. They needed to twist the mainsail.

* * *

Ariadne stormed into camp. "I'm afraid we are on the wrong side of the Loire, my friend. We are going to have to work together to try and gybe the *Selene* - turn her so she is facing northwards. If we don't, we are likely to pass England and head straight over the Dutch Republic."

Seamus seemed concerned by Ariadne's demeanour. "What's wrong, Ari? You seem mildly perturbed. Turning the sail is one thing easily rectified, but you seem a tad on the cross side."

Her steely gaze remained. "Aye, I just need to stay focussed until we are home. More questions have arisen, but I would talk with you about them then and not now."

Whether it was the talk of home or the struggle he sensed in her voice, Seamus roused himself from the ground. He shook off the mantle of solemn invalid and replaced it with the new swashbuckling adventurer they had found on the *Selene*. Seamus flashed her a cheeky grin, his ocean-blue eyes glinting in the sunlight.

"Together, then." He followed her to the mainmast.

* * *

The sail had been tied to the yardarm, the spar running horizontally across the mast, through a similar pulley system to the 'steering masts'. Yet, instead of attaching the bottom of the sail to a boom above the treeline in a similar fashion, they had just tied the sail off to trees either side of the mast - pulling it tight. To turn the *Selene* all they had to do was untie the portside rope attached to the yardarm and turn it so that the sail formed an angle against the wind, hopefully turning the flying forest. It was sound in theory, but no one had done this with a flying forest before, so the practice would be informative. Not to mention this was all happening above the canopy.

Seamus' head peaked out of the treetops. He had climbed the tree that the sail rope was attached to and was readying himself for disaster. Ariadne was there with him, they needed to both work together to twist the yardarm and steer the *Selene*. Seamus in his infinite wisdom had prepared for this eventuality and created another crude pulley system at the top of the tree. He had wrapped some rope around the tree tightly and tied off a loop, in case they needed to turn her. The plan was to untie the ropes holding the yardarm in place and thread them through the loop so that the rope could be pulled from the ground. With the yardarm free to move, they both just needed to work the ropes to turn the sail. If she and Seamus could manage it, injuries aside, they might be able to turn the *Selene* back into the wind - and back on course.

"Are you sure this is going to work?"

"Have faith, my friend, we shall have the *Selene* back on course in but a moment."

Seamus untied both of the ropes keeping the yardarm in place, while Ariadne popped her head above the canopy to check that everything was okay.

"Nothing seems to be amiss." She felt apprehensive about the whole affair, but she was still optimistic.

"Excellent, I've threaded the ropes through the pulley system. We can head down now. If we pull one rope, it will turn the sail one way. Pull the other rope and it will turn the sail back the other way."

"Seems simple enough." She cocked an eyebrow, remembering the time he fixed the crow's nest, then wincing at the thought of the shattered steering mast to starboard.

"I know that face, oh ye of little faith, Ari!" She watched as Seamus climbed down the tree trunk, shortly following after him.

They finally reached the ground. "I can't help feeling a little horrified at what might go wrong with this contraption." She grinned.

Seamus laughed, "What can I say, my inventions require a certain vision to appreciate. One that you aren't blessed with, it seems. I'd like to see you invent something, that way I can chuckle with great voracity at its failure."

"Just you wait, my friend. Before the day is done, we shall see who is the better inventor." She patted him on the shoulder. "Which one do we pull?" She looked at the ropes before her.

She watched as Seamus traced the rope down, then took hold of the relevant rope.

"You are sure?"

"Positive."

Ariadne grabbed hold of the rope with him. "Here goes nothing." She pulled in unison with Seamus, as they both braced for disaster. The cord didn't come easy. The wind pushed the yardarm as fierce as they pulled it back. It was inching its way back to them, however. She could see that Seamus was in pain, it was taking everything she had just to take the brunt of the pulling. Eventually, they twisted the sail into an angle against the wind.

"Tie it off," she shouted to Seamus, "I have it!" Ariadne braced for the extra pull as he let go to wrap the rope around the tree and secure it.

"There, let go." The bind was strong, the sail held in position.

"Wait here, Seamus, I shall check the forecastle in quick time." Off she ran, the wind brushing through her salty brown locks, her heart beating in her chest. It wasn't long before she reached the limit of the *Selene*, the edge of the forest breaking open, revealing the sights below. She peered through the exposed roots to the lands below, looking for the Loire on the portside of the island. *There it is.* Once she had grown accustomed to the sight again, she quickly placed it. The river Loire swept across the breadth of France to the left-hand side of the *Selene*. Chateaux periodically spaced out along it. They had flown further off course since she had last checked. Ariadne watched as she looked for evidence that the island was moving back into the wind.

The *Selene* started to howl an altered tune; the ground shook slightly. The Loire began to turn. *Huzzah!* The *Selene* was turning and in the right direction. Seamus had done it. It was time to give him his dues and to turn the mainsail back. She waited till the flying forest passed over the Loire and had started moving north—*time to head back.*

* * *

The sail had moved back into place with relative ease. Once Seamus had finished lording it over Ariadne, they rolled the anchor over to the aft of the *Selene*. She had found a perfect spot to place it. Some exposed roots, with no earth beneath them, easy enough to cut away in a pinch, with no need to roll it off the edge. The giant wicker ball had been attached to some rope and a makeshift winch.

"This is what happens when you let a real inventor on the island."

Seamus laughed heartily, "and what is this?"

"This is my winch, of course. Here look. When I found the cups I found this barrel in the late botanist's personal effects, and it gave me inspiration." Ariadne patted the barrel wrapped with rope. "When we need to lower anchor, we can cut the roots below it. Then, from here," she moved over to the end of the rope tied to a tree, "it's just a small matter of untying it and lowering it down to its full extent." She smiled triumphantly.

Seamus seemed impressed. "I see, and with it being on the thick branch there it allows the barrel to rotate freely. I am impressed! Good job, Ari."

Ariadne wasn't used to receiving praise, especially from someone she looked up to. Her face turned a bright hue of red. "I'm not saying it will be easy to do, but the two of us will be able to manage the weight. The barrel will allow for a slower descent."

Seamus mused over the winch. "Perhaps if we coiled the rope around these two branches over here, it would hold it in place better, so we only have to uncoil it one length at a time. That way, neither of us would struggle to unfurl the anchor."

"That sounds like a better idea than acquiring rope burns. If you could start coiling the rope, I shall start filling the basket with rocks, so we are ready for our arrival."

"Of course, they don't call me the fastest rope coiler in all the seven seas for nothing!" Seamus seemed proud of that fact.

"Who calls you that?" She asked incredulously

"The men," he stated matter-of-factly.

Ariadne pushed even further. "Which men?"

"Men in certain rope coiling circles."

"Ya fool." She walked off chuckling to herself as she went looking for rocks.

* * *

The Anchor had been suitably packed to the brim. It looked like it could break a ship in two as well as stop an island. She hoped. The two of them were now at the forecastle of the *Selene* taking in the view.

"The light has almost faded from this day, my friend." Seamus stood staring eagle-eyed into the distance.

"Aye, home beckons." Ariadne reminisced about their adventure.

"This whole ordeal has felt like our very own odyssey, don't you think?"

"Seamus, we haven't had to slay any beasties yet."

"Very true." He stood corrected.

"I think you still have the right of it though. Only, I feel as though this odyssey has yet to begin. This mere affair you and I have experienced was just the proving ground, to test our worthiness, to partake in the god's plans. I feel the real tests are yet to come, the real monsters still to set their scene."

Seamus thought about the things she had said. "I fear you are right, my dear friend. If we have learnt anything from this ordeal, it is that we can overcome anything that life wishes to throw at us. I feel we have both grown as people, as friends. Whatever this dastardly French king wants to throw at us, I feel that together we will be a force to be reckoned with."

"He won't know what's hit him when the *Selene* comes crashing down on his fancy French palace." She smirked.

"Do you want to know what else I think?"

"What's that," Ariadne asked curiously.

"I think I finally spy the white cliffs of home!" The two jumped for joy. They had made it, against all the odds. In a floating forest no less.

What a tale to tell the grandkids.

"Should we wait till we are at the cliffs themselves?"

188

"To stop? I have no idea! How much momentum could the old gal have?"

"I think if we are going to drop the anchor, now would be the best time to do it? Who knows what damage it would cause dragging it through London."

"You have the right of it, Ari."

"Are you ready to run?" She asked a tired Seamus.

He blew air out of his mouth. Seamus didn't seem to be looking forward to running again. "Lead the way!"

Ariadne raced through the forest, with Seamus trailing shortly behind. It wouldn't be long before the *Selene* was over the cliffs, and the anchor needed to be out to its full extent if it was ever to make any difference.

"Seamus, bring down the sail while I continue to the aft!"

"Aye, aye, cap'n." He grinned smugly as he split off from here and headed towards the mainsail.

Ariadne continued to run. It seemed to take forever. The trees whizzed past her in a blur as she made her way to the anchor. Eventually, she got there, out of breath. There was no time to lose. She began sawing at the roots under the anchor. It took a few moments, but she didn't have to cut through them all, just the main ones, because when she had done that, the weight of the anchor broke the rest. She watched it in a state of unease as the wicker creaked under the stress. Then, when she felt happy with the state of equilibrium reached, she moved over to the coiled up rope and began freeing it. She let loose the first length and watched the anchor inch down. *Steady as she goes.*

She began to uncoil the rope at a fast pace when she knew that the winch worked. It was at this point that Seamus rejoined her at the aft, also severely out of breath.

"Sail. Is. Down," Seamus wheezed, taking in a short breath with each word.

"It feels like we are still moving. Help me unleash this beast." Ariadne worked together with Seamus to let loose the anchor at a quicker pace. It wasn't long before they heard a distant splash, and they knew that they had done enough.

Ariadne looked at her friend. "The deed is done, my friend. Now we wait." They didn't need to wait long. The *Selene* was moving at a pace much quicker than either of them had anticipated. For when they moved to check down below, a terrible crash could be heard from below, then a disastrous jolt ran through the island, throwing them off their feet. The trees shook with disdain, and the island groaned in protest.

"Good gods, it looks like the anchor has hit the cliffs."

"Aye…" The island seemed to slow down, while the rope strained under pressure. Both Ariadne and Seamus stared at the winch, wishing that it would hold. She knew she was going to be sorely disappointed as the creaking intensified. Low and behold.

She winced as the barrel groaned like an angry stomach and flew like a cannonball between the two of them. The branch exploding into smithereens. It was rather pleasing to witness. *Selene* continued her journey on momentum alone.

"Well, that brings that to a conclusion. Hopefully, the old gal decides to come to a stop on her own." Seamus seemed hopeful.

"Let's check from the forecastle."

"I shall meet you there, my friend, the wind seems to have been knocked out of my sail."

Ariadne nodded in affirmation as she made her way towards the forecastle.

* * *

Ariadne stood at the forefront of the *Selene*, as she careened forward. The walls of London, fast approaching. She stood there with her arms folded as Seamus joined her. She wondered what the people were thinking as they watched the *Selene,* a flying forest, approach their homes. They had made it all this way, the least she could do was stop at the door. Someone must have been listening, because the wind died down, and the world stopped moving beneath them. They were home.

Chapter - 12 - The Parting of the Ways.

Jack stood on the aft of the *Neptune*, one foot resting on the taffrail, one hand stroking his spyglass. He was watching the horizon. He hadn't seen the light again, but he was sure that whatever was there still lingered. Sebastian had been keeping watch too, and he swore blind that he saw masts. It was enough for Jack. Someone was hunting them. He closed up the spyglass and popped it in his pocket.

"See anything, cap'n?"

Jack had let Sebastian take the ship's wheel. It wasn't his usual forte, letting another man touch his vessel in such an intimate way, but he had spent the last two weeks breaking her in across the North Atlantic, in every imaginable way. So he was fine with 'Big Seb,' as he now referred to the scholar, fingering the *Neptune* so thoroughly.

"Nothing, Big Seb." Jack felt frustrated enough to take it out on someone. He turned towards Sebastian to take the wheel. Sebastian rolled his eyes.

"I do wish you wouldn't call me that." His cheeks flushed a nice rosy red.

Jack shrugged with a grin. "What? It's an apt nickname. I just wish you wouldn't walk around with that thing hanging out. You're going to have someone's eye out with that thing. I, for one, do not think an eyepatch goes well with these garments."

"I was in my room changing!"

"Just because I gave you a room out of the goodness of my heart, doesn't mean I allow you privacy as well. You're going to at least have to," Jack paused, musing over the task, "sink the ship that is plaguing us."

Sebastian let out an incredulous laugh.

"Besides, you wanted to learn how to talk to the fairer sex?" Jack laughed out of his nose. "It's simple really, Big Seb, just let loose that sea monster in your pants, the girls won't need wooing with words."

Sebastian looked like he was deep in thought. "You really think that's all I need to do?"

Jack laughed, "I'm not saying just lob it out whenever you meet a cute girl," he paused for a second, "although I dare say that probably depends where you are. I know a few girls in Cuba that would very much initiate a little tête-à-tête if you showed them the goods." He remained in thought, reminiscing on past conquests.

As if to sway Jack from his current thoughts, Sebastian cleared his throat. "Do you think it is Bla...Edward Teach that stalks us?"

Jack gave him a sideways glance. "I wouldn't put it past him, to hold a grudge. He pretends to be the Pirate King, after all. I just can't fathom why he lays waiting on the horizon, just out of reach."

Sebastian mused over the conundrum. "Perhaps to instil fear? The apprehension of being hunted."

"Do you see me pissing in my breeches?" Jack forced a laugh.

"If there is someone following us, I should take the watch." Sebastian held out his hand to Jack.

"You always want to touch my things, Big Seb." Jack finally relented and handed him his spyglass.

Sebastian rolled his eyes at him as he took hold of Jack's piece and went to take over his watch. "Perhaps this is all some game, Teach is toying with us? I don't know how you pirates like to get your jollies."

Jack cocked an eyebrow at him. "This is the longest game of cat and mouse I have ever played, my friend. Besides, you know better than anyone how I like to get my jollies." He grinned and threw Sebastian a wink.

Sebastian had obviously learned to let Jack's humour wash over him, like water off a duck's back. "Indeed I do, you deviant." Sebastian was concentrating on the horizon. "If we are in agreement that Teach is hunting us. Then I postulate that it could be one of two things."

Jack glanced over his shoulder, his interest piqued. "Pray tell me your thoughts."

Sebastian twisted the spyglass. "Either Teach has caught an unfavourable wind," the scholar leaned over the taffrail to gain a closer look, "or he waits to see where we are headed." He held out the spyglass to Jack for him to take a look.

Jack waltzed over and grabbed the piece from his hand and focussed on the place Sebastian had been scrutinising. *There you are, hiding.* "Good eye, Big Seb, I see bloody hearts and horned devils. It seems the *Queen Anne's Revenge* is hunting us, those flags are unmistakable." He passed the spyglass to Sebastian so that he could double-check.

"You have the right of it, cap'n. A Horned skeleton spearing a bloody heart. Teach's ship?"

"Aye, the bloody scoundrel." Jack spat into the sea.

"What should we do?"

"The *Neptune* is no match for the *Queen Anne*, not alone, anyway. We could keep her at a distance for a few days, at least. Hopefully, this fortunate wind keeps up till we can get to the Azores. If we are drawn into a battle, I would much rather have the *Kingston* as backup and a favourable setting. If I remember correctly, there are a few spots in between those paradise islands, which hold a wonderful spot to scupper Teach's plans."

"Do we have the men for such a battle? With half the crew with Anney, we leave ourselves open to fatiguing the men running double duties."

"You leave the tactics to me, Big Seb, I shall leave the conquering of ladies in your more than capable hands." He smirked. Sebastian groaned. "In any case, we must catch up to the *Kingston* and inform Anney of our plans. Tell the men to unfurl all the sails, let's see how fast she can really go."

"Aye, aye, cap'n," Sebastian made his way to the main deck while he took back control of the *Neptune. Let's see what the Pirate King is made of, love.* He stroked the wheel's handles suggestively.

* * *

It had taken the good part of the morning to catch up to the *Kingston*, but through various signalling, the *Neptune* had managed to catch up with her. The ships had expertly manoeuvred to matching speeds and were now breaking through the waves of the ocean side by side. Jack stood on the rigging, grinning at the sight of Anney.

"Permission to come aboard, Cap'n?" He shouted over.

Anney had been preparing for his arrival once she knew they were to meet up. It was evident to Jack, anyway. She stood there decked out in her knee-high boots, tight breeches, and open shirt. Hands rested upon those curvy hips of hers, with her green eyes and red hair enticing him in, making his breeches feel as tight as the shirt she wore. *Bloody siren.*

"I can see you're ready to board me from here, Jack." She shouted over to him. Hector gave a slight chuckle, while Jack grinned even more.

Voice of a siren, too. "It does me well to see that arse of yours on the *Kingston*. You ride her hard like I taught you."

"I had to break him in, didn't I? Show him who his new master was." She stroked the taffrail. "We've been getting along fine, to be sure," Anney said with a grin. "Why don't you come aboard so we can have ourselves a proper conversation."

Jack checked the gap between their ships and seemed happy with the distance. He grabbed hold of one of the sail ropes and swung across to the *Kingston* from the rigging. Landing expertly on the main deck, to the chorus of a lonely 'Huzzah' in the distance.

"Thank you, that man." He took a bow to his audience.

"You always did know how to make an entrance, Jack," she grinned, "Shall we take this to my quarters?"

Jack eyed up the saucy vixen with a voracious appetite. "Aye, Lady Bonney, I think we ought to."

***

Jack and Anney slammed against the table, her legs wrapped around his waist. His hands were exploring the curves of her face and the softness of her flame-red locks, while his lips found hers. Tongues crashing over each other like waves licking up a hull. She was busy grabbing hold of his pert arse and trying her very best to pull him closer so she could feel the heat from in between his legs. *Gods, it has been too long.* He ripped open her shirt with an animalistic ferocity and a primal grunt. He buried his face into her chest and began to tease and satisfy his own desires, making sure not to be too rough. He knew she liked it slow and steady, but he just couldn't help himself. He had to have her now.

Her back arched as he kissed the soft, white skin of her breasts. The sound of her moaning made him even harder as she dug her nails into his bareback, scratching her mark on him. She wrapped her legs even tighter as Jack picked her up off the table and moved over to the bed. Kissing and biting softly up and down her neck, he could feel the goosebumps form on her chest. The desired effect he was searching for. Jack lay her down on the bed and unhooked her legs from his waist as he worked to remove her breeches.

"Gods, woman, how did you even get these on?"

"Shut up and take off your pants!"

Anney lay there raised up on her elbows, panting with sexual frustration. Jack smirked back at her while he unbuttoned his breeches and let them drop to the floor. "That's what I've been missing." A smile spread across her face as he walked towards her, her legs splayed, begging him to take her.

* * *

"So, to what do I owe the pleasure of your company?" Anney sat naked in bed, the slur apparent in her voice like she was utterly spent. Jack definitely was.

"It is time for us to part ways, love." He was busying himself, putting his breeches back on.

Anney leaned forward, more alert. "Truly? Like we discussed?"

"Aye, lass. It looks like I was right about our little shadow on the horizon." He pulled on a boot, then searched for the other.

"Teach," she said with a tiresome groan.

"The one and only. He stalks us from afar. Sebastian seems to think he has either caught a less than favourable wind, or he means to see where we are headed." He had found the other boot under the bed and was busying himself with that.

"Why would he want to know that?"

Jack thought about the question for a moment. "Well, he was headed east, according to Hector. Perhaps he means to see if we are worth the chase or to carry on with his own goals." He continued to look for the other garments that had been discarded in a frenzy.

"So, what do you plan to do?"

Jack paused his search and directed his attention to her. "In a few more days, we will arrive at the Azores, I mean to stay and fight. The two of us together would be a match for the *Queen Anne's Revenge*, I'm sure." He continued his valiant effort to find the missing shirt.

Anney scoffed, "and if we don't succeed?"

Jack mused over the idea of failure. "If it looks like we aren't going to make it, I want you to hide in that little spot we found the last time we were there." He had spotted the shirt on the chandelier above the bed.

"If I can find it again," she said with a doubtful tone. "That was damn near ten years ago." Anney thought more about the plan. "What are you going to do if I'm hiding?"

"If I'm not devilishly crushed by Teach, I'll lead him away from you. Give you a chance to make it to your goal. If he's after me, he probably won't come looking for you."

A look of anger flashed across Anney's bonny features. "You mean to play the hero with me, Jack Rackham, I won't let you sacrifice yourself for me."

"Watching you get mad makes me horny, love. Do it some more." A look of devilish smugness spread across Jack's face.

"We have come too far for this to be the end of our path together."

Jack sighed with a heavy heart. "Look, love, this was always the plan. You know that. Besides, if one of us is to lead our people back to their home, I would much rather it be in your very capable hands." Jack straddled her and held her protesting hands.

"But…" Anney sounded defeated.

He looked into her soul to try and fathom her protestations. "But what?"

"…I love you," she sighed, "I can't do this alone." Her body relaxed as the words she had held onto escaped her pouting lips.

He ran his fingers through her hair, trying to comfort her. "You won't be alone, Hector will be there by your side, and you have the best damn crew the new world has ever seen. Besides. He hasn't bested us yet, love. It'll take more than a black scab, like Teach, to take down this pirate." He grinned. "Now, where were we?"

"You were just leaving, I presume."

"Oh, was I?" a wild glint flashed across his eyes as he leant down to whisper in her ear. She shuddered with a pleasurable groan escaping her lips as he returned to seal the words he had uttered.

* * *

"I presume you and Anney got reacquainted?" Sebastian smugly suggested. Jack was back on board the *Neptune* after having a lengthy conversation with Anney and Hector about the specifics of the plan.

"Aye, that we did, Big Seb." Jack had returned with a more laid back demeanour. He was confident that the plan to lure their hunter into the Azores would work. He just hoped that Anney would stay hidden and not do anything stupid - like try to save him.

"I told the lads to take down the sails and break away from the *Kingston*. I presumed you wanted to give them some headway while attracting our friend on the horizon back on to our hook.

"We have spent much time together, my friend, you are learning well." Jack took back the ship's wheel from Sebastian. "Let us see if we can't lure him into a conflict on *our* terms."

The sun's myriad hues of yellow swept over the sky, followed by the shades of purple brought with the moon before the masts reappeared on the horizon at the start of the new day. As luck would have it, Jack had spotted the Azores in the direction they were heading, so everything was going to plan.

Sebastian appeared from the main deck, his black mess of hair and fuzzy moustache peaking over the steps to the poop deck. "Has she made it, Big Seb?"

Sebastian sighed, "Aye, cap'n, as far as I can tell, she's made it to the Azores and is lying in wait. I saw her disappear behind one of the isles."

Good girl. "I think it's time to let our pursuers gain some ground on us. Don't you?" Jack nodded to the scholar.

"Aye, aye, cap'n," he relayed as if understanding Jack's unspoken order, "let's get some of those sails down, lads!" Sebastian barked to the crew. "Let's put that scurvy worm in his place!"

"Huzzah!" The crew cheered in unison.

Jack grinned. He was impressed.

It wasn't long before the *Queen Anne's Revenge* was near, close enough to see that evil bastard grinning at the wheel. Luckily, the Azores were closer. Jack planned to lead Teach through the northwestern Isles, the Ilha das Flores, then, if he took the bait, southeast to the Pico Islands. The volcanic mountain imposing on the scenery. Where the *Kingston* should be laying in wait to ambush Teach. If all goes to plan, three ships will enter battle, and two will leave. Preferably theirs.

If all didn't go according to plan, he instructed Anney to head further south towards Ilha de São Miguel. Where, if she listened, she would hide till they passed. Jack hoped that she would see the bigger picture, though. It was more important that she survived the encounter than both of them dying in the imminent conflict.

They were fast approaching the Ilha das Flores, with Teach still hot on their aft. "Hard to starboard!" Jack shouted to the crew, working furiously on the main deck, as he rotated the ship's wheel to turn the rudder hard. The men heaved on the ropes, which turned the sails so that the wind would push the *Neptune* in a sharp motion to the right. She glided through the waters, masts creaking at the strain, her sails whipping in the wind.

Jack took her as close to the cliffs of the island as he dared, as he skirted around the edges, luring Teach into his trap.

"There's two, cap'n!" Sebastian cried wildly over the wash of the waves battering the hull.

Dread crept over Jack's heart. The *Queen Anne's Revenge* alone they may have been able to handle, but two was pushing it. "Are you sure?" He shouted at Sebastian.

"Aye, cap'n. I only caught a glimpse of it as we turned, but it was directly behind Teach's ship. We wouldn't have seen it until we turned away from their course." Sebastian sounded panicked, he understood the implications that were racing through Jack's mind.

They were almost past the Ilha das Flores, heading to open waters. "Take the wheel, Sebastian, make your heading east-southeast. Head straight for that volcano!" Jack let him take the wheel, before grabbing the spyglass and heading to the aft of the *Neptune* to check on the latest addition to the festivities.

"Straighten those sails, men!" Sebastian growled at the crew sweating away on the portside.

Jack extended the spyglass and scanned the island they had left behind. "Are you sure you saw two vessels?" He shouted over the crashing waves. The speed with which the *Neptune* was going caused his hand to bob up and down with the motion of each undulation of the sea.

"I'm sure, Jack! I would not have said otherwise." He could hear Sebastian's anger reverberating in his ears.

Jack fought the urge to berate the man; he did, of course, offer his allegiance to the cause. Somewhat. He moved over to the wheel to help calm him down. Jack placed his hand on the scholar's shoulder and the other on his hand on the wheel. He made a slight adjustment to the course and spoke closely in his ear so he could hear. "Do keep her steady, we wouldn't want to sail into the volcano now, would we? And remain calm, have I ever led us into a plan without a backup?"

Sebastian sighed. "Aye, cap'n."

Jack didn't have a backup plan. He returned to the taffrail with his spyglass. *Where are you, ya slimy bastard?* He searched the cliff line that they had first turned hoping to god that Sebastian's eyesight was poor. *There she is!* "Ship ahoy," he bellowed.

"What about the other ship, cap'n?"

Jack hadn't heard what Sebastian had said; he was too busy trying to find the horned skeleton spearing the bloody heart. *It's not there!* The ship that had sailed around the corner after them was not Teach's ship. He had to presume it was the other ship. "It's not him! It's the other ship!" The panic was setting in.

"Unfurl all the sails! Let's get some speed, boys!" Sebastian cried from the wheel. "Cap'n! Look to starboard!"

Jack was confused by Sebastian breaking from the plan until he lay his eyes on the *Queen Anne's Revenge* coming in fast on their right-hand side. "He must have sailed around the other side of the island to try and cut us off, that cunning bastard!" Jack raced over to the wheel.

"Good job, let's make sure Teach doesn't split us in twain! I wouldn't want us to feel like a sore maiden that's just bedded you, ay lad!" Jack gave a hearty laugh as he patted Sebastian on the arse. "Come on, lass," he shouted to the *Neptune*, "Let's show him what you can do in experienced hands."

As the *Queen Anne's Revenge* ploughed through the ocean, aiming directly into the heart of the *Neptune,* time seemed to slow down. Jack could spy the mad glint in Edward Teach's eyes over the roar of activity onboard the man's ship. He stood at the wheel full of confidence, bracing himself as the rest of the sails unfurled and the

Neptune lurched forward at a greater speed. The roar of the sea intertwined with the cacophony of the crew seemed to resume the normal flow of time. Fortune must have smiled over them. The *Queen Anne's Revenge* narrowly scraped the aft of the *Neptune*. He turned to watch Teach sail past, menacingly leering at him, as Jack took his hat off to him and gave him an unnecessarily large bow before returning to the ship's wheel. He could feel the heat of the hatred and anger burning into the back of his head.

"Well, that was fun!" Sebastian stopped bracing himself for impact and returned to Jack's side, a grin on his face.

"Oh did you enjoy that from your cowering position?" Jack sassily commented.

"You must admit it was a little close. I'm just glad I'm not the only one who messed up their backside." Sebastian went to peer over the taffrail at the damage. "Nothing that a little polish won't solve," he cringed.

"The fun isn't over yet, my friend. The battle has yet to begin!"

"What about Anney? She doesn't know that there are two vessels. If she fires all her guns on Teach's ship she'll leave herself open to retaliation from whoever is on the other ship." Sebastian returned to Jack's spyglass.

"Anney's a smart lass, I have every faith in her abilities. The *Kingston* is a fine ship too, and its crew is a talented bunch." Jack may have kept a collected exterior, but his interior was filled with worry for his lover. He made his way to the islands where Anney lay ready to ambush their attackers. Who were now both trailing behind the Neptune, matching her speed.

"It's the other ship," Sebastian shouted to Jack, "the one I sabotaged!"

"No prizes for guessing who sails that then." He snorted with derision.

"I couldn't really see in the dark, back on Monte Christi, but this lass has brown hair and even browner eyes!"

Jack nodded as Sebastian rattled off the description. "Aye, that's the woman."

"Good gods, Jack, she looks as fearsome as Teach. I fear we have well and truly incurred the wrath of these two." Jack could hear the panic creeping back into Sebastian's voice.

"Calm yourself, Big Seb, I have a few tricks up my sleeves." Jack grinned as the *Neptune* made its way to the group of islands fast approaching. He planned to sail down the centre of two of them, at least it looked like two. The island to the right consisted of the smaller island they approached and the massive volcanic island behind it, leaving a small gap for a ship to lay in wait. The long thin island to the left allowed no ship, caught in a crossfire, room to manoeuvre. It was either stay the course or run aground. He liked that he was giving his pursuers those options.

The *Neptune* threaded through the isles, the small one on her starboard, the long thin island to her portside. Edward Teach and Mary Read in full pursuit, their sails fully unfurled, chomping at Jack's slightly bruised aft.

Jack expected to see Anney and the *Kingston* as soon as he had passed the smaller island. They were almost there but he could see no sign of her. He rolled his eyes. "Trust Anney to be late to the battle."

"I can't see her, cap'n! She was supposed to be here?"

The *Neptune* was now fully adjacent to the gap where Anney was supposed to be, broadside exposed, ready to spring the trap. Yet, she was nowhere to be seen. Jack lost himself to thought. *Could she have left me behind? No, she wouldn't do that to me. Maybe she's in the wrong place? Where are you, my love?* His ship was now past the gap and was sailing along the edge of the volcanic island, the plan seemingly failed. Jack glanced back to see the *Queen Anne's Revenge* also pass the gap, with Mary's ship shortly behind it.

As if she had heard his cries, from between the isles, the *Kingston* burst onto the scene, crashing over the waves and smashing directly into Mary's ship. Anney must have hit a powder keg reserve because Mary's ship cracked in twain with a mighty boom. Shards of oak flying everywhere. Jack shuddered as the explosion rippled across the Azores, a wave of force unsettling them both on the *Neptune*.

Jack straightened his jacket as he surveyed the destruction caused by the *Kingston*. Mary's ship looked in a sorry state, it's mainmast had come down and looked to be taking on water. Not to mention the fire. As far as he could tell, Anney had wedged her ship into the middle of Mary's, her ship wrapped around the *Kingston's* forecastle. Other than that it seemed to be fine.

"Such an apt way for her to destroy Mary's ship. Broken in twain by her ex-lover." Sebastian smirked.

Jack chanced a laugh. "Even in the face of such destruction, you hazard a joke?" Jack paused, allowing the dust to settle. "Very good, my friend, you are learning." He grinned, patting Sebastian on the shoulder.

"What now, cap'n? It's just us and Teach."

"We can't take the *Queen Anne* head-on, we're going to have to employ some," he paused while he figured out how to phrase it, "unconventional tactics."

"Care to divulge the specifics?"

"Now is not the time to teach erratic manoeuvres. Trust me, Sebastian, I know what I'm doing."

The *Neptune* was almost back into open water with Edward Teach snapping at Jack's heels. He could see the whites of his eyes, his face seething with rage at the loss of his comrade. There was no doubt about it, he was coming for Jack's blood.

"Hard to port!" Jack bellowed down to the crew who were working the sails mercilessly. They had come to the end of the long thing island on the left, and Jack meant to steer sharply around it. As they sailed around the corner, another island came into view.

"That there is Terceira Island, the *Neptune* is going to lead Teach on a merry chase around it. When he catches up to us, I'm going to greet him with a forty-five gun salute from my broadside." Jack beamed with smugness.

"And that will sink the bastard?"

Jack laughed with a great ferocity. "Oh, Sebastian, you do tickle me with your humour."

Sebastian shrugged while throwing Jack a look of puzzlement.

Jack noticed his look of bewilderment and decided to clarify. "No, my friend, I mean to distract him while we make our escape. If all goes to plan, we will be able to hide in the place Anney was supposed to."

"Do you think it will work?"

"I have faith, my friend, of course, it will work." Jack adjusted his course so that Terceira Island would come upon the *Neptune's* starboard so that they could circle the isle by steering right. He gauged the distance between him and his hunter. "Good, the distance has opened up a little, that'll do nicely!"

The *Neptune* glided through the water towards its destination. The island that had come upon their starboard was another old sleeping volcano, the top overgrown with grass. Jack caressed the *Neptune's* wheel as he steered her around the edges of the cliffs that surrounded the island. Jack had now lost sight of the *Queen Anne's Revenge*; he hoped that Teach was still tailing him. Jack was looking for a specific cove with which to base his attack. He turned another corner to be faced with yet more cliff, until, "there it is!"

"Where?" Sebastian peered over the taffrail to the right. "I can't see anything, just a cliff face."

"Just you wait, Big Seb, all will become apparent." He grinned as he steered the *Neptune* seemingly into the cliff. Jack laughed as Sebastian braced for another collision. "Try not to mess up your breeches again, my friend." The ship glided into a hidden cove, much to Sebastian, and his trousers, surprise.

"Well, well, you are full of it today, Jack." Sebastian looked on in amazement at the surrounding area. While the crew pulled down the sails in such a manner that they could be quickly unfurled to make a speedy escape.

"No time to waste, Sebastian, ready the men to fire upon my order." Jack's demeanour changed to that of a pirate who means business.

"Aye, cap'n!" Sebastian burst into action, running down the stairs to the main deck, to make sure the crew was ready for what was about to occur.

Jack steered the *Neptune* so that she sat just inside the cove, with her broadside facing outwards. The cannons poking out of the portside, ready to unleash hell on Teach. She drifted to a complete stop, swaying in the water. The crew all lined up, staring at their leader, waiting for the order. Jack waltzed over to the portside taffrail and removed his cutlass from the sash around his waist, raising it in the air to command his men. If he had wanted to, he could have sliced the tension in the air as everyone waited with bated breath.

Jack watched, he waited and listened. His eyes never wandering away from that opening.

Everything all happened at once, as soon as the *Queen Anne's* figurehead appeared around that corner. Jack waited till he knew he would inflict the most damage, then as swiftly as he had drawn his cutlass, he swiped it down, giving the command to fire with extreme brutality. And it was brutal. The roar from the cannons was deafening, bloody and ferocious, the *Neptune* shuddered with pleasure as her entire broadside came alive with fire.

The effect was instant, especially this close up, the *Queen Anne's* hull exploded in an ephemeral symphony of sounds. She was wounded, Jack admired his handiwork, as he watched Teach scream the order to manoeuvre.

"Hard to port," came the blood-curdling cry of a wounded animal.

Then Jack knew it was time to act, and quickly.

"All hands! Full speed ahead! Make ready for cannon fire from the starboard!" Jack screamed his orders as if their lives depended on it. They did.

Sebastian seemed confused; he looked up to him on the poop deck mouthing the words. Jack knew what he was saying over the myriad of sounds drowning the scene, and the need for him to focus grew more apparent.

The *Neptune* quickly picked up speed, the cove provided a natural push from the wind hurtling around it. Jack knew he would be able to leap into action after the deed was done. As soon as they were out and back along the cliff walls, he ordered the crew to fire the starboard cannons.

Sebastian looked panicked as Jack screamed over the racket.

"Fire!" The cannons let loose, as the *Neptune* gave another satisfying shudder. The balls flew into the base of the cliff. Sebastian stood covering his ears, looking at what Jack had just unleashed. Jack's hearing returned just in time to hear the wonderful chorus of popping and cracking as the cliff wall destabilised and started to move, to shift and fall. The *Neptune* was far enough away to not take any collateral damage, but the *Queen Anne's Revenge,* who had resumed her attack, nearly had her forecastle destroyed. The high walls came crashing down, splashing into the sea, as Teach brought his ship to a complete stop turning as she did.

Not only had Jack thoroughly secured his place as Teach's mortal enemy, but he had provided a natural barrier to aid the *Neptune* in her escape. Jack stood at the aft, as he watched Teach try to recover his vessel and continue the chase. It looked like pandemonium onboard. He was satisfied that he had bought them some time to hide and continue their journey. Jack returned to the wheel and steered the ship around the island, away from the *Queen Anne's Revenge*.

* * *

Jack had found the spot he and Anney used to hide in. It was near an island further east than where they had fought Teach. It was perfect for keeping a ship hidden, and it was also good for intimate trysts. The place was a tall, hollowed-out volcano that Anney had taken him to many years ago. They used to lay in wait for passing ships and alleviate them of their goods. It had been a good life back then, not like now with them crossing evil bastards and skulking in volcanoes.

They had been holed up in there for a day now, the night had come and the sun had risen. He and Sebastian had taken it in turns to keep watch over the entrance, but nothing of note happened. Nothing to cause concern. The crew had picked themselves up and repaired what they could of the *Neptune,* and they were ready to embark when the command was given.

Sebastian and Jack stood on the poop deck both staring towards the open sea.

"Do you think Anney and Hector are okay?" Sebastian seemed worried.

"Aye, lad, I would know if they weren't. I think I'd feel it." Jack was calm. He felt he had a bond with both of them, that if ever it was broken, he would feel it. They had been through too much together for there to just be nothing. So he knew they would be fine.

"You know, I'm a man of science, Jack, but you know what?" He turned to Jack, "I believe you would."

"Do you think we've given Teach enough time to get bored and bugger off to wherever he was headed?" Jack was beginning to rely more heavily on Sebastian, he appreciated the candour he had developed. He also felt that if he let Sebastian in more, he would be more confident around the men. It was working. He felt strangely proud watching Sebastian work them. Taking the initiative with the *Neptune*. It made his heart swell. Just a little bit.

"Aye, Jack, I think it's time we carried on our odyssey."

"Odyssey? What's that?" Jack quizzed the man.

Sebastian turned to Jack and smiled. "I'll tell you on the way. Let's get out of here, my friend."

Chapter - 13 - Sightseeing.

Ariadne was home. The unmistakable River Thames snaked its way through the city in the distance, littered with boats ferrying goods up and down its length. Seamus peered over the edge of the *Selene*. She stood by his side, her arms folded, trying to figure out how to get them out of the predicament they now found themselves in.

Seamus sighed. "Well, at least we made it to London!"

"Aye, with no discernable way down." She unfolded her arms and leaned over the side.

Seamus thought for a while. "Could we not take all the rope we have left and tie it together to make another escape route."

Ariadne stopped peering over the edge and stared at him in disbelief. "You *know* how much rope I used for the anchor. We uncoiled the damn thing."

He kicked a stone over the side in frustration. "I know, Ari, this conundrum is just vexing. To be so close to home, yet still, so far away."

Suddenly the thoughts in her mind connected like the stars of a constellation. Inspiration had seeped into her mind, and it had spread to her face. She was grinning like a Cheshire cat. "You know what this means, don't you?"

Seamus looked worried. "Oh no, you couldn't mean…"

"Oh, but I do." She rubbed her hands together in glee.

"No, no, no, there must be another way?" Jack started to pace around, obviously racking his brain for an alternative.

"Oh, but there isn't," she laughed maniacally, "it's time for the *backup* backup plan."

Ariadne, of course, referred to the bird-like structure referenced in one of the journals. She had pointed it out earlier as another way to get themselves off the *Selene*, but Seamus was very adamant that the idea was to be used only *if* the rope was out of commission. Which it was. The rope and the winch system had been ripped out of the island when the anchor had caught on the sides of the cliffs. So they now had little choice in the matter.

"How would we even build such a thing?" He was trying to be as obstinate to the idea as much as possible.

"You leave that to me, my friend." The spark of life glinting in the cerulean of Ariadne's eyes. "I need you to find me the journal with the diagram."

Seamus blew air from his lips as he seemed to become more resigned to the idea. "Is this truly the only way?"

Ariadne ran up to the pacing captain and jumped on his back to try and cheer him up. "We can do this, ya landlubber!" She shook him till he acquiesced to her demands.

Seamus began to laugh, "Okay, okay, I give in." Ariadne jumped off, grinning. "What do you mean, landlubber? I am no such thing. How dare you! I was at sea long before you had even set foot on a ship." He jokingly knocked her with his shoulder as they walked back into the forest towards camp.

"Oh, sure! On the sea, no doubt. You and I are venturing forth into a new era, though. You need to get your airlegs. We can't be pioneers of the age of airships if you are afraid to take a little leap of faith off the edge of the *Selene*."

"Have our travels thus far not earned me, at least, some leeway?"

Ariadne pondered on his request. "Aye, maybe just a little."

Seamus grinned at her. "So how can I assist you in this endeavour?"

Ariadne cast her mind back to the journal. "Once we are back at camp, I'll look over the plans. From memory, I think we will need rope, some sail, and of course, the necessary branches for the framework. For now, though, I need you to collect as much rope as you can from the broken 'steering mast.'"

"It would be my pleasure." Seamus bowed as he drifted into the forest towards the starboard.

Ariadne continued on her hike alone. Without Seamus to bounce off she turned to memories of old once more, to reflect on her own past, and to consider the questions she would ask her mother if she deemed it necessary to visit her. The speculation was killing her, and it was getting her nowhere. Thankfully, it wasn't long before she was back at camp and rifling through the journals, looking for something to keep her brain occupied.

Where are you? She flicked through the pages. They were covered in mad drawings of insane inventions that could utilise the new material. All complicated, but this one was drawn haphazardly on the page. She felt they could do this themselves, with a little ingenuity. *There! Hmmm. It will take the right types of branches, and we shall have to figure out how best to steer them, but I think we should be able to handle this.* Ariadne grinned.

* * *

Ariadne admired her craftsmanship. She stood there, arms wrapped around her, one hand on her chin, contemplating what was missing. Seamus stood to the side, waiting for her approval, looking slightly worried that she didn't seem pleased with the construction. Ariadne scrutinised the main spines of the bird structures, checking it for breaks and impurities. She eyed the wings made from bent branches and bits of sail spread across them. They fanned out either side of the structures attached to support beams running perpendicular to the spines. She rustled them to make sure they were secured strongly enough. Finally, she examined the tails. The picture in the journal showed a sail mimicking a bird's tail feathers. She had done her best to recreate it.

Ariadne finally broke her silence. "We need to test them."

"Of course!" Seamus burst into action, climbing the nearest tree.

At the beginning of the project, they slung a rope around the surrounding trees to hold the spines in place to work on the birds in the clearing unhindered. All Ariadne had to do was untie one of the birds and let it float up to Seamus in the tree.

Seamus shimmied across one of the highest branches, adjacent to the clearing they were doing construction in, while she guided the bird to him.

"Now, remember to take hold of the straps under the wings. You can hold the branches if you want to, but the straps are going to be easier to fix." She shouted up to him.

"Duly noted, Ari," Seamus replied calmly.

Seamus didn't seem to mind throwing himself off a tall tree. She supposed it was the idea of flinging oneself off the side of a floating island, hanging half a mile in the air. She would be lying if she didn't feel the butterflies throwing up in her own stomach, but that feeling was engulfed by the excitement of doing something no one had ever tried before.

Ariadne watched as Seamus took hold of the tip of the bird's wings and pulled it across to himself.

"Careful, now. We don't want any more accidents." A flash of fear spread across her chest, clutching at her heart. Seamus' prior accident flashed before her eyes, leaving her with a mix of emotions that she wasn't ready for. She couldn't believe that she had let him go up there.

"Are you sure you should be up there? How is your chest? Is your strength up to it?" Then she flashed to just recently in the day, jumping on his back and fooling around. The flush of rose spread across her cheeks.

"I'm okay, Ari, don't worry. I wouldn't be up here if I wasn't. Besides," He let the sentence hang in the air as he too hung in the air. As he glided in a vector down across the clearing, over her head. Ariadne panicked as she watched him jump off the high branch and slowly fly over her like a bird. Seamus soared across the air like a leaf until he hit the floor softly.
Fear turned to jubilation as his feet touched the earth. Ariadne ran over to Seamus to make sure he was okay, checking him all over.

"Are you sure you are okay?" She needed to make sure her friend hadn't hurt himself any further. If they were to do this, she needed him in top shape—no extra damage due to her lapse in mindfulness.

"Ari, I'm fine," he laughed, "Now take this off me before she flys away."

Ariadne took hold of the bird and tied it back up to the tree.

"I apologise. It should have been me testing. It's not long since you were injured, and I got complacent." She searched for the truth in his eyes, the one place she had figured he couldn't hide from her.

"Look, we're a team, Ari. When one of us is adrift in a sea of emotions, the other picks up both oars and rows - agreed? I have your aft, always." Seamus beamed at her, his dimples melting her fears as always, and held out his forearm.

Damn you, Seamus.

"Agreed." She smirked while grabbing his outstretched forearm.

"We should name them?"

Ariadne cocked her head. "The birds?"

"Aye, we are about to swoop over the capital with them. When the Admiralty asks us what they are, we need something punchy. We are the pioneers, after all!"

She thought about it a little while. "Swoops?"

Seamus laughed sarcastically.

Ariadne mused further until a name spread its own wings over her mind. "Icarus."

He raised his eyebrow in a show of agreement, the smirk apparent on his face. "Agreed, Let's just try not to fly them too close to the sun."

She laughed at him. "I like this side of you. Promise me it won't end once we are back in London."

"Of course, this experience has changed us all. That is something I am not likely to forget. You and I are bonded for life, Ari, whether you like it or not." He grinned.

Seamus paused for a moment, seemingly lost in thought. "But, there are certain places I shall have to put up the façade. In front of the Admiralty, for example. Though, you have a way of bringing out this side of me. It shall never be far behind, my dear friend." A smile spread across his face, alleviating her fears.

Ariadne grinned as she patted him on the shoulder. "Good to hear."

"Speaking of the Admiralty, we have an appointment to keep. First, though, I would like to create some sort of waist strap on the Icarus. Here," she pointed to the midriff of the structure. "It's going to be a long way down, and we need all the support we can get. What do you think," she posed to Seamus.

"Excellent idea, Ari. Let's get to it!"

* * *

Ariadne and Seamus had both worked tirelessly through the night, the morning sun now illuminating the spring colours of

London below. Winter had finally thawed while they had been gone. It had left the green fields of Southwark, to the south of the Thames, beautifully exposed. They stood at the edge, peering down towards London, both of them with the Icarus tied to their backs around the waist. They had little choice because the Icarus' tail kept them from standing up straight.

"Any last words?" Ariadne grinned at a grumbling Seamus.

"Yes. If I don't make it. Go to my home in Whitechapel."

She raised her eyebrows, "Oh, fancy."

Seamus continued, "In the panelling behind my bedroom wardrobe, there are some journals, money, and deeds. I want you to have them."

Ariadne looked confused. "What about your relatives?"

Seamus turned to her. "The remaining family I have are not worthy of it, I would rather it go to you." She watched as Seamus dived forward as gracefully as a swan, leaving her with mouth agape.

"Wait!" She didn't even have time to prepare herself for the jump. *I am not getting left behind.* The fear and adrenaline pumped through her veins, while the excitement sent tingles through to her extremities and turned her stomach. Ariadne lept after him, eyes closed.

The wind rushed past her as she glided gently over the considerable void of air beneath her. She opened up her eyes to cast her senses over what she saw beneath as the cool breeze brushed her sun-blessed skin. The first thing that rushed up to her was the smell of home. The unmistakable stench of industry, there was nothing like it in the Caribbean. She had missed it. The fields south of the Thames rushed underneath her as she made her way towards Seamus. She had no idea where he was headed; they neglected to discuss that. She just presumed he had a plan.

Seamus turned in the air. His Icarus banking to the right, then levelling out. Ariadne needed to match his heading. She pulled on her right-wing strap, and the bird turned easily, the wind rushing in her ears as she did. Ariadne waited until she was facing the same direction as him and yanked on the left-hand wing to bring the Icarus level. It swung from side to side until she found her equilibrium and managed to level out too. She lifted her head up to scan the part of London they were headed and it soon became pretty apparent where their destination lay. The Tower of London.

Just north of the Tower, on the corner of Crutched Friars and Seething Lane, is where the board of Admirals worked relentlessly to administrate the many aspects of the Royal Navy. It seemed to Ariadne that Seamus meant to rouse the board from their slumber on this fine morning.

She pulled down on both wings in an attempt to catch up to Seamus. The Icarus dived dangerously, causing her stomach to lurch forward in an effort to escape the looming disaster. *Big mistake.* The wind rushed up into her face making it hard to concentrate on wrapping her feet around the spine to try and pull the bird level. *Some. Feet. Straps. Would have been useful.* The ground was fast approaching. Panic started to set in as she scrambled hard to hook her foot around the spine. She could feel it with her toes. Ariadne gave her body one last push, finally being able to connect with the spine. She scrunched up her body as if to crawl into a ball, bringing the spine with it, eventually levelling out.

She was now much closer to the ground than Seamus. He was still a little further ahead, though. *What a needlessly harrowing affair.* The sweat dripped from her brow as they passed over the Thames and into the sleeping city itself. The tower of London coming up on her right. Ariadne watched as Seamus expertly weaved his way around the building, coming back into view around the other side. *Showoff.* She kept her course true, *no more foolishness for me.*

The Tower now just below her, Ariadne's Icarus flew over the outer walls of the white tower. Since its construction in 1078 by William the Conqueror, the imposing place had been used as a jail for centuries. It was now being enjoyed to its full extent by King Charles, the cells being used to their maximum capacity. She watched the castle keep disappearing from under her as Tower Hill just north of the prison came up fast upon her. She braced for the gentle impact as the Icarus glided to the top of the hill.

Ariadne let out a sigh of relief as her feet finally touched the ground. She pulled out her dagger to cut the waist strap so she could stand up and search for Seamus, making sure to keep a hold of one of the wing straps. The Icarus hovered there while she scanned the sky for a lone sailor imitating a bird.

It wasn't long before she spotted him. Circling above her like a vulture looking for its prey. "Get down before you hurt yourself," she shouted quietly.

"I'm trying," he whispered loudly to her.

Ariadne spun round, making herself dizzy as she tracked the descending Seamus until he finally touched down on the hillside. She looked around for somewhere to hang the floating Icarus while Seamus stood bent over, not wanting to break or lose his own. She spotted a nearby metal railing outside one of the houses on the hill and moved to tie it up so it couldn't escape. She then ran over to aid Seamus getting out of his Icarus.

"Fancy moves there, sailor." Ariadne cut the waist strap so that Seamus was free to stand up and take hold of his bird.

He stretched his weary bones and yawned. It had been a long night. "What can I say, Ari, some of us are just naturals." He winked at her.

"Oh lord, just you wait. The next time we jump off a floating island, I'll show you natural." She was making bold claims she didn't feel she could back up. She smiled as she went to untie her Icarus.

They looked like a strange pair, she thought, as she returned to the sight of Seamus keeping his Icarus from floating away. *No stranger than the past week.* "Shall we go and wake the Admiralty?"

"I thought you would never ask. Shall we?" Seamus held out his arm so that she could slink hers around his.

They weren't far from the Navy Office. It was just a short walk, up Seething Lane, from where they were, and they would be stood outside the front door on Crutched Friars - just in time for breakfast. Ariadne was starving, her stomach rumbled at her like a cub testing out its newfound voice. "Do you think they will have scrambled eggs?" She looked hopeful.

"I'm sure they will have all manner of things. Maybe some bacon." Her mouth watered as he mentioned the tasty morsel. "Maybe some fried mushrooms." Her stomach purred like a kitten. Seamus paused. "Perhaps some kippers." Ariadne's stomach communicated with the rest of the whales.

"*Stop!*" She held her stomach with a sad frown.

Seamus laughed. "Okay, we're here. Time to act professionally." He straightened himself up the best he could, considering the circumstances, and they worked together to open the enormous double doors.

The Icarus tapped on the top of the door frame as they entered. Ariadne and Seamus glanced at each other. "Maybe we should tie these up outside."

He nodded. "Good idea."

They both tied their Icarus outside on the horse tether and continued back inside the building.

Someone must have heard the commotion they were causing because as soon as they reached the grand hallway with sweeping staircases, a man appeared. A man who seemed to be diametrically opposed to them in clothing and in manners.

Seamus coughed and straightened himself up further. "Good morning, my good fellow. I wondered if you might let the Admiral, Sir Thomas Allin, know that Captain Seamus Hawthorne and Lieutenant Ariadne Smith are here to see him." Seamus gave a big sweeping bow intended for royal personages.

The man looked them up and down with a look of pure disdain and repugnance. The indignation he must have felt, being ordered around by two people looking like ne'er-do-wells, must have been insulting for a man of his station. Which was apparent in the derisive snort he directed at them both. The man gave a curt nod and turned on his heels.

"I think that went well." Ariadne cringed.

Seamus shrugged. "Mayhap we should have gone home to change first?"

Several moments passed before the tapping of newly healed boots, echoing off the walls, could be heard making their way down the hallway from whence the man had disappeared. A different man appeared, whom Ariadne recognised but could not place, he wore a suit an eye-catching shade of merlot, and his cravat revealed his standing in society. Although the words that sprang forth from his mouth did little to uphold his image.

"Bloody hell, is that you, Hawthorne? How the devil are you?"

Seamus gave a deep, respectful bow, "Sir Thomas," he raised to greet the man, "It is good to see you in good health, and it seems, in better standing." Seamus motioned at the building he stood in.

Ariadne stiffened up when she realised to whom she now stood in front of. She, too, decided on an overly deep bow. "Admiral."

"Come now, Seamus, tell me who this delectable young creature is, and how can I get one of my own." Sir Thomas oozed charm. Some people spend their whole lives honing one skill, and this was most certainly his. The admiral chuckled while Ariadne blushed.

Seamus grinned at her, knowing full well she was blushing. "This is my Lieutenant, Ariadne Smith."

"Ah, yes, Smith. I am well acquainted with the Smiths. Your mother will be pleased to know that you have returned to England." Sir Thomas looked her up and down. "Although, maybe not in such a state of undress. What the devil happened to you two?" He stood, waiting for an answer.

"Maybe we should take this to your office, Sir Thomas. I think these matters are best discussed behind closed doors."

The Admiral cast his eyes over them again. "Perhaps you are right. First, you must change. The two of you are making my eyes sore. Seamus, there will be suitable attire in my wardrobe. Lieutenant, some of my wife's clothes are up there, you should be able to find something to wear." He nodded as he motioned them back to his room.

"My thanks, Sir Thomas." Seamus offered up the courtesy of a small bow, while she followed suit.

The three of them walked down the wood-panelled hallway, turning a few corners, before entering a roomy office. The place had a warmth to it, aided by the log burning hearth, the comfy high-back leather chairs, and the wall to wall collection of leatherback tomes. The portrait behind the oak desk was that of the admiral, in all his finery, posing heroically at his ship, in the distance, with his cutlass slung around his waist.

Sir Thomas had caught her admiring the painting. "Do you like it?" He smiled. "I've just had it commissioned. I felt like they captured my essence, don't you think." He struck the same pose.

Ariadne felt a little timid around the man, he was an admiral, after all, proprietary must be upheld. He was just so charismatic and familiar, *just like a certain captain.* She cleared her throat. "Very dashing, Admiral. I think they did a good job of capturing your good looks." *Did I really just say that?* She felt the heat sting her cheeks.

Sir Thomas looked impressed. "Someone's looking for a promotion, ay Seamus?" The two of them had a good chortle at that. The admiral moved to open a door in the back of his office, while his laughter died down. "Please, make use of my home away from home. You should find everything you need to freshen up and make yourself presentable. The maid has already filled the basin with warm water." He shepherded them through the door into his living space, closing the door behind them.

The room was just as opulent as the admiral's office; wall to wall wood panelling, luxurious four-poster bed, logs fuelling the fireplace, and a large porcelain basin. She admired the man's taste. Seamus had made straight for the admiral's wardrobe.

He pulled out the first suit he laid his hands on, looked it up and down, gave it a nod of approval, and proceeded to remove his tattered naval uniform.

Ariadne gave a little cough to affirm she was still in the room. Seamus turned slightly to her, remembering she was there. "Sorry, my friend, you should be able to find something in the wardrobe over there. These are all suits I'm afraid." He continued to remove his clothing while she admired his form, the heat emanating from her cheeks, giving the log fire a run for its money.

She shook herself out of the daze and moved over to the large wardrobe beyond the bed, trying to give Seamus some privacy. Ariadne opened the doors to gaze in wonderment at the selection of dresses on offer. She wasn't one for all this elegance. The dresses in here were all for women of a much higher social standing than her. She flicked through the line of finery until she found one she could bear to wear and pulled it out to check it. The gown was golden silk, something she could never afford, the bodice looked a little tight, but she could work with that. She wasn't too keen on the puffed sleeves, but it would have to do. The admiral's wife must have had a thing for off the shoulder necklines because that's the only type of cut the woman had. *No matter; this will do.* She threw the gown on the admiral's bed.

Seamus was over by the sink, rubbing perfumed soap on his skin, trying to wash a week's worth of dirt off. Ariadne sat on the bed, pondering Seamus and the admiral's relationship.

"You and the admiral seem to get along well. He reminds me of you a little."

Seamus chuckled loudly, "I would hope so. Nothing forges a friendship quite like the fires of war. It's only natural that he picked up some of my more charming characteristics," he added smugly.

Ariadne knew all too well the bonds formed during a battle. Her mind retreated to a darker time.

Ariadne's hand trembled as she released her grasp on the cutlass. She looked on in horror as the sailor tried to clutch at the blade in his back, the life slowly draining from his eyes.

What have I done?

The sailor's lifeless body slumped on the deck, revealing the almost defeated Captain Smith.

Her uncle lay on the deck, catching his breath. "You did good, girl. You ok, Ari?"

"Ari, what do you think?"

Ariadne turned to see Seamus now fully dressed in his new attire striking an imposing figure. She was so used to seeing the man in his tattered uniform. She was impressed. "You look smart, who knew a gentleman lay under all those rags."

Seamus admired himself in the mirror. "The man always did have impeccable taste. On the dawn of battle, against what felt like a hundred dutch vessels, Sir Thomas wouldn't lead the fleet into battle unless he was in a freshly pressed uniform."

"You fought in the St. James Day battle?" Ariadne was impressed. That was a well-fought conflict.

"Aye, that and those despicable barbary corsairs." Seamus' eyes turned glassy as he reflected upon his memories.

"There's a lot more to you than I thought, Seamus Hawthorne. I'm sure you have some amusing anecdotes that I would love to hear someday, but not right now. Right now, I need you to give me the room so I can get changed." She watched as he got the hint and shuffled out of the room with a slight bow.

Ariadne returned her attention to the gown, sighing as she stood up, letting her clothes fall to the floor. She pulled on the dress and adjusted the shoulders, so she looked more respectable and less like a busty bar wench - in the better part of town, of course. *For king and country,* she thought as she made her way back out towards the admiral's office. The boys were seated comfortably, debriefing, when Ariadne walked in.

"The *Daedalus* was a fine ship, she will be sorely missed. We'll find the bastards, Seamus, don't you worry. They will all hang for mutiny." Sir Thomas was red-faced. He looked as angry as she had when they were tied up on Anegada, struggling to free themselves.

Seamus stood up as soon she entered, his familiar smile putting her at ease, pulling out a chair for her to sit in. "Lieutenant, you look wonderful. Please, have a seat. We were just discussing the start of our adventures." Ariadne gave an uncomfortable curtsy before sitting down in the chair offered.

The Admiral was speechless, for once. As soon as she was seated, he began again. "I say, Lieutenant, you fit that dress a lot better than my wife does." He paused for a moment, then proceeded to voice the concern in his face, "Just don't tell her I said that."

Ariadne grinned as she started to feel comfortable in the presence of the admiral, "No promises!"

Sir Thomas gave a hearty laugh. "Don't lose this one, Seamus. She's got a fire in those ocean eyes of hers."

Seamus laughed at the sentiment, "I don't intend to. The Lieutenant has been instrumental in getting us here, I couldn't have done it without her." He glanced over to her.

"That reminds me, Hawthorne, how did you get here? There are no ships scheduled for weeks." Sir Thomas looked puzzled.

Ariadne saw Seamus struggling to make an understandable sentence out of the madness, she knew she would be. She interjected, "All in good time, Admiral," and watched as Seamus relaxed.

"Rightly so, where were we," the admiral paused deep in thought, "ah, yes, so you were marooned, on the island, you were sent to watch over."

"Yes, Admiral, that's correct. They had left us bound together with no supplies on Anegada. Thanks to Lieutenant Smith, we managed to free ourselves and plot our return to the mainland." She watched as Seamus considered his next words.

"Before I continue, Admiral, is there anything you can tell us that was left out of the original briefing? Perhaps some secret the king wished to omit?" Seamus leaned forward in his chair, while Sir Thomas thought on.

"If there was," Sir Thomas paused, looking up at them both to make the point clear, "there isn't," he stressed, "but, if there was a secret the king wished to be omitted, I couldn't tell you."

Seamus cocked his head and gave the admiral a look of bewilderment. "So, there isn't?" He looked over to her and shrugged.

Ariadne cleared her throat, "I think what the captain is trying to say is, did you know of any experiments taking place on Anegada? If so, did you know what they were trying to accomplish?"

Sir Thomas looked contemplative. "The king has become very insular, especially after the plot to kill him. That whole Rye House business has broken his trust. It's tough to gain an audience with him. Which is why I found it a tad odd when I was summoned to his court. The order came directly from the king, I merely passed it on to you. They made me the Comptroller, I control the flow of his Majesty's Navy. He doesn't tell me his secrets. I honestly know nothing of any experiments on Anegada, my good lady, I was just told to send you there - to protect his majesty's interests." The admiral seemed vexed.

Ariadne spoke up, "Admiral, we found things on the island, things that don't make any sense within the natural order of things. Things

232

that we think the king would want to know about. That he needs to know."

"What could be so important?" Sir Thomas cocked his eyebrow. "I need to pique the king's interest, to gain an audience. Things that don't make sense, and things you think he should know about, are not arousing my interest - yet."

Ariadne's mind raced, trying to decide on the best course of action. "If it's interests that need piquing, how about this. We found journals on the island, which brought light to new information. We believe there was an alliance between King Charles and King Louis - to create new materials for the war effort against the Dutch. We have cause to believe the French king went behind Charles' back and stole the results with a means to gain the upper hand against him." She paused, waiting for the weight of the issue to gain speed in the admiral's mind.

Sir Thomas was paying attention now. "Are you saying that the French mean to go to war?"

"Aye, we believe that the fruits of knowledge gained from the experiments on Anegada would place the Sun King in a most fortuitous and, might I add, prominent position to subject England to a most disastrous destruction." Ariadne was not pulling any punches trying to highlight the prodigiousness of the mayhem that would occur.

Sir Thomas was in a state of amazement and worry. "What exactly is it that you found on that island?"

"I think it's best that we show you, Sir Thomas." Seamus stood up from his chair and moved over to the south-facing window. He opened it up and looked outside briefly, before bringing himself in.

Ariadne knew what he was looking for, the *Selene*, it wouldn't be hard to spot. Seamus motioned to the admiral, "take a look for yourself, Sir."

Ariadne watched as the admiral walked over to the window and peered out. Moments passed before Sir Thomas pulled his head back in, his face a vision of complete befuddlement.

Sir Thomas sat back down with a wobble. "I think it best if you start from the beginning, and don't miss a single detail."

* * *

Seamus and Ariadne sat on Tower Hill after their rigorous recounting of the past week, with the Admiral. She needed sleep. The feeling of drowsiness hit her like a warm blanket enveloping her in its arms. Ariadne rested her head on his shoulder.

"Do you think it will be long before the king calls us to attend to him," she asked sleepily.

"Sir Thomas seemed to think it wouldn't be for a few days. He needed to go through all the proper channels." Seamus let out a yawn.

She rolled her eyes. "You'd think that he'd want to know about an imminent invasion straight away."

"Yes, well, it's all speculation from his point of view. Anything could have happened to the French ship that stole those documents; Shipwrecked, mutiny, waylaid by weather or even pirates," he reeled off the list of possible factors. "And, if the king is suffering from assassination attempts he's going to be extra cautious about any meeting he does have."

Ariadne shrugged. "I suppose. Should we perhaps go and catch up on our sleep then?"

Seamus turned his head to hers. "I cordially invite you to make use of my house while we sort this business out. There are plenty of rooms going unused, and it's close by."

She smiled. "That would be greatly appreciated, Seamus. It would be a strange feeling to be apart from you after spending our nights together under the stars, recounting our lives. Plus, I can't bring myself to face my mother yet. I need to organise my thoughts."

"Oh, and don't forget, someone owes me a day of hunting."

"Sleep, then hunt." Ariadne was so drained she struggled to get the words out.

"It's a plan!"

She smirked as they both helped each other up, and made their way towards Whitechapel.

Chapter - 14 - Bienvenue en France.

      Jack sat in the boat listening to the waves crash against the sides, they had finally made their way to French waters. He had taken up a new pastime along the way, reading Sebastian's journal. He liked the idea that someone was chronicling their odyssey. Sebastian had gone to great lengths to explain the meaning behind the word and the great journey that the Greek hero, Odysseus, went on. Jack, of course, saw himself as the Greek hero.

Betwixt the rise and fall of the ocean, a single sailboat made its way across the waves. It bobbed in time with the crescendo, inching ever closer to the white sands. The sea took in a heavy breath and released, the waves breaking the silence. Amongst the rhythmic lashing of the shoreline, two men, cloaked and hooded, worked the boat till it slid on the sand. The sea retreated from whence it came, it's offering made. For they were here, their long journey had ended. This was Calico Jack's time to shine.

"Give 'em the signal," the hood spoke unto the night.

"Aye, Jack." The other mass of cloth, moist from seaspray, removed its cowl to reveal his friend - Sebastian.

Jack removed his hood and watched as Sebastian removed a torch and some cloth from under his seat. The scholar pulled some flint from his waistcoat pocket and struck them together till a lone spark flicked onto the fabric, setting the torch aflame. He jumped out of the boat, signalling the *Neptune* in the distance as soon as his soles hit the ground.

Sebastian looked over as he stood, "Are you reading my journal again?"

Jack stopped what he was doing and closed the book firmly, placing it in the lining of his cloak. "I have to keep myself entertained somehow." He grabbed hold of the boat's side and launched himself out onto the shore, boots squelching as he did. Jack cast his eye on the horizon, his love hiding in the dark, the sails illuminated by the moon with a single light flickering on deck.

Jack had a look of pure bliss on his face and a sizable bulge in his breeches. "Look at her Sebastian, doesn't she just make you want to get on your knees and beg for more."

Sebastian looked somewhat disappointed. "I do worry about you sometimes." He shook his head with a look of sheer embarrassment for him.

The two watched the ship, while Sebastian waved the torch in the air until the Neptune's light was extinguished.

"I shall miss her. We had just begun to get to know each other intimately."

"She will be alright, Jack." Sebastian patted him on the back.

"Aye, and if all goes well, we shall meet again in Le Havre."

"Let us hope she, and the crew, don't run into any difficulty during their task. Passing for a merchant's vessel is easy enough, from a distance, but actually working the trade routes and striking up business along the channel is a formidable task."

"I have faith in the men, and they will do as I ask of them. Besides, keeping the *Neptune* in one spot for too long would be dangerous, if she can look like she's meant to be there conducting business, then she should be fine. While we conclude ours. The plan makes her easily available if aught goes wrong."

"Agreed, which is why I suggested it in the first place."

"Alright, don't get cocksure, Sebastian. We need to survive the next few days. Hopefully, they do too." They both stood and watched as the *Neptune's* sails, glistening in the moonlight, moved northwards undercover of the night.

Sebastian turned to Jack. "And what about your other lover? Do you think she made it to her destination?"

Jack thought deeply. "Knowing her, she'll probably be rallying the troops as we speak," he paused, offering her a silent prayer. "Let us be off, my friend, while we have the cover of darkness."

Jack and Sebastian marched up the shore, away from the sea, towards a small village in the distance.

"This town we are headed to. You know someone there?"

"Villeneuve-en-Retz, aye, a long time ago. I owe them a debt. Hopefully, the same family still lives within."

"Might I know the debt?"

Jack gave Sebastian a sidewards glance. "You may." Jack remained silent.

Sebastian laughed, "Well? Don't keep me in suspense, man."

He decided to acquiesce to the scholar's demands. "Very well. It's nothing really. When Hector smuggled Anney and I over French soil, a man, friendly to the order, gave us succour. They also aided us in gaining passage, along the coast, to Portugal before we disembarked to the New World."

"You and I have very different visions of what nothing is, Jack."

Jack breathed a heavy sigh. "Our lands were gone. Ravaged by war between France, conquered and divided, we lay upon the field of battle. To the victor the spoils - my homeland. Which is where our last stand took place. I was but a mere boy of no use to anyone, but that didn't stop me from wanting to fight. I donned my armour and held my sword high. Yet it was not to be." Jack fell silent as they approached Villeneuve.

Sebastian raised his hands, questioning the silence. "Well, what happened next?"

"Our families wished for us to be kept safe. They tasked a knight of the order, Hector, to smuggle us through enemy territory and take us somewhere we wouldn't be mercilessly slaughtered. I begged and pleaded to stay." Jack paused while the memory played over in his head. "Anney didn't put up a fight, she sobbed. I still remember the sound of the tears hitting the floor."

Sebastian seemed reluctant for him to continue. "Come now, Jack, you don't need to carry on. Let us take our minds to happier places."

"I am fine, my friend, I appreciate your concern, but I feel you must understand the full context of the accord you have entered into. I mean to repay all my debts, especially to the French, for the slaughter they perpetuated, for the executions of my kith and kin."

"Oh, so nothing impossible then," Sebastian added sarcastically, "Well at least my time with you hasn't been boring."

"Nor will it ever be, my friend, come, we are here."

They had reached a lonely farmstead on the outskirts of the town, the candles were lit, and the sound of conversation came from within. Jack gave a rapturous knock on the door.

"Now if I could only remember that damnable phrase," Jack mused.

Seamus looked panicked. "What?"

Ah yes.

The door opened to reveal a greying Frenchman, unmistakenly built for farming - Sun-drenched skin housed in a wall of muscle. He exuded suspicion as he took a measure of the men in front of him. "Bonsoir, puis-je vous aider?"

Jack cleared his throat, "Parlez-Vous Anglais?"

"Yes, of course," the man looked puzzled.

"I have a shipment of roses from Lorraine."

The man paused, his steely gaze staring into Jack's soul, before checking the surrounding area. Eventually, he stood aside as if to let them in. "The *Order* is late, but I will accept your business," he motioned for them to get inside, "Quick before we are the talk of the town. We may be a small village, but news travels fast on land."

Jack and Sebastian moved through the hallway to the living space, whereupon they were greeted by the man's wife and child, seated at the dining table, readying for the evening meal.

"Bonjour?" She seemed a little startled that two cloaked figures had entered her home, but her fears alleviated once her husband returned.

"Do not be afraid, Marion. These are friends."

"Renee! I wish you had told me we were to have company," she admonished her husband.

Jack removed his cloak so that he might better absorb the warmth from the raging hearth. "My good lady, please, do not be too upset with Renee. I fear we have set upon you at the most unreasonable hour, and we are very late. Allow me to make it up to you." Jack took hold of her hand, embracing it with his lips while giving her a slight bow.

Marion's cheeks flushed, but it seemed that imminent chastisement had been diverted - for now. "Can I offer you some food? We have plenty to spare, this year's harvest has been bountiful."

"That would be delightful, I'm sure that your cooking is the talk of the town. Allow me first to introduce myself," Jack released her hand and took a step back, "I am John Rackham of the Duchy of Upper Lorraine," he bowed again to her, "and this is my compatriot, Sebastian Bellamy."

Sebastian gave a little bow. "A pleasure to meet you."

Renee moved to pull out extra seats for them, "please, take a seat. You must have had a long journey?"

Sebastian laughed, "You could say that."

Jack eased himself into the chair, gaining some comfort while alleviating the stress of the travel. "I did not know your name the last time we met, Renee, but this is not our first meeting."

Renee looked uneasy. "Oh?" His eyes flicked towards his family

"Do not trouble yourself. We met at a different time. You did not have a beautiful wife and a wonderful little boy back then. How far you have come," he smiled towards Marion and the boy.

Renee seemed to be searching his memory but remained silent.

"I was but a boy when we first met, my companions were an older man and a girl."

The look of recognition dawned on Renee's face.

"Now you remember," Jack grinned.

"I never expected to see you again, young sir. To see you now, a man, it lightens my heart."
"Tell me, I remember the journey perfectly fine, but not why you helped us? Why would you endanger yourself?" Jack had to be sure they wouldn't cause him trouble once he and Sebastian had left.

"Lord Rackham, not all your people were destroyed by the French. Some found their way to lands far enough from the conflict to start again."

Jack understood now, "and so you did, my friend."

"If you are here now, do you mean to take back the capital?" Renee seemed hopeful.

"One step at a time, Renee. First, we must consult with the Order."

Sebastian was tucking into the delicious display on offer, while Marion and the boy sat on the side befuddled.

"What is this you speak of? Renee?" The woman was becoming increasingly confused at the events transpiring around her.

"Calm yourself, Marion, I shall explain all to you later," he pleaded with his wife.

Jack felt as though he needed to calm the situation he started. He didn't want to be the cause of familial distress. "Please, we mean no disrespect to you, my lady. I only came to repay my debts. I owe your husband a great deal. He took in my friends and I many years ago and protected us from persecution. Renee is a good man," with that Jack reached under his cloak and procured a generously large coin purse, placing it on the table in front of Marion. "For services rendered."

Marion seemed to be satiated. "Very well," she smiled, "please, speak freely. I will get my answers later."

"Thank you, my lady," Jack bowed his head in gratitude.

"You should try the food, Jack, it's delicious." Sebastian seemed oblivious to all going on around him as he cut off another wedge of cheese and drank some wine.

It was Jack's turn to shake his head in disappointment at him. "Not now, Sebastian."

The scholar shrugged at him as he continued to eat his fill.

"Where was I? Ah, yes. Tell me, Renee, does the order still operate out of Chateau de Brissac?"

"The Dukes of Brissac have always been sympathisers of the Lotharingian's plight, but whether the roses have been allowed to flourish there or not, I could not tell you."

"No matter, my friend. I must still try and connect with the Duke; whether the Brass Roses are there or not, perhaps he can tell me where I must search," Jack paused letting out a little sigh. "What about Nantes, are the king's men stationed there?"

Renee chuckled. "Aye, if you mean to take a boat up the Loire, I wouldn't bother unless you wanted to answer prying questions - which I'm sure you don't, my lord." Renee mused on the subject. "The Sun King has tightened his fist around France recently, bolstering the coastal defences, especially the port towns."

Jack felt a little setback, "I thought as much," he sighed. "Then, I fear I must impose on you further, my friend."

Renee raised an eyebrow in curiosity. "Of course, if I can help, just say the word."

"A bed for the night, and some horses?" Jack braced himself.

Renee thought for a moment. "We don't have any room in the house, but the stable would be warm enough. I'll have Marion pack up some supplies for the journey if you mean to keep off the road to Chateau de Brissac, they will come in useful."

"Thank you, my friend. Once we take back what was once ours, we will need good men like you." Jack and Renee shook hands over the table.

"Come, Sebastian, let us not keep them up any longer than we need to." Jack stood up to leave for the stable, while Sebastian watched him with a sausage in his mouth and sorrow in his eyes.

Jack bowed once again to his hosts and retired to the stable, while Sebastian grabbed hold of some bread and cheese, offering thanks and bowing as he followed suit.

* * *

Jack awoke to a warmth on his back and an arm draped over him, it seemed Sebastian had grown a little cold in the night. "My, my, Sebastian. How very bold of you. I wish you would at least court me if you are going to be so brazen with your affections."

Sebastian awoke with a startle, retracting his arm and rolling over. He stretched and yawned, "In your dreams, Jack," he chuckled as he sat up brushing the hay off his clothes.

"Nightly, my dear." Jack winked at him in the dawning light.

"Renee lied to us. He said it would be warm enough, yet there is frost on my moustache." Sebastian sighed as he stood up to stretch further shaking the stiffness from his bones.

"Yes, well, at least I was warm," he grinned at Sebastian.

The scholar rolled his eyes.

Marion appeared from round the corner. "I thought I heard voices. I prepared the saddlebags for you when I woke, your supplies are in there," she patted the bags on the side of the stable. Marion lingered quietly, as though she had something else to say.

"Thank you, my lady. Your kindness shall be repaid one day." Jack smiled as best he could with the sleep still in his eyes.

"You can repay me now, with a favour," she replied abruptly.

Jack's interest was piqued. "Oh?"

"Renee isn't up yet, I know he wanted to say his farewells," she seemed unable to bring forth the words.

Jack sensed this and wanted her to feel at ease. "Speak your mind, you are among friends."

Marion relaxed little, "We have a good life here. I don't want you getting my husband's hopes up. He told me everything last night, of the pride that swelled in his chest when he heard what you planned to do. I feel for you I do, but I have to think about what's best for Renee and my boy. If you tarry longer, he's of a good mind to follow you to whatever godforsaken corner of the world you mean to wage war," she sighed, "If you go before he wakes, I would be eternally grateful and consider all debts repaid."

Jack understood perfectly well. He gave the woman a nod of agreement. Marion gave him a relieved smile and went back inside.

Jack looked to Sebastian, the look in his eyes spoke volumes. "Is this what it is to be like wherever I go, my friend? Have I left it too long to return?"

Sebastian considered Jack's words. "I think that the time is right, whether the people follow you or not, I shall be there by your side."

Jack's gloomy demeanour was instantly replaced with a big grin. "Then let us ride, side by side, to Chateau de Brissac."

* * *

The two friends rode for days, o'er hill and mountain, through forest and field. Pushing their horses until their coats shone and their mouths frothed. Never a truer sign that they had pushed the stallions to their limits. The pirate and the scholar made their way across the French wilderness, never straying too close to the roadside, nor civilisation. Prying eyes doth make for a longer journey. Ahead of them lay a divergence in the path, a stone in the river. Would the Duke hold the answers they so sorely needed, or would the journey end in heartbreak? The uncertainty of possibility spurned their horses on, ever faster, to realise the answers they sought.

Jack sat under a tree, adding notes to Sebastian's journal, scratching at the pages with his adequately sized lead. The horses had complained, so they let them rest a while to take a drink from the nearby pond.

"What are you doing to my prose?" Sebastian tried to grab back his journal, to no avail.

Jack fended off the handsy scholar, "I'm just making it better," Jack turned back to the pages, adding a few more notes. "It's nothing too drastic, anyway, I just figure someone should make sure the facts are right, before recording our misadventure."

Sebastian held out his hand until Jack relented. "Okay, done. I haven't changed it too much. You are annoyingly accurate on some points, others you take liberties with the English language that make even me cringe," he put his lead away and passed it to the scholar.

Sebastian scanned the pages with a horrified face, "Big Seb has no place in this story, thank you very much," Sebastian pulled out his own lead and scribbled out some of the additions while Jack fell over laughing, "the others," he scanned the pages, "I can agree upon. It gives it a more romantic feel to it." He pocketed the journal.

Jack returned his attention to figuring out where they had ended up.

The journey was taking its toll on Sebastian, Jack had managed to stop him from falling off his horse at least twice on the journey from Villeneuve. They needed to rest and soon.

"Not to be a nag, but are we almost there? Our supplies are looking awfully thin," Sebastian checked the saddlebags with a gasp, "and we are down to our last bottle of red wine!"

Jack stood up and sauntered out into the open field, scanning the horizon for landmarks, "Our surroundings are starting to feel a little reminiscent. It's hard to bring an image of the place to mind, especially when it seems a lifetime ago." Jack strained hard to remember the few days he had spent there with Hector and Anney but to no avail.

Sebastian sighed, "Should I ready the horses?"

Jack shook his head, "No. Let them have their moment. When we are done at the chateau, we shall need to ride to Paris. That will be no easy task, for us or them." He returned to Sebastian.

Sebastian removed an apple from the saddlebag and fed it to his horse while stroking its wild mane. "I agree, the closer we get to the capital, the more likely it is we shall be spotted. We can scarcely afford to be detained, we have goals to attain, people of ill repute to meet with."

"What do you mean, 'ill repute'? These are my countrymen, my brothers in arms."

Sebastian held his hand up in protestation, "don't forget the shady women we mean to meet," the scholar grinned while Jack threw a stone at him, "it was a jest, Jack," he laughed.

Jack stopped pretending to be offended and returned to the matter at hand, "Aye, and we don't want anyone finding this on our persons," he removed the vial from his cloak and shook the small splinter of oak floating inside.

Sebastian shook his head. "That never ceases to amaze me."

Jack threw him the vial as Sebastian marvelled at it and continued expressing his thoughts, "Or asking why two Englishman are sneaking around the french countryside!"

"Nor that." Sebastian gave the vial one last shake and passed it back to Jack.

The rhythmic beating of hooves on grass could be heard growing louder through the forest to the west, then a voice echoing over the open lands shouted angrily, "Stop, Poachers!"

Jack held his hand to calm Sebastian, who looked ready to bolt, and waited till the man on horseback was within speaking distance. The horse came to an abrupt stop, a few feet in front of them, the hot breath from its mouth puffing out in misty gasps.

The Frenchman looked imposing with his fineries and his well-groomed hair, he glared down at them, taking in the measure of them. "You picked the wrong day to poach on the Duke's lands, you'll surely hang for this."

Sebastian was taken aback, "How did you know we were English?"

The man gave a derisive snort, "Please, I can spot a foreigner a mile off."

Jack held his hands up in surrender, "Come now, my friend, we are not poachers. Do we really look the type?" Seamus opened his cloak to reveal his well-tailored garments.

The man on horseback gave them both another once over before seeming to come to some sort of conclusion. "I know every face in these parts, but not yours. From where do you hail?"

Sebastian tried to stifle a laugh at the man's expense, "Surely, you jest with accents like these?"

The man remained stern-faced. "What are two Englishmen doing on the Duke of Brissac's lands?"

Jack grinned at Sebastian, before returning his attention to the man, "Ah, so we are here! Excellent. Be a good chap and take us to the Duke. We have travelled a long way to see him, and my companion and I are ever so tired."

"I'll take you to the duke, alright, he can decide whether you're a poacher or not." the man patted the butt of his flintlock rifle on display.

"No need for hostilities, to whom do I owe the pleasure of being in the presence of," Jack paused, waiting for the man to reveal himself to the two.

The man hesitated, seemingly deciding whether the two Englishmen deserved such information, he sighed, relenting, "Pierre, I am the Duke's veneur, how you say, huntsman."

Jack nodded, "Very well, Pierre, we shall follow you on horseback, if you'll allow us?"

Pierre nodded in agreement as he watched them mount their respective horses.

"Which way, my good man?"

The huntsman directed them to the northeast, compelling them to lead while he took up the rear. Jack felt a little uneasy with a stranger at his back, especially one stroking a rifle, but he decided to allow it - seemingly the only safe way to get to their destination.

Pierre motioned them forward, "Easy now, no sudden movements."

He and Sebastian led the way towards the Chateau de Brissac, with the huntsman following them closely. Jack gave a little chuckle as they made their way to the top of the hill, after realising that the Chateau was just over it. The horses galloped in unison, making their way towards the French estate. Jack couldn't help but admire the baroque architecture of the imposing chateau. It certainly was tall. "Tell me, Pierre, is the Duke compensating for something?" He nodded to the impressive size of the castle, cocking an eyebrow in amusement.

Pierre either missed the jest entirely or chose to ignore it, "The Chateau de Brissac was built several centuries ago by the Dukes of Anjou, passing from many families over the years. When King Henry came to power he passed the castle to Charles II de Cossé as a thank you for his help in bringing the king back to the throne, he also gave him the coin to rebuild it to its current grandiose scale. It has remained in the Cossé family ever since."

Jack was impressed with the huntsman's historical knowledge. "Tell me, Pierre, how is old Henri? Is Gabrielle keeping him on his toes still? The last time I was here, they were unwed, did he finally make an honest woman of her?"

"So you know some local history yourself, that doesn't mean you aren't poachers." Pierre still sounded unimpressed or unmoved by Jack's reveal.

"Very well, Pierre, we shall allow the duke to judge as he sees fit." The three made their way to up the path leading to the front entrance of the Chateau, finally coming to a stop and dismounting. The stairs ahead of them led to a small courtyard which brought them in front of the chateau itself, the two turrets either side of the door looming largely over them. Pierre nodded to the doormen posted on guard, who opened the large oak doors to allow them entry.

Jack made his way over the threshold with Sebastian, then Pierre, shortly behind him. The large staircase in front of them swept up gracefully to a landing that went both left and right. Making their way down the stairs, a man, looking like he had something stuck up his nose that he wished to sneeze out, descended towards them. Jack straightened himself up while Sebastian eyed up the decor, his mouth agape.

The new arrival peered at them over the top of his glasses. "Pierre? I was expecting no guests today. Who are these two clothed as if they are ready to skulk around."

Jack removed his cloak, handing it to Pierre as he was about to explain himself, and bowed profusely to the man on the stairs. "Henri Albert de Cossé, it brightens my heart to see you again. It seems like a lifetime ago when we last met. Allow me to reacquaint myself. Lord John Rackham, formerly of the Duchy of Upper Lorraine." Jack paused allowing the duke to process the information, "Oh, and this is my companion, Sebastian Bellamy."

Sebastian had stopped gawking and gave the Duke a respectable bow.

Henri's jaw almost touched the floor, his spectacles dropped from his face as he stood there shocked. After a few moments of speechlessness, the duke's whole demeanour changed, from that of an upper-class citizen looking down on his vassals to one better befitting an old friend. "John Rackham, as I live and breathe. I should have realised it was you, you look so much like your father." Henri moved off the stairs to inspect Jack further. "That will be all, Pierre, thank you for bringing me, my guests."

Pierre was speechless but nevertheless gave a slight bow and left the chateau to return to his own business.

Jack was struck with a resurgence of memories of his late father, "Aye, my father was a good looking fellow wasn't he," Jack's mood had turned sullen, "May his soul rest in peace."

The duke looked confused, "What do you mean, John, he isn't dead. I spoke with your father no more than a month ago. He is still residing on the outskirts of Paris."

Jack's mind was a blur, the duke was talking to him but the words became a hum in the background. His father was alive; he had spent all this time believing his father dead. His head was filled with questions; why hadn't he come for him? Was his mother still alive too? What should he do now? He tried hard to focus but his mind kept retracing back to the same thing, filling his mind. Hugo Rackham was alive.

Chapter - 15 - An Audience with the King.

"Control your breathing, draw back the bowstring, take aim." Ariadne stood by Seamus' side. She was looking down the arrow towards the makeshift target down at the bottom of his estate.

"You know, when I said you should take me hunting, I didn't expect to be hunting a large ham in my shrubberies." Seamus sounded slightly disappointed with his current state.

She hushed him, "You'll scare the prey away."

Seamus stopped stretching the bowstring and turned to stare at her in disbelief, then back to the ham.

"Concentrate, Seamus. How do you expect to hunt in the wild if you can't even fire a bow properly? Now listen to my instruction," she nodded towards the ham. "Focus, control your breathing, draw back the string, then take aim."

He relented, bringing his bow back up and pulling back the bowstring to his ear, just like she had taught him.

Ariadne examined him thoroughly. "Good posture," she tapped his elbow up, "Keep that high otherwise, you'll lose power in the shot." She was satisfied with everything else. She watched as he held his elbow in position. "Now, aim," she watched as he aimed down the arrow, "Make sure to allow for the drop, so aim a little higher." Seamus adjusted for the arc of his arrow. She smirked at him. "Okay, now I want you to exhale, and upon doing so, I want you to release the bowstring." She watched, and hoped, as he breathed in, then out, and at that moment, he released the string. The arrow flexed lightly as it left the bow, travelling in an arc to its target.

They both watched in anticipation as the arrow found its mark, with a thunk, in the fearsome ham.

Seamus jumped in the air with joy. "Huzzah!"

Ariadne patted him in on the shoulder. "Well done, my friend, now you can shoot with the same proficiency as a nine-year-old girl," she laughed.

"Hey! It's my first time," he said with a tinge of defeat.

A small woman appeared clad in aprons from the back of his stately home, her face smeared with a mask of flour. "Seamus dear, your apple pie is ready! Oh, and there's a messenger from the Navy Board here, something about an audience with the king."

Seamus looked to Ariadne with a glimmer in his eyes, "About time!"

Ariadne looked worried, "Do you think they'll be wanting some of our pie?"

Seamus shook his head from side to side.

"I thought so too." She danced up the stairs towards the house, Seamus following shortly behind, as they made their way inside, following the scent of apples in the air.

There it sat by the kitchen window, the golden crust steaming and the apple pieces glistening through the pastry lattice. There also stood the messenger sent by the Navy Board, who had wormed his way into the kitchen, obviously following his nose too.

Ariadne held up a finger, "No! Naughty," she huddled around the pie stopping his advances.

Seamus looked at the pie with a sigh, then to the messenger, feeling he should really see what the man had to say. "I assume the king is ready to see us?"

"I'm just the messenger, sir. I wouldn't know."

"Oh? And how is it that Mrs Tibbs knew exactly the nature of your visit," he questioned the man with a look of disappointment. Seamus grabbed the royally sealed letter, "You may go, tell the king we shall be along shortly." The man looked wantonly at the pie, Ariadne tucking into it with a fork, before thinking better of it and leaving with all his fingers.

Seamus ran his thumb over the royal seal, the Latin inscription catching his eye. *Defender of the faith. I wonder what God has to say about all this.* He broke the seal and proceeded to fold open the letter. The calligraphy was immaculate; it even sent chills down his spine. He loved an excellent bit of cursive. Seamus cleared his throat before reading the contents to the room, "His Royal Highness, King Charles II, formally requests an audience with Captain Hawthorne and Lieutenant Smith at their earliest convenience."

Ariadne had essential questions on her mind, "Do you think he means before?" she stroked the crust of the apple pie, "Or after?"

Seamus placed the letter down and walked over to Ariadne, placing a hand on her shoulder, letting out a little sigh, "before."

She felt defeated, placing the fork down. "Time to make ourselves presentable. It's not every day you meet a king.

Seamus hesitated, "Are you talking to the pie or me?"

Ariadne looked sheepish, "You, of course."

Seamus had a look of disbelief in his eyes before swiftly changing the subject, "I took the liberty of having Mrs Tibbs pick up some garments that I thought were more suited to your tastes. I saw how uncomfortable you were in the dress at the Navy Board, so there is nothing of that sort. Sadly, I didn't have enough time to have a new uniform made up. Hopefully, these will suffice," he beamed at her as the three of them made their way into the foyer.

Ariadne didn't know how to process the kindness, she had struggled to let Seamus do things for her on the *Selene,* and now that they were back in London, she felt a little overwhelmed. It was one thing when it was out of necessity, but she didn't know what to say when it wasn't. "Thank you," she smiled at her friend, "I shall find a way to pay you back as soon as *this* is over."

"You can repay me, Ms Smith, by taking me hunting. Properly this time!" He gave her a stern look, which quickly faded into a smile before making his way to the stairs.

Ariadne chuckled, "Consider it done."

Mrs Tibbs stood in the background admiring the interaction. Ariadne had caught her smiling in her periphery, "And thank you, Mrs Tibbs, for everything you have done to make me feel at home - especially the food," she grinned.

"You're welcome, dear," she pulled Ariadne to the side and whispered, "It's just nice to see Mr Hawthorne with a smile on his face. He seems to care a great deal for you."

Ariadne huddled in closer to Mrs Tibbs, "And I him. Just don't tell him I said that. We wouldn't want him getting overzealous with his diligence towards me."

Mrs Tibbs put a finger to her lips to seal the deal. "You just make sure he takes care of himself out there; God knows if you'll be back."

Ariadne gave her a warm smile and a slight nod.

Seamus was halfway up the stairs before he turned to the two conspirators in the foyer, "Oh, Mrs Tibbs, would you be a dear and call a carriage for us while we change."

"Of course, Mr Hawthorne." She shooed Ariadne up the stairs.

* * *

They had finally dressed into something befitting a royal audience and were on their way to meet King Charles. Apparently, when the king was in residence at Windsor Castle, he liked to hold his audiences at Hampton Court, or so Seamus had told her on the way through London. He looked smart in his naval uniform, decorated with numerous medals, which was rather impressive. She made a mental note to ask him about each of them, in greater detail, at some point. Ariadne was pleased with the selection of clothes he had picked out for her: the tight black breeches, buttoned white shirt, and a brown corset with gold buckles that sat snugly beneath her chest. She had also fallen in love with the dark teal jacket with gold inlays, which now adorned her shoulders.

"I take that you like the clothes I picked out for you," he said with a smug tone.

"Aye, you did good, Seamus." She patted him on the knee. "What do you think the king will ask us?"

"I presume he will want a full briefing of events that led up to us arriving in London."

Ariadne sighed, "That sounds tiresome."

"Yes, well, we did fly a forest halfway across the globe."

The carriage began to slow down and turn. Seamus looked outside the window. "It looks like we are finally here. We're heading through the outer gates, through to the main courtyard. Won't be long now."

Ariadne sat, tapping her knees.

Seamus looked at her with a smile, "Nervous?"

She ceased the rhythmic beating and took hold of herself, "What gave it away?"

"It will be fine, Ari, Don't worry. I'll be there with you. We'll get through this together." They both nodded at each other as the carriage finally came to a stop. The royal footman opened the door for them.

Ariadne stepped out first, with Seamus shortly behind her; she had never been this close to a royal palace before. She wasn't impressed. "Well, this is underwhelming. I was expecting something big and flashy for the king's residence."

Seamus admired the aesthetically pleasing archways of the inner courtyard. "Yes, well, architecture isn't everyone's cup of tea. Besides, this isn't his residence. This is where he holds court."

"Ah, yes, you mentioned that," she looked to the heavens for answers, "I blame the nerves for my memory," she grinned at him. Ariadne had noticed the royal footman to the side of them. He had been waiting patiently for a lull in the conversation to interject with formality, and it seemed to Ariadne that he was finally going to get his chance.

"This way, please, the king is expecting you." The royal footman gave a slight bow and a wave of the hand in the general direction he wished them to travel.

Seamus looked at Ariadne and swept his arm out in the same direction, motioning her to go ahead. She gave him a slight nod of the head and proceeded forward.

Ariadne was shocked; the inside of Hampton Court was far more overwhelming than the external - the ceilings at least. As she walked towards the king's court, she felt her neck strain from continually glancing above at the beautiful vaulted ceilings.

"Watch your step, Ari," Seamus whispered at her as she almost walked into a wall.

Ariadne focussed, they were about to come face to face with Charles Stuart, the king of England, and she was busy gawking at the ceilings. The two of them entered the courtroom finally, and they were met with a loud booming voice, "Presenting, Captain Seamus Hawthorne and Lieutenant Ariadne Smith of His Majesty's Royal Navy."

Seamus gave an overly enthusiastic bow, "Your majesty."

It was only until she followed Seamus' bow that she really paid attention to the man on the throne. Charles sat there, all black curls, a thin moustache, and a faint waft of sophistication. All wrapped up in his regal attire. Quite ravishing actually, maybe the rumours were true about all his mistresses. King Charles sat upon his throne silently. Ariadne thought to herself that he was allowing them a moment of reprieve, to allow his presence to wash over them.

Finally, the king took a sharp intake of breath, "I hear I have you two to thank for the island currently floating above the south bank of the Thames," he announced to the room with calm, soothing tones.

"Yes, your majesty, we do like to make an entrance." It seemed Seamus had thought a light quip might be well received, by the mood of the room.

Ariadne noticed that the king's face remained in the same placid manner.

"Indeed, maybe next time try mooring it up, closer to the ground so that way we can take a look." Charles didn't give them time to answer his own quip; instead, he continued with his own thoughts, "I received a debriefing from Sir Thomas, very thorough."

Ariadne's mind was awash, with a collection of emotions and feelings she had felt during that time, almost as if she were still there. "A lot happened, your majesty," she retorted, the levity now absent from her voice.

"Quite," he paused, "Frankly, this couldn't have come at a worse time. The bloody puritans are at my throat, telling me that this is God's punishment for my dalliance with Catholicism. God is taking back his creation, piece by piece if he has to until I repent! I don't have the stomach to tell them that I messed with the natural order of things. It will cause bloody outrage and would naturally have the same outcome or my execution. I ought to just dissolve the bloody lot again and rule on my own," he paused, "But I digress."

Ariadne watched as Charles seemingly shook off the vexations plaguing his court and straightened himself upon the throne. She cleared her throat, "Forgive me, your majesty, but if you are fully aware of the circumstances that led us here, then why did you summon us?"

A smile spread across the king's face, "Ah, yes, that brings me to the most concerning news that was whispered into my ears - namely the threat of war." Charles let the sound of his words reverberate off the court walls. "Since you know about mine and my cousin's secret experiments, I shall speak plainly. The puritans plague my court. They don't want anything to do with catholicism, even going so far as to try and deny my brother the succession of the crown. Now you are telling me that the Catholic King of France wishes to wage war on me? If they ever learned of this, there would be a resounding cry for a pre-emptive strike. I need actual proof that this is the truth."

Seamus spoke up, "Your majesty, we raced back here on the *Selene* because we believed the threat stated by your own scientist was credible. We dare not try to fathom the intricacies of France's foreign policy."

Charles leaned forward in his throne, rubbing his forehead, "Speak freely, Captain, why would my cousin go to war with me when we agreed to share the results? Divide up the spoils. We each needed the material to further the war against our enemies, enemies of the faith. Each nation had a stake in the union; each had something to gain."

Seamus laughed, "Very well, I shall speak freely. You and parliament fight amongst yourselves over religion, *your* own words. The nation can not run without a functioning government working together with their king," Seamus paused to check Charles' temperament, "Some might perceive the infighting as a weakness."

Charles scoffed, "You think England to be weak?"

Seamus held his hands up in protestation, "Your majesty asked me to speak freely. I am merely suggesting what others may perceive, not I."

Charles seemed to calm down a little, "Very well, continue."

Seamus nodded, continuing his postulating, "Now, your experiment bore results, terrifyingly unexpected results, but nevertheless, results that give one an edge. You only have to see what the Lieutenant and I cobbled together to understand the implications. If one single nation held this power, they would be unstoppable, beholden to no king or country. Can your majesty not see the allure of that?" He questioned the king. "As it stands now, you have the best fleet in the world," Seamus said with an air of pride. "No king would dare to risk going to war with the Royal Navy," Seamus paused, "Unless they had a far superior advantage."

Charles interjected, "Yes, but I do not wish to invade France. I have no issue with my cousin. He has aided me greatly during our Dutch campaign."

Ariadne spoke up, "Can you not see the fear that would spread forth from this? What is to stop you from invading France with this power? Once parliament understands the gauntlet which it could wield, they would bring forth a holy war of righteousness themselves. If you were a catholic kingdom facing a puritan government with this amount of power, I think I would be scared." She stopped, leaving the words in the air.

"Surely, there should be some cause for concern," Seamus added.

The king mused on this information with a sour look on his features, "As luck would have it, two special advisers came to my court a few days ago to corroborate your story. Speaking of a holy fire waiting to wash over England, to cleanse it of its unrighteousness."

Ariadne looked to Seamus for answers, and it seemed they were both confused with the king's revelation.

Charles continued, "They'll be here shortly. I had them looking over that device you constructed. What did you call them? Icarus? They were most interested in what you had brought us."

"Who are these special advisors?" Ariadne curiously asked the king.

"Foreign dignitaries, from the Americas, claimed to have first-hand experience of the French attacking another one of our joint experiments and severing ties with me, which concerned me quite a bit, as you can imagine. Then you come to me with a flying island and a similar tale, which adds more weight to their credibility."

"Foreign dignitaries," Seamus looked puzzled.

"That's right. They hail from the Duchy of Lorraine. Apparently, they were attending some business in the Caribbean when they came across an island on fire. They investigated and found a lone survivor, whom they brought back on board. He was a bit worse for wear, but he managed to relay what had happened before the poor fellow passed away. Their story sounds very much like yours."

"So, there were more islands like Anegada?" Ariadne questioned the king.

"Of course, Lieutenant, a king never puts all his eggs in one basket," Charles smiled at her.

Ariadne turned as the booming voice from behind them proclaimed the entrance of more people, "Presenting the Duke d'Arlon and the Lady Beatrix d'Arlon."

The king seemed more animated upon the arrival of the new guests, "Ah, excellent. Allow me to introduce you to Captain Seamus Hawthorne and Lieutenant Ariadne Smith."

"A pleasure to meet you both. We have heard a great many things about you." The Duke gave them both a slight bow.

"All good, I hope?" Seamus and the Duke laughed while Beatrix and Ariadne weighed each other up.

Ariadne examined Lady Beatrix. She could see why the noblewoman had caught the duke's eyes. Her flowing red locks and beautiful emerald eyes obviously made her stand out in a crowd. Beatrix dressed in a similar fashion to her own. She could admire a woman who preferred comfort over propriety. The woman had caught her admiring her clothes, and she grinned back at Ariadne with a wild glint in those green eyes.

"Not much call for dresses aboard a ship, as I'm sure you are greatly aware of," Beatrix eyed up Ariadne. "Allow me to introduce you to my husband, Francois," she motioned towards the Duke, beckoning him closer.

"Pleasure to meet you, Captain Hawthorne," the Duke and Seamus both mirrored a bow. Francois then turned to Ariadne, and something took over her body. She held out her hand for him to take as he bowed to her and placed his lips on her hand, "And Lady Smith, a pleasure I'm sure," he smirked. His dimples were prominent, and his incredibly blue eyes pierced through her soul, stirring something deep inside her. Her cheeks flushed with heat. Something about the duke seemed so familiar, but she just couldn't place it.

Ariadne squinted at Francois, "Have we met before, Duke?"

"Please, call me Francois, and no, I don't think so," Francois eyed her up and down, taking in every feature, "I think I would have recognised someone so beautiful," he grinned at her, those dimples melting Ariadne's resolve.

"Dear husband, leave the poor woman alone. Can't you see you're making her blush?" Beatrix rolled her eyes.

The king broke the tension, "Good, now that everyone is well acquainted, I shall tell you all why I have brought you here."

"About time someone got to the point, love," Beatrix moved closer to the king, "I grow very restless on land, something about the sea, the sway beneath my feet, it relaxes me," she seemed to lose herself in the moment as she swayed.

Ariadne was mesmerized. There was sensuality in the way Beatrix moved as if she were there on the sea. There was also something in the way she spoke, the cocksure way she conversed with the king. It was almost as if Ariadne felt excited that someone else was breaking down the barriers of propriety. The words brought forth from

Beatrix's mouth seemed to electrify the air, making the hairs on the back of her neck stand on end.

Seamus' voice brought her back around, rousing her from the euphoria, "I think what the Lady d'Arlon is trying to say is how can we aid your majesty?"

"Thank ya kindly, love." Beatrix grinned at Seamus, giving him a little wink.

"I have considered both your testimonies, both tell me a similar tale, both speak of a threat I should be concerned about," the king paused for emphasis, "But that is all they are, words. I need proof." He seemed to weigh each of them up before continuing his speech. "I mean to send you to Paris, as my envoys, to seek out proof of Louis' misdeeds. You have the full blessing of this court to invoke my name, if needs must, to gain an audience with my cousin. You won't be able to accuse him outright, but see what he has to say on such matters."

Seamus looked to Ariadne for support, "We would need a ship, your majesty, something fast." Seamus spoke his thoughts aloud to the king.

Ariadne had a thought, "What about your ship," she questioned the duke and his wife.

Beatrix looked heartbroken, "Would that we could, love. We had a bit of a run-in with some pirates. Our beautiful ship needs a bit of care and attention."

Seamus looked concerned. "Nothing too serious, I hope?"

"It's out of action for at least a fortnight," Beatrix had turned sullen, "We made sure to scupper their plans or piracy. They shall rue the day they thought it a good idea to try and steal our wares."

The king cleared his throat, "It just so happens that my shipbuilders are in the process of fitting a new vessel at Chatham. It should be ready within the week."

Ariadne nodded to Seamus, impressed, "I think I speak for the Captain and me when I offer our full support on this endeavour."

"Of course, your majesty, we shall get to the bottom of this diplomatic quagmire." Seamus gave a hearty bow.

Charles turned his attention to the duke and his wife, "I know I have no right to ask the noble people of Arlon for help in this matter. I stand on the precipice of war, and if we mean to avert this, I would greatly appreciate your assistance in the matter. I can not ask for help outside this court; to do so would spread rumour and gossip. If the puritans gain wind of this, we won't even need proof. They will wish to start a pre-emptive war with France; if I were to try and stop, it would surely mean my execution."

Francois looked like he was considering the king's words, until finally, it seemed he had come to a decision, "Say we acquiesce to your request, what would you have us do?"

"I would have you employ covert tactics, if possible, to uncover any documents or evidence pertaining to said deeds," the king waited for their answer.

The duke laughed, "So let me get this straight. You wish for us to sneak into France, gather intelligence regarding Louis' motives, then what? Sabotage? Theft? You would ask a duke and his wife to do these things," he scoffed.

"I shall speak plainly, Duke, so please do not take offence. Had we the time, I would word it carefully," the king looked them up and down, "Your attire betrays your title. In this court, you are the Duke and Lady d'Arlon. To the outside world, however, you appear as swashbucklers, not merchants. You bested a pirate ship in the Caribbean, without nary a scratch on you. I think what I ask of you is well within your means, sir," replied the king calculatingly.

Beatrix was grinning, "He's got a point, love."

Francois grumbled, "Very well, your majesty, you make a fair point. However, our help comes at a price," he motioned to the king.

"Name your price, and you shall have it."

The duke paced around the room, seemingly mulling over the king's offer. He paused his movements and faced the king, "In exchange for our aid in this matter, we wish to open agreeable trade negotiations between England and the Duchy of Lorraine."

Ariadne noticed, out of the corner of her eyes, Beatrix. A look of puzzlement flashed on her face. She admitted to herself that it was a bit of an odd request, but nevertheless, she decided to talk to Seamus about that later.

The king considered the duke's offer. "Agreed, in exchange for the aid in bringing this matter to an end, I shall open up trade talks with the Duchy of Lorraine."

"What about you, my lady? Care to accompany us across the channel," Seamus flashed a grin at Beatrix.

"The king had me when he mentioned chicanery," she grinned with a raised eyebrow. "It's bloody madness, I love it, I'm in." Beatrix seemed to be sold on the idea straight away.

Francois rolled his eyes.

The king moved in his throne, his discomfort apparent, "Then it's agreed. The duke and his wife shall accompany Captain Hawthorne and his Lieutenant into the heart of Paris. In an attempt to uncover any dastardly deeds that the self-proclaimed Sun King has set in motion. I shall allow you to act as you see fit. If there is proof that he means to attack, but it can be sabotaged, then do so. If not, get the information back to me as fast as the wind can carry you."

Beatrix chimed in, "Aye, if they let us come back," she rolled her eyes at the king.

"*If* that is the case and you don't come back within the month, I shall take that as my answer and make the necessary preparations in parliament," the King affirmed, "I have every faith in your abilities, especially the good Captain and his trusty Lieutenant. If they can fly an island across the North Atlantic to England, then I can rest assured that France won't be able to keep them tied down." He flashed Ariadne a grin.

"Have no fear, Captain Hawthorne is here," Beatrix chimed in.

"Indeed, If there are no other questions, I shall allow you to make your way to Chatham dockyard and await the completion of your new ship."

"Thank you, your majesty." Seamus and Ariadne bowed and made to exit the court, while the duke and his wife gave a slight bow as they exited behind them.

Ariadne could hear the king yawning as they moved away back to the courtyard.

"Well, that was unexpected, dear husband," Beatrix sounded slightly irritated, "What was all that business with trade negotiations," she asked Francois.

The duke replied in hushed angry tones, "Now is not the time."

Ariadne gave a side glance to Seamus, who looked equally as troubled with the conversation behind them. They had finally made it to the courtyard where carriages awaited them to whisk them away to their homes. Ariadne and Seamus turned towards their counterparts, "It was truly an honour to meet you both," Seamus took a hold of Francois' forearm, "Shall we reconvene in a few days? We need to discuss what we intend to do in Paris. Ariadne and I have a few things to take care of first before we commit ourselves to espionage," Seamus grinned with suave sophistication.

Francois shook in agreement, "Aye, that seems agreeable to me."

Seamus gave a bow to Beatrix before entering into the carriage.

"I'm looking forward to seeing what you're capable of, Lieutenant," Beatrix winked at her before jumping into her own carriage.

"Apologies for the forwardness of my wife, Lady Smith," Francois bent down in a bow. Ariadne couldn't help but lose herself in his ocean-blue eyes, she blushed as she curtsied. As Francois arose from his bow she noticed a wisp of golden hair in the sea of grey. The image triggered a memory deep inside her, she stood there stunned as Francois took his leave and entered the carriage after his wife.

It couldn't be him. What is he doing here after all this time? I need to speak to Seamus. Her mind raced as she jumped into the carriage. The sun was setting on Hampton court and she had lingered far too long on her memories, it was time to get some answers.

Chapter - 16 - Like Father, Like Son.

The words had been ringing in his head all evening, *Hugo Rackham is alive*. He had always thought the man was dead. He had heard from one of Hector's contacts of the disastrous results of the battle of Nancy - the last stand of the Duchy of Lorraine. *None were left alive.* Yet, his father lived, and according to Henri, was in contact with the Brass Roses. Why hadn't he sent for him? They could have been fighting this damn war together.

The duke had extended an invitation for them to stay as long as they required. Chateau de Brissac had a long history of being a neutral territory, where opposing forces could meet to parlay on terms. The last French king had met here with his rebellious mother, to try to avert a war she couldn't win, and the chateau had always been a meeting place for the Brass Roses during the old days. So the chateau was safe enough for Jack to let off a little steam.

"What has he been doing all this time, Henri? I've heard nothing from him for years. There's been no news from the Roses. Nothing at all." Jack took another sip from his goblet.

The duke sat at the head of the table, his servants filling it with various delicacies. Sebastian surveyed the table, biting his lip. "You must understand, John, in all matters of state, I must stay neutral. I wouldn't be a very good foreign diplomat if I took sides. While I have remained a friend to Hugo all these years, he has never put me in an unsavoury position. We share mutual respect; he doesn't divulge sensitive information to me nor I to him."

Sebastian was tucking into a particularly juicy breast of a pheasant, with a ponderous look on his face, "So what *do* you two discuss, if not politics?"

"I may stay neutral in matters of state, but I still like to know that he's doing ok. It's one thing to lose one's country to war, but then having to live amongst the victors while they divide up your home and hand it out as the spoils," Henri sighed, "It takes a toll on a man. I feel responsible for him, I couldn't do anything back then, so I do what I can for him now."

Jack understood how the duke was feeling. When he was a boy, he wanted to do anything but run away and hide. Now he felt the responsibility to do something, anything, to get back the land his people called home. "I'm sure he still appreciates the sentiment, Henri. I just wish I had been given a chance to aid him." Jack downed his goblet and poured more of the sweet wine into his cup. "Tell me, has my father ever mentioned me?"

Henri took a sip of his wine, seemingly deep in thought, "I recall asking Hugo how you were doing a few years ago. He seemed to think that you were doing well, that you were living life out in the Caribbean building some sort of merchant haven."

Jack was confused. *How could he know that?* "That was about five years ago, Henri. How could he know that when I haven't spoken to him for ten years."

The duke seemed to mull over the thoughts in his mind, "Hmm, yes, five years ago is when he last spoke of you. He seemed sullen, as I recall. I didn't want to push him too much on the matter. I fathomed it would have been a hard subject to talk on. Though you say, you have had no contact with him since we first met?"

"None." Jack's head started to fill with thoughts, answerless questions, "How could he know of my escapades if he wasn't there," Jack offered up to the room.

Sebastian cut off a corner of cheese and popped it in his mouth. Jack watched as he savoured the taste, the look of euphoria crashing over him like waves caressing the sand. Once the ephemeral effects of the food had ebbed away, Sebastian's face lit up as if he had an epiphany. "Someone was obviously keeping him apprised of your situation."

"Who?" Jack felt irritated. Why would someone keep this fact from him? His father was alive, and they were sending him missives about his movements. It was beyond his comprehension.

Sebastian poured himself some more of the red wine. "My best guess would be Hector." He popped a grape in his mouth and squashed it between his teeth.

Jack felt the anger swell inside his chest as he downed another goblet of wine. "Why would you think that? The man who raised me and brought me to the Caribbean to protect me, why would he keep this from me?"

Henri seemed to have a moment of clarity after taking a sip of his wine, "I may be able to shed some light on that." Jack and Sebastian both focussed on the duke. "Perhaps he was told to keep this from you. Think about it. What would you have done if you had known? Would you have come to France, pledging your allegiance to the cause? Do you think that's what your father wanted? *Or*, do you think that maybe he wanted you to come back to a home and not to war?" Henri paused, thinking further, "I know that if I were faced with a similar choice, I would want you to come back to your home," he smiled warmly.

Jack felt a little bit of the anger subside. *Is this why he didn't wish me to know he was alive?* A sadness washed over him. "You offer me counsel to think on, Henri, but in any case, Hector better have

276

survived the battle with Blackbeard and Read. It seems I have a few questions to ask him."

Henri finished his glass of wine, "Now, I feel I must take my leave of you. The night is meant for younger men than I," the duke stood up, keeping himself balanced, "Good night, my friends." He gave a slight bow before departing to his room.

Jack reached over to the rogue bottle of wine near Henri's vacant seat. He pulled out the cork with his teeth and sat drinking straight from the bottle. Tonight was to be a libatious one.

"Hey, leave some wine for the rest of us," Sebastian exclaimed.

The wine had flowed freely, the cheese even more so. This was France after all. Jack and Sebastian had discovered Henri's study and had brought in several bottles of wine to accompany them while they sat and discussed the finer points of the fairer sex.

"The next time we happen to frequent a tavern, I shall show you how a real man speaks to women." Jack sloshed his bottle as Sebastian laughed at him.

"We shall see, Jack. If it's anything like watching you and Anney trade innuendos, count me out!"

Jack let the last drops of wine drip onto his tongue. He searched around his chair for more, "Ugh, Sebastian, where has all the wine gone?" Jack slurred the words that tried their hardest to escape his mouth.

"Jack, as much as I find you an amusing drunk, I would not have you deplete the rest of the dukes' reserves of red wine. Especially now, we have no more cheese to go with it." Jack could feel Sebastian weep internally at the loss of the accompaniment

"God, Sebastian, must your love affair with food haunt us everywhere," Jack cradled his head, keeping the thoughts from spilling out.

"How about I speak on something other than food?" Sebastian offered him some reprieve.

Jack felt a calm in the storm as Sebastian teased at a change in conversation, "That would be music to thine ears."

"Your father." Sebastian drunkenly cackled while Jack groaned like a dying whale. "You know we are going to have to circumnavigate that problem at some point, whether you choose to deal with it or not."

"Yes. Believe me, I am aware," Jack pushed the sentence forcefully from his lips.

"Is that it? just, yes?" Jack groaned as Sebastian continued, "The way the Duke tells it, your father is coordinating the affairs of the Brass Roses from a residence on the outskirts of Paris," Sebastian waited for him to reply, only being met with silence, "What do we mean to do about that?"

"Sebastian," Jack searched for answers in Sebastian's eyes, "I'd be lying if I said I didn't feel a little betrayed. I feel cheated, Seb, not just the time I could have been with my family," Jack sighed, "I could have been helping the fool, strategise, or something." Jack felt the anger swell. Sebastian sighed, and before he could respond, Jack's thoughts came fast. "I don't know the man, at least I thought I did. I have this idealised image of a man in my head who died at the head of a battle charge. Dying for his country, his people," Jack changed the cadence of his tone, "This man has been hiding in Paris, doing what? Why is this the first I am hearing this?" Jack went back to cradling his head.

Sebastian placed a solitary hand on his head, the constant buzz in his mind slightly subsided with the implied comfort to his weary thoughts. Jack fought to form the sentence through the fog, "What am I supposed to think, my friend?" The scholar laughed.

Jack used every ounce of strength he had left to lift himself from his thoughts, "Why do you laugh at me?"

"Jack, come now. I'm not laughing at you. You and I are two very different people, but sometimes when I look at you, it's like looking in a mirror." Sebastian sighed as he stood up, walking to the window. "I do not wish to delve into too much detail regarding my own past because you are far too drunk, and you will not remember come tomorrow."

Jack strained to hold on to lucidity as he worked through what Sebastian had said, arriving at the only conclusion available. "Your father wasn't around either?"

"Aye, Jack, my father spent great swathes of time away from his family. He would come back for short periods, but I would not know the man. As I flitted through the years of my youth, my ideals and education were moulded to the setting I found myself in." Sebastian shook his head, "Even this is too much detail for you."

Jack felt curiously invested in Sebastian's story, "Come now, my friend, tell me more," he slurred.

Sebastian looked over to him, and Jack attempted his best impression of a sober pirate. It seemed to have worked because Sebastian continued. "Very well. Many years later, my father started to spend more time at home. I would find myself wondering about the early years, why he strayed so far from home, for so long? Should I ask the man what happened, or should I just leave it? I eventually plucked up the courage to ask him the things that had been burning away at my soul since childhood. Namely, why wasn't he there."

Jack felt he was getting to the vital part of the story. Even though his eyes wanted to shut, he willed his ears to stay awake.

"Do you know what he said?" Sebastian looked over at him; Jack was slightly incapacitated, "He said, *I always thought that the best thing I could provide, for your childhood, was the means for you and your mother to live comfortably.* I was astounded, here I thought that my father did not love me, that he had no desire to spend time with me." Sebastian shrugged and returned to sit next to Jack. "I feel Henri hit the mark; your father was just trying to provide the best possible future for you. Maybe he was trying to rekindle your legacy?"

Jack heard the words, and he heard Sebastian sigh, but his body had shut down. He was beyond responding. It was the last notion that he heard before he passed into oblivion.

* * *

Jack awoke in one of the many bedrooms that the Chateau had to offer. His head was pounding, and his vision blurry. It wasn't often that he let himself get in that state, but all things considered, he felt it warranted. He scrunched his face up as the light hit his eyes, and he turned to try and pull himself together. He could still feel it, the hum of the questions filling his thoughts. *Seems you can't silence them with wine.* He sat up and tried opening his eyes again. The room spun, slowly stabilising. Jack looked around the room with a half squint, noticing Sebastian asleep on the chair next to the bed.

Jack tried to order the thoughts in his head. He remembered getting so drunk he was asking Sebastian for advice. *God, was I drinking red wine again?*

"Sebastian," he threw a boot at the man who still owed him an answer.

Surprisingly, Sebastian awoke with a startle as the boot hit him angrily in the testicles. After he had subsided from the pain, he looked over to where Jack sat, squinting at him. "Good morning."

"I asked you a question."

Sebastian snorted, "You asked me a question. Do you think you were ready for the answer?"

Jack reflected upon the state he had got himself into, "No?" He wasn't sure; he certainly didn't remember anything Sebastian had said. He was only left with the subtle impression that they had bonded over red wine and cheese.

"You don't remember anything I said, do you." Sebastian shook his head. "Get up. We are going to visit your father today. You may not like the answers he has for you, but we have a nation to save, sailor. Steel yourself, ya idiot." he threw the boot back at Jack as he got up to get himself ready.

Jack was suddenly reminded of Anney. *What would Anney say about all this?* Jack sighed. *I hope she made it to England.* There was a pang in the place where his heart was supposed to be. He missed her. Jack dragged himself out of the bed while Sebastian cleared up around him.

"Do you think Henri has some cheese left for us to take," Sebastian asked inquisitively.

Jack rolled his eyes and groaned as he walked out of the bedroom door.

* * *

The three friends stood in the courtyard, waiting for Pierre to bring the horses round. The Duke had been awake for some time, or so he had told Jack, he liked to make himself busy when the mornings were brisk, and this particular morning was rather invigorating. Jack took in a gulp of fresh spring air. "Today smells like a good day, Henri."

"Hopefully, that bodes well for your reunion." Henri patted him on the shoulder.

Jack stared off into the distance, contemplating what his first words to his father would be, "We shall soon find out, my friend."

Pierre appeared from around the corner leading the two horses they had arrived on. They seemed well-rested and happy to see Sebastian, who patted his pockets when they were near, obviously hiding a treat for them.

Jack placed his thoughts to the background of his mind and turned to thank the duke. "Your hospitality has been much appreciated, Henri," Jack embraced the Duke's forearm with a firm shake.

"And the supplies," Sebastian added as he gave the duke a little wink while he too shook the man's forearm with gratitude.

Jack walked over to where Pierre stood with the horses, "and thank you for taking care of the horses, Pierre, apologies for our earlier indiscretion." Jack held out his hand to take the reins.

"Do not worry, Lord Rackham. We can not be too careful in these parts. I suggest you cross the Loire further inland, don't bother at Angers. The last time I was there, the king's men were keeping themselves busy bothering travellers. I believe the crossing at Saumer is quiet these days," the huntsman smiled.

The duke turned to start up the stairs towards the chateau, then turned back to the pair. "Oh and John," Jack turned to the duke, "Don't be too hard on the man. He's been through a lot."

Jack sighed, "Aye, and so have I."

The duke nodded, a look of sympathy glistening in his eyes, "Stay safe, my friends," and with that, Henri disappeared into the chateau.

Jack watched as Sebastian pulled an apple from his pocket, hiding it behind his back until his horse whinnied towards the hand that held the succulent fruit. Sebastian stroked its mane as he fed the treat to his four-legged friend. The scholar looked over to Jack, noticing his love affair with the horse. "Shall we be heading off, Lord Captain John Jack Rackham?. He laughed at Jack whilst dodging his advances as he chased Sebastian around the horses.

Once the chicanery had subsided, and Jack was out of breath he dignified Sebastian with an answer. "Aye, let us make way to Paris."

* * *

They had been riding no longer than it had taken the sun to reach its zenith, along the French countryside, when Jack spotted something in the sky. Jack stilled his horse and squinted towards the western horizon, "Sebastian, my head may still be a little groggy. Would you do me the honour of looking to the sky in the west?"

Sebastian pulled the reins on his horse to bring him close to Jack. He closed the saddlebag he was stuffing cheese back into and looked to where Jack was facing. "What is it?" he questioned while chewing on a particular creamy vintage of Roquefort.

"Something unusual just disappeared into the clouds. Wait a moment, it should reappear," the two stood there, staring into the sky, searching.

"Perhaps it was just a bird," Sebastian offered, "I can't…" he continued but was cut off by Jack pointing at something much larger than a bird bursting out of the clouds.

"There!" He pointed to a mass in the sky, bursting forth from the clouds. Jack moved his horse closer to Sebastian, took hold of his head, and guided it to where the mass was.

Sebastian sat with his mouth agape as he finally registered what Jack was directing him to, "What is that?"

Jack couldn't fathom what they were looking at, then a spark of inspiration blossomed in his mind. He patted his pockets until he found it, protruding down his trouser leg. "What were we doing last night, my friend?" Jack smirked as he carefully extracted the spyglass from his breeches. Sebastian rolled his eyes as Jack extended the scope suggestively and scanned the heavens for the mass again.

"Can you see it," Sebastian asked eagerly.

Jack strained his good eye through the scope, "Aye, it's moving fairly fast."

"Let me see!" Sebastian tried to grab the spyglass from him.

"Just you wait," Jack leaned out of reach, slapping his advances away with his free hand, "It seems to be headed this way, whatever it is. Here take a look," he handed Sebastian the device.

The scholar snatched the spyglass from his friend and quickly honed in on the mass, "It's a browny-green smudge in the sky. There, I solved the mystery," Sebastian grinned while continuing to watch, "Whatever it is, it's coming into focus as it gets closer." Sebastian removed the spyglass from his eye and rubbed the end. "I can tell you what I think it looks like, but," he paused, "you'll think I'm mad."

Jack snorted, "I know you're bloody mad, Sebastian, entertain me with your thoughts anyway."

"I think it's best if you take a look yourself."

Jack held his hand out for the spyglass until Sebastian obliged him. The object in the sky was now definitely clearer; it had an outline and features, and it wasn't exactly what Jack was expecting, so he made sure to go through every other thing it could be before settling on what it actually was. "Is that," Jack paused, his mouth agape, "Is that a flying forest?"

Sebastian was giggling as he had just been tickled, "I told you, madness," He flung his arms up in the air in exasperation.

Jack let slip a little gasp, "Seb, there's a sail on top of it," he exclaimed.

"I would say don't be absurd, but then we are watching a flying forest -- absurd doesn't quite cut it,"

Jack was sure that what they now faced was a flying forest with a sail, "Here look," Jack passed the spyglass back to Sebastian. He watched as the scholar peered at the oddity.

"Huh, I'll be damned, so there is." Sebastian took a short intake of breath through his teeth, "I don't know how to tell you this," he paused, leaving Jack hanging on his every word, "So I'll just come out and say it. There looks to be a woman on top of the sail."

Jack couldn't have grabbed the spyglass any quicker at the mention of a female. He had to see for himself. He looked towards the top of the sail with a disappointed sigh, "It seems she isn't there. Could you have been mistaken?"

Sebastian shrugged, "Possibly, we were up late drinking last night," he chuckled.

Jack continued to monitor the flying forest's progress, "This has something to do with the secrets we carry. The vial in my pocket and this island are one and the same. I swear my life on it."

Sebastian nodded, "I would say so. The experiments in the Caribbean were mentioned in the journals. The splinter of floating oak that seems to defy all natural laws. This flying island. They all seem to be from the same realm of strangeness."

Jack felt an uneasy feeling rising in his chest while he was listening to Sebastian. He had no idea how this would affect their plans, if at all. If there were people in this flying forest, whose side were they on, and what were their intentions? The thoughts raced through his mind, worrying him. Jack voiced some of his concerns, "Aye, and what realm would that be? Where do you think this forest has flown from?"

Sebastian shaded his eyes from the sun, "Judging by the direction of flight, west to east, I can only presume it came from the Americas - or at least that general area."

Jack was impressed by the notion, "You think that *thing* has come all the way across the North Atlantic?" He mused over the thought, "It seems plausible." Jack was lost amid a myriad of questions swimming around and around, searching for answers that did not come.

Sebastian broke the silence, "Bugger me, Jack, think what we could do with a fleet of those?"

"Seb, that and so many questions are running around my head right now. I wouldn't even know where to begin. This," he pointed at the island, "turns my head upside down and throws everything I know into the locker, it does." Sebastian looked bemused by Jack's floundering, "It just brings questions I can't even begin to fathom. The main question is - What in Poseidon's pissing arsehole is that?" Jack raised his arms to the heavens.

"Ha!" Sebastian snorted, "You have such a way with the English language."

Jack's mood turned to elation, "At least someone is amused by all this. It is still my goal to make you swear like a sailor." Jack placed the spyglass down momentarily and faced Sebastian. "I am glad you are here, my friend. I would not have liked to face all this alone. Words alone can not express my gratitude. It shall not be forgotten."

Sebastian grinned, still watching the forest, "Aye, ya bastard, that's what I'm here for. To keep you on this path that you've set us all on. Anney, Hector, and I are all counting on you."

Jack placed his hand on Sebastian's shoulder, a flash of confidence in his eye, "I shall not disappoint."

The scholar pointed to the forest, "What's it doing?" He looked confused as he stared into the sky.

Jack placed his eye back on the spyglass. "It seems to be rotating its sail," he strained his eyes. *It can't mean to turn into the wind?*

"They are jibing it, Jack. It's turning into the wind!" Sebastian sounded far too excited.

"I love it when you talk nautical to me, Seb," Jack grinned. He had to agree with the scholar, though, "Aye, that it is, slowly. It seems to be heading across the Loire - northwards."

"To England?"

"God knows, Sebastian. Wherever it's heading, it can't be good news." Whoever was flying this forest, Jack envied them. What he wouldn't give to be able to pioneer that method of travel. He thought about the buzz of excitement they must be feeling attempting such a thing, and it left him wanting.

Sebastian broke the tension, "Does it change anything?"

Jack looked over to his friend, "To the plan?" Sebastian nodded his head. "No. Come, let's pay my father a visit. He needs to know about this, and I have some long-overdue questions that need answering." Jack spurred on his horse with an almighty cry as they rode, like the wind was at their backs, to Paris.

* * *

"There lay a village, not too far from the outskirts of Paris, Fontainebleau. The Chateau de Bourron nestled here amidst the idyllic setting of this picturesque landscape. Behind tree after tree, the chateau peaked out, offering the impression that it was hiding from the local populace. In fact, it was, at least, hiding its occupant. Exiled; from his home, his family, his people, Duke of Lorraine, Hugo Rackham.

We rejoined our story at the dawn of the light on the third day. Our two heroes had ridden through the night. Calico Jack's steely gaze pierced the Chateau. This hiding place was fit for a king. Had his father been living in luxury this whole time? What had he been doing in this moated castle? Where were the Brass Roses? Our hero had a few questions for the recently revived head of his household."

"It'll do, I suppose, I mean, two heroes? The last time we did something worthy of a bard's tale, you were cowering and shitting your breeches," Jack grinned at him.

Sebastian huffed, "Fine, how about a trusty companion?" He scribbled on the pages of his journal, amending the prose. "One day, though, I'll do something to make you proud, my friend." He grumbled.

"Of that, I have no doubt." Jack had spotted the chateau from the hillside to the west of the forest, hiding it. So they were working their way through the trees at a slow trot, which the horses didn't seem to mind. They had worked them hard over the past few days' ride. Sebastian's horse had seemed happy enough, as long as there were enough apples for him to bribe.

"How is Olivia?"

Jack stroked the mane of his horse, "She seems fine. She'll be ready for a rest once we get to the chateau. She's done really well, haven't you girl?" he patted Olivia's neck.

"Here," Sebastian threw him an apple.

Jack deftly caught the fruit with one hand and took a bite before feeding the rest to his hungry horse. He had spotted the chateau a few moments ago. The sun rose behind them, sending shafts of light through the forest, the trees breaking its radiance. The walls of the Chateau de Bourron shone with such brilliance as the light reflected off its numerous windows. Jack turned to Sebastian to let him know, but before he could even open his mouth.

"I know. Not long now. Are you ready for this?" Sebastian threw the question at him like they were preparing to go to war, for they may very well soon be.

"Of course, I've had three days to mull on it," he uttered with a cockiness.

"Well, good because we are here."

The forest opened up, offering the full extent of the chateau's exquisiteness. Sebastian's jaw dropped while Jack felt the anger brewing. He remained stoic, however. Jack led the horse over the moat and into the courtyard. Olivia trotted sedately up the garden towards the two sweeping staircases, either side of the main door.

"Someone did well, out of the loss of their country." Sebastian's snide remark did not help his anger.

"Quite. Let's just go in." Jack and Sebastian tied up their horses to the staircase balustrades and approached the main doors, pushing them open. Nary a soul was about.

The hallways were quiet, dark. The sunlight had not yet hit them. They both moved through the rooms gracefully until Jack heard a cough in the distance. He looked towards Sebastian, who confirmed with a nod that he had heard it also. Sebastian pointed towards the direction the sound had come from, and they both went to investigate.

They came to another set of double doors, ornately crafted, with gold filigree on the handles. Jack looked at Sebastian for ideas.

"After you, my friend," he whispered, motioning to the doors.

The doors swung open as Jack heaved them apart to reveal the dining room. He made his way over the threshold and into the room itself. He noticed the large table in the centre, which was partially laden with food. As he scanned up the table to the head, an old man sat deep in thought, huddled in a warm cloak.

"And who might you be?"

Jack, for once, was speechless. He had thought of nothing else for the past few days, and he had no words. Hugo sat at the head of his table, seemingly deep in thought. The man looked broken, tired, dishevelled. Everything that shattered the image in his head. Henri was right. The years had been rough on the man.

"Well? Speak up, boy," he barked at Jack.

Jack's mind raced, searching for the answer to the hunched over duke's question. He looked at Sebastian before being somewhat inspired. "Lord Bellamy sent me. I'm his squire."

"Lord Bellamy?" Hugo looked up from the papers on his table. He had been inspecting a large map with pencil marks on.

"The Brass Roses, Duke, I'm here to take a message back to my Lord. Regarding how he should prepare?"

Something seemed to have unstuck a memory from the man's mind. He seemed preoccupied. Jack figured he could have used any name, and his father would have been none the wiser.

"Ah, yes, of course. Come be seated." Hugo motioned to the seats by his side.

Jack and Sebastian both bowed and moved to sit. Sebastian had the good sense to remain silent on the whole matter. As soon as they were seated, Jack cast his view over the documents to get a feel for what the duke was planning.

"How is Lord Bellamy these days," Hugo asked with a slightly sceptical tone.

"He is keeping himself busy, Duke. He awaits the day when we can finally take back our homeland. Long has he been vacant from his lands, as have we all. He wishes to do anything in his power to aid in the swift release of the French kings grasp on the blessed lands of the Lotharingians." Jack fuelled his lies with his own passions.

Hugo took a measure of the man in front of him, the first time his face had left the table. Jack couldn't look him in the eye. He would lose it if he did. He didn't even know why he had started this fictitious tale, but he was in it now. It served a purpose if nothing else. If he knew his father was working towards the liberation of his home, he could go easy on him. If he had been lining his own pockets to keep himself in the comfort he had become accustomed to for these past ten years, he would be served with a reckoning.

His father finally broke his own silence with a heavy sigh. "As do they all, young squire. It brings a tear to my eye every time I hear the pleas of our knights. Desperate to aid in a cause which has no way of succeeding." Hugo placed down the map in his hands. "There are no plans to take back the Duchy of Lorraine, the rightful lands of old king Lothar. Please tell Lord Bellamy to stand down any designs he has. We can not afford to anger the French. That will be all." Hugo returned to his map, paying them no more attention.

Jack's cheeks flushed with flame. The anger filled his insides like a volcano, waiting to erupt. "Nothing!" He slammed his fists down on the table, shattering the silence, the thud echoing around the hall.

"Excuse me, squire." Hugo packed the last word with pompous venom as he peeked over the top of his map staring at Jack.

"You are not excused," Jack volleyed back, "nor by *our* people," he shouted at his father. "You have sat here *hiding* for ten years, your tail between your legs, in the lap of French luxury, and you have nothing!"

"How dare you!" The duke shouted back.

"No! How dare *you*!" Jack stared at the man in his cold-blue eyes, his resolve staying intact, "I have spent my youth away from my family, my people, my lands! I thought you were *dead*! Yet here you are. Alive, growing fat." Jack swiped the plates of food from the table while Sebastian looked fearful for the man.

The duke stood up, rage filled his face, "You come to my home, and you slander my honour. You have no idea how heavy my heart is. Where were you boys, when I stood in the Vanguard, my brothers in arms by my side? Where were you when the Brass Roses lay dying at my feet? Those were *real* men," his voice faltered as he steadied himself with the table, "They knew the courage and fortitude it took to stand against your enemies. Especially when they knew *damn* well that none of them were going back to their homes." Hugo took a moment to collect himself.

"I would have stood with you!" The duke looked at him, confused. "That choice was taken from me, like everything else. When I found out you were alive, I came here hoping you had not been squandering your years. That a plan was being put in motion to take back our lands. Yet I find this," Jack motioned to the table. "I could have been helping you, instead you have been doing nothing."

"Who are you, that you would say these things to an old man? There is nothing that can be done. Our lands are gone. I live here in exile, never to leave, upon punishment of death. What can I do?" Hugo coughed uncontrollably, the weakness of his age soothing his rage.

"Who am I?" Jack looked at Sebastian briefly before returning his attention to his father. "I am Lord John Rackham, son of the Duke of Lorraine, Hugo Rackham, and I will tell you what *we* will do."

Chapter - 17 - The Past Revisited.

Ariadne sat across from Seamus in the carriage. She had spent the last few moments bringing forth the memories of her encounter with the knight and her grandmother on the Sintra Mountains. The Duke d'Arlon had a striking resemblance to the Knight, if not a little older. She had to be sure. *What does this mean? If he and the knight are one and the same, maybe I can get some answers to my own past. This is too much of a coincidence. First, my memories resurface, and now the characters that played parts in my history come to reprise their roles.* Ariadne looked over to Seamus, who was watching London go by. "Seamus, remember when I said that something was troubling my mind, back on the *Selene*?"

Seamus awoke from his mesmerized state, pulling himself away from counting the cobbles. "Hmm?"

The rain dripped from Ariadne's hood as she stood holding her mother's hand.

The memories were coming fast now, flashing before her mind's eye. "The memory I had, on the *Selene*, when we passed the Sintra Mountains. The Order of the Brass Roses, the knight with the curly blonde hair and the wonderful blue eyes. My grandmother, Lady," she sifted through her memories, "Lady Francis, or Smith, whoever she was."

Seamus looked more alert now, the day had been long, but she needed her friend's counsel. "Aye, I remember. I remember you had another memory surface that you wanted to talk about. Is this that?"

Ariadne shook her head, "No, but I shall get to that." She bit her lip in frustration, "This concerns the Duke d'Arlon. I believe he and the knight, the one I met at the monastery, are the same person."

"I see." Seamus looked deep in thought. "Well, the time of the knight has all but passed. There were only a few older countries in Europe that held onto such a romantic tradition. When the world no longer needed them, it makes sense that he would find other work. Mercantile ventures can be highly lucrative."

Ariadne laughed, "You believe me? Just like that? I thought I was going mad."

"But, of course, my friend. If you say it is so, then it is so. You have no reason to lie. I trust you." Seamus was acting all matter-of-factly.

She breathed a sigh of relief. "Perhaps, it is as you say. Yet of all the people in this world, it can not be a coincidence that he has come back into my life a second time." Ariadne stared into space. *The rain dripped from Ariadne's hood as she stood holding her mother's hand. She could hear shouting in the distance. Horses galloping.* "Maybe he holds the key to my other memories."

"Ah, yes, the one you wished to wait to tell me." Seamus had focussed all his attention on her now.

Ariadne attempted to bring the memory forth, squeeze every bit of detail from it. "This memory is more slippery. All I seem to be able to recall is a collection of images and sounds." She was frustrated. It was hard enough with what they had been through, but now she struggled with her own personal issues.

Seamus seemed to sense the anxiety building up inside her. "Take your time, Ari, breathe." He placed a hand on her own.

She looked into his eyes, his smiling face calming her. "It was when we were flying across the Loire. I saw several Chateau dotted along the river, but there was one that stood out. As I stood in the crow's nest, my mind wandered. I saw myself standing in the rain, holding my mother's hand. Then I heard shouting in the distance," She strained her mind but could not focus the sound.

"What were they shouting?"

Ariadne shook her head, "I don't know. The next thing I heard was the sound of hoofs on wet mud, getting closer and closer. I turned to my mother, and she was searching through the rain, looking for something." Ariadne could feel the squeeze of her mother's hand in her memory. She looked down to see Seamus' hand holding on tight. "I remember the look of relief on my mother's face when a carriage broke through the storm, and we were able to flee." She sighed, "From whom, I do not know."

"You know what I'm going to say, don't you?" Seamus stared at her as she tried to look away.

"No," she groaned.

Seamus laughed under his breath, "No, you don't, or no you don't want to?" He clasped her hand with both of his. "I don't know what hardships you and your mother have been through, but I know that the only way you are going to gain peace of mind is to talk to her. I'm confident that she will be able to shed some light on your past and maybe even some on the duke. I know she sent you off to sea because she couldn't deal with you, but life is too short to waste time holding grudges from the past. Before you know it, you'll be dead and buried."

Ariadne sighed like a woman who had accepted her fate. "Why must you be so wise, like an old owl?"

Seamus recoiled. "Why must you always lace your compliments with ageist slights?"

"Oh come, Seamus, my impoliteness merely masks our familiarity - our bond," she rolled off her tongue.

He curled his lips into a coy smile. "Fine. Then I no longer need to impress upon you the sense in your next steps." She grinned at him. "I feel that I already know the answer, but if you require the company, I am more than happy to hold your hand through this ordeal."

Ariadne watched outside the carriage window as London passed them by. "No, I fear this is something I must do on my own."

Seamus nodded, "I figured as much, very well," He rapped on the carriage wall nearest the driver, "Whitechapel, posthaste, my good man." Seamus returned his attention to her. "You will spend the night at my home; Mrs Tibbs will be pleased to see you. I don't think she has had anyone compliment her cooking as much as you for as long as I can remember. Then, in the morning, we will both take a trip to your family home, and I will peruse the local scenery while you speak with your mother. That way, I shall be close by if you require this wise old owl." He grinned in that way he liked to do.

"Do I get one of her famous breakfasts?" She sat, looking like the cat that was about to get the cream.

"If you're a good girl," Seamus paused, "then yes."

"To Whitehcapel, posthaste driver!"

* * *

It had been one of those mornings, the kind where you drag it out as long as possible. Ariadne had not had one of those types of mornings for as long as she could remember. Mornings on board the various vessels she had the privilege of serving on had always been early. Even when they were marooned on the *Selene,* she arose at an ungodly hour. Some might even say she was keeping today's planned activities at a great distance.

Yesterday's debriefing had left her with ravenous lust for food; her body's hunger must have finally caught up with her. Luckily, she was greeted in the morning by Mrs Tibbs' sausage, eggs, and bacon. If that didn't cure it, nothing would. She had said goodbye to Seamus' housekeeper, who had laden her with a brown parcel filled with leftovers. The delicious package now accompanied her in. It bounced along as the carriage made its way over the cobbled streets of London towards Southwarke - towards her family home.

The carriage slowed as it made its way over London Bridge, through the numerous people going to market, then through the square where all the stalls were set out. That was one of the few things she missed about coming home. She loved the hustle and bustle of market day, where people from most walks of life mingled together. It was a far cry from the solitude and silence of the *Selene*.

"This is where we part ways, for now, my friend."

Seamus had been there as silent support since they had left his home. She had been mentally preparing for the meeting and had totally forgotten that he was leaving her to it. It was probably for the best. "Aye, are you sure you don't want to come in for some tea?"

Seamus laughed. "You will be fine, Ari. I would only divert attention away from the true matter at hand. I would rather you have a clear mind when we embark on this mission for the king." He exited the carriage and turned, "Don't forget, I am not far away if you truly need me. I shall meet you in the market once you are done."

Ariadne nodded at him, a grimace adorning her face. "Agreed. I shall see you soon." Seamus closed the door and rapped on the side, giving the all-clear to carry on the journey.

Eventually, they came to a stop. Ariadne opened the carriage door and stepped out directly into a puddle. She rolled her eyes. *It begins.* The manor imposed on its surroundings, tall and expansive. A lot of room for one person. The garden was still well kept, and the flowers were blooming. She had fond memories of helping her grandmother plant much of what she now saw. But those memories were not why she was here today. "Thank you," she said to the driver as she handed him a coin. "Don't leave me alone," She muttered under her breath. It was already too late; the carriage was bobbing its way back through Southwarke. She was home.

Ariadne caressed the intricate design on the oak door. It had been a while since she had seen it, but the eagle had adorned her family home since as early as she could remember; it had become worn with age. It had always been a habit of hers to touch the crown atop its head for luck. This time, though, it didn't provide much of a challenge - she was now a fully grown woman after all. She raised the knocker and let go, allowing it to bounce on the door. The din rang through the house as she stood there nervously, waiting for someone to answer. Ariadne could hear footsteps approaching. She straightened out her clothes, making herself look mildly presentable. The door swung open to reveal an old, well-dressed man, fumbling for his glasses. Placing them on his face, he allowed his eyes to focus.

"Ms Ariadne, is that you?"

The old butler used to chase her around the garden when she was young. She would raise all sorts of hell to bother her family. Now he seemed a ghost of the man he once was; Ariadne didn't think he would be chasing anyone around the garden. His eyes still shone with the same green-hued liveliness, though. "Higgins, it's good to see you. Have you been keeping well? You've still got that sparkle in your eyes," she exclaimed.

Higgins chuckled, "Thank you, Miss." He beckoned her in.

Ariadne crossed the threshold and felt a sudden chill take control of her body. "It feels like someone has walked over my grave, old friend."

He looked at her like she was talking her usual shite, like the old days when she was a small nuisance. "That'll be the draft, Miss. Come in, come in, Let's keep out the brisk morning air."

She moved further in, allowing the old man to close the door behind her. "Is mother here, Higgins?"

"Why yes, of course, she's in the back garden tending the Roses. They've bloomed beautifully this year. I shall let the mistress know you are here, my lady."

"No, don't trouble yourself, Higgins. I'm sure it will be a lovely surprise for her." Before the old butler had even a chance to object, she had whisked past him. She made her way through the hallway towards the back door while Higgins went about his business.

Ariadne inspected the familiar walls, still full of old pictures, none of them of her. She rolled her eyes in exasperation. The back doors were open. She moved through them and searched for the woman who gave her life. It wasn't hard to spot the harpy. There she was, a thorn amongst the roses. "Hello, you old witch."

Her mother didn't need to turn around to know it was her. Who else would greet their mother in such a way? "I thought I could smell sulphur. Did Satan send you to claw me back to hell with you?"

Ariadne smirked. "No, he sent me to torment you instead."

"No change there then?" Her mother stood up, wiped the soil off her hands, and turned around. "You look thin. Are you eating enough?"

"Yes, mother."

Her mother looked at her sternly, possibly trying to discern whether she was lying or not. It was true that they had hardly eaten on the *Selene*, but Mrs Tibbs had seen to it that she had caught up somewhat. *Oh no! I left the package in the carriage!* She groaned internally.

Her mother walked towards her, giving her a loose hug. "How was your trip home?"

Ariadne could tell that her mother was getting the pleasantries out of the way so she could go back to her roses. "It was eventful, but we made it back in one piece."

She nodded, "Will you be stopping? I'll have Higgins set up the spare room."

That was the last thing Ariadne wanted to do. "I can't, mother, I have business to attend to. We are being sent on a mission by the king, a perilous mission, hopefully, to avert a war." She hoped to sound important, maybe to try and elicit some sort of feeling other than hate from her mother.

"Then what can I do for such a notable person?" She didn't seem impressed, typical Christina Smith.

Ariadne sighed, "I have questions about my past. I would be glad if you could shed some light on what troubles me before I leave for France."

Christina cocked her eyebrow, "Whatever would you be doing there?"

"That's for the King and me to know, and for you to keep your beak out," she scowled at her mother.

Christina looked down her nose at her, "Very well, but be warned. There are tumultuous affairs occurring over the channel. Watch your back." She looked stern - unusual for a Smith.

Ariadne cocked her head and gave her mother a weird look, "What does that even mean? 'Watch your back?' What have you heard?"

Her mother shrugged in that way that absolved her of all responsibilities. She had made an effort; it was up to Ariadne to figure out the rest. That was usually what her shrugs meant. "I just hear things, nothing more." She trailed off, "Anyway, what is it that you came here to ask me about?"

She could tell her mother was getting bored already. She kept huffing and looking around the garden. "Do we have to do this outside?"

Christina sighed, looking inside the house and back to Ariadne, "I suppose I could have Higgins make us some tea."

"Oh, only if it's not an inconvenience," Ariadne said with an air of incredulousness.

Christina walked over to the back door, "That's what he's paid for darling. Higgins," she shouted, the sound reverberating through the house, "Tea, in the parlour."

"Yes, ma'am," came a call from the aether.

Ariadne followed her mother back into the manor, "Wonderful, I wouldn't want to dirty the house properly."

Christina gave her a glance over the shoulder as they walked through the dining room and into the hallway, "God knows where you have been. I would rather not have Higgins keel over cleaning up after you. He has enough work keeping up with the dogs."

A thought dawned in Ariadne's head, "Speaking of dogs, how is Aunt Sophia?"

Her mother scoffed, "Since your uncle, Tiberius, went and got himself blown up by the Dutch, Sophia has had to remarry."

Ariadne tried to look interested, "Oh, anyone I know?"

Christina rolled her eyes. "Some witless clerk in the commons. She's not getting any younger, I suppose. It was either that or go live on the streets." She chuckled to herself.

Memories of Ariadne's first Captain flooded her mind. "My uncle was a good man. She would have found it hard to find another man with his courage and tenacity under fire."

Christina paused before the parlour door, "On that, you and I can agree. He was very good at dealing with troublesome women." Higgins came shuffling in and passed them with a tray and some tea.

"Yes, well, he had you as a sister. I'm pretty sure you put him through his paces before he got to us," she fired the insult across Christina's bow. It must not have registered because she made her way into the parlour and made herself comfortable in the chair with the window view. *At least she has something interesting to look at when she gets bored with the conversation.*

"So, how can I help ease your worries?" Christina took a sip of the fresh tea that Higgins had been pouring for them.

Ariadne moved into the parlour and sat down directly in front of her mother so she could ruin her view. She didn't know where to begin. She took a deep breath and exhaled slowly, "I suppose the best place to start would be the memories of the pilgrimages, Grandmother and I would make to the Sintra monastery in Portugal."

"Wonderfully pointless waste of money," Christina rolled her eyes, "What about them?"

Anger flashed across her eyes. Her grandmother practically raised her. She didn't get to insult her memory. "Selene didn't think they were pointless, and neither did I." *Calm yourself, Ari.*

"Yes, well, we shall have to agree to disagree on that one. You didn't have to deal with the finances after she was gone," her mother said pointedly.

Ariadne sighed, recomposed herself, and decided to get this over quickly. She didn't want to be here any longer than she had to. "Tell me what you know of the Brass Roses?" She wasn't sure, but she swore she could see a flash of recognition in her mother's eyes.

Christina shook her head, "Nothing comes to my mind."

Liar! "Are you sure? Grandmother seemed to have a great reverence for one of their order, at least."

"His name?"

Ariadne wondered whether to even bother telling her. It was worth a shot, she supposed. "Francois d'Arlon." There it was, again, another flash of recognition crossed her mother's face.

Christina shook her head a second time, "No, sorry. I don't recall anyone by that name."

Ariadne sighed, "Very well." She knew her mother was hiding something, but she couldn't figure out what. She didn't want to push the meeting to its conclusion quite yet, especially when she had more questions to ask. Angering her mother now would end the conversation swiftly.

"Surely, that wasn't everything?" Christina was getting fidgety and playing with her fingernails, sure signs that she was hiding something and that she wished to be anywhere but here answering Ariadne's questions.

Ariadne knew she was wasting her time; she wasn't expecting any revelations from her, although it was worth a try. She thought she might have better luck with the memory of her mother and a young Ariadne, but she wasn't holding on to any hope. "I recently found myself travelling along the Loire."

Her mother interjected, "In France?"

"Yes, where else?" Ariadne looked incredulously at her mother. Christina shrugged. "One of the chateau we came across triggered a memory I had long forgotten about."

"Do tell." Christina sipped her tea.

Ariadne pulled the memory to the forefront to relive it while she gave a running commentary for her mother. "I was only young, about eight or nine. We were standing outside a chateau in the rain. I held your hand. You looked worried; you were searching for something." She looked into her mother's eyes to take a measure of her, nothing. Christina stared out of the window as much as she could. "We were being hunted. I could hear shouting and gunfire. I remember being so scared."

Her mother had stopped looking out of the window and was actually focussing on Ariadne, looking genuinely concerned. "What happened after that?"

"A carriage appeared out of the rain and whisked us away. We were finally safe." She looked at her mother, waiting for her to illuminate the darkest recess of her memories.

Silence. Her mother stared into space, "Well, that all sounds very excitable. Are you sure it wasn't a fever dream or perhaps a nightmare?"

Ariadne grew tired of this outright denial. She became frustrated and angrier with each new word that would extricate itself from her mother's mouth. "No, mother, you were there. What happened to us? Stop with these charades and speak the truth. For once, tell me something that will help me." She slammed her fist down onto the side table, rattling her teacup.

"Ari, I do not recall such events ever occurring. I would also appreciate that you watch your tone with me in my own house." Christina glared at her daughter.

"Mother, I can see it in your eyes. Why would you keep the truth from me?" Ariadne's frustrations were getting the better of her; her voice began to falter. She sighed for what felt like the hundredth time since she had entered the manor. She looked pleadingly into her mother's eyes, "Mother, please."

Christina relaxed her shoulders, seemingly releasing some of the tension in the room. "You were very young, I always thought that you wouldn't remember because you never mentioned it since. I sometimes wish I didn't," she sighed. "Château de Brissac is what you are referring to. We lived there with your father. The night you are referring to is the night he was killed by French bandits. You and I fled together, we barely made it out of there alive after they stormed the chateau. Luckily, one of our guards had the foresight to sneak into the stables and bring the carriage around. After that, I felt that it was no longer safe for you and I to stay there. So after your father was buried you and I made our way to England to live with your Grandmother."

Ariadne felt like she had been punched in the gut. She was speechless. She knew her father had died many years ago, but she had no idea that she had been there in those crucial moments.

Christina broke the silence, "I never thought I would see the day that Ariadne Smith had nothing to say."

"I'm just shocked. Why have you never told me this?" Ariadne was still reeling. She was finding it difficult to find her centre and remain composed.

"I relive it a thousand times in my own mind. Why would I want to bring more credence to the memory by stepping through the past with you? We both nearly died, Ari. The night was traumatic enough. Why would I want a child to live that moment over and over in her mind? It's hard enough every time I look into your eyes I am reminded of my beloved," a single tear traced a line down her mother's cheek as she, "the life draining from his face and the moments we stood in the rain fearing for our lives."

There it was, Ariadne thought, *the elephant in the room finally exposed for all to revel in.* She felt an emptiness in the pit of her stomach. "Is that why you can't bear to be in my presence?"

Christina wiped the tears from her eyes. "Ari, I," she paused.

Ariadne butted in before she could get the rest of the sentence out before her mother could destroy her anymore. "Don't bother, mother, I understand." She stood up to leave. "Thank you for your time."

Her mother stood up, pleading with her. "Ari, wait! Let me explain."

"You've explained it well enough." Ariadne could not look at her mother in the eyes. "I have a prior engagement to attend to." She stormed out of the parlour and into the hallway. Ariadne opened the front door to leave, but as soon as she did, the wind blew harshly, like someone had barged in, nearly ripping the door from its hinges. The uneasiness she had felt when she had first entered had returned as the wind blew through the house and up the stairs. After those moments of initial unbalance, the wind died down a little and grew quieter. Ariadne paused in the hallway.

Suddenly, a creak from upstairs resounded through the house. Ariadne looked to the parlour. She could not see her mother, but Higgins was there, clearing up the mess. Her reckless attitude to exploring the unknown was clearly chomping at the bit. She felt rooted to the spot and felt the immense urge to run up the stairs and face her fears. *The devil may care, but I bloody don't.*

Ariadne nervously inched her way up the stairs, heart beating away in her chest. She measured each step carefully, navigating the creeks and cracks in each tread, hoping not to alert the presence upstairs. She eventually reached the landing with a cold sweat upon her brow.

Her fingers slipped from the rail, finally losing grip on the one thing keeping her steady. The words ringing from her mother's mouth were still fresh in her mind. Another smaller creak made her jump but also alerted her to the noisy door, the wind whipping through the air. Selene's old room. She walked over to the door to feel a pocket of warm air enveloped her, taking the edge off her nerves a little. She fingered the doorknob tentatively, giving it a slight push, just enough to reveal any intruders. Yet there were none. The wind died down completely as Ariadne broke the veil to Selene's inner sanctum. *Someone must have closed the front door.*

It was just as she remembered. The curtains were drawn and the light from the tall window cascaded over the four-poster bed, which had been freshly made. There was no dust in sight. Higgins had obviously been keeping himself busy in here. It almost felt as if she wasn't gone, but she knew in her heart that she had been gone a long time. Ariadne sat on the bed to calm herself, the emotional battle of words with her mother had exhausted her, both mentally and physically. She reminisced about the time she spent here as a child. The lessons she learned. She sighed to herself. *How times have changed.*

Ariadne stood up and walked over to her grandmother's dressing table. She loved to sit and play with the things that adorned it. Ariadne moved the chair to sit down, to take a look at the woman she had become. She could see the features she had inherited from Selene, prominent cheekbones, sparkling eyes, brown hair. She missed her. *What would Selene Smith do?* She asked the mirror, but no answer came. Ariadne sighed and got up to leave. A creak came from the floor as she stepped on the boards next to the chair. *A loose floorboard?*

Getting onto her knees, Ariadne pushed on one edge of the board, which lifted up the opposite end. She removed the loose part of the floor to check underneath it. Nothing. Ariadne plunged her hand into the darkness, her fingers finding the edge of something leather and worn. She extracted the item from between the joists to discover a journal. Ariadne sat back on the chair and ran her fingertips across the cover. *Is this Selene's?* She opened it up to find a folded letter just inside the journal. The nerves had returned as Ariadne unfolded the letter.

Dear Ariadne.

* * *

It was her grandmother's handwriting. Ariadne had quickly closed the letter; she couldn't have read it there. Not if there was a chance her mother had found her in an emotional mess. Especially not after their heated exchange. She did not want to give her the satisfaction of thinking she had caused her state. Ariadne had left the manor briskly; she tried to distance herself as far from her mother as possible. So she had gone looking for Seamus in the market close by. She had found him bartering with a rather rotund purveyor of alcoholic beverages. He had waved to her, so he knew she was there. She decided to sit on a nearby bench and wait.

The market was still bustling, but all Ariadne could hear was the muffled sounds around her like she was surrounded by four walls. Her attention had been focussed solely on the journal she now kept in her inside pocket. Ariadne could feel her heart beating away next to it, pushing her closer to reading it. This really was not the time, but when would it be, she thought. It was now or never. Ariadne reached in and pulled out the letter.

Dear Ariadne, What are you doing sneaking in my things? It's good that I taught you to be inquisitive. Ariadne chuckled to herself and continued reading. *There is so much I wish I had taught you, but I'm sure you are doing just fine. Despite what your mother thinks, I know that you've grown into a fine young woman. Yet, my deepest sadness is that I am not there to see it. There is so much more I need you to know before I leave this mortal coil. Even though I have indeed passed by now, I can still let you know what your mother doesn't want you to know.*

Suddenly, Seamus appeared, making Ariadne jump a little as she quickly scurried the letter away inside her jacket pocket. He had returned carrying something that she highly suspected was for the maiden voyage.

"What was that?" Seamus asked curiously.

"Oh, nothing." Ariadne felt a little sheepish hiding something from her friend. "It's just a letter."

"From who?" Seamus came to sit by her on the bench, the bottles he had procured clinking together in the wrapping.

Ariadne chuckled, "Rum?" Seamus nodded at her. He must have been waiting for her to stop dodging the question. "Ugh! Fine." She pulled the letter from out of its hiding place. "I found Selene's journal hidden away in her room. I haven't had a chance to read it because as soon as I opened the cover, a letter, addressed to me, dropped out."

Seamus raised his eyebrow, "First thing's first, my friend. Did you get the answers you needed from your mother?"

"Some. She was rather elusive, as I figured she would be. We got into an argument over the reasons why she can't stand to be around me."

"I'm sorry, Ari," he draped an arm over her shoulder.

She cuddled into him before sitting back upright again. "I found out why my memory was triggered when I spotted the Chateau de Brissac over the Loire. We lived there for a while before it was attacked by French bandits. Not only did they murder my father, but they would have killed us too if we hadn't escaped the night."

Seamus looked aghast, "Good lord, Ari. I don't know what to say."

"It's fine. It happened a long time ago. At least now I know why my mother can't stand to be in the same room as me."

Seamus gave a nod and a look of understanding, "She is reminded of the event constantly. I do not like to admit it, but I went through a similar stage when I reminded myself of my own family. The memories of them alive and well made me angry. Until I couldn't bear to remember them." He sighed. "It is different now, though. Just give your mother time. Hopefully, imparting the knowledge to you has opened the path to reconciling with the present."

"We shall see." Ariadne wasn't hopeful for that. Her mother was stubborn, just as much as she could be.

"And the letter?" Seamus seemed to approach the topic with a bit more tact.

Ariadne opened the letter back up. "It's addressed to me. The bit I read, she just talks about her regrets, but then she goes on to say that she wanted to tell me something my mother didn't want me to know."

"Well? What are you waiting for? Read on."

Ariadne found the spot where she had been interrupted and carried on reading. *"She doesn't want you to understand your legacy. Christina thinks it is too much for a young girl to understand but I know you better. You are smart and strong, and I feel the contents of this letter and journal will lead you to a better future for your family and your people."*

Seamus seemed confused. "What does she mean 'your people'?"

Ariadne had no idea what she meant. She continued reading. "*I feel as though my time is short, so I won't try and explain everything in this letter. The journal will explain everything. All my love, always. Selene.*" She turned the page over to check the other side - nothing. "Looks like I'll have to read the journal to unlock the secrets my mother was keeping from me."

"Then we shall do it together, my friend. Though, I'm afraid we must be off soon. I have arranged for the carriage to pick us up at midday to take us to Chatham," He looked towards the sun, seeming to gauge the sun's position, "And time is short."

"Very well," she placed the letter and journal away in her jacket pocket, "A mystery to unwrap later then." It was at that moment their carriage pulled up to them to whisk them away. Ariadne entered while Seamus spoke to the driver. It wasn't long before the two of them were on their way to the dockyard to meet their new ship.

* * *

Chatham Dockyard, a delightful place filled with England's wooden walls. Ariadne stepped from the carriage and took a lungful of fresh salty sea air and freshly cut oak. "Smell that, Seamus? That's the smell of the best fleet in the world."

Seamus popped his head from the carriage door, "Hard to forget, my friend, it reminds me of the *Selene*." He stepped down and joined her.

Ariadne could see the *Selene* looming on the horizon. "I wonder how London is coping with a floating mass of island imposing itself south of the Thames?"

She reminisced about the time she had thought it a dream when the *Selene* was plucked from Anegada. "Probably as well as we first did on that fateful morning."

Seamus chuckled at her. "I suppose so. Tell me, did you uncover any new information from your grandmother's journal?"

"I couldn't bring myself to read it. I fear if I do, then I will not be of any use on this mission. I need to come to terms with the revelation of my father's death first, as tempting as the mystery of my past is. It isn't relevant to our current predicament."

Seamus nodded in agreement, "Upon our return then?"

"Aye, as soon as we are safely back on English soil." She grinned at him to let him know she was somewhat coping with everything. He gave her a slight smile in return. She wasn't fooling him. She decided to change the subject - the perfect sidestep. "So, where were we supposed to meet Francois and Beatrix?"

"Here, my friend." He waved his arms around in front of him. "The *Trumpet Tavern*. They must have been here a few days. The letter they sent arrived while you were polishing off Mrs Tibbs' breakfast. It said to meet them where they would be staying."

"Let's waste no time then." Ariadne motioned for Seamus to lead the way.

The Tavern was an absolute dive, and full of seamen. Exactly what Ariadne had expected to find. She thought back to her own time at Chatham and could never recall fraternising in the shady pubs that lined the dockyard. *Good, I would have had a terrible time, going by this tavern.* She spotted them fairly quickly, they were cosied up in one of the dark corners of the place, animatedly chatting away.

Beatrix spotted them first. She waved them over with an enthusiasm she wasn't used to from other women.

"Well met, strangers," Beatrix exclaimed obviously three or four pints in, "You took your time recuperating."

Seamus gave Francois and Beatrix a little bow. "It's good to see you in high spirits, we had some business to attend to that couldn't wait, I'm afraid."

Francois stood up to embrace them both, "No problem at all, my friends. You come at the most opportune of times. The Oracle is nearly ready," he exclaimed.

Ariadne saw a glint of excitement flash in Seamus' eyes. "Is that what they're calling her?"

"Aye, as soon as we arrived, Bea has been keeping tabs on her progress. She's a mighty fine ship, captain." Francois grinned at Seamus.

"How many guns?" Seamus finally managed to get some words out. Ariadne bet he couldn't believe his luck.

"Oh, she's a beasty, captain, one hundred guns. She'll surely protect us if trouble should raise its ugly head," Beatrix drawled off, in that way that made everything sound erotic.

"Can we go see her?" Seamus licked his lips.

Ariadne rolled her eyes.

Francois stood up with his tankard, "Aye, I don't see why not. Let's go see how the lass is getting on." With that, he marched out of the *Trumpet Tavern* with Beatrix in tow.

It wasn't long before the four ambassadors found the ship that they would be taking to France. Ariadne and Seamus stood there, their mouths agape. Francois was right, she was beautiful with curves in all the right places. She wasn't going anywhere fast with all that weight, but wherever she wanted to go, she would do it in style. Seamus looked loved up. Ariadne poked him in the ribs, "Come on, let's not keep her waiting. You got that rum?"

"Most definitely." Seamus dreamily waltzed towards the *Oracle*.

Ariadne almost forgot to add, "And don't lose this one!"

Chapter - 18 - The Sun King.

Jack watched as Hugo fell back into his chair. The truth was out now for all to see. The words still echoed in the dining room. The shock on Hugo's face was as apparent as the palpable tension in the air. Jack let the information soak into the atmosphere. He now stood there in front of his father, the Duke of Lorraine, waiting for him to say something. Hugo's eyes filled with emotion as he looked upon his son's face.

"Mine own flesh and blood has returned to me." Hugo sat there, taking him all in. "You have grown up big and strong, my boy." He spoke with the timbre of a man living with a thousand regrets.

Anger flashed across Jack's mind once again, "You would have seen that had you sent word for me to return after the battle!"

Hugo closed his eyes, nodding slightly at the sting in Jack's words. He sighed, "That is one of my deepest regrets, not seeing you grow up. It is also the one thing I am most thankful for that you weren't there for the battle or its devastating aftermath." Hugo's eyes turned glassy as he turned inwards, reflecting upon the loss. You were not there to see countless knights of the Brass Roses cut down in a quick cleaving motion."

Henri's parting words echoed around Jack's mind. He took a breath and calmed the rage bubbling away at the surface. "Tell me more. I would know what happened."

"With a thousand knights on horseback, the Brass Roses looked formidable. Nothing could stand against their might and valour in battle; they had proven themselves a hundred times over. I trusted every single one of them with my life. We were cocksure -- we knew the land, and we knew in our hearts that we would win."

Jack interjected, "And the French washed over you, battering the stalwart defence of the Brass Roses, like the sea. Wave after wave of soldier crashed upon you, till there was none left alive. Or so Hector told us." He wanted to stick that in there, to let his father know that he knew what Hector had been doing.

"Aye, Hector told you what I asked him to. If I had told him to tell you that I was alive, what would you have done?"

"You know damn well that I would have found a way back to you. I would have helped you take back our home."

"Exactly, and what would a boy of ten do against the entire might of the Sun King? Die?"

Jack grumbled under his breath. He knew his father was right, but he was still angry at him.

Hugo continued, "Our home is no longer our own; it lays occupied by French forces. We are exiles from our own lands. Again!" Hugo's anger made a brief appearance before being subdued by a coughing fit.

"Sorry to interrupt, but I haven't been keeping track of French relations. Why does Louis have such an urge to mount Lorraine like a buxom wench?"

A smile spread across Jack's face like it had no business being there, especially in his current state. It found a way to invade his face, nonetheless. "Let me enlighten you, Sebastian. My father has always been, how should I put it," Jack thought for a moment, "Anti-French, in his policies. He picked the wrong side in a French internal conflict in his youth, and he's been paying for it ever since."

"I see you've picked up a knack for oversimplifying matters." Hugo rolled his eyes, while Jack shrugged, "Yes, I backed the losing faction in the Parisian conflict. I was exiled for many years, while Louis occupied Lorraine until the sixties when I came back. Thanks to the Holy Roman Empire. Do you know why Louis is the Sun King?"

Sebastian shrugged.

"Because he thinks the bloody sun shines out his arse!" Hugo scowled.

Jack nearly burst out laughing before he remembered he was cross at his father.

"He thinks that all the lands should come under his reign. The damn Sun King had started to move into a position to start another war with the Holy Roman Empire and the Dutch; we were just in the way of much bigger things. I knew our defeat was at hand, I knew there was no way we would survive this time, so I sent John and Lord Bonney's girl away. I didn't want them to have to deal with the consequences of the path I had chosen."

Jack felt sorry for the man; his rage had subsided. He had no real reason to be angry anymore. He was just doing what he thought right. The man was correct, there was nothing to come back to, no way of fighting against that kind of power, but his father had no idea what he had been through, what he had seen.

"Why did you choose this path again if you knew it led to destruction?" Sebastian seemed very curious as to the Duke's decisions.

Hugo continued, "I have always been in an alliance with the Empire. They stood for values better than those that came from Paris. I was bound to defend her interests. I always have." Hugo sighed, "I knew we didn't stand a chance, but the men were brave and confident. We lined up on the field of battle and waited. The beat of the French war drum did not break our resolve, nor did their insurmountable numbers." Jack noticed the look on his father's face He had seen it before - inescapable horror. "The arrows bounced off our shields, and the sound was deafening. Then, before the din of that had subsided, the roar of the spearmen came all too quickly."

Jack felt he needed to tie loose ends up, "But you survived."

"Aye, I wish I hadn't. Being forced to walk past the men who had died for my cause, men I called brothers, is not a thing I would wish upon any man." There was no anger left in the room, only sadness.

"So they captured you? Forced you into exile? Put you somewhere they could keep an eye on you."

"They had me guarded at first. As the years went by, they lost interest in me. The Brass Roses all but decimated in the battle.

"You say 'all but'?" Sebastian quizzed him.

"Yes, my friend, few still remain, but they are scattered to the wind. In hiding. Just like Hector. How is he, by the way?"

Jack was pained by the question. "I sent him with Anney to England. At least I hope."

"You did what?"

Jack sighed, "I have not forgiven you, nor do I ever think I will. You let me believe you were dead." Hugo nodded in acceptance, "but I do believe you could do nothing from here. Given what you have been through. If I had been in your position, I wouldn't have been so bloody stupid with my allegiances, especially not twice in a row" His father conceded to that point. "But I don't agree that there is nothing that can be done now." With that, he extricated the vial from his person and slid it across the table towards his father.

Hugo looked befuddled. "What is this?"

"The answer to our predicament."

"If the answer is a lump of wood in some water, I'd love to know what the predicament is."

"It's not in water."

"What?" Hugo shook the vial; the splinter of oak bobbed around it. "Perhaps some other solution then? Perhaps alcohol."

"Open it," Jack grinned and watched as his father uncorked the vial. As soon as he had, the wood began to float out of the container and upwards. Hugo caught the piece of oak before it flew away and placed it back in the vial.

"What witchery is this?" Hugo seemed shocked.

"No witchery. Science. We came across a French vessel in the Caribbean. Some pirates had attacked them, left them for dead." Jack could feel Sebastian's eyes burning holes into the side of his head. "They had taken all the goods and left a lone survivor. Sebastian here managed to coax some information out of him. Apparently, they were on a mission from the Sun King to steal all information that he and the English king had been working on in the Caribbean. Experiments with trees, making them light to build faster ships. What they didn't count on was making this." Jack pointed at the vial. "Material that flies like a bird."

"So the French and the English were working together over there, and Louis decided to stab the alliance in the back? Aye, that sounds like him." Hugo shook the vial again. "Is this the only evidence you have?"

"No. Sebastian and I buried a chest of documents that we found on the French vessel, pertaining to the whole thing, on an Island near Tortuga. We didn't want to chance bringing them with us, just in case."

"Smart," his father smiled at him. "So, what was the plan? Pitch the two against each other. You say that you sent Anney and Hector to England. With a view to what? Tell the king that they had seen first hand the treachery of the Sun King. Tell Charles to go to war with France?"

"Aye, then I would come to France, seek an audience with Louis and tell him that Charles had caught wind of his schemes and was on his way with an Armada, that I had managed to salvage some of the documents."

"Sounds like the plan hinges on whether you can convince two kings."

Jack sighed, "I have every faith in Anney sweet-talking Charles. I hear he likes the ladies. I'm not so bad with words either; they can drip honey when I want them to. But, there was something that we did not plan on. Something that we don't know whether to be worried about or not." Hugo sat, not saying a word, waiting for Jack to finish. "As soon as we set off from the Chateau de Brissac, we encountered something in the sky."

"What exactly?"

"A mass of earth with a forest on top, flying through the air as if it were a normal day."

Hugo squinted.

"I know how it sounds, but the forest, the experiments and journals, and that which you hold in your hand. They are all linked. They are all omens that a change is coming. I can feel a great war on the horizon, and we must stand at the precipice to seize any advantage we can so we can take back our home."

"So you expect me to believe that forests are flying around out there in the sky, like some sort of fever dream?"

"You hold some of the proof there in your hands."

Hugo held the vial to the light and shook it, allowing the splinter inside to bounce around again. "You are telling me that this little thing could help us get our lands back?"

"Can you not see the applications such a material could be used for? Imagine a fleet of flying airships; they could go anywhere, attack anyone. Kings would go to war over such power. We have witnessed first hand the effects of their experiments, seen with our own eyes what they can create. I have no doubt that with a little whisper in the king's ears is all that it would take, they will be more than willing to go to war - Leaving Lorraine vulnerable."

Hugo sat, contemplating his son's words. "So, you mean to set the French against the English."

"Aye, keep them busy like the French is keeping the Holy Roman Empire busy with the Turks while they steal more lands in between them."

"You've been keeping abreast of current affairs?"

"Henri and I had a little chat; he loosened his lips once he'd had a bottle or two of the red."

Hugo laughed. "You would use the French's own tactics against them? There is something poetic about that; I like it. It might work," Hugo sighed, "If we had an army with which to march with."

Jack sat deep in thought, "What about the remaining Brass Roses?"

"Fifty knights at most, those that were away on diplomatic duties, not enough to make a difference, I'm afraid. Don't get me wrong, I would rate one Brass Rose to ten normal soldiers, but even that would not do."

"Mine and Anney's crew are also quite formidable. That would make it another one hundred on top of that."

Hugo scoffed, "I bring highly skilled knights. You bring merchants."

"You have not seen them fight, downright vicious they are, I would pledge my honour on any one of them matching your Brass Roses." Jack had a thought, "What about Lord Francis?"

"My brother? Not a moment goes by that I don't lament on Nicholas. I'm afraid to say he passed just as you left for the Americas." Jack felt a little taken back. To have last his uncle and not even known for so long. Hugo moved over to console his son, only for Jack to wave him off. "I'm sorry. I know it must be hard, the wound will never heal, but I still feel the loss. If it makes you feel any better, his family migrated to England soon after. Nicholas was persecuted here by the previous French King, this was no place for them, so they escaped in secret and fled to safer lands." Hugo stopped talking and seemed to be deep in thought.

Sebastian had been quiet for far too long, and since he had worked his way through the food, it had seemed like he wanted to throw in his thoughts. "If we used guerilla tactics to take back the capital, it would take longer but would manage it with fewer men."

"That sounds reasonable, but extra time would give the Sun King time to divert some of his forces," Hugo added, then seemed to wander off into thought, "But what if we created diversions in a port town?"

"You would have us create a diversion to pull the French Reserves in the wrong direction. Giving us more time to carry out our skirmishes and secure Lorraine?" Jack was impressed that the old man still had a tactical mind. "What kind of diversion?" Jack was curious. He liked that the plan was becoming solid, but it seemed to be spreading the men out thinner.

Hugo sat up and started shuffling his papers around till he found the one he must have been looking for, "Well, I have not been completely useless with my time here," he gave Jack a stern look over his papers. "The remaining Brass Roses I have kept busy in various parts of the continent. They've been whispering in my ears like little birds."

Jack grinned, "You sly old seadog, there's still life in you yet!" he slapped his thigh.

Hugo chuckled at the sight of his son beaming at him. "Quite! My contact in Le Havre, for example, has been sending me concerning reports." Jack's interest was piqued. "The port has been busier than usual, seeing all sorts of unsavoury characters arriving and departing."

"Nothing unusual for a port, especially if they are anything like the ones in the Caribbean," Sebastian added as he helped himself to a lonely bottle of mead.

Hugo nodded at Sebastian, "This is true, however," he huddled closer to the two as though the walls were listening, "Unsavoury characters don't usually draw the attention of the Sun King." Sebastian gasped unnecessarily while Jack just stared at him. "He's been making regular trips to the port town to meet with this man."

Jack took the mead from Sebastian and poured himself some, "Does your Rose in Le Havre know who this man is?"

Hugo sighed, "No, whoever he is, he has cloaked himself in anonymity. My contact has not been able to ascertain his name or even what he looks like, just that he has been in and out of Le Havre over the past year. The only distinguishing feature they can ascertain is the name of the man's ship."

"Oh?" Sebastian stopped drinking long enough to listen to the next sentence.

Hugo shuffled the papers and maps about, seemingly searching for the relevant document on the table in front of him. "Ah, yes, here it is. The vessel in question goes by the name," he paused, allowing the suspense to build, "the *Queen Anne's Revenge*."

Jack stared into space, "I'm going to need something stronger to drink."

Sebastian spat on the floor.

* * *

Hugo had been very cagey about whom he had received the intelligence from, but he was all too happy to point Jack in the right direction. So he and Sebastian had made their way to Le Havre to attempt to figure out what Edward Teach was doing consorting with French Kings. They stood at the corner of the most reputable looking tavern, near the docks. "Skulking again, eh, Jack? People will think you like hiding in the shadows with me, where no one can see," Sebastian wiggled his eyebrows suggestively at him.
Jack was peering around the edge of *La Roseraie*, the right direction Hugo had pointed them to. "Pay attention, ya scallywag. We are here on business. Save your sexual frustrations for inside." Jack nodded towards the entrance of the building.

"What do you mean? What do you see?" Sebastian slapped him on the arse as he moved past him to get a better view. Jack jumped with a sigh and nodded at the mass of lovely ladies swarming into the tavern.

Sebastian was mesmerized until he must have had a thought, "Are you sure the *Neptune* will know to keep away?" Sebastian suddenly seemed concerned.

"Aye, Seb, they're smart enough to keep away if they see trouble, not to mention the *Queen Anne's Revenge* in port," Jack thought on,

"I think they would even stay close by if they spotted her, just in case we need them."

Sebastian was getting restless; he was sighing a lot more than usual and blowing air through his teeth. "Are you sure this is the right place?"

"My father's contact said that Teach's men usually frequent this tavern when they are docked. So I guess we just have to wait till some of them show up, question them, and hope one of them gives the game away in a haze of drunkenness."

Sebastian rolled his eyes emphatically. "Well, I've only seen women, and I mean beautiful women, coming in and out of La Roseraie so far." Sebastian seemed to continue to ogle the beauties.

Jack took in a short breath, "Well then, lead the way, Big Seb. We might as well have some fun while we wait, instead of *skulking* about."

Sebastian eagerly bounced around the corner, like a predator pouncing on its prey, making his way towards the doors of La Roseraie. *This lad has been too long at sea.* Jack followed him shortly behind, amused by Sebastian's excitement.

"Looks like you'll be able to teach me how to talk to women finally! While we wait on Teach's men to show up," Sebastian spewed out with giddiness.

Jack nodded while muttering under his breath, "Something tells me I won't have to," as he noticed the quality of the ladies going in for himself.

"Hmm?" Sebastian wasn't even bothered if he clarified his mumble because he had continued bouncing along into the tavern. Jack and Sebastian stopped dead at the threshold, the door swung open to reveal wall to wall of French maidens all doting on the few midday patrons that couldn't seem to leave.

"Where to begin," Sebastian whispered in awe.

Jack spied the woman behind the bar, "How about some information first?" Jack sauntered towards the bar, leaving Sebastian to look disappointed at not satisfying his urges first. The innkeeper was slowly cleaning tankards ready for the busy period. "Deux bières, merci beaucoup."

Sebastian looked at him, impressed. "Been brushing up on your French, Jack?"

Jack shrugged, "When in Paris."

The women behind the bar looked them up and down. Her auburn hair flowed down the sides of her soft face and onto her considerable chest in rivulets, while her hazel-toned eyes *were* something to write home about. The swirls in her iris seemed to mesmerize Sebastian, or, at least, that's what Jack assumed he was gawking at. Jack brought him around with a swift stamp on the foot.

Sebastian reeled in pain, "What?" he exclaimed in agony as he hopped about on one foot.

"Don't just gawk, my friend. First lesson," Jack smirked at him. "The ladies don't take too kindly to being stared at. They prefer confidence, charm, intelligence and if all else fails, tell them there's a reason you're called *Big Seb*." Jack laughed at his own hilarity.

"Go on, try using your words on these fine ladies while I talk to the proprietor." Sebastian sauntered off, trying to look confident.

"Your friend knows this is a brothel, right?" The woman spoke to Jack in English heavily laden with a French accent.

Jack flashed her a charming smile, "Not yet, but I don't want to spoil his fun," he grinned at the woman while she placed two tankards down next to him. "The name's Jack Rackham, a pleasure to meet you," he cocked his head and threw a glance at the woman in a way that asked her for her name.

"Abigail. My family and friends call me Abby, but you are neither. Ms DeRose is fine," she exuded sassily.

Jack couldn't help but laugh out loud.

"What is so funny?" Abby looked slightly hurt.

"It's a little on the nose, don't you think?" Jack scoffed

"I don't know what you are insinuating," She seemed to have grown bored of his lack of conversation. Abby moved to leave him there.

Jack grabbed hold of her wrists, stopping her from leaving, but as soon as he had, two burly Frenchmen wormed their way out of the woodwork. Abigail motioned to them to hold their insinuated assault, "Extricate yourself from my personage." She looked at him in such a way that he felt he would've lost his hands if he had kept his hands on her for a moment longer.
Jack held his hands up in an apology. He was so sure she was the contact that he had to test the waters. "Now what was that damn phrase," he spoke aloud, "I will go, wherever," he tapped his head,

333

trying to mentally release the rest, "the wild Rose will bloom." He sat there waiting as Abby stopped dead in her tracks.

She turned around to face him, "Quiet, you idiot. You don't want everyone to hear."

Jack looked around at the number of people in. "I don't think that's the return phrase. Are you a turncoat for the other side?"

Abby scoffed, "Fine, you'll find that Le Havre is rife with Roses."

Jack looked pleased with himself, "Then I'm in the right place. No wonder my father didn't want to tell me about you."

Abby's eyes lit up like she understood, "I see it now. I couldn't be sure at first. You can't be too careful, but you have your father's face. He visits in person as regularly as he can to gather intel," she whispered.

Jack laughed, "I bet he does," he looked Ms DeRose up and down.

"It's true, he has a few favourites. Some that your friend seems to have worked up a thirst for."

Jack glanced over to see Sebastian covered in ladies. "It's been a long journey. Let him have his moment. I don't know when he will get a chance again." Jack slid a gold doubloon across the table and watched as Abigail's eyes grew as large as the moon. She bit it to prove its validity. Seemingly impressed at the sight of real gold, she nodded to the girl sitting on Sebastian's lap, who slid off and waltzed over towards the bar. The air filled with the heavy scent of flowers as the woman approached, making Jack's head swirl, and his senses come alive. *God help him*, he thought.

Abigail passed a tankard to the girl, "Jasmine, the monsieur is to have a good time; make sure he feels as though he is wooing you."

"Oh, there's no problem there, mon amour," she sauntered off, giggling.

Jack smirked, a proud feeling swelling in his chest. His friend had changed so much from those first days on the *Kingston*. His attention returned to Abigail, "Where were we? Ah, yes, the *Queen Anne's Revenge*."

Abigail hushed him, "In the back." She nodded to one of the walls of meat that had wormed their way out earlier, who came to take her place at the bar. Jack followed her into a small back room furnished with a round table surrounded by chairs. "Sit," she pointed to a chair across from her. Jack obeyed. She pulled out a bottle of something that looked strong from a draw, poured it into two glasses, and slid one across the table to Jack. Abigail then raised hers in the air, "To the fallen."

Jack raised his glass, "The fallen." They both knocked back the brown liquid. Jack could feel the burn all the way down to his stomach. It had been a long time since he had the chance to sample some French whiskey. After the moment of silence had passed, Jack decided to break it. "I see a round table, yet no knights."

"What is it that you see before you?" She asked angrily. "Just a woman, or maybe a tavern wench? What about a harlot?" Her eyes glistened as the words curled off her tongue, lashing him relentlessly. "I feel the same loss as you, my home, my people. The *merde* I have to put up with to help the cause, and you come in here disrespecting *me*! I am as much of a knight as my father was. I follow the same code of honour, as does any Rose! You *will* recognise the knight at this table." She slammed her fist onto the table in demand; the glasses bounced with anger.

Jack was taken back. He hadn't feared for his life like this since he had angered Anney. Luckily he knew how to defuse the situation, "I fear we both live in the shadow created by our fathers," Empathy. "You feel as though you will never live up to the standard set by yours, and I fear I will never be able to win back what he has lost." Jack sighed.

"Do not pretend to know me, pirate. I know what you've been doing while your father and the Roses have been working towards a goal."

It was Jack's time to be angry, "Oh, and what would that be? How close to taking back the homeland are we? We have men to take her back? No? I didn't think so. Yes, I may have whiled away my time as a pirate, but at least I have a plan to take back the capital. Maybe you should focus more on gathering intelligence on the threats that are relevant, like Edward fucking Teach, rather than the man that sits before you."

Abigail poured another glass of whiskey and knocked it back; she seethed from the burn, "It looks like we both have reason to be angry."

Jack poured her another glass, then topped his own up. "I am not here as your enemy. I am here as a friend. Help me, Knight DeRose. Help me win back our homelands."

Chapter - 19 - Nothing to see here.

The crescent moon illuminated Ariadne's homeland as it hung low in the night sky. She had managed to convince the work crew to allow them to spend the night on board before the crew showed up in the morning. It hadn't taken too much effort to get her travelling companions to spend the night, *splicing the mainbrace*, either. Wherever there was rum involved, sailors weren't far behind. The *Oracle* was in good company, the finishing touches would be completed by midday, and Seamus' new crew would definitely be broken in by then. So they would be free to set sail and find out what, if anything, the Sun King was plotting.

So here they sat, around the captain's new table. They were already one round of rum down, and Seamus was busy topping up their glasses to the brim. "So, Francois, tell me about this pirate you bested. Captain to captain, did you make the bastard suffer?"

Francois chuckled, "Well, you'll have to ask Bea, she's the captain of our vessel." Beatrix looked a little sullen at the mention of the battle, but it was only fleeting once she realised Ariadne was looking at her in awe.

If Ariadne needed anymore to love about Lady d'Arlon, this was it. At the mention of a woman taking charge of her own ship, she sobered up a little. "You are the captain?" She was jubilant, finally, another woman at the forefront of naval command, just what the world needed.

"Aye, love, he's an old ship, but he knows how to treat a lady. I'm still a little sore about the damage, but time heals all. That and the king's shipwrights," Beatrix exclaimed.

Ariadne was eager to hear about the battle. "It must have been a vicious assault?"

"Downright bloody, it was." Beatrix took a sip of her rum. "We were running some goods from the Americas, a small convoy of two ships. The trip across the North Atlantic is long and arduous, as you both know. It's also damn well dangerous - pirates lurking around every wave, every island. One night we spotted a lone light on the horizon and thought nothing of it till it wouldn't leave us alone. We knew they were hunting us, so we hatched a plan. The other ship would lure them in while we hid in an archipelago off the coast of Spain. Surprise them with our broadside cannons," she grinned, "but there wasn't just one of them. There were two. We were ahead, turning into our hiding spot when Francois saw them both. Mean ones at that, tall walls and rows of guns like the teeth on some damn Kraken!"

Ariadne was on the edge of her chair. Something was mesmerizing about the way Beatrix wove her tale, and it had her enthralled. "So, what did you do?"

"Well, we couldn't communicate with the other ship anytime soon. So we had to hatch a new plan. I trusted that the other captain would be able to think on his feet. Luckily, I was right. He drew them in as planned, and we lay in wait around a small island. Small enough for us to see them coming. When the two pirate ships had disappeared into the island, I knew it wouldn't be long till they came out the other end, so I gave the order to unfurl all the sails. Gather as much wind as possible. He lurched forward with great ferocity as if Poseidon himself were at his aft pushing. We made our way towards where the scurvy sea dogs would reappear. We sat and watched, moving closer and gaining more speed."

Ariadne sat, waiting with bated breath. She was lapping up the prose like a hungry bard. "Then what happened?"

"Well," Beatrix leaned forward, "We were getting closer and closer, but still nothing. Then, just as I was about to call the men to drop sail, our other ship burst forth from the island's cliff walls and flew past the opening. She was quickly followed by the first pirate ship, then, just as we thought the plan was going to hell, out came the second pirate ship! So we braced for impact." Beatrix looked to be lost in the ghost of the memory until she shook herself free from reminiscing with exuberance, "the noise as the two ships collided was unlike anything I've ever heard, with added explosions to boot! Sure enough, we split the ship in twain."

Seamus laughed hard, slapping his thigh, "Good show, that woman!"

Francois decided to speak up, "Aye, as soon as we hit the bastards, we must have hit the reserve powder kegs because the starboard side was blown to smithereens. Bea and I were tossed aside like some child's ragdoll from the force." Francois laughed. "As soon as we regained our senses and our footing, we boarded their vessel with great care. There was no telling what dangers lay in wait."

Beatrix took over, "We crept through the smouldering wreckage. She was clearly taking on water, and most of her crew lay in tatters. It was a nasty sight." She sighed into her cup. "Just as I thought it was all over, it most definitely wasn't. A cutlass struck from nowhere!" Beatrix struck out across the table with a pretend blade. Ariadne and Seamus gasped, brimming with astonishment at the tale. "That would have been the end of me had it not been for the quick reactions of my dear husband."

"Aye, I may be old, but I can knock the rust of my bones when it matters." Francois winked at Ariadne, sending her stomach into a flutter. "I saw the blade thrusting forth! So I quickly flung my own blade forward, only just managing to deflect the cowardly captain." He flung his own pretend blade out and mimicked the deflection. "It gave Bea enough time to put up her guard and defend against her attacker."

"She was hiding behind some crates like a coiled up viper, ready to sting," Beatrix exclaimed.

"She?" Seamus reiterated.

"That's what I said, love. The captain of the ship that was making its way to Davy Jones himself was a woman, tits and all." Beatrix clarified smugly.

Ariadne piped up, "I only know of two female pirates. Notorious they are. Anne Bonney and Mary Read. Both wanted by His Majesty for many counts of piracy and other crimes."

Beatrix smirked. "Aye, well, this must have been Mary Read because if it had been Anne Bonney we probably wouldn't be here to tell the tale! I hear she is a vicious one!"

Seamus shuddered, "I can only imagine. So, then you went toe-to-toe with this Mary Read?"

"Of course! It was a rousing battle for the ages. We danced up and down the deck," Beatrix mocked swordsmanship in the captain's quarters, "swung from the rigging trading swords, and we fought along the taffrail." Ariadne's mouth was agape.

Francois scoffed at Beatrix, "Really, girl?"

Beatrix rolled her eyes. "Well, fine. We fought hard. It was nearly a loss," Beatrix lost herself in the moment again but then caught herself and carried on, "She's a feisty fighter that one, dirty too. If it weren't for Francois at my back, she would have bested me, no doubt."

Ariadne felt as though she were there with her in the battle; she felt mentally drained from the story. "So, you slew her?"

Beatrix was quiet now. Francois looked over to her and patted her on the shoulder. "No. The other ship returned, much worse for wear, it seemed, our other ship must have given him something to think about, and he had come limping, wounded. Just as Bea was about to deal the killing blow, Mary flung some powder in the poor lasses face and flung herself over portside onto her passing companion's ship."

Seamus hit the table in frustration making the glasses rattle. "Did you manage to get the name of the offending ship?"

Beatrix broke her silence, "Aye, that we did. It was none other than the *Queen Anne's Revenge.*"

Ariadne didn't know all the pirates, but she knew the bad ones, mainly because of her time in the Caribbean, and this was one of the worst. "You made a lucky escape then. Thank God, you left with your lives." Ariadne grabbed hold of the rum bottle and poured everyone another helping. "Here's to the pirates that plague our seas, may they all rot in Davy Jones locker!"

They all raised their glasses to shouts of *here, here,* and each toasted by downing their measures.

* * *

It was with heavy heads and weary eyes that Ariadne took to the main deck of the *Oracle*. She had been awoken by the bang and clatter of the shipwright's tools finalising Seamus' new ship. The *Oracle*'s sails were down, and tools were strewn across everywhere, but even in the dawning light, she was magnificent. Her aft was ornate and patterned with gold lining, and the figurehead was the most beautiful she had ever seen - a woman dressed in greek robes, her arms outstretched showing the way. She rubbed the sleep from her eyes and walked up to the nearest worker.

"Mornin', Lieutenant. Should be finished soon." The man gave her a little wink.

Ariadne sighed with relief; she didn't know how much longer her head could put up with the banging. She didn't want to have to throw herself overboard to escape it, but needs must when the devil drives. She bothered the man some more, "What time are the crew due?"

The shipwright looked over to the dock, "Right about now. That's them, over there." He pointed over to the group of congregating sailors. They looked to be a rowdy bunch.

Ariadne panicked once she had realised what her priorities were. She needed to wake up Seamus and get him ship shape. They had been up a long time last night, swapping yarns, and they had worked their way through both bottles of rum and then some. She couldn't let the new crew see their captain in a rough state, although it would fuel another humorous anecdote at the captain's table. *No*. It would definitely be a poor start for Seamus' third ship. "Thank you, sir." She rushed back to the captain's quarters. Upon opening the door, they were exactly where she had left them. Seamus was draped over a chair; a bottle still hung from his hand. Francois was sat on a bench at the side of the cabin with Beatrix laying on his lap. All fast asleep.

She crept silently over to Seamus. "Seamus! Come on, rise, and shine!" She shook the captain like a rag doll.

Seamus' moan reminded her of the Selene's first noises when she finally broke free from Anegada. "What's happening?" Seamus shook himself awake.

"The crew are here. Time to put on a good show." Ariadne grinned at him as much as she could with a sore head.

"What? Already?" Seamus leapt from his chair like someone had just poured a nice cold bucket of bad news over his head.

"Aye, they are all lining up to meet you. Time to sober up, somewhat." Ariadne started to try and straighten out his clothes.

"One moment, my friend." Seamus ran over to the window at the aft of the *Oracle* and proceeded to lose the contents of his stomach into the sea below.

Ariadne grimaced at the sight of Seamus bent over the window, throwing up. "Beautiful." Once he had finished, Seamus ambled back over to her, wiping his mouth. "Feel better now?"

He nodded, "Much."

She looked him up and down, straightening his uniform as she did. "You look like you went a few rounds with a great white," she straightened his hair, "but it will have to do."

Seamus checked himself out in the full-length mirror near his bed. He shrugged, "I've looked worse. What should we do with those two?" He nodded over to Francois and Beatrix still soundly asleep.

Ariadne thought about grabbing a bucket of seawater but then thought better of it. "Let them sleep. They are the ones that are going to be sneaking about once we reach Paris. They are going to need their wits about them if they are to be effective," she rubbed her head, "And I do not feel very witty at the moment."

Seamus grinned at her reflection in the mirror, "Indeed. We drank a fair bit last night, but we had a good night getting to know our fellow ambassadors."

She watched as he finished sorting himself out in the mirror. "Ready to face the men?"

"No." Ariadne laughed at him. "Next time, remind me not to try and outdrink you." Seamus headed out onto the main deck with Ariadne shortly behind him.

They both made their way to a man who was talking to one of the shipwrights. The lean, black-haired man with trimmed beard and moustache to match seemed like he might be able to handle himself in a fight. He seemed too busy talking the ear off of the worker to notice them until they got close.

The man stood to attention as soon as he registered them. "Ah! Captain Hawthorne and Lieutenant Smith, I presume? Permission to come aboard, Captain?"

"Master Crockett, *I presume*." The man gave them both an overzealous bow. "The board sent your details ahead of you - very impressive, I might add. Welcome aboard."

"Thank you, Captain Hawthorne. I have strived to serve with the utmost diligence. I am glad it shows in my record." Crockett gave a slight smile.

"According to the letter I received from the Admiral, you served on board the HMS *Resolution* during the St. James' Day Battle. She was a courageous ship; it was heart-wrenching to see her burning at the end of the battle."

"Indeed, Captain. The crew fought bravely till the very last, but in the end, there was nothing that could be done to save the crew or the ship." His smile had gone, "If it weren't for the *Cambridge,* I would have been floating in those waters till Davy Jones himself came to take me."

"You may not remember me, but I remember you, Crockett. I was aboard the *Cambridge* briefly at the end of the battle. I remember the bittersweet feeling of victory tinged with the feeling of loss for our comrades."

"Thank you, Captain. It means a lot that you remember our legacy." Crockett smiled at Seamus.

"It said in the letter that you had served in several other minor conflicts also."

"Aye, Captain, me and the lads have fought the lot of 'em at one time or another." He looked rather smug at the fact.

Ariadne felt the need to enquire further, "What about the French?"

Crockett nodded, "Aye, we've danced on a few occasions."

Seamus grinned, "Very good. You are a credit to the Royal Navy. If you show as much zeal aboard the *Oracle* as you have in your service, then you and I shall get along fine."

Crockett gave a little bow, then looked to have had a thought. "Are you expecting the French to get a little fruity with us?"

Ariadne was unsure of his phrasing, but she got the right of it. "Hopefully not, but we must remain alert and prepared." Ariadne gave the Master an understanding nod.

"Of course, Lieutenant Smith. The crew and I will get you and the Captain where you need to go, and should there be trouble; we'll give 'em hell!"

"Excellent, have the men make themselves at home, Mr Crockett. The *Oracle* is at the dawn of her odyssey; she will need men who know how to appreciate a fine ship to guide her." Seamus stood by the taffrail, caressing the oak, "Bit different this oak, ay Ari?" He returned his attention to the Master, "Muster the men once the shipwrights have departed."

"Aye, Captain." Master Crockett beckoned the rest of the crew waiting on the dock. Ariadne watched as they all made their way up the gangplank with their various trunks and baggage and took in the *Oracle* with awe.

Seamus whispered to Ariadne, "Let's let them get acquainted with her.

Ariadne nodded. "Should we go see how our friends are doing?"

"I think that would be quite pertinent, my friend." He beckoned her to lead the way.

Ariadne burst into the captain's quarters with Seamus. She was filled with the excitement of starting a new mission and of being aboard the *Oracle*. Things were finally looking up. Francois and Beatrix had not moved a muscle, not even with all the commotion out on the main deck. She made her way over to Francois to try and wake him gently. She took a moment to look over his features. The memory from so long ago flashed across her mind again. Ariadne was positive; this was the same man from her memory. Although the other memory had quite clearly been missing some elements, maybe the memory of the Sintra mountains had been too. There was only one thing for it; she would have to ask him. Not now, though, later.

Seamus whispered to her, "What are you doing?"

Ariadne snapped herself out of the trance she had unknowingly put herself in and shook the duke gently. "Time to wake up, sunshine." The effect cascaded along the bench. Francois roused himself from his slumber, stretching, then Beatrix yawned and blinked back into existence. The two slowly brought themselves around.

"Is it time we should be off, Ari?" Francois said sleepily.

"That it is, Duke. Our crew is getting to know the *Oracle*, the shipwrights are almost done, and then we will be ready to make headway to Paris."

Ariadne grinned as Beatrix sat up and looked her way. "What's got you so happy? Anyone would think you were glad about the circumstances of our little trip across the channel."

She smirked to herself, "After spending time on the *Selene*, it's just nice to be back on a normal ship floating on something I understand."

Beatrix stood up and stretched out her curves to their full extent, achieving the whole euphoric state of pulling every muscle in any shape other than that which it had been cramped in overnight. "Aye, I bet it feels good to feel the sway of the sea beneath your feet; there's something sexual about that. There's no other feeling like it, well, other than," Beatrix trailed off as she winked at her.

Ariadne blushed and tried to change the subject quickly. "It's a much quicker journey up there, in the clouds, and there is something quite disconcerting about being disconnected from the earth. At least if you fell overboard, there is something for you to fall into relatively safely. But up there," she shuddered, "Endless blue sky. I dare not think of falling to my doom over the side."

Seamus interjected, "Don't even remind me of the troubles we experienced on the steering masts."

"Or the mainmast," Ariadne added.

"I do envy you, though. I wish I could have been there to experience that. I doubt I would have coped as well as you - managing to fly an island all the way from the Caribbean and coming to a stop at your doorstep."

"As Seamus pointed out, it wasn't all plain sailing. It was scary at first. Everything we knew about the world got turned upside down. Everything became normal; then, we uncovered the plot. Then things started going wrong. I'm glad Seamus was there with me," she looked over to him, "I think we kept each other sane."

"And alive!" Seamus added.

Ariadne continued her train of thought, "I do miss her, though, the *Selene*. I feel as though we got to witness something special, to be on the cusp of a new age, flying through the air like a bird. That feel of the cool mist on my face as I passed through a cheeky cloud." She lost herself in the memory - a smile spread across her face.

Beatrix snapped her out of it, "I must admit, you have me curious, but give me that nice gentle sway of the waves any day." She looked over to Francois, "What about you, dear husband, air or sea?"

Francois thought for a moment. "I spent much of my youth on solid ground. I think I prefer the earth beneath my feet rather than the sea."

"That's not the question." Beatrix chided him. "Would you rather be on an airship or a ship that sails the seven seas?"

This was Ariadne's chance to ask the duke about his past without looking too strange. "Tell us of your youth, Francois, have you always been a merchant?" She could feel Seamus' side glance burning into her. Beatrix frustratedly gave up on getting her answer and went over to nudge Seamus out of the way so she could make herself look presentable.

"Not always, my lady. Before I met Bea, I was a military man, you might say. I upheld the honour and the traditions of my brothers in arms, fighting many battles for my homeland. To protect and serve my king." He stared off into the distance, a sombre look in his eyes. "But that was many moons ago. I try not to dwell on the past for too long."

Ariadne felt she had to be tactful here; if she was wrong, she could put the duke in a foul mood that would not bode well for the rest of the journey. "I can sympathise." She went to sit by Francois. "There are parts of my youth that have recently been brought to light. Memories unshrouded upon our journey," the images flashed before her eyes, "A recent conversation with my mother shed more light on it. Still, it has made the memory too unbearable to recall, even now." She paused to push the memory down into the depths, or at least dust until the carpet till she had time to deal with it. "Yet, the journey also unblocked happy memories from my youth, but they are patchy and only pose more questions than they answer."

She had hooked him. Francois looked intrigued, "We have a bit of time if you wanted to talk? Maybe four heads can solve what one can not?"

"We flew over the Sintra mountains on our way back home. I recollected the times I had visited there with my Grandmother, you see, we used to make a pilgrimage there. My grandmother Selene would say that it was to pay homage to the order of monks that lived there, in a monastery, for helping us. She also said it was to help preserve both our legacies so that they may never be forgotten." Ariadne thought, "I guess it's a terrible thing to leave nothing behind in this world for others to remember you by. You are never truly dead unless someone remembers you or your deeds."

"Never a truer word has ever been uttered. Your grandmother was a wise woman."

Ariadne nodded, "Aye that she was."

"So, what's the part that has you answerless?"

"Well, she would never tell me the specifics of why this order helped us. Parts of my history remain covered, for now. There was also a mysterious knight there who seemed to know Selene. He told us he was part of the Order of the Brass Roses, and he was there just as we were - paying homage to the monks."

"And did your mother have anything to say about these things?"

Ariadne huffed, "No. She played dumb, but I knew she was hiding something."

"Well, I'm afraid I wouldn't even be able to point to this monastery on a map, let alone tell you of its order of monks. And the only knights I have ever seen were in history tomes. The order of knights has long been dead; I'm afraid, my friend." Francois patted her on the shoulder. "I'm sorry, Ari. Maybe time will unlock the answers you seek." Ariadne had been paying attention to Francois' features, looking for any twitch, movement, or grimace that would betray the words he spoke. But alas, his face was devoid of any such tells.

At that exact moment, there came a knock at the door. Seamus raised his eyebrow and walked over to the door. He opened it to reveal the master stood to attention. "Ah! Crockett. Have the shipwrights completed their jobs?"

"Indeed they have, Captain. I've mustered all the men ready for you as requested."

"Excellent, Crockett. We shall be out momentarily."

The master gave a little bow and left them to it.

Ariadne turned to Seamus, "Are you ready for this?" Seamus gave her a little nod. He moved out onto the main deck as she, Francois, and Beatrix followed him to greet the crew. They all lined the deck now, eagerly waiting to exchange pleasantries with the captain. They were a very different bunch to the last crew she and Seamus had. They exuded confidence and seemed very well presented—the exact polar opposite of the crew that left them without a ship on Anegada. Ariadne's eye was dragged to the one female crew member, as she was sure it had caught Seamus' attention. She watched as he made his way down, inspecting them, stopping every now and then, passing on some inane platitude to boost morale. She had seen this a dozen times before, but only once with him. Seamus was a bit more standoffish this time. Maybe he had learnt his lesson. She honed back in on his conversation - he had just reached the only lady in the lineup.

"To whom do I owe the pleasure." Seamus seemed to do his best to appear charming.

She seemed nervous. "The pleasure, Captain?"

"It is good to see another woman taking a stand in the Royal Navy. So far, I've only had the pleasure of Lieutenant Smith, and she has been an asset to me ever since she has been under my command." Ariadne flashed to all the times she had commanded him and chuckled to herself.

Crockett broke the awkwardness, "This is Cecile. She's our gunner, Captain. I have every faith in her abilities. If we run into any trouble, she will keep us safe."

Seamus looked impressed. "I looked forward to working with you."

Ariadne watched as Cecile managed a smile, "Thank you, Captain."

Seamus walked to the mainmast taking in the display of seasoned seamen. "I am glad," he bellowed, "that I had a chance to see you all in person. For our mission relies on each and every one of you," he pointed to a few of the crew. "We are heading into potentially dangerous waters. Our success will rely on you all working together as one." Seamus marched up the line slowly, "Our mission is to investigate the Sun King's intentions. I am sure you are all aware of the island now floating above London, well, me and my companions here," he waved his arm in their direction, "strongly believe that Louis means to use this new invention to wage war," he shouted across the breadth of the *Oracle*, "and that can not go unanswered." Seamus marched back up the deck. "So our gracious king is sending us to try and deal with this diplomatically," he turned briefly to Francois and Beatrix, "and perhaps a few un-diplomatic methods." Seamus turned back to the crew, "But I, nay England, expects every man," he looked at Cecile, "And woman will do their duty." Seamus stood, admiring them with a warm smile on his face. "Make me proud to call you my crew!"

Seamus took one last look and walked over to the master. "Have the crew prepare to set sail. Our destination is Le Havre."

"Of course, Captain, straight away." Crockett gave Seamus one of his small bows and went off shouting commands to the crew.

Ariadne beamed at Seamus. "That went well, I thought."

"Indeed. Although, I fear the true test is yet to come." Seamus stood at the helm with Ariadne to one side and Francois and Beatrix to the other as the *Oracle* prepared to take her first steps into the briny deep.

* * *

It wasn't long before the *Oracle* had reached French shores. The sun had reached its zenith, and the Channel had been plain sailing. Ariadne had been keeping an eye on the crew and watching them work on the new ship, much to her satisfaction. She looked up to admire Seamus, who had insisted on steering the ship on her maiden voyage. He was busy talking to Francois while Beatrix was busy chatting to the gunner down on the main deck. Ariadne moved to the forecastle and joined Crockett to get a better look at Le Havre in the distance.

"Lieutenant." the master gave her a slight bow of the head.

"See anything suspicious, Crockett?" She stood with her arms folded, casting her eyes over the port town.

"Just the usual activity, though, I fear we should be careful. I spot a few ships that don't belong." Crockett handed her his spyglass.

"Oh?" Ariadne looked through the device towards Le Havre. She scanned the names of the vessels currently docked, mostly French names bar a few. Only one of them vaguely stood out to her. "I feel as if I should know this vessel." She couldn't think where she had seen it.

"Aye, It belongs to a pirate from the Caribbean. Though, what he would be doing here, I care not to fathom."

"Lucky for him, we aren't here to arrest pirates, though, he is duly noted. Make sure you give him a wide berth, Crockett. Dock the *Oracle* at the other end of the dock if you have to. We don't want to cause a scene." Ariadne passed him back the spyglass.

As Ariadne made her way back to inform the captain, Beatrix came bounding over. "See anything concerning?"

"Just some pirates, Bea, nothing to worry about." Beatrix gave her a slightly worried smile as she sloped off towards the front of the ship.

Ariadne jumped up the stairs to the poop deck two steps at a time, eager to tell Seamus her news. He smiled somewhat smugly as she approached. "I remember that smile. Did the captain enjoy himself?"

"Very much so, my friend."

Francois laughed heartily.

"What news from the forecastle?"

"Apart from pirates docked in Le Havre, it's nothing much to worry about. Might I suggest we dock to the far end of the western dock," she said nonchalantly.

Francois snapped from his laughter instantly. "Pirates? Who?"

"The name of the ship Crockett spied was," Ariadne was interrupted by the sudden appearance of Beatrix, who had come running up towards them. They all waited while she caught her breath.

"It's the *Queen Anne's Revenge*. He's here. Edward Teach is in Le Havre."

Francois looked fiercely angry, "Take her in slowly, Captain. This is the bastard who fled our fight with Mary Read."

"What would a notorious pirate like that be doing all this way from his territory in the Caribbean?" Ariadne was puzzled. She was sure she was missing something but couldn't quite put her finger on it.

Francois stood at the taffrail, scrutinising the ships in the dock. Bea moved over to him and placed a hand on his shoulder, seemingly in comfort. "It's too much of a coincidence, Bea, he can't be here for anything else other than that."

"And you had no wind of this in Monti Christi?" Beatrix asked her husband.

"None! But why else would he be consorting with the French?"

"I don't know, old man, but we are going to find out." She patted him on the arm in consolation.

Ariadne and Seamus stood side by side, watching the scene play out until Seamus spoke up. "By the tone of your conversation, are you trying to tell us that Edward Teach, otherwise known as Blackbeard, is in league with the Sun King?"

"Bah!" Francois spat on the poop deck. "Don't call him that. It only adds to his mythos!"

Beatrix turned to face them, "It would seem so. We must tread carefully from here on in. Teach is an evil bastard, and if he's here," she sighed, "then so is she."

"Pirates in league with the Sun King, this doesn't bode well, Seamus. Bea has the right of it, we should be careful."

Seamus seemed to be weighing up his options. "Tell me, Francois, do you know of a place in Le Havre where we can gather intel before we proceed?"

The duke stared off towards the port for a moment before breaking the silence, "Aye, I know a place. The man who used to be my merchant contact in Le Havre runs a nice tavern near the dock. Goes by the name of *La Roseraie.* We should find what we need there."

Chapter - 20 - When all hope is lost.

Sebastian stood on a street corner that they had never frequented but was now looking like a familiar haunt for the duo. "Are you sure this is where they are meeting?"

"Positive. Abby and I had a lengthy discussion," he grinned and wiggled his eyebrows at Sebastian, "Teach has been meeting here with the Sun King throughout the year."

Sebastian surveyed the dismal rotting wet timbers that formed the most miserable meeting place Jack had ever seen. "This place? This warehouse?"

"It's just a trick of the light, Seb. I'm sure, on a nice sunny day, Kings would flock to have a meeting here. It just so happens that we are here on a miserable day."

"Right," Sebastian didn't look convinced. "Oh well, the worst thing that could happen is we waste a couple of hours here while Teach and Louis have their meeting somewhere else."

Jack sighed, "What can I say? the Knight was quite convincing." He faced Sebastian, "Besides, you haven't told me the tale of your evening."

Sebastian turned a bright shade of pink with an added cheeky smile. "What happens between 'Big Seb' and his companions stays between the extremely satisfied participants."

Jack didn't know if he could raise his eyebrows any higher, try as he might, he could not convey how surprised and fascinated he was, all within the confines of his facial dimensions. "Colour me impressed, my friend. *Companions* at that, you'll be the talk of Le Havre, nay

France. When news of your big cock gets around the ladies *will* come flocking. Do you have a business card that you could perhaps leave in the taverns?" Jack couldn't contain his laughter any longer.

"Oh, Jack, some men have it and others," Sebastian looked over to Jack, "Just don't. It's fine, I still love you."

Jack felt as though the wind had been removed from his sail, his laughter died as his friend's words settled in. "Oh really? You think because you've bedded a few whores for sale that you are now God's gift to women?"

Sebastian shrugged at him, "If the cap fits," he grinned at Jack. He watched as the cogs turned in Sebastian's brain. "What do you mean whores?"

Jack's eye had been caught by four hooded figures making their way towards the warehouse, "Be quiet now, Seb, we shall discuss this later. We have company." There was no way of telling who was beneath the hoods unless Jack went over and just removed them. That wasn't an option. There was one person leading three others, at least, it looked that way. "The one upfront must be Teach, I'm sure of it. The other three must be his Lackeys," he whispered to Sebastian. "Let us see if they enter."

"What are we to even do if it is them?"

"Obviously spy on them, figure out what they are up to. Why they are colluding. What's in it for both parties? The basic things, Seb."

"And what if they don't happen to have a conversation which lays out all their main points conveniently for us?"

"Well," Jack grinned, "then we improvise. It's been a while since we caused a ruckus, do you feel up to the task?" Jack held out his hand.

Sebastian grabbed him by the forearm and shook him vigorously, "Aye, I do believe I am."

Sure enough, these were the men they were looking for, at least, they were the ones that entered the wonderful seafront location and closed the doors behind them. "Teach or not, they've gone into the place where Abby said his men were moving crates too. If only we could see what they were transporting." Jack searched the warehouse's facade, it was a fairly large building, big enough to hide an army of pirates. The sides rose high, and a sloped roof circled a raised level with windows above it. "There must be some way we can get inside without being spotted?"

Sebastian looked around. "Perhaps we should just wait to see if Sun King arrives? So we aren't caught between the two."

"And what if he isn't coming and we've missed an opportunity to figure out what's going on inside?" Jack quietly blasted back.

Sebastian grumbled to himself. "We need to play this safe, Jack. If we get caught, who will take back Lorraine?"

Jack wasn't listening to him. "We'll worry about that once we are in." Jack had spotted an opening above the sloping roof, "There." He nodded towards it. "We can use those crates to climb up to that window and have ourselves a nice little bird's eye view of the whole thing," he smiled.

Sebastian gave up arguing his point. "I suppose we would be free from discovery should the king turn up." He looked around, "It's better than standing in plain sight watching the door." He gave Jack a nod of reluctant approval.

Jack led the way. Crates had been stacked on the side of the warehouse, offering a convenient makeshift set of steps leading to the roof. Once Jack had reached the edge of the roof, he turned back to make sure Sebastian hadn't run into any issues. He grinned as he watched the scholar struggle up, eventually reaching his side. Jack whispered to him, "Crawl up here. The tiles will be slippery." After a challenging ascent, they had finally reached the raised level. Jack looked through one of the windows, spying a landing, where they could watch from above. Luckily for them, the sun had positioned itself nicely. The warehouse was mostly illuminated apart from a few nooks and crevices covered in darkness, though what they saw below was mostly covered in sheets. The warehouse seemed like any average-sized building from the outside, but it seemed to be much larger on the inside from up here. "Are you seeing this, Seb?" Jack whispered.

Sebastian nodded to him, "It seems the warehouse is actually several joined together. It also appears to be set deeper than the floor level. Look," he pointed to where the entrance was, "There are stairs leading down from where the hooded men entered."

The warehouse itself contained several large objects, wrapped in dust sheets. He didn't like to wildly guess, but they looked familiar. These were surrounded by crates of all different sizes, piles of timber and tools strewn about the place. "I have a bad feeling about what is under those sheets." Jack scanned the interior, just beyond the window. The raised level ran around the outskirts of the warehouse leading to steps down either end. Jack knew they would be safe inside and still able to snoop undetected. "Let us head inside, my friend. We will be safe enough, I promise you." Sebastian gave him a curt nod.

Jack crawled through the large open window and into the warehouse itself, making sure to step lightly. He helped Sebastian squeeze through the gap, and then the pair of them slowly made their way to the rail that marked the edge of the walkway. "This is a much better view," Jack whispered. "Can you see them?" Jack scanned the warehouse looking for the man he believed was Edward Teach.

"There," Sebastian pointed towards the back. There seemed to be offices behind one of the large sheeted objects.

"We should head closer to see if we can hear anything." Jack made his way towards the back of the warehouse, carefully measuring each step. He didn't want to be caught, and there was no way of knowing what kind of mess they would find themselves in if they were. The only thing that mattered was finding out what was going on here and how it involved the king. Maybe it was a coincidence that the Sun King and Teach were here at the same time. To think that they were in league would royally bugger up his plans to put the two kingdoms against each other. Jack's mind raced, trying to think of the reasons why he would be here at the same time as him. *Calm yourself, John.* He needed to take one thing at a time. First, they needed to find out who the hooded figures were. The rest they would deal with after.

It took a while to make it there without being detected, but they both now stood directly above the now unhooded men. Jack and Sebastian peered over the rail to take a sneaky peek. Fury raged over his face, recognising the man below him instantly. "Long black curly hair, beady fucking eyes, ugly bastard," he whispered with venom between his teeth, "That's him, Edward Teach."

"I have to agree, Jack, that's him alright." Sebastian crouched back down below the rail. "What do we do now?"

"They seem to be just waiting, so we wait too," he whispered angrily.

"Do you recognise the others?"

Jack studied their faces. "I recognise the big lout from the dock in Monte Christi, you remember, the drunken fool who nearly discovered us sneaking about?"

Sebastian nodded at him, "Aye, I remember you finding excuses to push me into dark corners away from prying eyes."

Jack stifled his laughter. "Goddamnit, Seb, not here. We need to focus."

"What about the others?"

"Nobodies, I might recognise some of them from our other exploits with Teach."

Sebastian sighed. "Well, I guess we just have to wait until something happens."

Jack stood vigil for what seemed like hours. He spent at least one of those hours praying to any god that would listen to make Teach's head explode. No one was listening. He had been watching them like a hawk; the *pirate king* seemed to be getting rather tetchy. *Good, that means he's waiting on someone.* He couldn't imagine they had just come to stand in a warehouse in silence for the day. Just as he was about to go down there and give him some shit, a hatch in the floor opened up to reveal two nondescript mean-looking royal guards and one fancily-dressed French king.

"There must be secret tunnels underneath the warehouse," Sebastian whispered his thoughts to a concentrating Jack.

Edward broke the tension down on the floor that had obviously been building up during the wait, "Finally, I was beginning to think you were trying to make me angry."

"Is that any way to speak to a king?" Louis asked the pirate in a way that showed he wasn't afraid of his aggression.

"Is that the Sun King? He looks like a feminine version of King Charles," Sebastian observed.

Jack nodded and whispered, "That's him, Charles' cousin, Louis."

"Listen here, Louis, none of this would have been possible without me. Look at all I have helped you to create." Edward waved his arm in the direction of the large sheeted objects. "I should at least warrant a modicum of respect and punctuality."

"And should all go to plan, you will be well rewarded for your efforts." The Sun King interjected.

"I hope so because I ran into a lot of trouble on our last journey - Lost a ship and crew. Ships are easily replaced, but reliable crews are like rocking horse shit, especially in the Caribbean." Jack had clearly vexed Edward dearly, and this pleased the pirate hiding on the walkway above them.

Louis raised one royal eyebrow, "Nothing you couldn't handle, I'm sure?"

"I'm here, aren't I?" Edward snapped back. "Just some pesky nuisances." Jack seethed silently from his hiding place. "Once work has been completed on our project here, no one will stand in our way again."

"You seem a little vexed by this pest. Are you sure I don't need to worry? Because I can find another pirate to aid me if you can't keep your end of the bargain. I'm sure the barbary corsairs would give me less cause for concern."

"No, don't concern yourself. This pest took something from me, and I don't like it when people take my things."

"Nothing important to the plan, I hope?"

Edward's anger flared up as he marched towards the Sun King, stopping just in front of his guards, "I said it's nothing to concern yourself with."

"Oui, oui, fair enough." Louis walked over to the sheets, his guards shadowing his movements, "You know, when you came to me over a year ago with a tale about Islands floating in the Caribbean, I thought you mad. Then you told me what you had squeezed out of my own alchimistes and I still found it hard to believe. That my cousin and I had forged a new material beyond anything that we could have hoped to achieve. It was beyond imagination, beyond comprehension. Then you broke open the crate of the material you had brought, and I could see my plans to conquer Europe realised. A fleet of ships made from this material, unhindered by borders, able to attack ships at sea and armies on land. No one would dare try and stop me with that kind of power."

Sebastian and Jack looked at each other, needless to say, a little worried. "If this happened over a year ago, then there is more to this than we know, Jack. There could be countless floating islands out there."

Jack whispered, "I'm not worried about floating islands. It's the mysterious object under the sheets that's worrying me."

Edward laughed, "You know what I like about you, Louis? You dream big. That's something you and I share in common." The tension between the two seemed to have been quelled for now. "As long as I get what you promised me, I don't care what you conquer, hells, why stop at Europe? With a fleet of these things, there will be no limit to what you can achieve."

"One step at a time, my black-hearted friend. Tell me, how well is the construction proceeding here in Le Havre?"

"See for yourself, your majesty," Edward sneered as he nodded to his three lackeys, who proceeded to pull the sheets from the first bay.

As the sheets fell, Jack's worst fears had been realised. They had been hiding a frigate, and he could only presume that was what waited for them underneath the other sheets. They looked slightly odd, but he had to believe, from their conversation, that it had been constructed from the same material that he had found in the vial. *Are these air-ships?* This one looked to be tied down with a rope to stop it from floating into the roof. He hated to say it, but the craftsmanship was arousing. It just looked like a fancy frigate, but this one had many more sails, at least, he guessed that was what the yardarms on the side and back were for. It reminded him of what it would look like if a ship had fucked a fish, this would be the offspring. The sails were in the same place as they would be on a fish, the flippers on the side, tail on the back.

Sebastian looked at him in amazement, "Looks like a ship had sex with a fish," he whispered.

"She is Magnifique!" Exclaimed Louis excitedly. "You will be able to fly her, yes?"

Edward looked cocksure, "Of course, I've been dying to get my hands on this one in particular. I'm waiting for your engineers. Your little ambassador tells me that he will send over an engineer to teach me once they've completed the mechanism. He seems to think that without it, they would just fly on one level. I've given them the night off, though, while we have our little tête-à-tête. Mistakes are made when sleep calls, and we can ill afford them in our venture. I guarantee you they'll be ready come the big day."

"The big day," Sebastian mouthed questioningly at Jack, who just shrugged at him in return.

"It has been a long struggle, but all the little pieces of our plan are finally falling into place." Louis finished admiring the airships and turned to Edward. "There is just one little hiccup to overcome something that I need you to deal with."

"I'm listening." Edward stood there, his arms folded.

"The harbour master tells me that my cousin has sent envoys, ambassadors if you will, to investigate vicious rumours that have made their way to his court. I need you to make them disappear. When they don't return, Charles will realise something is wrong, but by then, it won't matter because nothing can stand in my way with these at my command."

"Why can't your guards make a few of Charles' lackeys disappear?"

Louis seemed to be growing impatient with Edwards' questions, "You know I would execute lesser men for such testing of my patience?" Louis calmed down a little, "I don't want to cause a scene in Le Havre. If one of them were to escape or word should get back to England, they would send the entire Royal Navy over here and blow the place to smithereens."

Edward shook his head and sighed a little, "Fine. I'll have Ms Read command our little fleet to blockade the port. Nothing will leave Le Havre while *we* flush out these *hiccups*."

Jack remembered to breathe. He stopped paying attention and turned to Sebastian. "I think it's time we leave. Looks like we need to alert King Charles' ambassadors that trouble is coming for them."

"I agree. We shall discuss how much shite we are in once we are out of this dismal place." Sebastian got up to make his way back to the window and out. Jack watched as he took the lead, using the rail to take some weight off his feet. Neither of them expected the railing to break away, and neither had expected Sebastian to fall off the walkway to his doom below. Yet, peril often wants to happen during Odysseys, Jack thought, as he tried to grab hold of Sebastian's free hand in slow motion. He clutched at Sebastian's fingertips as he fell over the edge, and the last image he saw of him was the fear in his friend's face as it disappeared below the walkway.

Time sped back up, and Jack flung himself to the edge for that final attempt at grabbing hold of him, but alas, he was already a groaning mess in a pile of boxes. Sebastian had smashed them all open as he impacted, and lengths of oak were floating away into the roof space. The commotion had alerted Teach and the Sun King, who were rushing to extinguish the intruder. Panic gripped his mind he didn't know what to do, he couldn't leave his friend there to be butchered by the rabid dogs now inching their way towards him. He searched for something to help, anything, he couldn't lose Sebastian. A second of eternity passed, and then he heard in the distance,

"Leave," Jack looked down to see Sebastian looking at him, pain in his eyes, "Go, there's nothing you can do. Carry on the fight, my friend."

"I won't leave you!" Echoed through the warehouse.

"You must. The rose must continue to bloom." Sebastian passed out, and his body went limp.

Shit, shit, shit. "I *will* come back for you, *brother,*" Jack shouted into the air.

"Up there, too, another rat!" Reverberated off the walls.

Jack knew time was short; he took one final look at his companion and pushed himself to his feet. Spurred on by the ever louder footsteps, he ran for the window they had entered. His mind raced as he made his way along. He felt numb, grief-stricken, but he needed to keep going, get help, come back and save Sebastian, sabotage the ships, warn the envoys. His heartbeat fast in his chest as the shouts of spy and rat ran through the air. As he got closer to the window, he had a wild idea. The timbers had floated towards the walkway near the window, and they would provide him with extra time if what he was thinking went off without a hitch.

Jack grabbed hold of one of the lengths, which surprised him with how light it was. The shouting was getting closer. He turned to see the guards and Teach's lackeys up on the walkway running towards him. Jack took a few steps back, aimed for the front door, and took a running jump over the rail, into the void of the warehouse holding the timber aloft. He glided through the air in a nice pleasant arc to the entrance, much to his amazement. Once his feet touched the steps in front of it, he let go of the timber and ran out of the double doors. Closing them behind him, he pushed everything and anything he could in front of them to slow them down and bolted for somewhere to hide. He needed help. He required a Knight.

* * *

La Roseraie appeared in front of him as Jack ran around the corner. The plan had just become too convoluted; he had not prepared for any of these eventualities. Though he felt extremely naive that he expected everything to go the way it had in his head. Maybe he should have given his father more credit than what he had given him. He felt embarrassed now. Once this was all over, he needed to go back to Chateau de Brissac and have a long talk about their next steps. His feet pounded the dirt as the doors to the tavern grew closer. First things first, he needed to save Sebastian.

Jack burst through the doors, out of breath, resulting in him scaring the girls. Abby stood at the bar, probably wondering what trouble he had brought to her doorstep.

"What the hell is going on, Jack. You look like the devil is chasing you." The knight moved from behind the bar to his side.

He fought through the gasps, his lungs burning, "They caught Sebastian. I need your help." The scrapes of chairs in the corner made Jack look up from his bent-over position.

"Jack, is that you?"

He shook the tired blur from his eyes and focussed on the voice in the darkness. Relief spread through his heart and a grin across his face as he locked eyes with a well dressed Anney, a sophisticated looking Hector, and two others he had not seen before. *Remind me to make an offering to the God that pulled this out of his arse.* Jack had watched the plan go to shit with his own eyes, but things just got interesting.

Chapter - 21 - Look to the skies.

Ariadne stood staring at the facade of La Roseraie, the wind had picked up a bit, and the sign with the painted Rose was swinging back and forth. A woman, who she might have described as in a state of undress, rushed past her, giggling and blushing as Francois gave her a wink. The walls of the tavern belied its age, the timber frame was old, but the whitewashed walls were freshly painted. *Someone had given them a lick of paint recently.* The smell emanating from the tavern wasn't like any she had encountered before; she found perfume and hints of leather warmly cascading through the open door where she expected stale ale and sweat. "This is the place your merchant friend owns?"

"Well, it has been a few years, but I hope so." Francois looked worried now. He must have only just this minute considered the fact that it *had* been a while since he had spoken to his contact, and perhaps he *didn't* still run the place. "No, it will be fine. Judging by the calibre of the patrons, whoever is running this place is in the same line of business." Beatrix grinned at the duke.

"What do you mean?" Seamus looked puzzled.

"Let's just head inside. We won't find any information about Edward Teach out here. Unless he decides to saunter past and stop for a little chat about the tides or the weather." Ariadne rolled her eyes and entered the tavern. She was as confused with the internal decor as she was with the outside. The place had shelving, books adorned the walls, which is probably where the leather smell came from. Several fireplaces were lit around the central area, offering up quite the warm setting for the gaggle of women relaxing on the chairs chatting to the men. A bar situated itself in the back corner. The place was well lit with candles, and bottles lined the wall behind the smiling woman stood beckoning them in - away from the door.

"Come in, ladies and gentlemen, take the weight of your feet. Pull up a stool. I'm sure your feet are weary. What can La Roseraie do for you on this fine morning?"

As Ariadne made her way towards the woman, she began to smell the scent of jasmine getting stronger. Her senses were being sent on a wild ride that she didn't want to get off. She dare not think how the boys were coping in here. She gave a quick glance at a smiling Seamus, who seemed to be doing just fine. Francois leaned in to whisper to her.

"Let me do the talking; I know this woman." He then spoke a little louder, "Or, at least, I know her father. How are you, Abby? Where is Jacob?"

Abby strained her eyes at the man before her. "Do I know you, friend?"

Francois laughed heartily. "We have met, but I wouldn't be hurt if you didn't recognise me. After all, I last saw you when you were this big," Francois held his hand horizontally to his thigh, "let me see, you must have been four or five."

It was like a light came to life in Abby's brain. She now had a look on her face that relayed recognition, "Blonde curls and blue eyes, I remember you. You were quite the handsome chap back then." Beatrix's head snapped towards the proprietor.

"Hey! He still is."

Abby laughed, "Of course. I'm afraid I must apologise. While I remember your features, I do not recall your name."

"Francois d'Arlon at your service," the duke gave her a bow. "This is my lovely wife Beatrix and our companions Seamus Hawthorne and Ariadne Smith."

"Well met." She sighed, "I hate to be the bearer of bad news, Francois, but my father passed away several winters back." Francois looked sullen; his usual smile had been replaced with a depth of sadness that Ariadne hadn't seen yet from him. She stepped over to comfort him with an arm draped over his shoulder.

"Thank you, but I'll be fine. The roses wither more and more every year."

Like a bolt of lightning connecting the earth to the heavens, Ariadne's memory awoke with Francois' words. She felt like she was beginning to put the pieces of the puzzle together. Abby had remembered his features, blonde curls, blue eyes, same as her memory. He mentioned the roses withering. *Could he mean Brass Roses?* Whoever this man was, grief had let the mask slip from his face.

Francois must have noticed the look in Ariadne's suspicious eyes and the doubtful look on her features. "La Roseraie, named after her father's family name - DeRose. The family grows smaller every year. Upsetting times."

Her suspicion subsided, for now. Ariadne decided that it was time to move things along. She had all the time in the world to navigate the lies. War seemed imminent, especially if pirates were involved. "If your father has passed, do you still run in the same business?"

Abby looked carefully at each of them, "And what business would that be?"

Ariadne leaned in. "Information, of course," she whispered.

Abby nodded to the burly men who stood over by the stairs. They got up and proceeded to have a quiet word with all the men in the tavern, who in turn stood up and were led upstairs each by a buxom wench. The floor remained clear now, bar those ladies who remained to entertain themselves. "Make yourself comfortable. I'll be over shortly." Abby moved away from the bar and went to whisper to the apparent protection.

There was no doubt now, in Ariadne's mind, what this place was - a brothel. *This must be how Abby gets her information. Impressive really.* She turned to her companions and nodded over to a dark, secluded corner, "Shall we?"

"Miss DeRose has quite a nice setup here. It reminds me of my office at home." Seamus seemed to be looking at the books arranged on the wall as he passed.

Beatrix smirked, "Even with the whores?"

Ariadne burst out laughing as she sat down, "I've seen the man's office. I can attest to its dreariness - not a woman in sight unless you count Mrs Tibbs. I'm positive *she* would have a thing or two to say, to these men, about the proper way to woo a woman."

"Food." Seamus had clearly gotten over the joke at his expense.

Francois agreed with a nod. "Definitely food."

"So let me get this straight." Ariadne turned to the duke and his wife, "Abby runs a brothel. Her *ladies* and I use that term loosely, ply the men with drinks and costly fornication. In return, their loose lips provide intelligence that could potentially sink a ship, or tell us the whereabouts of Seamus' innocence and even let us know if Teach has been waltzing around Le Havre?"

Francois nodded in agreement, "Indeed, my lady, any and all information that passes through Le Havre, filters through *La Roseraie*."

At this crucial juncture of understanding the machinations at work in Le Havre, another element was thrown into the mix. Everyone's attention was drawn to the man who had just burst through the doors of the tavern, trying to catch his breath. Beatrix was the first to react, as she jumped from her chair, with a look of pure elation on her face.

"Jack, is that you?"

This Jack looked desperate and relieved, which was a new mix of emotions by anyone's standards, especially Ariadne's. She watched as Beatrix ran to him, leaping to fling herself around the out-of-breath man as he stood up to meet her.

"I knew you were alive! I kept telling Sebastian, *there is no way she would let a little thing like that break her,* and here you are." Jack squeezed Beatrix's arse, "God, I've missed you."

Beatrix sloped off him. "Now don't you go getting all mushy, you know I wouldn't let Davy Jones claim me. We have too much to do, love." She grinned at him.

Francois coughed, bringing Jack's attention to himself. Jack waltzed over to him and embraced him in a tight squeeze, "It's good to see you too, you handsome devil." Francois was glowing with happiness. This man obviously meant a lot to the Duke and his wife. Ariadne finally had a chance to appraise the man. His clothes were tattered as if he'd been long on the road, his hair long and scruffy like he'd been at sea for longer than anyone should have to be. Through the exterior roughness, though, there lay a charming face and a wild glint in his eyes that she recognised in herself.

"And who are these charming fellows?" Jack focussed on them.

Ariadne could feel his gaze take the measure of her. She felt as though there was cotton stuck in her mouth, preventing her from introducing herself. Seamus saw her struggling and interceded on her behalf.

"My muted friend here is Lieutenant Ariadne Smith." Seamus patted her on the back and moved forward to shake Jack's hand, "Captain Seamus Hawthorne of His Majesty's Royal Navy. A pleasure to meet you, sir."

Jack scoffed, "It is good to see you in pleasant company, but Sebastian needs our help."

"What happened, Jack?" Beatrix looked worried.

"Wait, Royal Navy? I assume you are the envoys here to see the king?"

"Yes, why?" Questioned Ariadne.

"Even you, Anney?"

"Aye, we are all here to see if the Sun King's been a naughty boy, but when we noticed that Teach was here, we decided that this was a safe bet. We are here to find out what those two scoundrels are up to and find proof that they are going to war with England," Beatrix emphasised.

"Oh, I see, well then you are in luck. You are all royally fucked. Before the scoundrels captured Sebastian, we learned about their plans." Jack waltzed over to take a shot of something that was on Abby's bar, "Then, Louis asked Blackbeard to take care of you himself. Seems that you are a hiccup in his plans that he wishes to quash."

"What proof of this do you have?"

"Well, if we stay here talking for much longer, Teach's men will start searching each building for me, and when he finds the ambassadors to King Charles as well, he'll have us all killed. Is that proof enough for you?"

Ariadne was angry, "I knew we should have come here at the head of a fleet!" She kicked a chair over.

"How is Charles supposed to believe our words if we have no proof?"

"Trust me. With the frigates I saw in the warehouses, you won't have to wait long. Louis and Teach will be soon flying over London blasting down its walls."

"Trust you? We don't even know who you are?"

"Oh, me, love? I'm just Jack Rackham, fearsome pirate of the Caribbean, Lord of a fallen Duchy." Jack gave an obnoxious bow, "Pleasure."

Ariadne was just about to blow her top, *Flying frigates! Pirates!* However, she didn't get a chance to voice that anguish because as soon as Jack bowed, musket fire ricocheted off the walls of the tavern. The glass shattered and blew over the tables. Chaos ensued. The sounds of muskets being reloaded emanated from outside as those inside La Roseraie cowered behind overturned tables.

"What the fuck is going on?" Abby screamed.

"Looks like it didn't take Teach long to find me," Jack said calmly and swiftly. "I assume you have a back entrance?"

Abby nodded as she made her way towards the door at the rear. Jack beckoned them all as he followed her. Their escape was challenging, but eventually, they made it to a dingy back alley with the sound of firing further away and less concerning.

"Is everyone ok?" Seamus was checking Ariadne for holes.

"Aye, Francois and I are good," Beatrix exclaimed.

"Francois?" Jack looked to the group in confusion.

"Story for another time, perhaps?" Beatrix said sarcastically.

Jack just grinned at her.

Abby turned to Jack, "You say that Teach and the king captured your friend?"

"Yes, he fell from a walkway onto some crates, and they came for him."

"And he is alive still? Merde." She brought a finger to her lips as Ariadne watched her mind turn with the beginnings of a plan.

"I guarantee it, that bastard is as stubborn as I. He won't die until he's bedded me, that's for sure." Jack revealed, causing Beatrix to snicker.

"Very well," Abby replied. "My men and I will save your lover. You need to secure passage out of here while you can. We will meet you at the dock."

"No, I can not let you do this for me. Sebastian was my responsibility, my friend and I let him down," Jack protested.

"You can not get captured. You must continue the fight. Do not throw your life away and don't try to stop me. Secure the passage. For your Sebastian, for my father, for the Brass Roses," Abby embraced his forearm, "For Lorraine."

Ariadne had no idea what was going on, but she recognised the Brass Roses. Pride seemed to swell in Jack's eyes as he and Abby exchanged unspoken words of respect.

"I owe you more than I can repay, Knight. We will meet you at the dock." Abby nodded and ran off in the direction of the warehouse with her men.

Seamus spoke up, "One day, we will have a long discussion about what is going on here, but for now, we need to get back to the *Oracle* and secure her."

"You might have some trouble there, Captain. Teach mentioned sending his lapdog to blockade you in Le Havre."

Beatrix's attention was piqued as she turned to Jack, "Who, Read?" She said with an anger Ariadne had not seen in her. She didn't even know that Beatrix was capable of such rage.

Jack nodded to her. "Well, we shall see if she is ready for another battle. I, for one, will not be put down like a rabid dog. We shall fight till we have no more breath in our bodies. What say you, Francois?"

"Aye, Bea, wherever you and Master Jack go, you will always have my sword arm as old as that may be."

Jack turned to Ariadne and Seamus, "What say you, officers of the Royal Navy? Do you want to stay here and get shot at, or do you want the chance at living a full life for another day?"

Ariadne turned to Seamus, "I think we gave it our best shot at diplomacy, Seamus, better to live today and fight another."

"You and I differ greatly on *our best shot,* but I agree if we stay here any longer, they will kill us on sight. I think that proof enough that the Sun King means to wage war on England if his first act is to kill its envoys."

Jack smiled. "Then we are in league; let's secure this *Oracle* of yours and hope to God she's a good ship."

Seamus swelled with pride, "Oh, she's the finest!"

"Show me."

The group ran. They ran until their muscles ached. Until the breath from their lungs burned. They weren't alone in their escape; Teach's men chased them, firing volleys of musket fire around every corner. Corners of buildings exploded as musket balls whizzed by in a cacophony of sound. The good thing about Le Havre was that it wasn't that big, so their little jaunt to the docks didn't take too long. Yet, it still felt like they were in an eternity of death-defying dodges and superfluous sprinting.

"There she is, the *Oracle*." Seamus managed to get out between wheezing breaths.

"You were right, Captain; she is a mighty fine ship. It will look lovely, in pieces, when Louis' air-ships attack it from the skies."

"Seamus! Look!" Ariadne pointed to the ships aligning in the bay.

Jack cringed. "That'll be Mary blockading us in. We're too late."

Ariadne waved to Crockett, who was onboard the *Oracle,* but he must have heard the commotion and seen them coming, for everything was ready for a quick getaway. The men seemed riled up and ready to start a fight with the ships in the distance.

She heard the cries of Cecile, the gunner, shouting in the distance as they ran up the gangplank. "Just get me close enough. I'll blow their silly French hats off!"

Jack seemed impressed by the vibrancy of the crew, "I like that one. Can we keep her?"

Seamus growled, "That one is mine, pirate, and don't you forget it."

Crockett barked over the musket fire, "Shall we set sail, Captain?"

"No, my friend, we are waiting for allies. Break out the matchlocks and hand them out to the men with the steadier hands. We must draw a line in the sand and dare the bastards to cross it."

"Aye, aye, Captain." Crockett reeled off some orders to the men, and they ran down into the hold, returning shortly with muskets under their arms. By this time, Teach's men had lined up on the dock and fired at the *Oracle*'s crew. Jack grabbed hold of one of the muskets and stood firmly at the taffrail loading up as the others were distributed, and the men shored up in defensible positions.

"Fire at will, men," shouted Seamus over the din. "Give our men the time they need to free themselves."

"Huzzah!" Came the unanimous call from the deck.

Ariadne took up a position by Jack's side. If being out in the open firing wildly was good enough for him, it would do for her too. She wasn't going to get shown up by some Buccaneer. Jack turned to see her there and gave her what she felt might have been his most dashing smile, but it paled in comparison to the ones she had seen before. Teach's men were pushing forward. They were running out of time. "Jack," she shouted.

Jack looked to the advancing scurvy dogs, "I know." He bit his lip and aimed down the barrel, firing into the closest pirate. "That should buy us mere seconds until they are brave enough to send in another idiot."

"I don't know you, Jack, you being a pirate disagrees with me. But you came to warn us and probably saved us from being riddled with holes. So, that buys you some time," Ariadne took another shot, "But as soon as Teach turns up, he's going to throw everything he has at us to take us down, especially on the Sun King's orders. We can sit here and take our chances with them," she nodded to the increasing amount of pirates now present on the docks, "Or you can watch me show you why the Royal Navy keeps kicking your lots arse in the Caribbean. We deal with this Mary Read." She watched as Jack weighed up his options.

Jack turned to look at Francois and Beatrix, a solemn look in their eyes. He gave them a nod. "Do it. Unfurl the sails, let's get out of here and punch a hole through Mary bloody Read again."

"I promise you, for what it is worth, that they will not have died in vain."

"Oh, they will not die, Lieutenant, we will meet again. I have faith in that."

Ariadne turned to Jack, placing her hand on his shoulder and giving him a nod of agreement. "Captain!" She ran over to the poop deck, "Let's show these ships trying to block us in what we think to that." She bellowed it out so the whole crew could hear.

Ariadne stood in awe as the sails were unfurled and filled with wind. She was mesmerized as Jack flung a small powder keg into the gathering pirates and fired upon it with a grin on his face. The crew must have realised what he was trying to do and started doing the same. Cecile was the first one to get the shot on target. The explosion caused a tremendous rousing of maniacal laughter on the main deck, heightening everyone's spirits.

Ariadne observed as the *Oracle* slowly slipped out of the dock and made her way to the four ships which now blocked her way home. She watched as the crew worked as one moving the guns in place, ready for the ensuing battle. Ari eyed Seamus; the look of pride spread across his face as he steered towards the pirate blockade. She watched as Jack finally hit his target as he stood at the aft, daring Teach's men to fire at him. She noticed the looks of bewilderment spread across the crew as a frigate parted the clouds and started flying haphazardly towards them.

Panic started to set in and spread like wildfire amongst the crew. Teach was coming for them, and there was nothing they could do to stop him. Ariadne witnessed the crew scramble for more muskets, which was the only thing they could use to protect them from the menacing frigate. Jack stood at the aft, his spyglass to his eyes, shouting at them, looking joyful. Ariadne tried to focus on what he was calling, but she couldn't hear. She ran from Seamus' side, through the distressed sailors, until Jack's voice became clear.

"It's Sebastian! God knows how he did it, but he's flying that damn machine."

"What? Give me that." She snatched the spyglass from Jack, and sure enough, as she placed the device onto her eye, there was a man, beaten and bloodied with a big grin on his face at the wheel. Stood next to him, a woman who looked remarkably like Abby DeRose. "Friendly vessel," Ariadne shouted at the top of her voice. The message passed all along the main deck back to Seamus. The looks of panic and fright started to turn to jubilation and wonder as this airship came to the aid of the *Oracle*.

The frigate glided through the air towards them, the sails at the side turning, putting it into a dive. Ariadne felt mild panic as she thought it was going to fly right into the *Oracle*, but then just as it reached her, the airship pulled up, furled her sails, and came to a stop. Ropes were thrown over the side of the frigate, and the *Oracle*'s crew tied them along the taffrail to secure her.

Then, who she could only presume was Sebastian popped his smug grinning face over the side of his vessel. "Need a hand?"

Jack just stood and laughed for what seemed like a while. "You bastard, you had me worried for nothing. You just wanted to be the first to fly the damn thing. I can't believe you would put yourself in danger like that just to best me."

"A pirate does what it takes, Jack, you know that." Sebastian smiled. "You coming up?"

Jack didn't seem like he needed much coaxing. He was straight up the rope. Ariadne followed quickly behind; she wasn't going to let him have all the fun. She climbed and climbed till she reached the name of the ship, stopping briefly to admire it, before jumping over the *Swordfish*'s taffrail and joining Jack with his friends.

Ariadne watched as Jack embraced Sebastian, squeezing him to the tune of a groan, then wrapping his arms tightly around Abby for all he was worth. "Thank you, Abby. I owe you my life." Ariadne cleared her throat as she watched their exchange, "Ah, Sebastian, you haven't met Lieutenant Smith." He patted her on the shoulder. "She was one of the envoys the Sun King wanted dead."

"Oh, I see. I take it this blockade is for you? Shall we show them what we can do, love?"

Jack turned to Abby, a glint of amusement in his eyes, "Is Sebastian talking to the ship?" Abby just shrugged at him with a smile.

That was the last thing Ariadne saw before explosions erupted from above. Before she had the chance to look up, to see where they were coming from, she felt an impact near where she stood. The brute force knocked her and the rest of the crew off balance, sending her midair, desperate to find her footing.

Before she could, darkness enveloped her as she drifted into the mental abyss.

The End?

Printed in Great Britain
by Amazon